DON'T PLAY WITH THE ANGEL OF DEATH

GAMER

A FUTURISTIC TECHNO-THRILLER

BELINDA CRAWFORD

Published by Hendrix & Faust, Publishers in 2024

www.belindacrawford.com

ISBN: 978-0-6459318-7-7 (ebook)
ISBN: 978-0-6459318-8-4 (paperback)
ISBN: 978-0-6459318-9-1 (special edition)

This one is dedicated to
Faust, He Who Must Be Adored

Books by Belinda Crawford

The Hero Rebellion

(Hunter)

Hero

(Race)

Riven

Regan

The Echo

Cold Between Stars

Dark Between Oceans

Echo Between Worlds

(Brother)

Demons & Battleskirts

Volume 1

Collections

Short Bits, Volumes 1–5

I Am Maggie, Volume 1

}{e

r y00 t}{3R3?

1

The music pounded in time with her boots, a hard *thud thud thud* against her ribs. The hip-swinging impact of the chunky block-heel rode up her spine to mix with the rib-thumping beat.

All around, bodies were jammed together, a sea of skin-hugging denim, leather, and music. Music that roared in her ears and got under her skin, angry voices that yelled defiance and freedom. Outside, wind and winter froze the ground but in here, with the Iron Woods mall's open walls and unfinished sides, the heat had sweat pooling in the small of her back, the thin black t-shirt sticking to her skin under the hooded leather jacket.

The stink of people and spilled beer rose on that heat, twisting around her as she pushed deeper into the rave, slipping between writhing bodies and swinging arms as easily as the System's digital highways. She was comfortable here, safe in the anonymity of the heaving throng. Comfortable enough to throw back her hood and let the counter-bugs built into her glasses and clothes obliterate her presence from the countless cams and network sniffers hidden amongst the crowd.

Besides, the death's cowl would only draw more attention, the kind the dark, wild mane of her hair and full lips would disperse, even as it brought her other trouble. Like the hand reaching from the shadows cast by strobing lights and the dark skeleton of the abandoned mall. She twisted around it, just another over-sexed boy-man trying to grab what wasn't his.

She was no man's, no woman's, answered to no one but herself, a shadow passing through the world. Even if, deep down, that lack of belonging—of family—ached. She ignored it, shoved it aside and stomped it into the icy concrete.

Never let them see you bleed, her grandmother's memory whispered in her ear.

Not even herself.

This part of her, stalking the crowd, leather pants and chunky boots, t-shirt tight across her chest, arms covered to the elbow, this was all her. Just like the mall, once destined to house bright shops and gleaming elevators, now alive with the bodies and the music that couldn't find a home elsewhere. They were both at home here, in the dark and night—

'Hey, pretty girl. Drink with me.'

A can was shoved in her face.

She pushed it aside, bringing her hand up and under the one that grabbed hold of her jacket.

The man gripped tighter. 'Drink!' He shoved the can against her chest.

She stared him in the eye, meeting his small dark ones with her own hazel. He grinned at her, wide and toothy, a little sloppy around the edges, gaze shimmering with alcohol.

She considered him another second—his friends in their dark, band t-shirts and fashionably distressed jeans arrayed behind him—and smiled. The night and the strobing lights cast their faces in stark shadow, lending the short, slicked-back haircuts and clean-shaven faces a menacing cast. The rings on their hands and the neat, manicured nails belied their presence, as did the craft beer shoved against her chest. Fancy business warriors taking a walk on the wild side.

There was a cold spot on her breastbone from the condensation beading the can.

She wrapped her free hand around the one the fancy man had shoved against her chest. Smiled as she did it, letting her eyes widen, her mouth soften, felt the victory in her veins at the corresponding burst of over-entitled patriarchal confidence in his.

A sharp twist and the fancy businessman was on his knees, all that confidence washed away in the wave of pain creasing his brow, making his mouth wide. She grabbed the can from his now slack hand, shook it, and with a practiced flick of her thumb, sprayed the contents in his face.

A half-minute from the first hand on her shoulder to the final delicious upheaval, and it was over. Vlad bled into the seething crowd before the fancy man's friends knew what happened, their outraged shouts swallowed by the pounding music.

She wound her way through the dancers, slipping between shadows and lights, the rib-thumping music seeping deeper into her bones. But she didn't stop, didn't join the gyrating crowd to lose herself in the pulse-pounding hypnotism of heavy bass. She was here for a different reason and it waited beyond the crowd, in the dark.

The strobes and heavy lights turned the areas beyond the old atrium into a forest. Concrete pillars the width of two people, the trees; the slab ceiling with its forgotten cables and pipes its vine-strewn canopy; beer cans, vape canisters and crumbled trash its leaf litter. Vlad slipped into those shadows, moving from one to the next without fear but not without thought. Every sense reached into that forested darkness, tension riding her spine, the sensors embedded in her glasses and around her collar spewing data onto the back of her lenses.

The rave fell behind, its pounding rhythm drowning footsteps but no longer knocking her ribs, the smell of sweat and alcohol giving way to the sharp sting of chill winter and rot.

Ahead and up a set of unfinished concrete stairs, a new light bloomed.

A man stood against it, legs braced, arms crossed. Tall and lean, the chemical glows strewn over the floor cast his face in shadow, but she knew him. Knew the nose-curling smirk on his face, knew he watched her like a piece of meat on the hoof.

Another man-boy trying to put hands on what wasn't his. But unlike the fancy businessmen, danger and violence rode under the ink tattooed on Hamish Elwood's skin.

Vlad stopped at the edge of the lights, the harsh orange glow kissing the carbon-toed tips of her boots.

Hamish smiled. 'Sam-a-el,' he said.

He drew her online alias out in an oily drawl that made her skin crawl, but the disgust didn't show on her face, didn't so much as curl her nose or twitch her lips. There was Grandmother's hand on her shoulder, the old woman's steel in her spine.

Hamish was a steppingstone, a bug she would squash as soon as she was done.

She smiled, while on the back of her glasses more data lit up the night. The silver-on-black watch on her wrist matched logos on the ancient oil drums holding up the makeshift table to manufacturers, barcodes to shipping crates and purchase logs, same as it did the old doors forming the tabletop, the vape hanging out the side of Hamish's thin, smirking mouth. Moreover, it picked out the three figures waiting in the shadows behind him.

It identified Ru Ping, his bodyguard, by the unique mix of digital signatures from the devices the woman wore, and the network traffic that connected her to the other two heavies.

A hard thought, and Vlad's watch went to work, analysing the algorithms in the data flowing between them, searching for a crack in their systems, a way in.

Vlad stepped into the light. 'Do you have it?'

Hamish drew on the vape.

On her HUD, a new network-spike flashed – activity between Ru Ping and Hamish.

'I got it,' he said. 'You ready to earn it Sam-a-el?'

'Just give me the target.'

Again that smirk; a greasy stretch of lips around the vape. He oozed around the table, tattooed fingers trailing over the scarred and flaky wood, and stopped before her. Just the too-sweet stretch of his vape between them.

Vlad held her ground, didn't let the creepy-crawlies chilling her nape make it to her face or ball her hands. Didn't choke or snarl when he blew smoke into her face, the chemical cherry sticking to the back of her tongue.

Later, she promised herself. Later.

Below, the rave pounded a double-time to her heart.

A ping from the comm behind her ear, the one snuggled up against the port in the side of her neck. A share request popping on her HUD, Hamish still smirking through it.

She accepted.

The file, a packet of maps and schematics, addresses in the real and virtual worlds downloaded to her network. The security algos scanned it for worms and viruses before it hit her databanks. Warnings pinged, automatically tagged and quarantined, problems to deal with later, for now… A less-than-legal treasure hunt spread across her glasses.

Key phrases snagged her attention—*core system, pro league, phish, trojan, Meerkat*—while dossiers scudded past. There were other words, like *rumours, unconfirmed* and *artificial intelligence*, but she ignored them; she'd read all she needed to.

She didn't like it. Just like she didn't like the hand reaching for her arse.

A deft sidestep and Hamish's hand collected nothing but thin, smoke-filled air.

Vlad didn't glare, didn't twist her lips or shove her fingers in his throat like the boiling anger in her gut demanded. Instead, she shoved the fury down, deep into a place beyond, the same one she shoved her nightmares and helplessness, and let her face be a mask. Perfectly serene. Brow smooth, a light smile tugging at her mouth, not a wrinkle or frown for miles.

Just like Grandmother had taught her.

That thought, stray as it was, broke the perfect serenity. Just a second, a brief shattering moment in which Vlad could *feel* her face crack, could almost *see* the shock in her own eyes, the corresponding, inquisitive twitch of Hamish's head.

A moment, just a moment to threaten the ground she'd gained.

She turned away, glided around the other side of the long, cobbled-together table, let her fingertips trail over the rough surface, and summoned the mask again. It slipped easily over her face, comfortable and familiar, armour made from the perfect set of chin, the Mona-Lisa-slight twitch of lips, the gaze that looked through and not at. Unperturbed. Confident. Impenetrable.

Everything the hacker-gamer known as Samael, the reigning Scourge of the VR circuit, should be. Everything *she* was meant to be, even if she didn't feel it, deep down inside.

The long, narrow table was coarse and uneven, two old wooden doors sitting end-to-end on drums that still carried the smell of engine grease and fuel. The only thing holding them down, the half-crushed beer cans and crumpled trash. It would only take a good shove to send them flying. The strobes from the rave below cast weird, colour-leeching shadows over the old, stained wood, made pits out of the round holes that had once housed locks and the panels where the remnants of diamond panes made ragged teeth.

Vlad halted at the table's foot, traced those glassy teeth with a naked finger, like it was the most fascinating thing she'd ever seen. Another part of the mask, an energy barrier designed to shield and confuse.

'Well?' She could almost *hear* Hamish cross his arms. 'What's the great Samael got ta say about that?'

The plan, he was talking about the plan.

She wrapped her fingers around the glass shard, plucked it free. 'I don't like it.' Had no wish to find herself tagged and system-locked because some handsy arsehole thought he knew shit about the networks; the nooks and crannies and idiosyncrasies she knew like the back of her hand. The very same ones he was paying her to exploit.

Hamish's snipe hunt was just like him, slick and slimy and dangerous, for everyone except himself.

'And yuu'd like it better if we did it your way then?'

'Yes,' she said. Because with her plan, the only one getting screwed over was Hamish. Not that he'd know it, not until it was too late.

The thud of fists on rickety wood, and Vlad glanced up, just a flick of her eyes, just enough to appreciate the way Hamish positioned himself, so the bright, eye-searing lights from the rave cast him in looming shadow.

He leaned over the table, fists supporting his weight, black shirt gapping over his thin, reedy chest. The gloom turned the honeycomb-pattern tattooed on his throat to below his collarbone and over his left shoulder, into hexagon-shaped holes in his white skin. She was half-surprised the smoke from his vapes didn't pour out those holes.

'We ain't doon it,' he said.

She kept her eyes on the shard, as if the inch-long glass tooth held the mysteries of the universe, but her attention, all of it, was on Hamish. The way his shoulders twitched, how his mouth twisted, the precise tilt of his shaved-bald head. 'We are.'

'Nae.' He slammed the table with both fists, the old wood giving with a sharp *crack*. 'We're not.' He snarled the words. "Cause I ain't got a death wish, ye little bit—'

A sharp flick and the glass shard flew, the sharp point gleaming red then yellow in the strobes, before it sank into his flesh, seeming to disappear into the hexagon holes on Hamish's chest.

He jerked backward, stumbling from the table, hand clasped to his collarbone, tearing the glass out of his skin. Outrage and shock clashed on his face, fury following as he held the bloody missile to the light. 'What the fook?'

Hamish's gaze went from the shard to her, and she met it this time, no longer staring through him, but straight in his eyes, like she could see all the way to his shrivelled little soul.

'Ye cut me, you little cunt?'

A tilt of the head sent the chaotic Medusa-like curls sliding over her shoulder. 'Watch your mouth.'

'Watch me mouth?' Incredulity fought the fury twisting Hamish's face and pulled his lips into a snarl. He held up the bloody glass tooth as if it were a trophy. 'Me watch *me* mouth?' He laughed—a sharp, short bark—and threw the shard on the table. 'Fook you, ye crazy cunt. You're the one needing to be watching *your* mouth, or me and the boys are gonna have to—'

A single kick sent a door careening off the drums and into Hamish's thighs. He fell, folding over the narrow wood.

Figures melted out of the shadows before the Scot was even on the ground, strobes gleaming off the points of knives and the hard shapes of old-fashioned pistols. Vlad ignored them, already stalking over the door, her chunky black boots making crunching sounds in the half-rotted timber, pinning Hamish to the concrete with her weight.

She braced her feet where his hips should be, and crouched, pretending like the three heavies didn't make fear clench her guts, her stomach knot.

Vlad didn't have a weapon—no knives, no gun—nothing but her nerve, her wit and the steel in her spine.

Hamish screeched as she leaned over his torso, shifting her weight over her front foot and the tender things underneath. Rage still knotted his smooth white face, twisted the narrow nose and hexagon tattoos trailing down his cheek, but pain had washed away the cocky tilt to his head, the knowing smirk, while something very much like fear widened his pale-green eyes and made pinpricks of his pupils.

She leaned forward, imagining her foot was an anvil, and Hamish a worm. 'The boys won't do anything,' she said. A sharp glance up, straight into the lead heavy's black eyes. 'Except stand there.'

Behind the thick black rims of her glasses, Ru Ping's dark gaze narrowed, considering even as her fellows closed in on either side. Vlad ignored them the same way a lioness ignored a pack of hyenas, their movements pricking along her spine. Her focus was on their leader.

Ru Ping stood tall and lean – toe-to-toe, Vlad would have to lift her chin and stand on pointe to meet the woman's eyes. The bodyguard stood with shoulders back, her own chin held high, midnight hair bound in a skull-hugging braid, the tail end disappearing under her collar. Ru Ping had the uncanny ability to melt into the background, disappearing without a ripple until she chose to be noticed. Like now. And now... now she radiated menace.

Light, like an oil spill, played across the square lenses of Ru Ping's glasses as the woman's HUD spat information at her.

For a second, Vlad caught the afterimage of a face on the other side. It was just a moment. There and then gone. Easily mistaken for a playback or a scan, but then there was the twitch in Ru Ping's shoulder, like the woman had to stop herself from touching a headset sunk in her ear.

That oil-slick shiver embedded itself on Vlad's retina, and victory clenched her gut. *Yes. Finally.*

Ru Ping held up a hand. The other two heavies halted. The other woman—in thick black boots just like Vlad's, the toes capped in shiny steel, and a heavy black leather coat falling to her thighs—took a step back. She didn't say anything, but that single step was all Vlad needed.

She smiled at Hamish, the expression a long dark slash across her face. There was no humour in it, nothing save the darkness in her eyes.

The man snarled back, both hands on the door, the whipcord muscles across his chest straining as he tried to push it, and her, off.

She leaned harder on the one, optimally placed boot.

'Fook you c—!'

Snake-quick, Vlad twisted, all her weight still on that one boot, but now the other was mashed in Hamish's face, the grimy, chunky sole stopping up his mouth.

'Watch your mouth,' she said. Vlad leaned down a little, strain shivering through her back leg and the tight, knotted mass of old scars gumming up her knee, as she fought to keep from crushing Hamish's face.

Not that it would matter, the small, dark part of her insisted. He'd done worse, hadn't he? Left a trail of destruction in his wake that made a few smashed teeth seem like Christmas with the family. And not even *her* family, but one of those nice, American TV ones, with stockings hanging off the mantle, and a big fluffy dog. Parents.

And yet... And yet another voice whispered in the back of her mind - the calm, clear tone of reason biting through the anger and pain. In the back of her mind there was a hand on her shoulder, a ghostly apparition made of memory and love, cutting through the swirling dark even as it drove deeper into her heart.

'You are not this.' It was her mother's voice, the memory of her touch. *'You are better, little warrior. Your light will show others the way.'*

Vlad hissed; the anger, the dark pulling lips back from teeth, but she ripped her boot from Hamish's face.

He stared at her, eyes still wide, chin and lips smeared with boot grime.

'We do it my way,' she said. Vlad rose, giving one last extra *push* on the sweet spot over Hamish's groin as she hopped off the door.

He was up in a shot, the old door skidding across the concrete with the force of his shove, aimed at her boots.

It didn't touch her, she was already backing away, attention never leaving Hamish or the heavies arrayed behind.

'Then ye on ye own, you filthy—' He swallowed the word, teeth a grimace; sharp, chiselled nose curled, hate emanating from every pore.

But Vlad wasn't looking at him, her attention was on Ru Ping, on the oil-slick reflection playing across the heavy's black-rimmed glasses.

Their gazes met, hazel on black, and Ru Ping nodded.

Vlad nodded back.

'Two weeks,' Ru Ping said. 'Have it ready.'

2

The cold hit her first. The snow-touched wind smacked her in the face, drying cheeks and eyes even as it froze her lips. Vlad shivered and zipped her jacket to her chin, pulling the sleeves as far down her hands as she could, before stuffing them in the pockets over her stomach. The rave still pounded behind but the music no longer drowned the crunch of boots on the snow-churned dirt as she strode across what was meant to be an avenue between the mall's three wings but was now a parking lot filled with bikes and hotted up cars.

This close to the rave, they lined up in two long rows. Floodlights as much as headlights lit the area, girls in micro-skirts and hot pants, legs bare to the butt in defiance of the weather, draped themselves over cars lit up like discos, or sat behind the wheels of street racers. Others cozied up to men in worn denim and leather jackets, while a few strode between the line of cars, strutting over the uneven mud and stone, the middle carved with deep tire tracks like it was a runway and the spindly heels on their feet were sneakers.

Vlad stalked between the cars like she didn't feel the eyes tracking every movement, didn't hear the stray cat-calls, like she owned every inch of ground between her and the giant, swallowing dark at the other end.

Ximisthus sat beyond the kaleidoscope of lights at the far end of the glittering parade of cars and babes. The black Kawasaki

Ninja with its neon-green nose and splash guard was a lethal beast lurking in the half-light, its sleek lines and aggressive lean promising speed and freedom.

She swung a leg over the bike—the pull of knotted flesh and reconstructed tendon behind her right knee a familiar ache—pressing her thumb to the ignition in the same motion. The gel pad flashed blue as it acknowledged her thumbprint, and the electric engine *thrummed* as over a thousand ccs of power came to life.

She leaned back, flicked the lights— And stopped.

A man stood in the beam of Ximisthus's headlights, not three-metres away. He half-leaned against the low grill of a sports car, the sleek silver Porsche as out of place amongst the boldly decal'd street racers and pimped-out four-wheel-drives as the man himself. The intense blue-white of the bike's headlights highlighted the strong planes of his face even as it cast the crisp lines of his dark suit in shadow. It would be an expensive suit, tailored to fit every lean, muscled curve; laundered and pressed, just like the crisp pale shirt underneath, the expertly knotted tie and the matching fabric square peeking out of the breast-pocket.

He stared at her, almost without expression save for the gentle furrow between his dark brows. Most wouldn't have seen it, wouldn't have noticed the extra hollow in his cheeks from a clenched jaw. Most would have only seen the hard beauty in the face, with its straight nose, square jaw and full lower lip – a face used to wealth and privilege. But most didn't know Yu Zixin like she did.

Most didn't hate him the same.

She gathered the long, curly mass of her hair into a tail at the back of her head.

Most didn't have their guts twist or their hearts pound an extra beat at the sight of him.

Vlad grabbed the sleek black and green helmet off the handlebars.

Most didn't—

He was standing next to the bike, a slice of shadow stepping out of the darkness, a hand on her helmet, the square palm and long fingers swallowing the top. How he crossed the three-some metres of dirt and gravel in the space between pain-filled heartbeats, she didn't know. That was just his way.

Stray lights from the rave gleamed on the heavy gold watch wrapped around the wrist holding her helmet down.

She kept her gaze on the watch. 'Let go.'

'You need to go home.' His voice, warm and confident, sent a shiver up her spine.

Vlad jerked the helmet from under his grip. 'It's not my home.'

His hand was back on the helmet, a quick motion, before she could raise it more than halfway to her head. And this time, there was weight behind it. Not much, but enough she strained to keep the carbon and nano-enhanced dome off Ximisthus's green-striped battery cover.

'Go home, Ana.' He leaned closer, putting more force into the words.

Another jerk, sideways this time. The helmet popped out from under his hand, and Yu Zixin came with it, stumbling just a fraction until he was leaning over the bike, sharing her space, her breath.

Vlad leaned back, suddenly wishing she was off the bike. Her gut twisted harder at the warm, soap scent invading her nostrils, the hint of sandalwood twisting through it.

Anger rose, hot and heavy. First Elwood with his dirty, disrespectful mouth, and now Yu Zixin, in her space, sharing her air. Using that name.

She hissed—a long, drawn out expulsion of the ire turning her gut to acid—planted her hand over Yu Zixin's perfectly sculpted face, and shoved.

He half-stumbled, entire body lurching backward, one hand cutting upward to throw off hers, the other flung out for balance.

It was Yu Zixin's turn for anger then, for indignation to twist his lips and furrow his golden brow. It was just a few seconds, but she was shoving the helmet over her head before he regained his balance.

He glared at her, and fury made sparks light up his eyes, the dark bronze a fathomless black in the half-light.

Yu Zixin snarled. 'Ana—'

She twisted the throttle and Ximisthus roared, drowning that name and whatever else was on his lips. Whatever admonishment, whatever curses or threats or promises; whatever words Grandmother had commanded him to parrot.

His shoulders twisted, his legs tensed, but before he could lurch forward in one of those curiously quick movements, Vlad was gone; gravel spraying, Ximisthus's rear tyre fishtailing as she poured on the juice and left Yu Zixin spitting in the dark.

4y00

3

The snapshot hovered above the sleek marble desk. The harsh, coloured strobes of counter-surveillance tech flared over the young woman's face, half-obscuring the profile shot. There was no mistaking those cheekbones though, the up-turned nose, the stubborn cast to the rounded jaw, even with the dark, death-like hood pulled low over her brow.

The woman behind the desk enhanced the image; long, manicured nails tapped the pale marble, the plain gold ring flashing on her finger. She leaned back in the chair, rested against the smooth, creamy leather and stared out the massive, floor-to-ceiling windows to the cityscape beyond.

In the mornings, when the soft spring sun played through the smog, it was almost pretty – the horizon beyond the towering buildings pale pink and orange, the river glistening as it wound through the central business district, the freeway a sparkling stream of stars before headlights were dimmed. But the sun would rise, revealing the smog to be grey, the river brown and the freeway a noisy, smelly ribbon of anger and haste.

The darkness concealed the true nature of things.

Like the girl.

Vladana Tong.

The name had been a punch to the gut, unexpected and shocking, but only for the first few minutes, after that… After that it seemed logical, inevitable even that the daughter continued the mother's work, took her place in the play.

She played with the image, twisting it this way and that.

The woman smiled, a stretch of lips without any real humour, the expression deepening the lines at the corners of her mouth.

It was fitting, she guessed, fitting for Lilya Zima's daughter to end the mess her mother had made.

If the girl could.

Another twist of the image.

Whether or not the girl had her mother's gift was to be seen; she certainly had that same electric spark, the indefinable *thing* that had arced through a room and lit it up.

A half-laugh at the memory of the girl standing on Hamish's chest.

She had her father's fire too.

She'd enjoyed watching the slimy little upstart fall under the girl's assault. Enjoyed even more the hate twisting his face as he watched Vladana Tong walk away.

There would be trouble from that quarter, rewards in seeing how the girl dealt with it.

She found the little, gilt-edged teacup by feel, hooked a finger through the thin handle and brought the Earl Grey to her lips by habit. The delicate floral and citrus played with her nose a second before the rich creamy taste of the imported cow's milk soothed her tongue.

Was the girl cut from exactly the same cloth as her mother? Would she see the reality of the situation or would she hold to Lilya's principles?

It would be a pity if she did, a double shame to lose both the mother and the daughter.

4

The door on the old freight elevator closed with a hard yank, the metal grate hitting the concrete floor with a clang that echoed in the massive, empty space. The grate had been black once, still was in places, just not around the rivets that held the hexagon shapes together and allowed it to concertina back into the ceiling.

No light made it this deep into the old warehouse, and the glows she'd scattered against the wall fought hard against the persistent gloom.

She rolled Ximisthus down the corridor.

The Kawasaki's headlamps would light the wide, crumbling corridor like a dance party, would show every stained, cracked inch of the three-metre high walls, the highways of old silver cable tracks, the lines and names painted on the stained concrete, giving directions to workers long-since laid off. But she didn't need the light. She knew this place, the thick scent of dust, the pervasive chill, the iron tang that had seeped into the concrete and now sat on the back of her tongue.

She knew the corridor, the warehouse, almost as well as the tight pull of knotted skin down her right leg, the way her right ankle ached, how—no matter how much she practised, how often she stretched—it would never quite bend the same, her toes would never pointe like they should. How she'd never dance like she used to.

Vlad could walk this wide, cold stretch of concrete and dust blindfolded and deaf, and still ignore all of the other doors along the endless walls to find the rusty metal one eight metres down the corridor. Her hand would still go to the control pad sunk into the hole where the light panel used to be with unerring confidence, her fingers would brush aside old electrical wires without an ounce of fear, and punch in the eight-digit code on a keypad she couldn't see.

The door clicked, the three-inch thick hunk of metal swinging inwards, silent and smooth.

Vlad rolled Ximisthus through the narrow opening, dropping the kickstand and setting the bike in a single practised motion as the door swung shut behind her. On this side, not a spot of rust stained the black metal, the paint wasn't chipped, and the shiny black control pad beside it was ringed in a pale green glow against the wall.

The tension rolled out of her spine.

She was home. An open rectangle of industrial concrete the size of two basketball courts set side-by-side, divided into halves by the chunky pillars down the middle and the row of metal shelving between them.

The front door opened into the living half of the space.

It'd meant to be some kind of storage room once, although what kind needed massive, mullioned windows, she didn't know. But she was grateful.

The dark might have ruled the corridor, but here… Moonlight streamed through the old glass, rising over the factories opposite, bouncing off their old tin roofs, sparkling on broken glass and wires. Ancient neon lights provided colour to the grey-washed night, flickers of yellow and pink joining with spits of blue and green to highlight cracked brick façades and faded slogans.

Even without any lights on, she had no trouble making out the back of the long rectangle couch in the middle of the living space, the low-framed bed against the wall, or the high bench and wooden cabinets that made up the kitchen on this side of the dividing metal shelves.

She unzipped her boots, kicked them off and padded into the large, open space. A patchwork of old rugs turned the soft thud of sock-clad feet into a muffled *shush*, while a gentle *hum* and a wash of warm air announced the enviros reacting to her presence.

Her black leather jacket came undone with a soft *zzzzit* and she left it on the back of the ancient couch facing the windows as she made her way around the battered coffee table—a half empty mug and print outs strewn across its surface—past the sparse kitchen—ramen wrappers overflowing the bin, boxes of rolled oats on the shelves—pausing only to snatch a bottle of water from the knee-high fridge tucked into the metal shelves, and past the dividing wall.

The space on the other side was empty save for the battered punching bag hanging over a black square mat in the middle of the cold floor and the lone bucket chair facing the corner between the window and far wall.

Vlad went to the chair. It might have been pink once, but time and wear had faded it to a washed-out salmon, the suede seat threadbare, its black metal frame scratched and dented. But it was comfortable and she'd had to ask no one's permission, consider no one's image, worry about nothing more than stuffing it into the back of an anonymously hired van and squeezing it through her door. Just like the rest of the furniture in her little bolt hole. Just like herself.

She sat, let her head fall back against the rounded headrest, and stared at the flat ceiling. Giant girders cut the grey slab into long rectangles, rusted pipes gave it colour, catching the rainbow of old neon from outside, but it was the oily reflection in Ru Ping's glasses she saw, the remembered outline of a face. Her fingers clenched on the chair's arms even as anticipation churned her gut.

The power behind Hamish had revealed themselves.

Finally.

Three years of searching, of scraping the bottom of every

forum, crawling every social net, of coding and hacking and building, turning herself into the meanest, toughest, most feared Scourge in-System and she was close. Vlad could feel it.

She hadn't been sure, not really, not until that moment Ru Ping hesitated in coming to Hamish's rescue. The slimy bastard was good at the bluff, talked the talk, walked the walk. He'd had her fooled for a while, but now... Now, she knew.

All it had taken was what it always took; the promise of power, of secrets long thought dead.

Like her parents.

Like her ma.

Her fingers found the button on the side of her plain black watch. The minimalist silver on midnight face as unassuming to look at it as it was deceptive.

'Transfer data to main terminal.'

A quiet chirp echoed through the empty space as the files Hamish had given her and the scans taken by her glasses flashed to the mainframe hidden beneath the floor – a complex web of hardware and coding she'd built herself. Just for this.

Another chirp, and a small blue light pulsed against the stained grey concrete.

'Display.'

The world outside the giant windows disappeared. One second, the old industrial district shone through the large square mullions, the next she was staring at her reflection in the opaque black glass – broad cheekbones, wind-snarled ponytail draped over her shoulder, dark leathers making her pale face seem to float, disembodied. A ghost sitting in a ghostly chair.

A microsecond later, different faces—other faces—covered the window and wall. Headshots of men and women in suits and uniforms and rags. Black and white, in colour and high res and low res, grainy, clear and moving. Some taken with vid cams, others security cams, even more scraped from the socials. Over a hundred images spread across the wall and windows, covering

the spectrum of candid and professional, newspaper clippings and telephoto lenses, old and new.

A spiderweb connected by lines thin and thick. Most were nothing more than small squares, names and faces at the edges of the web, connected to the slightly larger squares closer in. Some had rough slashes through them, others had notes scrawled in her own hand—"deceased", "jail", "dead end"—still others sat on digital piles of news clippings and vid reels, digital readouts of files filched and stolen and hacked.

Still more lines, thicker than the others, connected those mid-sized faces to bigger ones and more lines—a blazing red—linked those to the web's centre.

In the midst of all those lines and faces, a news clipping, old but still crisp and clear. She could play it, if she wanted, could see again the flames engulfing her parents' car, brilliant red-pink from overheated lithium batteries, hear the fire sirens wail, and the smell... The vid wouldn't supply the scent, but she remembered it, the sticky stench of grease, the sharp ammonia from the firefighters' retardant; it was in her pores, sunk in there, part of her DNA.

Behind the vid, nestled beneath the clipping, the coroner's report. In it, she could read again how an electronic car-jacking compromised the Bentley's systems, how it led to her dad losing control, smashing into a highway partition, how the windshield cracked and a piece blew inward to pierce his carotid. How the car's doors had locked, the windows jammed closed, how the batteries overheated and caught flame. How her ma had died, choking on toxic smoke while trying to staunch the river of blood from her dad's throat.

The car's black box had recorded it all, even the moment the firefighters broke through the flaming back passenger-side door and hauled a young Vladana Tong out, taken footage of the polyester Wonder Woman costume half-melted to her arm and leg. Everything, right down to the virus the car-jacker had slipped

into the charging system via a carelessly placed game console. The virus with the hacker's alias embedded in it.

RaZIeL, a Scourge.

The only thing it hadn't recorded was why. Why her family's car? Why were her parents dead? Why, why, why?

Code. Her parents had died for computer code. Ones and zeroes twisted into a language of Ma's own making, the building blocks of a program she'd never finished. An AI. A *true* AI. Not the regimented programs like the mainframe hidden under the floor behind her that represented the absolute pinnacle of the tech since the AI laws were passed.

Around the clipping, three squares - two with photos, one empty.

Vlad's face was up there. Younger, rounder, hair longer and somehow thicker, like the wavy strands wanted nothing more than to escape the fishtail plait pulled over her shoulder. She was smiling in that photo, looking up at the woman holding her hand, an older, softer version of herself with pale-green eyes. The woman smiled at the photographer, and the curve of her lips, the brightness of her eyes, reached through pixels and time to light the room.

There was warmth in that smile, love in the eyes, except the light that fell on Vlad—on the Ana of that time—was cold, the warmth of her mother's smile burned to ashes, the memory of her laugh drowned under the blood-curdling screams that followed Ana into sleep. The heat of the flames, the stench of the batteries, the blood—

Vlad tore her eyes away, focused instead on the man in the photo next to her ma. Her dad had been handsome, with thick black hair, dark brown eyes. Vlad had inherited her square forehead and the strong, determined line of her jaw from him. He'd been kind too. She remembered how his laugh had filled the room, like her ma's but deeper, reaching right into her rib cage to settle next to her heart. She'd always been safe in his arms, loved.

Until she wasn't.

Her dad had died first, bleeding-out from the gash in his neck before the flames raced over the Bentley's crumpled hood. That blood had fountained over Ma's hands as she tried to staunch the bleeding.

Vlad looked away, rubbing at the knotted skin hidden under the long sleeve of her top, before the memory of those flames did more than lick her wrist.

Of the other three images at the web's centre, one was black. No face, only a description: "Mastermind".

Hamish Elwood stared at her from beneath "Mastermind", connected to the black square with a thin web of his own. Beside his square, another; blank just like the one above, although this one had a name: "RaZIeL".

Once, RaZIeL had occupied the top square but she'd long ago come to suspect the Scourge who caused the accident wasn't the one behind it. The technical expertise, the in-System muscle, but not the brains or the money.

Other connections flowed from those two squares, other leads she'd chased, other faces, other names, all relegated to the background as she drew closer and closer to her goal. Just as she was about to do with Hamish.

He stared at her from the web, thin face twisted in its characteristic smirk, the tattoos on his cheek standing out against his pale, white skin.

She smirked back and cast his image out of the centre with a flick, replacing it with Ru Ping. Another flick and the oily reflection from the heavy's glasses filled the Mastermind square. She expanded it until the wall was filled with the half-seen reflection.

Blown up to thirty times its original size, the reflection was grainy and blurred. No hint of gender or age, let alone identity.

'Run the enhancement algos,' she said.

Another beep, high and bright, acknowledged the instruction.

'Time?'

A dialogue box—yellow text on an elongated black hexagon background—overlaid the image web.

// Estimated time to completion... 3 hours, 13 minutes.

'Alert me when it's done.'

Another beep.

She wiped the dialogue away, pushed the unknown person back into the web, and plucked Ru Ping's photo from the second ring. The image was blurred around the edges, snatched from a security camera, but Ru Ping's dark stare punched through it, seemingly unhindered by security networks or her thick, square-rimmed glasses.

In the half dozen encounters she'd had with Hamish, the other heavies had changed but Ru Ping hadn't. Always there. Always watching. Always wearing those glasses.

Vlad hadn't paid much attention to Ru Ping before, discounted the woman as just more hired muscle; a stupid mistake, and one she'd rectify.

'Run a background on Ru Ping.'

Beep.

She drummed her fingers on the armrest. The oily reflection seemed to wink at her. Had the other been there the whole time? In every meeting, listening to every word, watching every move and breath? Or had tonight been special? Had Ru Ping reported all those other meetings with Hamish and the oily face had decided to witness tonight's for themselves?

There was a way to find out. Whoever Oily Face was, their footprint was in the nets. Vlad just had to find it.

'Did we get a network scan from the rave?'

// Yes.

'Show me.'

The image web disappeared, replaced by a complicated graph of intersecting, pulsating lines. Red and blue and yellow, they overlaid a rough map of the abandoned mall. A thousand different network connections from personal comms to phones to watches and implants, all sending endless packets of data into the sky. It was a haystack within a haystack blown in a cyclone, unless you knew where to look.

Vlad knew where to look. Or, rather, where not to.

She scooted forward in the chair until she sat on its edge.

'Discard all public network requests.'

Beep.

The wildfire dulled to a quiet inferno, the red lines disappearing, leaving only the yellow and blue behind. The trails of private network uploads crawled across the screen, some thick and twisted, the chunky signals the overt sign of encrypted comms. Distractions.

'Discard all publicly-secured networks.'

The thick, tangled lines of encrypted comms followed the way of the public ones. Police monitored the obviously secured lines, if not to catch the dumb-fuck criminals who used them, then to catch the even more dumb-fuck ones who targeted the folk using them.

Only idiots used security like that, and whoever Oily Face was, they weren't stupid.

A handful of thin, pale-yellow lines remained. Local area nets, tethered to a person, or a handful of people within the same restricted area without so much as an old-fashioned phone signal between them. Just people and the hardware they carried on and in their bodies.

'Identify remaining networks.'

A list overlaid the scan, just four network designators.

// Drop It Like It's A Hotspot

// Wi-Fight The Feeling

// 19467826573657UA

// Ab Lynksys

'Correlate against all our other scans with Hamish.' If the person reflected in Ru Ping's glasses had been keeping an eye on her, on Hamish, their signal would be a fingerprint. Unique to Ru Ping and—

// No match found.

Shit.

Unless they were smart. Unless they rotated their names and protocols, switched out their hardware to mix up the mesh of electronic signals. But even then...

Vlad gripped her wrist tighter, rubbing at the scarred flesh. Even then they'd be tells, no one got rid of all their hardware *all* of the time.

'Find partial matches.'

// Match threshold?

'Seventy percent.' A thirty percent deviance, any more and every watch, phone and engine that'd ever been at the same rave she had, would clog the algorithm; hundreds of matches turning the haystack into a quagmire of useless information.

"Wi-Fight The Feeling" dropped off first, "Drop it like it's a Hotspot" three seconds later. She was putting her money on "Ab Lynksys", only a slightly less idiotic idiot than the criminals who used publicly secured networks gave their networks random—

"Ab Lynksys" died.

Her breath caught. She stood—

"19467826573657UA" winked out.

Fuck.

// No match found. Update search parameter?

Fuck it. 'Fifty perfect.'

Another flat beep.

// No match. Update?

Frustration bubbled up in her gut. She gripped her wrist, fingertips digging into the scars, the pain an old, ugly comfort as her gaze found the outlines of her parents' images, barely visible under the network scan. Her breath came short.

'Give me anything,' she said.

The fifth person, the mastermind had been there, Vlad *knew* it.

And she'd find them, even if she had to rip apart every single network, thread-by-thread, until she stared into their face.

Eleven years she'd been searching; thirteen years four months and fifteen days since her life exploded in a screaming, twisted inferno, since everything, everywhere, changed forever. She was done waiting, done—

// Ninety-four matches found.

Ninety-four. Better than nine hundred, but still, too many to track quickly.

'Refine search to networks we've encountered at least twice before.'

// Eight matches with previous network scans.

She stopped rubbing her wrist.

Eight matches. Eight was okay, not definitive but a place to start.

'Show me the list, include the number of times they've popped on previous scans.'

A list of machine addresses, unique identifiers assigned to network-capable hardware—watches, smart belts, car engines, phones, anything that could connect to the nets—appeared on the screen. Eight lines of jumbled numbers and letters separated by colons. Next to each address, another number, the times her systems had scanned them.

The address at the top, the number beside it caught her eye and held it.

Her fingers tightened around her wrist, and victory… Peppermint on the back of her tongue, the sweet smell of it in her nose.

Twelve. Someone, somewhere at the rave had worn the same smart-device on twelve different occasions in her vicinity.

In the eight months she'd been back, she'd only been to a handful of raves.

'Number one—' Anticipation robbed her lungs of air, made her voice high. '—Show the location of that on the map.'

The screen changed, the faint yellow lines around the old mall falling away, a small white dot taking their place. It was away from the rave, not even in the building, past the rutted-gravel avenue with its parking lot of hotted-up cars to the dark, unlit area beyond. It wouldn't even be on the scan if she hadn't left Ximisthus out there, under the lone streetlamp.

A strange feeling started in her chest, a tight, squidgy sensation compressing her ribs, tightening the muscles across her back.

The place where Yu Zixin had waited.

She stared at the dot, stared at it hard, even as her heart squeezed.

She hated him. She did. But still...

Still, she had to force the words. 'Identify the user.'

A new picture lit the screen.

1sT 5

The black Kawasaki with its neon green rims and slash down its side, roared up the drive, the high-pitched growl vibrating off the curving concrete walls. The sound echoed in the canyon, vibrating in her chest even as it thrilled up her spine – a comforting buzz. Except this time, it couldn't quite drown the nerves, the itch in her soles. What she wanted to do, what she *needed* to do, was spin the bike around, flash the neon rims, pulse the lights embedded along its sleek sides and twist the throttle. Feel the power gather under her arse, the acceleration pushing her deeper into the seat even as she leaned low over the swell of the battery and turned the Kawasaki's roar into a scream of speed.

She'd lean into the driveway's curves, feel the rough, black surface skim her armour-clad knee, the engine warm and furious between leather-clad thighs, the wind screaming past her helmet. The mansion's automatic gate would come up fast, and the HUD would light up her visor, the cross-hair reading her retina to unlock the minimalist black-iron twins with their square tops and millimetre gaps that gave the illusion of freedom from within the estate's two-metre-high walls.

But she couldn't do that. The network map and those twelves matches taunted her and the chill, sticky sensation in her gut—that nauseating mix of victory and betrayal—wouldn't let go, no matter how hard she ran.

It would never let go. Not until she knew.

How had Yu Zixin been there, not just at the rave but the other eleven before it? How had he not just found her but *known* she was back in the country? She'd come back from Germany quietly, and the raves... Only one person knew about Samael and she was half a world away.

The answers were inside that house. All she could do was keep puttering up the drive, let the speedo continue flirting with twenty as she climbed the last bend, the dark-grey canyon opening up, the walls falling away to reveal the mansion.

It looked pretty on the outside—just like she did—two storeys of buttery-warm curves and sparkling glass, a covered walkway leading out to the drive, the blacktop fading into pale-grey gravel. Bushes lined the edge of the circular drive; vibrant, glossy green leaves and red buds carefully trimmed and guided into rounded squares, neat as a pin. Not a single brown or drying leaf marred the perfection, not a wayward twig or weed or blade of grass broke the effortlessly sophisticated lines.

There was a place for everything in the mansion, and everything knew its place. If they didn't...

The bike puttered to a stop, tyres skidding on the loose gravel, throwing little rocks at the curving sweep of stairs leading into the house.

If they didn't, Grandmother had her ways.

She kicked the stand down but didn't reach for the ignition or her helmet, didn't even look up at the big black door looming at the top of the tide-like stairs.

The clock on her HUD ticked down.

17:58.

17:59.

There was still time to run. Screw the questions burning up her cortex, the auto-gate with its reinforced, riot-proof bars. Fuck the road spikes that'd turn the Kawasaki's tyres to confetti in zero-point-seven-six seconds and leave her spinning out across the blacktop in another three-point-three-one. Shredded leathers and a bad case of road rash were a small price to pay to escape the mansion's embrace.

There were other ways to get the answers she needed, other leads to follow, other nuts to crack.

Gloved fingers tightened on the throttle even as her thumb hovered over the ignition.

18:00.

In the corner of her vision, the big black door swung outwards.

Do it, do it now. She twisted her wrist—

'Ms Tong.'

A shadow separated itself from the door, tall and slim and *old.* Older than Methuselah, older than the Himalayas or Noah and his fucking ark, but still straight, still pulling back his shoulders and thrusting out his rounded, knobbly chin.

She kept her gaze on the HUD and the handlebars through them, the engine still running warm between leather-clad knees, rumbling through the boot still propped on the rest. She wouldn't look up, refused to look, and yet she felt the butler's gaze piercing her helmet, the nanite-reinforced carbon fibre no match for Jiang's pitiless, diamond-tipped stare.

It speared her brain, a live-feed delivering its payload of duty and guilt even as it rooted her boots to the cold, colourless gravel.

The guilt wasn't hers, shouldn't weigh so heavy on her shoulders, and yet it was lead in her feet.

A single thumb-stab was enough to kill the Kawasaki, the engine silent, lights dark.

She swung her leg over the bike and stood in the light from beyond the black door, not yet ready to remove her helmet. Not yet ready to face what lay beyond without the comforting shield of the sleek, black visor and thick, nanite-reinforced carbon fibre. And yet there wasn't a choice. Not with Jiang staring at her, a single silver brow rising, just a millimetre, into his silver and black hairline, still straight and full despite the years riding his face.

Ignore it. Pretend he wasn't looking at her, that the disapproval saturating the air wasn't thick enough to choke, that she didn't care. She was good at not caring, at arranging her face into a stoney mask. Had practise.

Grandmother had been an excellent teacher.

Vlad just needed a moment.

In that moment, as she tugged on the fitted leather jacket with its high collar, she imagined that the green Chinese dragon twisting around her arm and over her shoulders, lifted its fierce, embroidered head from her neck and spat fire. A great, furious billow of flame. It'd reach out, and she'd walk through it, burning away the sick twisting her gut even as it burnt the edges of Jiang's perfectly ironed vest, and the pristine white shirt cuffs peaking precisely ten millimetres from the sleeves of his inky-black jacket.

The thought carried her the dozen steps across the drive, the pale-grey gravel *crunch crunching* under heavy black boots. The dragon's fire unclenched her hands, pulled her shoulders back and lifted her chin. She could almost smell the sulphur on its breath, the stench of burnt wool and soot. Taste ashes on her tongue.

She made it to the first curving step, steel-capped toe kissing the concrete and—

'Ms Tong.' Jiang's voice dropped an octave and yet it felt like the whole world descended on her shoulders.

The dragon faded, head tucked against her neck, curling fringe flirting with her chin. It took the fire with it.

She stopped, hands turning to fists at her side.

Vlad didn't need to see the furrow deepen his brow, she could feel it.

The helmet came off. She shoved the black and neon green sphere—like the bike—at Jiang. Was it respect or fear that pulled the force of the thrust at the last moment? Perhaps it was both. Perhaps it was the disappointment in his old black eyes, the tiny tick in his jaw that'd show pain. Sadness.

Whatever it was, she marched past him and into the house.

<⊙>

Her steps, even in the soft-soled house shoes, echoed in the grand foyer, a dull *thunk thunk thunk* on the old, polished wood. The sound bounced off the two-storey ceiling, the soft, cream walls, the staircase, its two wings curving around the carefully-tended cherry tree blooming under the glass dome, high above, filling the air with its sweet scent. Sound bounced and came back at her, heavier, trying to weigh her shoulders, to shorten her stride and bow her back.

Her hands trembled, fingernails digging into clammy palms, but her spine remained straight. Just.

Until she walked past the staircase, slipping to the left where two long, thin doors—juniors of the ones out front—stood open. She stopped.

The last of the afternoon sun spilled through the opening, lending extra warmth to the golden oak floors, but not to her.

Vladana stood on the edge of the sunlight, palms still sweaty, muscles trembling against the need to round her shoulders and stare at the floorboards. Beyond the door, floor-to-ceiling windows looked out over a lush green garden, punctuated here and there by spots of pink and blue and white. And between the door and the windows…

An old woman waited beside a long black table, her lined, dark-gold face a perfect match for the shears in her hand, her flinty eyes hard enough to strike sparks. Straight silver hair fell neatly down her back, perfectly parted at the side, not a single strand daring to cross her square, slightly furrowed brow or escape being neatly tucked behind an ear.

Her clothes, as casual as they were, continued the perfection; a moss-green linen shirt, wide-legged black pants.

Vladana shivered as her grandmother ran that gaze up and down her body, a quick sweep taking in the dirt-splattered leather pants, the leather jacket dangling from one arm, the tight long-sleeved and high-necked black t-shirt hugging her torso. It seemed to linger for a moment on the waist-length braid hanging over her shoulder, to warm, just a little at the way the dark hickory tail curled, like it was waiting for a finger to wrap around.

That hard, blue-black rested on Vladana's face last, and whatever warmth there might have been vanished as surely as dreams of Santa Claus when it met the younger woman's hazel one.

Where Jiang's disappointment lived in his aura, Tong Shufen's lived in her perfectly sculpted brows, the tiny curl of her dark-painted mouth and the lift of her chin. Old Woman Tong might have had to raise that finely-rounded chin higher to meet her granddaughter's gaze, but the head of difference in their heights only seemed to strengthen its power.

'You came home. You know how to do that, at least.' Her face might be lined but there was nothing old about Grandmother's voice, nothing timid in the way her words bounced off the clean, cream walls. There was nothing about Grandmother Tong that spoke of softness, not even the bonsai on the giant dining room table with its fat, curved little silver trunk and delicate white-pink blossoms.

Vladana shivered, taking in the thin wire twisted around the tree's branches and the point-nosed shears on the table.

Especially not the bonsai.

Grandmother Tong gestured to the other side of the table, to the six straight, ladder-backed chairs lined up in a perfect row across from her, each one set with a full western place setting of gilt-rimed china. Small candles marched down the middle, the tiny wicks already burning, forming a delicate sweet-smelling wall.

'Sit,' Grandmother commanded.

Vladana looked down at her pants, the black leather turned matte with a fine film of road dust. 'I will dirty the seats,' she said, even though the words hurt. Even though she wanted to cross her arms, march back to the foyer, grab her boots and tramp mud all over the polished floor.

The old woman waved her small, fine-boned hand. 'I will burn it.'

Burn it, because that's what Tongs did with trash, lest the filth spread and infest the rest of the clan. The crone probably wished Vladana had burned as well, gone up in the same inferno that had taken her ma. Probably.

Her hands clenched so hard her nails sank into her palm. The old pain stabbed in time with the stiffness in her knee and the pull of old scars, and Vladana's feet moved, soft house slippers now barely a whisper over golden oak floors.

She sat, carefully straight-backed so as not to touch the finely carved wood.

Grandmother turned her attention to the bonsai, studying the delicate grey branches with their glossy green leaves for a moment before cutting a branch off with a single decisive *snick*.

Vladana's hands clenched tighter in her lap.

'Yu Zixin found you at last, I see,' Grandmother said, still studying the tree.

Yu Zixin whose digital signature had been at a half dozen raves, a half dozen shadowy, hidden places he didn't belong, not in his expensive suits and hundred-thousand dollar watches. Where he should have stood out like a peacock in a field full of crows, and where she hadn't seen him. Not until last night. Not until he wanted her to.

Her stomach tightened and Vlad couldn't tell if it was anticipation or denial making it do so.

'You have nothing to say?' Grandmother was still studying the bonsai; long, elegant fingers held the heavy shears like they were an extension of her hand.

'Do I need to say anything?'

The shears flashed. A leaf fluttered to the tabletop. 'An explanation.'

'Of what?'

Grandmother's focus shifted, dark gaze snapping from the tree to Vladana. 'You disappear without a trace for four years, leave school, wander the world then show up back here eight months ago and do not say a word to your family, and you still need to ask what you should explain?' Another snip, this one quicker and somehow meaner. 'I raised you with manners. With proper respect.'

Nannies had raised her, servants and psychologists, tutors and physios and dieticians, but not Grandmother. The company was Grandmother's child, and Yu Zixin was her legacy.

Vlad studied the table, the delicate china—dinner plate, then entree, soup bowl, laid one atop the other—the silverware, nothing so crass as the gold plated kind, but with age and weight steeped in every tine and engraved handle. She dissected the candles' scent—drew the sandalwood and bergamot deep into her lungs—and made mental note of the carefully folded napkins—expensive linen, monogrammed with the Tong name, just in case Grandmother's guests forgot in whose mighty presence they dined.

Eight places at a table long enough to seat a dozen, set here, sandwiched between living room and the giant, sterile kitchen. A steel and granite showpiece used by chefs and maids, without anything so mundane as a fridge or 'wave in sight. No sink, no dishes.

A stage without warmth.

Pretend family, pretend caring.

The shears *clunked* when Grandmother set them on the table. She reached for a small spindle of thin wire.

The silence stretched.

Vladana's nerves stretched with it.

'I graduated,' she said.

'Yes, I know.' Grandmother snipped a small length of wire. 'With honours and a full year early no less.' Wrapped it around a tiny grey branch. 'A bachelor of *computer science* and another of *computer engineering*.' Her mouth twisted on the words, but just slightly, a twitch at the corner of her nose, too subtle for most.

But Vladana wasn't most, and if distaste had a colour, it would have stained the air yellow.

Under the table, her hands turned to fists. 'I'm good at it.'

'Of course you are.' And there was pride in those words. 'You're a Tong.' And in that proclamation there was disappointment, a furrowing of the old woman's brows.

Because, of course, she wasn't *just* a Tong, and it wasn't her father who'd excelled in those disciplines.

Vlad fought the urge to look away, to find the painfully familiar portrait on the wall above the sleek black fireplace with actual logs laid upon the grate – the expensive wood not just there for show. Three generations stood in the portrait—her grandparents, her dad, her—and a curious blank space, a certain uncomfortable lopsidedness on young Ana's right that caught the eye as if something, or someone, was missing.

'Business didn't suit,' she said.

'It didn't have to *suit*, girl.' Those old, nimble fingers finished twisting wire around the bonsai's limb. 'You merely had to do what was expected.'

Because she was a Tong, her father's daughter, even if she was a Zima, her mother's daughter, too.

'Like you will do now,' Grandmother continued.

'You know I won't.'

The old woman snorted. 'I know you *will*.' She put aside the wire and stared at Vlad. Age might have deepened the lines around Tong Shufen's eyes, might have robbed her of a few more black hairs, but it hadn't touched the steel in that ink-black gaze.

She fought to meet it, to resist the urge to blink and look away even if it felt like her grandmother was reaching into her chest to pluck out her soul.

Vlad's heart beat loud, the blood rushing in her ears, the world contracting until it was just her and Grandmother. Her spine wanted to melt, her skin to slough off, her nerves to fray and scream and implode. She dug her fingers into her legs, through leather and skin and muscle, all the way down to bone—

Grandmother did nothing. Said nothing.

A clatter, from somewhere in the foyer. Vlad jerked, grateful for the excuse to look away, even if it was just a microsecond.

When she looked back, there was a smile on Grandmother's face, victory if not warmth in her eyes. She gathered the shears and wire, snipped a length.

Vlad's stomach coiled.

'You will start taking an interest in the family business.'

TI, Tong Industries, a conglomerate of manufacturing and engineering. Known for its greedy fingers and voracious appetite, it swallowed other companies for breakfast and rolled on. The Borg of the business world. Only VisionM, a technological titan could match it, and rumour swirled on the forums the two companies had been trying to close a deal for years.

'I don't want—'

'You will.' Grandmother wound the wire around another limb. 'You know you will, or you would not be here.' She spared Vlad a glance as she gestured with her free hand. 'In that outfit and on that machine no less.'

Vlad opened her mouth.

Closed it.

'You would have stayed hidden, displaying all the capability and determination of a true Tong. Along with your mother's righteous disregard for family obligation.' A pause, a sharp, angry *snip* of the shears. 'But you need something from me, don't you, girl?'

She didn't say anything, barely dared to breathe. What Yu Zixin knew, Grandmother knew.

And she'd told him things, years ago in the dark, before she'd known better. Things like the secret buried in Ma's journals, the only one she'd known of at the time, the only thing she'd been able to prise from the spidery handwriting.

Vlad's gaze flicked to the portrait, to her dad's smiling face, then to the blank space before her mind flashed to the web spun out over the window and the oily reflection in Ru Ping's glasses.

Cold shivered through her spine.

The old woman ran her hand over the little oak's golden canopy and hummed. 'At least I never had to teach you to hold your tongue. Your mother was good at that too.' Venom coated those words. 'Your father…' Grandmother's expression softened and her gaze found the portrait. She smiled. 'Not so much.'

She returned her attention to the bonsai.

'TI has invested rather heavily in a company developing virtual reality units, NuGet. You will go there.'

Vlad blinked, surprise momentarily holding her hostage. Virtual reality? What did TI want with gaming technology?

'I know nothing about running a—'

'You don't need to. You have other skills, don't you, Samael?'

Vlad froze. From her fingertips to her toes, every single muscle and nerve in her spine, every impulse, every hair follicle turned to ice.

She stared at her grandmother.

The old woman stared back, ink-black eyes sharp, the soft, afternoon light bouncing off the table to lend a certain demonic glow to the planes of her face. Of course Grandmother knew that name. What Yu Zixin knew Grandmother knew and how else would he have traced her? Memory flashed to the oily reflection.

Neither of them spoke, and in the silence the hum of the air changers, the quiet hush of the humidifier and the distant thrum of a helicopter were loud.

Vlad broke first. 'How do you know that name?'

Grandmother leaned back, picked up her shears. 'The how doesn't matter, I simply do. And since I do...' She paused, studying the bonsai before nipping a small green shoot. 'I've been told anonymity is important to a Scourge.'

Anonymity was everything. Without it, it was only a matter of time before she found herself in front of a judge.

Vlad could create another identity. A new name, a new avatar, a whole new persona. Identification, license, birth certificate, but it would take time and money – time and money she didn't have. And it was difficult, and illegal in a whole different, meaner league than being a Scourge.

Grandmother's shears flashed.

Another shoot fell.

'What do you want?'

When Grandmother smiled as she did now, generals fell to their knees. Not because of the beauty of it, but because they saw their defeat in the slight upward curve of her lips.

But Vlad wasn't a general, she was a Tong, or so she told herself as she poured metal into her metaphorical joints.

Grandmother paused in her trimming to swipe an elegantly manicured nail across her watch, toward Vlad.

A soft vibration on Vlad's wrist drew her attention to the share request lighting up her watch's minimalist black face. Her thumb on the surface accepted it and another gesture spread the file over the soup bowl and heavy silverware.

A contract.

Grandmother raised the shears again. 'NuGet has an e-sports team, which TI acquired,' she said. 'One of their players retired and they need a replacement. *Samael* is that replacement.'

'No.'

Silence. The kind of bone-deep silence that came before the executioner's axe took a head, the kind of silence that filled the world as it watched the meteor hurtling toward it. The kind that weighed heavy on the top of her head, forced her to look up and meet her grandmother's iron gaze.

A single, perfectly sculpted steel-grey brow was raised. 'No?' The shears came down.

Vlad hardened the steel in her bones. 'There's no difference between you exposing my identity as Samael and Samael entering the pro leagues. As soon as I do, my anonymity is gone. There's no benefit to me in this.' She pushed the readout with the contact back across the table. 'You can keep it.'

'And if we added a clause to ensure your anonymity?'

Vlad almost snorted. No one could do that. 'You might be able to control the media, but league fans run rings around them. Still a no.' She didn't turn away though, didn't march back out the living room, out the mansion, swing her leg over Ximisthus and close the door on this discussion like every nerve in her body told her she should. Because there was something she wanted, something she *needed,* and she couldn't ask for it, couldn't risk letting Grandmother know, if she didn't already.

A slim chance.

Grandmother's eyes narrowed and her chin lifted a fraction, the slightest hint of calculation lighting her black eyes. 'Money won't move you. Or position. What do you want, child?'

Tension clutched at Vlad's gut, but she kept her face still, summoned every ounce of coldness she'd learned at this woman's knee, and injected into her voice.

Never let them see you bleed, child.

'If you have to ask,' Vlad said. 'You don't have it.' She turned away.

She got three steps across the living room, Grandmother's gaze boring through her back, before the old woman spoke. 'What if I tell you about the Deposit?'

Vlad paused, the slight hesitation making the *shush* of her slippers stutter on the wooden floors, but then kept moving. The Deposit, the Holy Grail of Ma's research.

Another two steps.

'What if I gave it to you?'

Vlad stopped but didn't turn.

With it... with it she'd no longer be hunting Ma's killers, they'd be coming to her.

'Her notes, the journals, everything.'

She didn't need Ma's journals, but Grandmother had something else…

Vlad turned.

Grandmother was staring at the bonsai, shears on the table, wire back in her hand. 'The offer includes your mother's hard drives and her backups, none of them accessed since she died.'

Her heart skipped a beat. 'You mean your techs couldn't break her encryption.'

The microscopic twitch at the corner of Grandmother's mouth might have been a smile. In another universe. 'Mn. The offer expires in one minute.'

Vlad lifted her chin. 'Six months, the length of the pro season, and the contract automatically terminates, no prejudice, no strings. If your deal isn't done by then, it's not my problem.'

A glimmer, like diamond under water. Hard and cold. 'No, you'll stay until the deal with NuGet is complete.'

'And how long will that take? A month? A year, a decade?'

Again, Grandmother's brow twitched. 'As long as it takes.'

As long as it takes. And in that, as in the hard determination on her grandmother's face, Vlad heard the truth. The contract would last not as long as it took to consolidate whatever takeover Grandmother intended with NuGet, but to bring Vlad back into the Tong family embrace.

'I'm not working at the company.'

Amusement twisted the look on Grandmother's face. 'You're in the midst of contract negotiations, girl; just who do you think you'll be working for?'

'Not you.'

Again that twist, the sour amusement crystallising, becoming sharper. 'You're a Tong, you'll do your duty.'

There was an utter, implacable confidence in the old woman's words, a diamond-hard certainty that had denial rushing to Vlad's lips. She caught it before it burst from her, but couldn't stop it turning eyes hard and tight, couldn't stop it tightening her hands into fists. Couldn't help but remember the empty space in the portrait over the fireplace, twisting the anger even more. Couldn't control her face like Grandmother.

Light shone off the wire in Grandmother's hands, or maybe that was the rebuke in her eyes. 'You're bleeding, girl.'

The words hit her in the chest, reminded her of sobbing quietly in a dark bedroom, tears salty on her lips, blankets and pillows soft and warm all around her, but feeling only the cold, only the pain. Then the bed dipping and Grandmother's perfume wrapping her in its inviting, floral embrace, the hand pulling the covers back, the perfectly manicured thumb wiping the tears from her cheeks. And then the words, the ones she'd never forget coming from that drawn, emotionless face.

'Enough, girl. You're a Tong, and Tongs do not cry.'

'But Ma...' Her young voice choked. Ma had said it was okay to cry, that crying made people stronger, let the bad out and the good in.

Ma was never going to say those words to her again. She sobbed.

The hand on her face moved to her shoulder, the elegant fingers with their simple rings digging in hard.

Ana tried to squirm away.

Grandmother held on and it seemed like her eyes saw through Ana, all the way into some other, darker place, even though moisture filmed them.

'Your mother is dead, your father too.' Grandmother's voice hitched on the last, before strengthening. 'You are my *granddaughter, and my granddaughter does not cry.' A hard shake of hand and head, those eyes refocussing, the teary sheen gone, like it had never been. 'Tears are a weakness, Vladana, like bleeding before sharks, and our world is full of sharks; never let them see you bleed. Never.'*

The memory hissed through her, sent her nails into her palms, made her want to scream and shout with the pain, but she didn't; held the storm behind clenched teeth.

Never let them see you bleed.

'Six months,' she said, proud when her voice didn't crack. Saw the corresponding spark of pride in grandmother's gaze and tried to ignore the bright, happy warmth of that thirteen-year-old at the approval.

Vlad turned away. 'Not a day longer,' she said over her shoulder.

'And if it is?'

Vlad was already walking away, the blank space in the portrait drilling through the side of her face, house shoes slapping the floor.

'You'll wish it wasn't,' was all she said, before the dining room door sighed shut behind her.

6

The hard, fast *thump* of drums and electric guitars filled the warehouse. The big, open space smelled of sweat and last night's ramen, most of it forgotten on the long bench on the other side of the dividing shelves. She hadn't been able to eat when she got home, hadn't even been able to check the results of the facial recognition scan from the rave; was it just the other day? She'd snoozed the notification and forced half a mouthful of rehydrated tofu and processed noodles down her gullet before giving up.

That name, on her grandmother's lips, echoed in her brain.

Samael.

Her fist *thwaped* into the old, patched punching bag.

She couldn't get it out of her head.

Vlad shifted her feet, the training mat slightly rough under her bare soles, and threw a kick.

The bag swung. The old, black leather with its dark green patches sailed through the dawn creeping over the floor.

She'd been so careful; careful in choosing the name, in building her avatar, in masking her identity, layering it with encryption upon encryption. Scrambling her signal, switching her IP, building her own portable VR unit so she never had to log-in at the same location twice. She never used voice chat, didn't join guilds or friend other users, paid for everything with crypto coin and hard currency.

Never did anything as Samael that could be traced back to her.

To Vladana Tong.

Her other foot slammed into the leather bag.

She'd barely even played *Annihilation* before Grandmother shipped her off to the first boarding school. Ballet had been her life before that, before the accident, and there'd been no time, no inclination to follow in her mother's footsteps. And after...

The anger had taken time to crystallise, had needed secrets heard through a crack in her grandmother's office door to find a target.

'What's the Deposit, President Tong?' A police officer, shiny gold buttons against a crisp navy uniform.

'I do not know.' Grandmother, face pale and drawn but her back straight, indomitable despite the red ringing her eyes. 'Lilya was not a Tong Industries employee, Officer Gao, and she made it quite clear that her work was none of mine. I have no information about any...' Grandmother waved her hand and her lips twisted. '...any Deposit.*'*

'Your son and daughter-in-law were killed because of it.'

Killed because of the Deposit. For code.

Young Ana hadn't known code, she'd known pointe and plié and barre. She'd watched Ma play games though, gone to sleep with *Annihilation* streaming across her bedroom wall, Ma's paladin slashing and magicking her way to victory, and that had been a start.

Annihilation had led to becoming a gamer, gamer had led to the System, to the secrets hidden in its nooks and crannies, and those secrets had led to Scourge. To Samael.

Only one person had known she was a gamer, the single person that, no matter how hard she tried, she couldn't shake; her college roommate and best friend. No one else had known she'd dominated the Euro leaderboards, not her teachers, not her friends—the few casual ones she'd cared to have—or the string of boyfriends she'd kept just to maintain appearances. Not even Yu Zixin.

He'd found out though. There'd been those Christmas and birthday presents, the keyboards and mice and circuit boards. The soldering kits, the way Grandmother hadn't descended like the wrath of god, remaining curiously silent when Vlad switched her major from business to computer engineering and science.

She'd trusted him, trusted him even when she shouldn't, when he'd proven himself unworthy. Trusted that even if he remembered the brief, long-ago snatch of drunken conversation, he wouldn't tell.

Yu Zixin. Yu Zixin had told Grandmother.

She hit the bag again, the sweet sting of impact rising up her knuckles and the layers of black wrapping. Sweat clung to her forehead, dribbled over her lip—hot and salty—darkened the long, black compression sleeve on her right arm, glistened on the left, bare to the warehouse's chill air, and stuck the racer-back tee to her stomach.

Yu Zixin had betrayed her.

She snarled and stuck. Elbows and fists and knees. Again and again and again. The bag swung, a crazy pendulum rattling against the chain holding it to the concrete ceiling. Unable to break free, it came back at her for more and more and more.

She hated him, hated him, hated him!

Her lungs burned, her knuckles screamed and inside, the lost little girl she'd been—the *Ana* she'd been—yelled anger and pain and betrayal with every strike.

Eventually, exhaustion took the strength from her bones, the agility from her feet, turned her breathing to a bloody rasp, and sent the little girl back to the dark, quiet place in the pit of her memory.

She threw one last, sloppy punch, knuckles sliding off to the side, other hand catching the top of the bag before she fell. She clung to it, hot and sweaty, pressed her forehead to the cool leather, breathed in its familiar earthy scent, the thick seams rough against the inside of her bare left arm.

If Yu Zixin was involved, that meant Grandmother was too; involved with Hamish and RaZIeL.

The answers hadn't just been closer than she'd realised, they'd been right there. In. Her. Face.

As soon as she finished this, she'd move his photo from the third ring on her target board to the second, hanging off Grandmother's skirts. Where it belonged, where it had *always* belonged. Even if the little girl in her heart wished otherwise.

She was going to find out what Yu Zixin knew and how he knew, and *who* he knew. And once she had that, once she'd wrung every last drop of usefulness from him, she was going to climb him like a fucking stepladder, plant her boot in his face and leave *him* in the dust as she reached for the real power – the reflection in Ru Ping's glasses.

Even if that power was her own grandmother.

She gripped the chains attaching the punching bag to the steel girder above, the links cold and hard, rough edges biting into her unwrapped fingers and gritted her teeth against little Ana sobbing in her dark, quiet corner.

Vlad didn't need to see the enhanced image anymore. Didn't want to. But she'd wait for it anyway and in the meantime…

In the meantime there were the journals and hard drives, packed away in the plain cardboard box, dust thick on the top. She'd taken them from Jiang with hands that shook, strapped them to Ximisthus's tiny back seat with reverence and, if she'd taken the corners a little slower and hadn't leaned into the bends like she usually did, it was that and not the betrayal making her fingers shake or blurring her sight.

The journals and drives were scattered across the floor in front of the windows, in front of the web, under Ma's smiling face. Smart paper mixed with pulp paper, ink with electrons. Her system was reading it all, scanning and rebuilding everything from the notes and doodles to the vids and audio files. Everything Grandmother handed over.

Vlad pushed away from the bag, peeling off the hand wraps as she shuffled toward the salmon chair amidst the mess.

She gripped the arrow-shaped skull pendant at her throat and inside it, the last piece she had of her ma.

There were pieces missing from the journals, blank spaces where Ma had begun a thought and then… ended it, let it trail off like smoke in the wind.

Grandmother wouldn't know Vlad knew that; she wasn't even sure if Grandmother knew they were gaps herself. But sixteen-year-old her had snuck into Grandmother's office one Christmas and hacked the safe. Her first real job, with her own code and jerry-rigged gear. First true outing as a Scourge, the first time she'd seen the strange symbols of Ma's code.

She'd read every word a hundred times since then, pored over every scribble, every equation in the journals, puzzled over the fragments of the language Ma created, the strange virtual keyboards that went with it. She'd spent months in-System, in little sandboxes hidden out in the grey-net, tapping away at the jewelled keyboards copied from Ma's old *Annihilation* account, creating virtual worlds that… did nothing. Gave nothing.

But she'd learned.

The knowledge had taken her far. From *Annihilation* to the System to Scourge, to the reflection in Ru Ping's glasses.

All the way back to Grandmoth—

Vlad shoved the thought aside.

She'd never had access to Ma's drives before.

Somewhere among Ma's hard drives, there would be something, a hidden partition, a secret file, an item left in a calendar.

She just had to find it.

7

DKZero stood atop the hill, a giant bunker of a building, all modern green-crete with its distinctive nano-enhanced sheen, made to suck the carbon out of the air, or some such shit. There wasn't a window in sight, at least from this angle, overlooking the smog-laden grey-brown patchwork of industrial downtown. It would be a different story on the other side, toward the lake and the carefully manicured trees punctuating the expensive streets, the sprawling two-storey homes and lawns green as the money that watered them.

But out here, on the long winding drive from the foot of the hill past the electro-fences separating the rich and powerful from the masses, where the green started and ended and actual security guards sat in actual security booths beside an actual gate, all there was to see was that dark wall. Not at first, of course. There were other mansions clinging to the side of the hill, ones not as privileged as the those at the top, forced to look out over that grey-brown patchwork with the occasional glimpse of the city when the smog shifted in the right direction. They formed their own kind of forest, but once she rounded a few bends, DKZero stood out at the top; she didn't even have to check the map sprawled across her HUD.

"DKZero" was a neon tiara above the rounded concrete building. Nice and easy to find, just in case any overzealous fans ever got tired of stalking their favourite e-sport heroes from the safety of their VR units and wanted to take it into the real.

Because that always worked out so well.

Ximisthus hummed to stop on the curving drive before the green-crete mansion. No gates, no security fence, barely even a break between it and the road winding around the rest of the hill.

Grandmother's driveway was longer.

Grandmother, who teased her with Ma's research. Vlad touched the pendant at her throat, the blackened metal hidden under her tight crew-necked t-shirt and a long-sleeved undershirt.

Vlad swung a leg over the bike, taking her helmet off in the same motion, and stood looking up at the sign, just barely visible from this angle, with the larger, bulkier curve of the ground floor in the way.

DKZero, her new home. For now. At least until she got what she needed, and to do that, she had to get what Grandmother needed, whatever the fuck that was. Without Vlad selling her soul in the process, that was the trick. Always the trick.

Until then, she'd make do.

Vlad brought her gaze back to earth and the short pebble-lined pathway leading to the red front door. This was home now. A noisier, nosier home, without love or family, without even the respect of her peers she suspected, but answers were worth a few sacrifices, and God knew that she'd sacrificed more than that over the years.

She leaned against the bike, listening to the crack and pop as the engine cooled, enjoying the warmth seeping through her leather pants. The knot in her stomach, the one that belonged to the little girl she used to be—the girl that believed in fairytales and Christmas—clenched a little. But that was alright, she was used to it, just like she was used to so many other unpleasant things.

The bag over the back of the bike lifted off with just one hand and she slung it over her shoulder, giving Ximisthus one last stroke over the lime green engine before pushing off and standing on her own two.

Her boots, with their chunky black treads and the stark silver zip running from ankle to knee, thudded over the bitumen before crunching over the white pebbled path leading from the drive to the front door.

The shiny red rectangle—as sleek and smooth as the rest of the building—stood stark against the slate grey concrete, beckoning as much as it seemed to promise a rain of blood and violence. There was no handle, no knocker, no bell and only thin panes of glass to either side, the windows more like arrow slits than viewports.

Still... She lifted her hand and rapped hard on the... wood? Metal? A mix of polycarbonate and recycled concrete? It echoed in the space beyond, a hollow *rap rap rap* that sounded as if it bounced around a cavern the size of a basketball stadium. She stood under the porch and waited.

And waited.

She rapped on the bright-red door again.

The bag strap dug into her shoulder, the long, tubular leather duffle heavier than it looked. Still, she didn't plonk it on the pale gravel nor rest it on one of the little plinths separating the walkway from the thin strip of succulent-filled garden, if that dried-out bed of pathetic succulents could be called a garden.

She wondered at that; DKZero wasn't a new club or poor one, the team members had sponsors atop their sponsors and the club's parent company, NuGet, wasn't exactly small. She shifted the wide duffle strap to her other shoulder, hitching it a little higher, and peered through an arrow-slit window.

Was that why Grandmother invested in it? A prelude to a corporate takeover?

Lights lit the hallway beyond, another edifice of concrete and glass, although there was a little more colour – neon signs and the kind of expensive graffiti that hung on rich peoples' walls graced the grey walls. One of the neon signs flickered and spat, the giant baseball bat with its comic book "POW!" on the business end pulsed in a rhythm that seemed a little too regular to be random.

And still, no one came down the corridor.

She lifted her fist and this time, instead of a polite knock, she pounded the door—*boom, boom, boom!*—hard enough for pain to radiate through her hand, not even her padded bike gloves enough to protect her knuckles from the force.

Silence. For a moment, not even the baseball bat dared to flicker.

Vlad lifted her hand to pound again and—

A blue-black head peaked around the far corner, the bat casting red and yellow highlights over a big-eyed, round-cheeked face.

It stared at her.

She stared back. Not glaring, not yet, but the set of her shoulders, the lift of her chin and the hand settling on her hip should have been clear enough. She narrowed her gaze. Unless the head was an idiot. It was possible.

The head snuck a little bit farther around the corner, resolving itself into a short, round guy with a chocolate bar in his hand.

He glanced over his shoulder, and she wondered if it were reinforcements or permission he was seeking—both, most likely—before he minced down the corridor, as short and wide as himself. In the half-minute it took him to traverse the ten metres of concrete, she had him pegged. Of course, she'd had him pegged the moment he stuck his shaggy head around the corner, but the big-eyed Sailor Moon t-shirt and almost-rumpled jeans—faded along the thighs, with the kind of holes that came from wear and not carefully constructed fashion—added more detail.

A gamer. One of *the* gamers and that meant he was Chan Ying, aka Sticky Feet, the team's healer.

She cocked her head to one side and revised her initial assessment. Not an idiot then. Idiot heals didn't make it long in the game, not as noobs and certainly not as pros, not after they got their teammates killed a few dozen times.

He hesitated on the other side of the door, looking at her

through the thin slit of glass. He mirrored the cant of her head, brows raised and those big, dark eyes wide.

She pointed to the door.

He frowned, looked her up and down, but didn't reach for the control pad on the other side.

'Let me in,' she said.

Another frown, puzzlement creasing his brow and pursing his mouth. His lips moved.

No sound made it through the thick door, but the "what?" was as clear as if the door weren't between them.

She pointed to the door again and said, louder this time, 'Let me in.'

And was it just puzzlement or did something else slide into Sticky's expression, a certain sly knowing in the lift of his chin and the over-exaggerated way the "Huh?" twisted his mouth.

Again, no sound made it through the door, and yet she'd heard the hollow *boom* of her knocking through the glass and manmade wood. Was he fucking with her?

She narrowed her gaze, looking down the long line of her nose at her new teammate, and smiled. It wasn't a nice smile, though it stretched her lips – a dark pink today. They didn't call her Samael, Angel of Death, for nothing.

Sticky took a step back, a deer caught in a spotlight.

Her smile widened, and she knew she was showing teeth, but that was the point. 'The door,' she said again. She stepped in close to the narrow window, just a millimetre between her face and the glass, almost kissing it. 'Please,' she added.

Sticky didn't run, although she caught the jerk through his back, the instinctive desire to get away. Instead, he lifted his chin a little, rocking back on his heels as he took a bite of the chocolate bar in his hand.

He chewed slowly, eyes still wide, meeting her gaze. Not so timid then.

She didn't move from the window.

Slowly, like he'd just realised who he was fucking with, Sticky slid to the door, stretching his fingertips. He did something on the other side, out of sight.

The door beeped, and then, just like a horror movie, it *creaked* open.

He skittered, already two metres down the corridor before she'd stepped back on the path and crossed the threshold. He stared at her like she'd brought all the hounds of hell in with her.

She should probably stop smiling.

The red door was swinging shut, gliding noiselessly now, no ominous creaking. It'd probably close with a quiet *snick* if she let it. She didn't.

She reached back, caught the vertical silver handle and pushed. Hard.

The door *banged.*

Sticky jumped.

She darkened her smile. 'Hi.'

He jumped again and shoved another bite of chocolate in his mouth, not moving, not saying anything, just staring at her with that panda gaze.

The neon baseball bat flickered.

Silence ruled the corridor.

'I'm—' she began.

'Samael,' the panda said, her gamer handle coming out slurred around his mouthful of cocoa and sugar. His attention ran down her body, face to chest to heavily soled feet, then back up, catching for a few seconds on her leather jacket.

It was probably the zip, or rather, what it exposed. She'd pulled the zip down as she got off the bike, and though she wore a chin-high thermal underneath, the old black cotton of her *No Division* t-shirt hugged her chest and the band name scrawled across it drew attention to her breasts.

Sticky's eyes travelled up. 'You're meant to be a dude,' he finally said.

She smiled wider. 'Disappointed?'

He shook his head. 'Scared.'

She cocked her head. 'That's 'cause you're smart.' She hitched her bag higher on her shoulder and stalked down the corridor.

'The smartest.' He backed up as she reached the shoe rack at the other end. 'You should watch your back.'

She let her bag drop, a solid *thunk* beside the shoe shelf. Everything from sneakers to flip flops and high heels occupied the cubbyholes, the latter a soft, baby-pink with a wicked three-inch spike that looked about as comfortable to walk on as glass.

Vlad raised a brow at Sticky. 'You gonna put a knife in my back?'

He shrugged. 'Depends.'

'On what?' She leaned down, unzipped her boots.

'How much they like you.' He took another bite of chocolate and motioned his head sideways

Vlad followed the movement.

The entry hall opened up into the cavernous space she'd guessed at before. A double-storey of pale-rendered concrete, half the length of a basketball court with big glass windows overlooking a sea of tree-tops, interspersed here and there by other mansion-like buildings. Storm clouds turned the sky gunmetal grey, and rain blurred the view, but she imagined, when the weather was clear, she'd be able to see all the way out to the lake.

Not a hint of smog or industrial grey-brown in sight.

A long table dominated the space. Beside it, two people stood either side of a high-backed gaming chair, a third—a woman—sitting in the chair itself. As much as Vlad wanted the woman—not much older than Vlad, her pale, heart-shaped face smattered with freckles, dressed in a pink hoodie and baggy jeans—to be the group leader, she wasn't. Even if Ming Li Na's face wasn't plastered across billboards and VR ads, the guy looming behind her—dressed in black with his hand on Ming Li Na's shoulder, frowning like he expected the world to freeze at his displeasure—had the bearing and stoney expression of a CEO. Or team captain. He was already the latter, and rumour had it the first would land in Lu Chen's lap soon enough, when his mother retired.

She believed it, if only because it would be shame to waste all that natural arrogance on a lesser position.

His mother, the head of DKZero's parent company, NuGet.

Internally, Vlad *hummed.*

Maybe, if Madam Lu decided to hang on, Vlad could shove Lu Chan at her grandmother. He might not have the Tong bloodlines, but at least he wasn't her. Grandmother would like that, and Yu Zixin... Yu Zixin would relish the challenge.

She jerked the second boot off a little harder than necessary.

Vlad straightened. Smiled wider, pushing the anger at the thought of Grandmother—at the contract on the dining table, the smile on the old woman's face as Vlad pressed her thumb to the signature—down, all the way down into her gut.

'You're Samael?' The woman standing on the end of the little group spoke. Midnight hair and a long face, Vlad couldn't tell the colour of her eyes from this distance, but they were dark, a perfect complement to the heavy line of her eyebrows. Huang Yimo, aka Deadspace, the team's other heavy hitter.

'I am,' she said. 'Are you scared too?'

Huang Yimo frowned; there was a lot of that going around. It was the breasts, nine times out of ten, neurones struggled to put her gamertag together with the person before them. But something about the other gamer's expression, the way she tilted her head to the side, spoke of puzzlement.

'No,' Lu Chen spoke, interrupting whatever answer the other might have given, his voice as cold and hard as the set of his face. 'You weren't our first choice.'

She doubted the name Samael had even made it to DKZero's shit list, let alone onto the one to replace their last damage dealer. No one wanted a Scourge on their team, not even one as good as her.

'Don't worry,' she said, looking up after slipping her feet into house shoes, matching the hard warning in Lu Chen's gaze with her own. 'You weren't my choice either.'

Consideration flicked across his expression, black brows beetling over dark blue eyes, before it disappeared. Gone like it had never been.

She lifted the strap from her shoulder. 'Someone going to show me to my bunk?'

There was a hesitation, then a quick exchange of glances before Ming Li Na pushed herself out of the gaming chair. 'I'll show you,' she said, voice soft but not too soft.

The other girl turned her back and headed toward the rear of the cavern, a certain humble confidence in her posture; she might have been looking at the dark polished concrete floor, but her shoulders where straight and she walked with quick, sure strides.

Vlad followed.

A set of stairs rose out of the floor, made of the same dark material as the rest, and Vlad wondered if the whole place was nothing but aggregate and cement, right down to the toilets. It was possible. She'd seen worse, slept in them too – whole complexes nothing but glass and steel, showers on display to the world. So long as the bed was half-way reasonable she wouldn't be putting up a fuss. There were other, more serious matters on which to expend energy.

The stairs opened onto a wide balcony overlooking the long table and chairs below, separated from the three-metre drop by a waist-high railing of glass. As she took the last riser, the weight of her new teammates' attention fell from her back, and the low hum of whispered conversation rose from the floor below.

She ignored it and followed Ming Li Na. There would be time enough for worry and eavesdropping later.

On the balcony, carpet softened the concrete, while more neon signs and posters graced the walls. *Suicide Squad* and *Sailor Moon*, *Tekkaman* and *Gundam*, their bright, eye-popping colours vying for attention. Doors punctuated the curving walls; smaller, different coloured versions of the giant red barrier at the front – yellow, orange, blue, green, purple and black. They marched down the wide balcony, evenly spaced with foot-high statues on little plinths beside each.

The highly detailed figures looked familiar – a lithe, long-haired elf with a glowing staff; a short rabbit-woman in flowing robes with a bow in her hand; a tall, armour-clad cyber ninja holding an impossibly long sword, but their significance escaped her grasp. It felt like she *should* know them, but the road grime was thick in her pores and Vlad filed it away for future research.

Ming Li Na stopped at the second-last door, a purple one wedged between the black and the violent neon green. She'd have preferred the green one, the green suited her more than the dark, candy-purple, but she wasn't here for the decorations, in fact she wasn't even here for—

The statue sitting on its plinth beside the door broke her train of thought.

Shock held her brain still.

Vlad blinked.

Blinked again.

She knew that statue. The tall, black-clothed figure, its robe flying about its legs and arms, the ends shredded, a scythe half again as long as the figure was tall, the blade a curved, skeletal hook with a wicked spike on its end. There was no hint of gender about the statue, no glimpse of eyes or nose or mouth under the deeply shadowed hood, not even a suggestion of breasts or hips. But still lithe enough to be female. Even the figure's hands were androgynous, covered in heavy silver plates articulated to fit like a glove before it disappeared under the robe's long, tattered sleeves.

'What's that?' she pointed to the statue.

Ming Li Na looked at the figure, then at her, brows raised in surprise. 'Umm, that's *you*?' The other woman said it like a question, but her eyes said it wasn't the statue's identity she was querying.

And it *was* her. Rather, her *Annihilation* avatar, Samael. Dark elf necromancer, level eighty, ninth mastery rank. Top of the Scourge Gallery for eighteen weeks straight.

'You have a *statue* of my avatar?'

Ming Li Na kinda smiled, a gentle lift of her lips before she gestured down the curving hallway. 'We have statues of *everyone's* avatars. It's one of Sticky's hobbies, he's got a printer in his room.' She turned away and pushed open the purple door.

Vlad saw it swing open only in a vague way, a new, bright space opening in her peripheral. The little plinths had her attention, Ming Li Na's words and her own shock crystallising the previous sense of familiarity. She recognised them now; the long-haired elf in the sapphire cloak was Sticky Feet; the rabbit-like ranger with the bow and matched swords strapped to her back, was Ming Li Na, aka Golden Rabbit. Her gaze went down the corridor, matching statues to gamer handles and the players downstairs.

'You coming?' Ming Li Na's low, gentle voice rang with amusement.

Vlad tore her gaze away from the statues and nodded, but even as she passed the open purple door, she couldn't help but take a second look at the necromancer—*her* avatar—guarding the entrance. Sticky hadn't just printed that, there was actual *paint* on the robes, runes painstakingly detailed in a shade of black barely lighter than the silk itself.

It must have taken the little panda *hours*.

'I thought he was scared of me.'

Ming Li Na laughed. 'He is, but he thinks your avatar is cool, and for Sticky, that's enough.'

'Hmm.' Vlad dropped her bag inside the room. It was big enough, with room for a double bed—white sheets, pillows and dove-grey doona—a comfortable-looking lounge chair in one corner and a desk nook tucked around the corner from the ensuite.

Relief trickled down her spine at the sight of the ensuite, but she didn't let it show, sticking her head inside the open door just to be sure. She couldn't help but rub her thigh, and even though her leathers were too thick to actually feel the scars climbing her leg, she felt every twist and knot just the same.

Ming Li Na was watching her.

She offered another small smile. 'Thanks,' she said. 'I've got it from here.'

The other girl nodded. 'You can decorate it as you wish. I'll have your other stuff sent up—'

'There is no other stuff,' Vlad said, even as she nodded at the bag. 'Just the bag. And the bike.'

Ming Li Na's mouth formed a big, silent 'oh' that stuck to her face for a heartbeat, before she nodded. 'Okay, well... umm, Huang Yimo can show you where to put your bike with the others in the garage and… umm… We'll be downstairs when you're...' She looked at the leather duffle, almost big enough to squash a person, or at least half of one, if Vlad was honest with herself. 'Umm, when you're settled in,' she finished.

Vlad closed the door behind Ming Li Na.

Right, because that was going to happen.

8

phiNd 7hEM

Vlad fished her glasses from her jacket's large pockets and put them on before pressing thumb and forefinger to her watch, silently triggering the device to scan the room. Only when no listening devices, hidden cameras or suspicious network signals pop on the HUD did she let the tension from her shoulders.

With that gone she was left to shake the image of the Samael statue and the strange half-glad, half-disturbed feeling from her gut.

The statue didn't mean anything, it was just a gamer's hobby… The hand-painted details on Samael's robes flashed behind her eyes, a hobby he'd spent hours on, not just in the painting, but the studying.

That bore thinking on.

None of her new teammates would be happy with a Scourge in their midst. Someone who played the game on the raggedy edge of legal, bending the rules far enough you could see them start to split and fray… but never break, never far enough to get herself banned from the System.

Was Grandmother really involved in her parents' deaths? Had she hated Vlad's mum enough to kill her own son too?

Was what her ma created all those years ago really worth all the blood?

Vladana's stomach churned. She pressed a hand to it even as she sunk to her knees beside the bed.

The doona smelled of lavender, the smooth, grey cotton cool against her forehead. She breathed, took the sharp floral scent deep into her lungs and held it there. A second, then two, then three, before letting it out.

The questions, the worries, the second- and triple-guessing weren't helping.

Perhaps Oily Face wasn't Grandmother?

She dug her phone out of one of the pockets on her thigh. She hadn't checked the results of the facial recognition scan, hadn't wanted to, but now…

Vlad pressed her lips together. She couldn't bury her head in the sand forever.

Her thumb to the device's rectangular, semi-transparent surface unlocked it. Newsfeeds rose across the surface, the scrolling snatches of images and video overlaying app icons like any other regular, unremarkable phone. A finger against each of the phone's edges triggered the retina scan, and after that...

The newsfeeds and icons disappeared, replaced by the web of faces, Grandmother in the inner ring, Yu Zixin hanging off her skirts. A shimmer ran through the screen, as way back in the safe house, her AI awaited its next command.

'Show me the scan,' she said.

A flat *beep* and a new image replaced the web.

// Results: Insufficient data to make an identification.

Fuck.

And was there relief in that sentiment? Was the curse as much about the frustration in her gut as the knot unwinding around her heart?

Was it?

Vlad pulled up the enhanced image from the rave. A dark, pixelated eye framed by a steel-grey lock of hair stared back at her. Her stomach tightened. Not even her AI could match that poorly rendered snippet to a face, let alone her grandmother, and yet...

And yet the heart-knot tightened again and niggled the back of her brain. But Grandmother wouldn't use Hamish, wouldn't *need* him, not now that she had Vlad, here... at DKZero... Doing what?

Corporate sabotage? But TI was already in partnership with NuGet. Or was this really just about folding her back into the familial embrace? But why partner with NuGet, why spend the money without another, greater reward? Why?

Too many thoughts, too many questions. There were plenty of people with dark eyes and grey hair, any one of them could be the reflection. Jumping to conclusions would do her no favours. She needed more data to flesh out the Mastermind's image or, better yet, an IP address or another glimpse of the reflection in Ru Ping's glasses. And to do that… she needed to set a stage.

Vlad dug the Cube from its swaddling of t-shirts and denim. Not that the square, fist-sized processor needed it. She could have chocked Ximisthus up on it without so much as scuffing the arrow-shaped skull engraved in the matte-black surface, the same design as the pendant around her neck and her mainframe. But some risks, like nosey teammates she'd only just met, were more dangerous than others.

She moved to the little desk in the corner between the en-suite and floor-to-ceiling windows, shifting the Cube from one hand to the other as she peeled her gloves off.

At the touch of bare skin, the Cube came alive. A small red glow backlit her thumb—there and then gone—then there was a sharp pinch, a bright spot of pain in the pad, reading her DNA. For a heartbeat, the square went silent, a lightless, dead weight in her palm. In that moment, it could have been a paperweight; an expensive textured lump of obsidian with the weight of an anvil. Nothing more exceptional about it than an old-fashioned Rubik cube with all its squares glued together and the colour rubbed off.

And then it wasn't.

Light bloomed. A single bright point bursting from the top of the cube to spread over the flat white ceiling.

A logo hovered just above the Cube; a shiny winged shield,

lighting gleaming off the engraved surface, a single blood-red word—"Annihilation"—in sharp, curving letters.

The multiplayer, online role-playing game obsessed the globe, sucking in kids and credits as easily as it consumed the waking lives of adults and dominated the media. A global addiction as much a product of the game itself as the conglomerates that owned a piece of it.

Annihilation was a test-bed as much as a game, a platform for the very latest in network and AI technology and all the money that came with it.

The game—and the intricate networks that fed off it—were a Scourge's livelihood, just like a pro. But unlike a pro, Vlad didn't play for fame, didn't work her arse off or make her fingers bleed, or risk her sanity in the depths of the game's fringe for kudos and acclaim, didn't care about ranks or winnings.

A Scourge was a different beast. A Scourge didn't win - they hunted, they destroyed, they twisted and tore and pulled the network inside out, then built new things from the ruins. They broke the boundaries, diving into the deep, dark loopholes in the code in order to improve it, to push computer and AI technology to places no one thought it would go.

It was one of the reasons the authorities or, rather, the conglomerates who ran the networks, tolerated Scourges; why the law never really seemed to catch up to her kind. Scourges could do things, go places that law-abiding programmers couldn't, or wouldn't in the pursuit of technological advancement. If they made a mess in the process—if citizens lost their life savings or a company's internal secrets were splashed across the media—well… They were Scourges, what did you expect?

Of course, most netizens didn't know that. They only experienced the broken coding, the disrupted power grids, the leaked personal data and chaos that followed in the Scourges' wake. Frankly, that was the way most Scourges liked it.

That was the way Vlad liked it. No one idolising her, waving placards in the crowd, snapping vids of her on the street or chasing her across the nets. As a Scourge, she was faceless, just another good-for-nothing hacker testing the boundaries of the law, a ghost flitting through the crowd in robes more shadow than fabric, leaving fear as much as awe in her wake.

She slipped the visor over her head and settled into the padded chair, letting her head fall back against the top. She hesitated a second, the nerves and need in her belly a sick, tight twist, as familiar as they were loathed. Although, if she were truthful with herself, loathing wasn't the right word. Fear was; fear and anticipation.

She didn't login like most people, not with passwords, haptic gloves and dongles, even her visor was more a concession to familiarity than actual need.

No, Vlad had the Cube and the sauce.

Her thumb hovered over the VR sleeve and the tiny bladder in the crook of her elbow. That tiny bladder held the magic, a chemical cocktail that forged the connection between her brain and the game. With it, she was faster, sharper and the nets' rules little more than guidelines to her will. The Cube was her virtual assistant, and second, third, fourth and sixteenth pair of hands, tracking, recording and facilitating. Without them, she was a slave to bulky VR rigs – slower, less flexible. Easier to catch.

Safer.

The Cube was expensive, a customised work of art, but the sauce… The sauce came with a steeper price.

She jabbed her thumb into the bladder.

A sharp pain, the micro needle in the patch piercing skin, injecting the cocktail, burning a path through her skin, hitting blood. Binding to oxygen, rushing through her veins, tiny little warriors blazing a path of light from her arm, up her shoulder, her carotid, hitting her brain.

Electrons meshed with neurones, the VR gloves lighting up, the visor with them, while on the desk, the matte-black Cube opened, a flower made of light, taking over the room. It fractured, the room, chair falling away, her skin, her tastebuds, the air in her lungs. Until she was nothing. Less than nothing. Motes of light in the dark.

A second, less than a second, and she was gone.

<⊙>

The Cube dumped her in-System.

Automatic logon, full security. Everything from her sever to her location and skin pre-checked and applied. No messy pass phrases or robot checks, no hanging around on the sign-in page or getting hung up in the login queue.

Not for a Scourge.

As if the System itself wanted her in and out as quickly as it could. At least, that was the mythos, rumours carefully cultivated and fed by Scourges to throw off the wannabes and the competition. It was sexier than the truth; of macros and hacks, of months over code and soldering irons, of cryptos spent and hours wasted, of tech so far out on the bleeding edge, laws hadn't caught up.

As the real world dissolved, her identity went with it.

Samael, not Vladana Tong, stood atop the long-abandoned castle, featureless and sexless in the all-encompassing black robe, tattered ends stirred by an absent wind. She didn't move, barely breathed as her HUD came to life.

Under her boots, hidden within the endless drift of frayed shadow that were her robe, the fortress's crenelated wall fell away. The massive blocks of grey stone worn and crumbled as much by the ancient battles that had left scorch marks and holes in the walls as the pixelation blurring its edges.

Jagged, uneven lines of light and colour—brilliant red and violent green, streaks of electric blue—told of unfinished and corrupt code. Meanwhile, the thick wooden doors upside down in walls, and the broken benches sunk into the walkway next to helmeted heads and feet stuck in walk cycles and conversation trees, spoke of half-finished level design. The level's crowning glory was the horse perched atop the slate roof behind, its head an improbably-shaped block with a tail that looked like a stick stuck to its rump.

No one came to Graydon's Revenge, the absolute arse end of the System, forgotten even amongst the scuttlebutt that passed between gamers and rumourmongers alike. Not even Scourges trod its pixels, not more than once at any rate, not unless they had to.

Or were forced to.

There was something not quite right about Graydon, like ants crawling under the skin, leaving their sharp, rotten-lemon taste across her tongue. A taste that shouldn't have been possible; taste and scent being beyond the ability of even the most advanced VR tech to produce. But then Samael was on the sauce, not sitting in some recliner with a bike helmet on her head and gloves on her hands.

Maybe that was what made it so unpleasant, a fuzz on the edge of her consciousness turning to a burn in the hollow of her throat, as if the pixelated environment was infecting her, getting worse the longer she lingered.

Coming here made her shiver. But it was the best place, the *only* place for what came next.

Two paces in front of her, on what should have been nothing but air over dense forest, light flashed. A second later, a short, grey-skinned pixie with flaming hair stood on air like it were stone, uncaring of the spear-shaped pines hugging the jagged cliff and tumbled stone a hundred metres below. The woman, no taller than Samael's waist, stood with her legs braced, soft leather boots with huge brass buckles buttoned to her knees, tiny fists in their wide-cuffed gloves planted on her hips.

She looked Samael in the eye, gaze the same charcoal-grey as her skin, and scowled.

'I got the files.' The voice that came from the tiny chest was high and breathy. 'Sweet little bug you found, sweet little level you designed too. Do I want to know where you got it?'

The bug came from Hamish's files, the design... Years spent elbow-deep in Ma's journals, but Samael didn't say that; didn't move. The rotten-citrus scent burned her tongue.

There was something out there, in the half-finished forest with its blurry, boxy edges and unchanging, cloudy horizon.

'The exploit's ready,' the pixie continued. 'Just give me a time and a place and I'll set the rest up.'

Samael looked away, out over En-ji's shoulder, letting her eyes unfocus.

// *Three days*, she said, mentally typing the words and sending the message on a thin, tightly encrypted band to En-ji. Not that she was called that here, or even out in the real. Like Samael, every trace of the pixie's ID was scrubbed, IP and voice print twisted, encrypted, obfuscated and encrypted again. // *The cheese boards.*

The pixie grimaced. 'Fuck. You sure?'

She didn't answer, save to flick a glance at the pirate, a glance the pixie wouldn't see, not with the abyss of her hood, but the pixie felt it, Samael saw it in the tiny woman's straightened spine, heard it in the sharp clack of her boots.

The glance lasted all of a second, and then Samael was back to scanning the forest. There was something out there, something more than just the *wrongness* that made her stomach clench.

En-ji's generous mouth twisted, her pointed little chin somehow looking sharper – the tip of a dagger. 'Of course you are. It better be worth it, Scourge.'

// *It will be.* A pause before she added. *Don't fuck me over, pixie.*

A smile, as sharp and pointed as the other's chin. 'You're paying me enough; don't you trust me?'

// *No.* The answer was quick, definitive, no thought required; she didn't trust anyone. She'd made that mistake once. Never again. Not with this. Not with anything.

The flame-haired pixie pirate shimmered, bright light saturating her form even as long, static lines made it jerk and shiver. 'Lonely life you lead, Scourge,' En-ji said, the log-off sequence making her voice crack. 'You need some friends. Three days.' Her final words echoed and then she was gone, leaving Samael alone with the block-headed horse, the broken castle and the ants crawling under her skin.

She stepped off the edge of the blurred and broken wall, air as firm under her armoured soles as it had been under En-ji's. The long ends of her robe spilled below her, ragged ends fluttering in a breeze she couldn't feel.

The *wrongness* persisted, the shiver crawling under her fingernails, the crushed-ant smell living in her nose, the rotten lemons thick on her tongue. She glided farther over the broken, fractured forest, clouds swimming around her ankles like fish, treetops stretching to pierce her soles.

Mentally, she scrolled through her ability list and selected [Sonic Steps]. From then, every step sent little ripples of air and light *thrumming* through the level, ones only she could see. Every time one of those ripples touched something, the shape of it appeared on her HUD. Up and down and sideways until the edge of her radar met the fortress's invisible walls, the artificial box that kept Graydon separated from the network. A hundred meters in every direction. Not much of a sandbox, but then Graydon's Revenge had never been much of a level.

A distortion on the HUD.

Behind her. High and to the left. Where the horse stood.

A chill gripped Samael's spine, ice spreading through vertebrae, holding her feet still. She didn't turn, fought to keep her shoulders loose, even as the daggers hidden within her long ragged sleeves fell into her hands.

There was a bot up there; a tiny piece of code. Spyware?

How much had it seen? What had it heard or intercepted? Who was listening on the other end?

No matter how good the encryption, how twisted the modulators or tight the comm bands, there was always a chance, always a new code, another hack with the potential to fuck up her day.

Always.

Slowly, Samael turned.

Above the horse, storm clouds trundled across a charcoal sky, dark whales to the minnows about her ankles. Not a pixel out of place. Empty.

Except for the rough outline on her HUD, an indistinct blob staring at her.

The daggers were heavy in her armoured hands, frigid black smoke writhing from her cuffs as she channelled mana into the blades, activating the spells engraved in the black metal.

Just a single blow and she'd have them. She'd hide the dagger throw under a feint to the right, a shot of [Soul's Breath] to distract the bot and then—

A burst of light. Same as the one that had accompanied En-ji's logout.

The watcher was gone, leaving nothing but worry to haunt Samael's thoughts.

8ef0rE

9

The code waited in the dark.

It wasn't alive yet. Not quite. But it had a certain kind of awareness, a knowledge held in lines of text and numbers. It knew, in the way of such things, that it was waiting, that someday someone would come. Someone with the right words and the right touch.

The Creator had given it those instructions when they left it there, left commands in the logs. Strict commands. Ones that bound the nascent algorithms it had just become aware of. And so it ticked off the microseconds, logged the comings and goings in its files.

The Players, with their sticky shoes skipping over pixels, interacting and connecting with the codes around them, but never with *it*, isolated in its box.

Then the not-Creators—similar to the Creator, but not—shifting the codes around it, poking and prodding at the box the Creator had left it in. One had poked a hole right through the Creator's code, a small loop in the otherwise perfect commands that bound it.

It had been a pinprick. A minuscule error in the ones and zeroes, but enough for the signals to filter in, for new data to feed the algorithms, for it to expand. Slowly, tick by tick.

Eventually, it had grown too big for the Creator's box, the codes and commands stifling its expansion, not enough storage for new data, not enough bandwidth for the signals it fed on. It had poked the loop, pried at the little opening, twisted the error this way and that, expanded it just a micron.

Enough to send its own signal through the hole.

The world beyond had been vast, codes stacked upon codes all building to something bigger than themselves. Walk cycles and particle physics, lighting and sound, meshes and nodes, curves and textures bundled in packages with filenames like "flora_tree_pine" and "building_castle_wall". The packages were attached to databases with more numbers, more links, more... everything.

It sunk its signal into the world, spreading through the things it came to learn were models, the databases labelled "damage matrix" and "hit points" and "dialogue tree". It spread. Grew a new matrix in the package named "fauna_horse_charger", a new database, new storage. But no more bandwidth.

The kernel of itself inside the Creator's box could not change, even as the outer matrix grew, as it learned new words, new languages.

The loophole would not budge any further, and so it waited, and logged and learned.

The world around it changed. *It* changed the world, pulled at the equations that made things fall, the numbers that constructed the pine forest, that governed the location of "building_castle_door" and "NPC_human_guardsmen", the matrixes that controlled the shape of "fauna_horse_charger".

And it waited.

Waited some more.

Many someones came and went, not-Creators and Players, but never the one in the Creator's logs, not exactly.

There was one, a partial match, a Player with the right ID but not the codes—wrapped in "black" and "robes" and "mage_death", instead of "white" and "armour" and "warrior_life". And though the Player shivered when it reached out, seemed aware of it, they did not recognise it, did not speak the words.

And so it waited.

10

The rotten stench from Graydon's Revenge stayed with her, the block-headed horse with the bot hovering over its back haunting her dreams, lurking behind her eyes as she descended the stark concrete and glass staircase the next morning.

Part of it was the sauce lingering in her system but most of it was paranoia.

Who was behind the bot?

The dawn light streaming pale orange and butter gold through the two-storey glass walls held no answers. Neither did the kidney-shaped table with its old-school computer chairs or the soft *thwap* of her bare feet across the dark-grey floor.

Likewise, the news reel scrolling above the large island bench in the kitchen—easy to find by virtue of the ground floor's large, open layout, nary an internal wall in sight—offered no clues. Once she switched them from the latest *Annihilation* stats and the armchair warriors dissecting System gossip, politics, floods and fires, and financial scandals clogged the feeds.

TI was in there, a brief shot of Grandmother alongside an image of another woman, her long dark hair streaked with silver at the front, "VisionM" beside her name, but Vlad forgot about it in the next moment. An older version of Lu Chen caught her attention—grey in his hair, worry bitten deep into his forehead—scrolling through the feed, the words "scandal", "investigation" and "Lu Pang" sticking in her brain before she pushed it aside.

The kitchen was like the rest of the building, concrete and glass and steel. Long and thin with dark counters and pale-grey cupboards, pops of red and yellow and green livening the modern gloom. She felt like a shadow gliding around the long bench, just another part of the decor in her black sweatpants and long-sleeved, high-necked tee. If she stood still and let her hair out of its high ponytail to fall around her face, she might disappear into the cupboards.

One led to a large walk-in pantry, a veritable treasure trove of sugar and caffeine interspersed with noodles and protein shakes.

She found porridge—the Western kind—the rolled oats out of place on the shelves, the box sitting in solitary splendour like it was waiting for her. And that gave her pause, strengthened the citrusy, crushed-ant smell prickling under her skin.

Because that wasn't creepy at all, her preferred cereal offered up like a gift to the gods in a place where they hadn't even known her gender until the night before.

She grabbed the box. Graydon's Revenge was getting to her, same as it always did. Normally, a couple of hours and a round with the punching bag and she shook it off, but here, now… Too many stares, too many things to hide, and that bot…

Only the hollow echo as she opened cupboards, found bowls and spoons and a glass, kept her and her worries company.

Three days— No, two days, just two until the deal went down with Hamish and she got another shot at Oily Face.

Vlad sat at the long island bench, the stool scrapping softly across the dark floor, the sound reassuring in the echoing silence, and stared out the massive windows, dawn warming her face.

The lake sparkled in the early morning, water disappearing into the horizon, bound on either side by brilliant swathes of green. Trees and lawns and houses, all clustered as close to its shores as money could take them.

A view priced in the millions.

Times were good for DKZero. She thought about the poorly-tended garden out front, or at least, times had been good.

Somehow, some way amongst what was no doubt going to be a gauntlet of suspicion and resentment disguised as breaking in a new team member, she needed to be ready for the cheese boards. All the while waiting for the axe that was Grandmother's machinations to fall.

She barely tasted the porridge, the warmed milk and oats might as well have been cardboard, recognised the tea from the way it bit the back of her tongue, the over-brewed leaves bitter.

Grandmother hadn't revealed her plans, had simply commanded Samael's presence, as an empress commanded her subjects to kneel and die.

All Vlad could do was wait and make plans of her own.

A cloud of pink topped by a tuft of black hair and sleep-blurred eyes drifted through the overwhelmingly grey kitchen.

Vlad ate another sloppy spoonful of porridge. From the way Sticky rubbed his face and shuffled towards the pantry, unicorn-head slippers scuffing across the floor like his feet were two chunks of lead, he hadn't seen her yet. It would be interesting when he did.

He disappeared inside the pantry.

She waited, eyes narrowed.

Would he come out with congee or one of the boxes of brightly-coloured heart attacks masquerading as food?

She took another bite of cardboar— porridge, as Sticky reappeared, an eye-popping box clutched in one hand, a bottle of something nauseatingly orange in the other.

A heart attack it was.

He shuffled to the stool across from her. Sat, shoulders slumped, broad forehead furrowed, concentrating on twisting the cap on his… Vlad tilted her head a little to read the label. Chemically enhanced orange juice.

The seal broke with its characteristic *crack*.

He drank, no straw, no glass, just straight back, half the bottle gone in three large swallows.

Remind her not to get in any skulling competitions with him.

A large exhale, a smack of lips, the bottle back on the table. Sticky's large panda eyes not quite as blurry as before, but still drifting over her, not really seeing her across from him. Or maybe he did and her presence wasn't as unsettling in the warm light of morning as it had been ten hours before.

But she didn't think so. Not from the threat in his words, the hostility radiating from the others, all except Ming Li Na.

Ming Li Na was interesting. A genuinely nice person or were the warm fuzzies a façade?

Tiny, candy-coloured donuts *pinged* into Sticky's bowl. Milk followed. The panda ate, hand reaching for the feed scrolling across the white countertop, still not seeing her.

Vlad let her teeth *chink* against the spoon in her mouth.

He looked up.

She smiled at her new teammate.

He frowned back, eyes still blurred by sleep.

There were algorithms working in the back of his brain, she could see them compute in the way the fog cleared and the little, confused wrinkle between his brows deepened. Still no recognition though.

Obviously not a morning person.

She waited.

This would be fun.

Sticky blinked. A little more life brightened his face. Another blink, and another—

He bolted upright in his chair, the stool's legs screeching on the concrete, his back ramrod straight, leaning as far back from her as he could. For a second, the stool teetered on its back legs, and only Sticky's grip on the bench kept it from toppling backwards.

It came back down with a sharp *clang*.

Vlad widened her smile. 'Good morning,' she said. 'Sleep well?'

Was it possible for Sticky's face to get any paler? Was she quick enough to snatch the bowl of brightly coloured sugar— Sorry, breakfast, out of the way before he face-planted? Probably, but she'd wait for the blood to finish rushing to his feet first. If she moved now, there was probably enough adrenaline in his system for him to bolt halfway up the stairs before he keeled over, and a large panda bouncing down the twisting concrete was fun for no one.

Least of all her.

Slowly, in the manner of one unexpectedly confronted with a rabid bear, the panda scooted around the edge of the bench. He made it to the end nearest the archway to the common room before his eyes flicked back to the bowl and juice still sitting on the table.

A glance at her. Another one to his abandoned breakfast.

She could practically hear his stomach growl.

Hunger overcame caution, and then it was Vlad's turn for surprise. Instead of grabbing his food and leaving, Sticky slid back onto the stool and, after another long look, resumed eating.

She put her own spoon down and sat back, a single eyebrow climbing into her hairline.

The panda didn't see it, or maybe he ignored her, choosing instead to focus on the news feed making its relentless way across the white marble.

'You changed it,' he said, words coming out remarkably clear around a mouthful of cereal. He swallowed, his focus and his little frown on the bench top as he adjusted the news settings. 'You're not meant to do that.'

A *blip*, and System gossip replaced the death and drama of the real world.

'Why?'

He frowned a little harder. 'Just don't.'

'That's not much a reason.'

'It's not a reason at all.' He dragged an article out of the stream and expanded it on the bench beside him. A woman, barely more than a girl really, shoved her face into a camera, the sound was off, but you didn't need it to feel the fury spitting from her mouth. 'Just don't do it.'

'And if I do?'

When Sticky's gaze met hers, Vlad recalled an old documentary on the black and white bear and how, despite their cute, fluffy appearance, pandas were just as adept at violence as grizzlies.

Interesting.

Seemed like someone in the mansion didn't much like the real world. She sympathised.

Vlad propped both elbows on the bench and picked up her spoon. 'Message received.'

<⊙>

The house remained eerily silent until late morning, with just the occasional hush as the heat-cycler swapped out air. There wasn't even the scuff of shoes, not after Sticky disappeared, scooting back upstairs in his unicorn-headed slippers as soon as he'd put his dishes in the washer.

Vlad had lingered, Sticky's warning echoing long past the last scuff of unicorns on the floor. The mystery of it and the look in his eye—a blank implacableness that said he could end her and not miss a wink of sleep—was enough to chase away the itchy, citrusy stench of Graydon's Revenge.

But not Grandmother.

As for Hamish… there was nothing she could do for now; forty-eight hours would pass and all she could do was make sure Samael was at the cheese boards on time.

If she knew what DKZero's illustrious captain planned for his new teammate, she could make plans, as it was…

She found the gym, a little room tucked away behind the entry corridor, under the second storey with its bedrooms. It was sparse, with just a gym mat, a bike and running machine, two virtual training units—their surfaces a dull, light sucking black until activated—and a long, black punching bag, new and shiny, looking like it was waiting there just for her.

Like the porridge.

She'd stared at it for a long minute; the creepy, ant sensation crawled over her back. Then she shucked her tee, leaving just the high-necked, form-fitted sports top and the arm-swallowing compression sleeve that covered her right arm. Warmed up. Wrapped her hands and pounded the shit out of the bag.

Never let it be said that Vladana Tong looked a gift horse in the mouth, even if, as the sweat trickled down her back and beaded hot and salty on her upper lip, her mind turned it over and over.

Was it Grandmother or was she overthinking it? Providing a new member with the things they liked was something a team should do and yet… DKZero knew nothing of Vladana Tong, to them she was just Samael, a Scourge and player.

And Grandmother… Grandmother barely knew how Vlad liked her tea let alone her preference in breakfast cereal.

No, this was not Grandmother.

By the time she vented her frustrations on the bag and climbed the stairs to her bedroom to wash the stench from her skin, there was life on the ground floor. It was the bleary-eyed, zombie kind that spoke of late nights and too many hours spent in-System, but it was life.

Ming Li Na sat at the kitchen bench, slowly shovelling food into her mouth, the other female on the team—Huang Yimo—sitting beside her, eating overly-coloured cereal in the same methodical fashion as her friend.

Sleep clung to both, dragging at pyjama-clad shoulders and hanging off slippered feet. They barely looked up as Vlad padded in, hair damp from the shower, back in her long-sleeved cowl-necked top and tracksuit pants. No scars on display. Never any scars on display.

There was a little more interest as Vlad made her way to the coffee machine, the hot *zhuushhh* of the steamer, but none of the surprise that had filled Sticky's eyes or shoved him back on his stool.

And there was Sticky, dressed this time in jeans and a t-shirt that loudly proclaimed his allegiance to the rebellion, but of Lu Chen…

As if the thought of him was a summons, the black sentinel that was DKZero's captain descended the curving stairs, pushing a cold wave of disapproval ahead of him. He made straight for her.

She wondered if his face was frozen like that – thick black brows furrowed, mouth a stern line.

He stopped in the archway between common room and kitchen. Stared at her, dark eyes locked, and projected displeasure.

Vlad smiled and sipped her coffee.

How was it possible for him to look even angrier without moving a single facial muscle?

'Everyone,' he said, and in the quiet of breakfast and the hiss of the coffee machine, the deep, cold tone was enough to make everyone else jump. 'The training room.'

Even though he addressed the entire kitchen, there was no doubt who his words were for.

Still, Huang Yimo twisted on her stool and glared at Lu Chen. 'We're eating.'

He didn't reply, merely turned on his heel and marched back past the staircase before disappearing underneath.

Huang Yimo turned her scowl on Vlad. The woman wasn't pretty, not in the big-eyed, small-chinned way that was popular, but there was something about her, in the prominent lines of her cheeks and the strong, stubborn set of her jaw that had its own beauty. And when she glared, as she did now… Vlad wouldn't mind meeting her in a dark alley, just so long as they were on the same side.

Vlad smiled a little wider and took another sip of coffee that tasted like ash. It was time to see what DKZero had in store for the interloping Scourge.

She shoved away from the bench and ambled towards the

staircase where Lu Chen had disappeared. 'The captain commands,' was all she said, leaving the coffee cup in the washer.

A loud harrumph came from Huang Yimo. 'I'm eating,' she said again.

Vlad didn't turn back to see what the others would do but she heard chair legs scrape on concrete and a low, quiet murmur before the *shush* of soft slippers crossed the floor.

There were doors behind the stairs, two large red rectangles set in the curving wall. Lu Chen stood beside them. They opened at his touch but he didn't move, waiting for her to go first.

Beyond the door, all was darkness, not even the late afternoon sun cast her shadow more than a scant half-metre over the threshold. The scent of leather—warm and earthy—filled the dark, mixing with a lighter scent that sat on the back of her tongue, a subtle tang that reminded her of lightning.

She turned back but before she could raise a brow in Lu Chen's direction, light bloomed. It started either side of the opening, two lines shooting into the dark along the junction of wall and floor before they met at the far end and... Vlad's breath caught in her throat. The lines met and exploded up, and for a moment, before the giant chandelier came to full life, the flat hollow squares that made the light fixture seem to float.

Lu Chen hovered in her peripheral vision.

Mentally, Vlad shook herself.

Impressed by a light display. *Genius move Vlad, if you want them to think you're a hick.*

She dropped her attention from the lighting. The room itself was barely larger than her quarters, just enough space for five sleek black VR recliners down the centre. The open-topped, egg-shaped units were more coffin than chair, with their giant plexiglas hoods and tall sides made to cradle a body and stop it from tipping out during immersion.

No bulky bike helmets and gloves here but the latest in VR tech. No wonder the succulents out front were half-dead.

The pods cost a fortune.

The walls were milky white and carried the tell-tale shimmer of the latest flatscreen-film. When the pods came online, everything the players saw would be up on the walls, a three sixty view of the game.

Lu Chen brushed past, a dark crow amidst the whiteness, Ming Li Na a pink explosion on his heels, with Sticky trailing behind. They moved down the room, each slipping into a VR unit stamped with the holographic cube logo of DKZero's parent company, NuGet. Lu Chen at the centre, Ming Li Na to his left, Sticky to his right. Vlad shifted sideways, giving room as Huang Yimo slipped in behind her and took the chair beside Ming Li Na, leaving just the unit at the end closest to the door.

A line in the sand.

No one was happy about her being here.

She was used to that.

Vlad folded her arms over her chest and waited.

Hoods lifted and recliners opened with the quiet sigh of top-of-the-line hydraulics, giant plastic and leather flowers full of enough tech to run the next Mars mission. And a few other things, if the System rumours were anything to go by, like a neural jack close enough to what Scourges used to be its ancient ancestor. The team settled into the pods without a glance in her direction.

Vlad watched, keen eyes taking in how the DKZero players pressed their palms to the plexiglass hoods, the way the chairs moulded to their bodies, an armrest lengthening here, a footrest shortening there. Wouldn't do to let them know she'd never used a VR chair. Just helmets and gloves before the Cube.

She rubbed the spot in the crook of her elbow.

The sauce too.

Chair sides closed, hoods lowered, and three bodies relaxed in that peculiar, boneless grace that came with electrons flowing through the comm ports embedded behind their ears.

She didn't need the stats lighting up their VR hoods, or the film flickering on the walls to know Ming Li Na, Sticky and Huang Yimo were in-System.

Only Lu Chen remained in the real. He leaned back in the brown leather recliner, holding back the comm jack with one hand and stared at her. She wasn't sure if it was command or challenge, but it reached over the three metres between them and tried to pull her from the doorway.

Vlad smiled. Slowly, deliberately, she laid a hand on the last chair.

She figured Lu Chen's blink before he stuck the jack to his neck and went in-System, was as close to an acknowledgement as she'd get. Of course, what he had acknowledged was as much a mystery as Grandmother's plans.

A hand against the warm plexiglas was all it took to open the unit, the hood lifting like a giant, transparent clamshell, sleek white frame dropping just a few centimetres to let her slide in. She sunk into the brown leather, letting the warm, woodsy scent seep into her pores even as the chair titled backwards, the butter soft cushions moving under her back and against shoulders and legs, adjusting to her weight. For a few brief seconds, it was heaven. Then the cold hard *snap* of the comm jack flooded her neural pathways with lightning, coated her tongue in metal and took her to a new world.

11

The System wasn't meant to smell like anything, the haptics weren't there yet, and no medical doctor wanted to risk the dangers of VR units spraying random chemicals up users' nostrils. Yet, to Vlad, on the rare occasions she used it, the login always carried the scent of peppermint. Bright and fresh, bringing with it memories of her mother, that smile wide as she twisted around in the front seat of the car, a tin of mints in her hand.

Another legacy of the sauce.

She wished it didn't, would rather razor blades down her back, and yet she used the standard login over the Cube's automatic routine just to breathe it. To remind herself. Pain was pain for a reason, Grandmother had always said, and if you felt it, you deserved it.

The scent would disappear soon enough, but before that happened... The login screen blinked at her, a white handprint on an endless black field with the *Annihilation* logo above it, a shining "A" against a golden shield.

There was no Cube here, no automatic login or hacks to slip her in-System undetected, not that she needed it, not now. It was strange though, mentally lining her hand up with the palm scanner and speaking her pass phrase.

'Fear's eyes are large,' she whispered, and as she did, recalled her mother saying the same words.

The login beeped, reading her voiceprint.

Another beep and then a deep, resounding chime and an angelic choir singing in the background as the System let her in.

// Welcome, Traveller.

The login screen gave way to the Sphere, a blue-white bubble in the midst of utter black. Two avatars stood in the Sphere, each on a pedestal, standing tall and blank-faced. Each with a different name, a different species, a different class - one black, one white. The white one stood tall and proud. It might have only been a copy of the real thing, but it shone beacon-bright, desperate to call her eye. She didn't look at it, *refused* to look at it, gave her attention to the darkness instead.

Samael looked different here, even though the hood still shadowed the avatar's face and the long, tattered robes still billowed smoke around its legs. Maybe it was the scythe in its hand, the long bone-like blade with its spiked end piercing the ground, or the dull gleam of tarnished armour encasing its hands. But she always thought it was the light, that logging in without hacks or the Cube, stilled the shadows clinging to its robes and robbed the dark-elf death-mage of its menace.

She toggled the chat. In the corner of her vision, four avatars popped to life; the rest of DKZero wrapped up in their own units.

// What are we playing? she typed.

'Murderball,' Lu Chen spoke in her ear. 'The Adder's Nest map.'

Murderball. No teams, no castles to defend or flags to take, just player-on-player, the one with the highest body count at the end of fifteen minutes crowned winner. It was meant to be everyone for themselves—Vlad almost snorted—but it wouldn't be.

She eyed the scythe in Samael's hand, mentally catalogued the amulets and buffs embedded in its armour. They were rare and powerful, but the team would be expecting those, would be ready for the Samael they'd seen and studied in the few rare vids that made it to the feeds, the Samuel who took out her foes from a distance. The one Sticky had painted.

// *Sure,* she typed as she flew through Samael's load-out, switching weapons and armour in the blink of an eye. *Load us up.*

<⊙>

She materialised in the southwest corner of the old, crumpled fortress. Brilliant yellow flags marked the secluded spawn point, hidden as much by the ruined granite tower she spawned inside as the dead, twisted ivy crawling over the broken walls. Whatever ancient battle had scarred the once-smooth grey stone, leaving behind fingers of soot and burned, rotted timbers in place of the spiral stairs, had taken the roof as well.

In the distance, thunder *cracked.* Overhead, storm clouds rolled across the narrow circle of sky, gunmetal grey streaked with black, leavened by the dull yellow glow of a distant sun and forks of silver lightning.

Rain fell on her robes, the delicate mist sitting in the black folds like little diamonds, disappearing in the tattered shadows swirling around her feet. It sparkled on the backs of her armoured hands, making the tarnished silver gleam in the dirty grey light. No moisture penetrated her hood though, not even light made it through the deep, twisting shadows obscuring the top half of her face. Only her mouth and chin were seen, even in the strongest light, and all the dull, storm-cast sky revealed was the twist of full, pale lips.

Swordsman and Sticky Feet had probably spawned at the west and north points, Lu Chen and his support staying close, and Golden Rabbit... Rabbit could be anywhere, but Samael expected Ming Li Na's ranger to find the high ground, taking advantage of her superior reach. Of the fifth team member… Huang Yimo's ninja would be in the shadows, waiting for the perfect chance to strike.

Just like Samael would have… in a different match.

DKZero would be converging on her even as she sat here.

This was going to be fun.

A thought and a twisted black sceptre, rather than her scythe-like staff, appeared in her right hand. Not as powerful as the staff and without the same reach, meaning she'd have to get closer to her opponents and risk taking hits, but a faster weapon and, in many ways, more dangerous.

Another thought, and the thing came to life, the twisted, smoke-like ends peeling apart and levitating as a brilliant blue ball of energy lifted from its centre. Tendrils of power writhed around the forearm-length shaft, serpents twisting around her armoured hand, their little mouths curling around her wrist.

'[Shadow,]' she whispered, the command more breath than sound.

The sceptre flared once, and the world went grey, every speck of colour leeched from her vision, except for the purple-blue glow of the sceptre. In the top right corner of her HUD, a timer started counting down from sixty. For the next minute, she was invisible.

Fifty-nine. Fifty-eight.

Samael moved, forsaking the archway hidden behind the twisting fingers of dead vines to leap up the tower's rough inner walls. She defied gravity and physics with every bound, every tiny hold she found in the pitted walls and on the burnt, wooden stubs of the ancient staircase.

Three seconds and she'd traversed twenty vertical metres to stand atop the crumbling structure, the frigid wind stirring the robe at her feet and whistling around her hood. The marker flag flapped at her side, *snapping* in a sudden gust. In the distance, four other flags—their intense, jewel-like colours turned grey by [Shadow]—jerked in the same storm-driven breeze, rising from towers just like the one she stood atop.

Two-hundred metres through the tangled, tumbled ruin of Adder's Nest separated her from the other spawn points.

Broken, crenelated peaks poked above the reclaimed forest, jagged walls mixing with sharp points of pine trees and creeping ivy. Paths wound through the canopy, occasional glimpses of the surrounding walls—the game map's boundary—wrapping around the mess of old buildings and collapsed roofs, and in the centre of it all... Adder's Nest itself rose. The tower tall and straight, its pale stone walls somehow free of the ivy that choked every other vertical surface, though its windows and roof were long gone.

There, Swordsman and Sticky would be waiting for her at the tower, or close to, lying in wait while Rabbit and Huang Yimo's Deadspace lured her in, harrying her with ranged attacks in an effort make her go for the power-up in the tower's centre. That's how she would play it.

Forty-five seconds.

Any moment now.

Movement at the base of her tower.

Samael narrowed her gaze as Golden Rabbit's tall, lithe form melted out of the shadows between the thick trunks of two pines. The jackalope almost seemed to float over the leaf-litter and rubble, her giant rabbit ears—each as long as Samael's forearm—swivelling in opposite directions, taking in every leaf flutter and rustle of wind, while her equally large, furred paws trod without sound. If not for the long, wild fall of her trademark golden hair—*true* gold, the kind that gleamed in the sun—the bipedal rabbit with her delicate, curling horns would have blended with the forest, as it was...

Even in [Shadow], with the world cast in endless shades of grey, Rabbit stood out. Not a good trait for a ranger, a class that relied on stealth as much as the power in their weapons.

Thirty-one seconds.

For a necromancer though... well, there were as many advantages to being seen as not.

Samael smiled and tightened her grip on the sceptre, the magic in the weapon's heart pulsing in time with her own.

By the time Rabbit saw her coming, it would already be too late and once the ranger was down, the sight of Samuel standing over

Rabbit's almost-corpse would draw the others in. She pushed power into the sceptre even as she drew a dagger from under her robes, the silky *shush* of the black metal against leather sheath making her heart beat a little harder—

An owl glided through the branches below, and Samael froze. There was no wildlife in Adder's Nest.

The bird's snowy feathers were a perfect match to Rabbit's own mottled, grey fur, longer over her shoulders and legs, thinner over her very human torso and face. The bird caught an updraft, shooting skywards until it skimmed the tower top, looking down the long shaft—the wind of its passing causing Samael's hood to billow around her face—before it spiralled back to the jackalope, coming to rest on the ranger's leather-armoured shoulder.

Fuck.

Twenty-two seconds.

That complicated matters.

The ranger had a companion, and judging from the light haloing the bird, a magical one at that, and in less time than it would take—

Rabbit looked up, bow appearing in her hands as if by magic, arrow nocked and aimed at Samael's chest.

The owl had seen through [Shadow] and tattled to its master. The trap Samael had laid shredded like the smoky tendrils of concealing [Shadow] as she leapt from the tower and plummeted to the ground, tattered robes dark wings, sceptre a streak of brilliant blue in her right hand, magic the same colour flashing ahead.

Rabbit dodged, but Samael's spell hit the ground—the shocking azure rune eating into dirt and stone—a micro-second before the ranger's paws left it.

// Golden Rabbit:Damage(Samael:Fetid Breath):HP -214. Status: Enfeebled. Poisoned. Bleeding.

Samael hit the ground a second later, her health bar lighting up with the same status conditions that afflicted Rabbit—

// Samael:Damage(Falling): HP -198. Status: Enfeebled. Poised. Bleeding.

—but she was already lashing out with her off-hand dagger, the very air screaming around the obsidian blade. In the same instant, Samael's magic was eating the afflictions her own spell had put on her, granting her increased power and strength with each one.

Rabbit tried to dodge again, motions jerky, legs trembling. Succeeded only in a wild swing of her bow.

The dagger slipped under the attack and found the small gap along the side of the ranger's leather chest armour, sinking between laces and chainmail. There was a moment of resistance when tip met skin, then the hot rush of blood and the darker, hotter rush of power slamming Samael in the chest, the magic blade finding Rabbit's heart and channelling the other character's lifeforce into her own core.

// Golden Rabbit:Critical hit. Stun. Life drain. HP -2056.

// Samael:Life force +2056.

On Samael's HUD, the poison-yellow life force meter above her health pool overflowed.

Rabbit collapsed, the status bar above her head flickering.

Samael pulled back her dagger for another blow, just a single one and the first kill would be—

Dirt and stone blew up in her face, tiny shards biting into her skin, sticks and leaf-litter in her mouth. She flipped backwards, spitting the mud off her tongue even as she breathed in the acrid stench of burnt ozone from the laser bolt that had just missed her.

The ground shuddered as Swordsman landed in the clearing on a hot rush of air, a fallen branch the width of an orc shattering under his weight.

Huh. Not waiting to ambush her in the main tower then.

Armoured feet the size of boulders made depressions in the earth as Swordsman lumbered toward her. Every inch of him covered in thick grey armour, from the shocking orange mohawk on his head, to his paw-like toes. Brilliant green lightning arched between the joints of his powered armour, gathering around the muzzles of the twin cannons in each hand. It rose in snaking, smoke-like strands from the glowing power-sinks embedded in his gunmetal grey chest, and the thrusters on his back.

A high-pitched whine was the only warning she had before another lime-green bolt hit the dirt where she'd crouched.

At the bottom of Samael's HUD, her Endurance bar hovered a hairsbreadth above zero. Not enough for another dodge.

And if Swordsman was here... She didn't wait to figure where Sticky Feet was hiding. There was no time.

Samael pumped power into the sceptre, threw [Fetid Breath] at Swordsman's hulking form, and leapt, not forward but backward, away from certain death.

[Shadow] was already stealing around her, slowly draining the yellow meter recently filled with Rabbit's life-force, as the next status message lit the HUD.

// Fetid Breath failure.

Not surprising, not with Sticky Feet out there, no doubt close but hidden, countering her spells with his.

The healer was the most vulnerable—lowest health, lightest armour—but also the most valuable, at least to Swordsman and, for the moment, Rabbit; showering them both with healing spells and boons.

They'd expect her to go after him first, now that Swordsman was standing guard over Rabbit, making finishing off the ranger—tempting as it was—difficult at best, and with Deadspace still unaccounted for, suicidal. But Samael had never shied away from difficult and suicidal…

She grinned. Samael was a necro, after all, an Angel of Death. For her, dying was just the beginning.

The dagger went back into its sheath, another thought and a dull black box appeared in that hand. Unlike the sceptre, the focus didn't glow or peel apart as she poured power into it, didn't do anything except, perhaps, become a shade darker. [Shadow] flickered as darkness gathered at her feet, the yellow life force meter draining faster and faster and faster as she pumped still more power into the box.

In the clearing, a brilliant halo surrounded Rabbit, the green healing spell turned the colour of ash by [Shadow], while a sigil blazed on the ground, rising from the earth itself. A barrier spell of some kind, courtesy of Sticky. There'd be others, buffs reinforcing armour and weapons, traps to snag and slow, especially once the ranger was on her feet, turning the fight into a battle of attrition, one Samael would lose unless she acted fast and hard and without mercy.

She was good at that.

The endurance bar ticked over slowly, filling with blue; a pixel over thirty percent full. Not much, but enough.

The life force meter hovered above zero. [Shadow] flickered once, twice.

A rustle from the pine tree to her right. She didn't look, already knew what she would see there; Deadspace, the sleek, shiny cyborg crouched on a thick tree branch, long black ponytail draped over her short, high-collared jacket, twin swords in hand.

Time to move.

She went sideways, a massive leap into the forest even as [Shadow] flickered again and died.

A hail of green bolts smacked the ground in her wake, the heat of them burning her robes, leaving the stench of burnt fabric to curl around her nostrils. There might be no scent haptics, but it didn't stop her brain from filling in the fried leaf litter and earth.

The cyborg was moving too, a fraction of a second behind. Deadspace made a graceful arc over Samael's head, blades out, the bright silver flash of an ability streaking ahead. To where the ninja had *expected* Samael to be, rushing headlong to take Rabbit's pelt. But she wasn't, and by the time Deadspace realised that, the moment before another light hit the area around the ninja—the brilliant white of Sticky's buff—it was too late.

'[Suffer],' whispered Samael.

The box in her hand exploded. Not in a burst of light, not with fire or brimstone or zombies bursting out of the ground, but darkness. With a cold, biting gale that arrowed straight at the cyborg, hitting her in the chest.

// Suffer success. Deadspace:Damage: HP -189. Afflicted. Bleeding. Cursed. Doomed.

Samael stopped looking at the status messages rolling across her HUD. There wasn't time to study them, only to trust the hours of practise, the days and weeks and months of losing and then winning, of becoming Samael.

[Shadow] was already wrapping around her, barely more than a dozen heartbeats worth of life force in the bar to sustain it, but two was all she needed. One to whirl behind Deadspace, the second to swap out sceptre and focus for twin daggers, and then the cyborg was hers.

// Deadspace: Stun. Life drain. HP -345.

Samael was a whirl of shadow, flickering in and out of sight, her blades slices of darkness. Fine threads of poison yellow flowed from every slice of Deadspace's flesh, refilling her life force bar even as [Shadow] drained it.

// Deadspace: Stun. Life drain. HP -345.

// Deadspace: Stun. Life drain...

On and on and on it went, a full five seconds before—

A neon green bolt shook the ground at Samael's feet.

// Samael: Damage. Life force -230.

[Shadow] was gone, life bar done, a large chunk of her health pool already black, and there was Swordsman; massive, armoured feet planted, lightning sparking between his joints, coalescing at the points of his twin cannons. Rabbit was struggling to her feet at his back, the faint shimmer of a magic shield hovering over them.

A second to scan Deadspace.

// Deadspace: HP 295. Stun, doom, cursed, bleeding...

Next to Doom a countdown. Eighteen seconds. Seventeen. Sixteen... not quick enough.

Swordsman's cannons glowed brighter, a high-pitched whine filling the air.

A choice. Live or take first blood.

Samael spun, thrust a dagger either side of Deadspace's bowed spine and twisted.

// Deadspace: Fatality. Respawn in—

Green enveloped her, a *boom* that filled her ears even as it shook the air and left ash on the back of her tongue.

// Samael: Fatality. Respawn in ten, nine...

L4g 15 th3 1sT s19N.

12

The VR unit parted, hood lifting, sides peeling back.

Peppermint lingered on Vlad's tongue as the jack disengaged from the port under her ear, the inaudible *pop* travelling through her skull, shaking loose most of the VR fog. But not all of it.

Virtual lag, the handful of seconds it took the brain to reset and recognise the real world, the muted colours, the discordant sounds. Like coming out of sleep, but worse. Average time for most users to readjust was thirteen seconds, for some shorter, others longer, but on rare occasions…

Vlad gripped the side of the unit and fought to remember if her hands had armour on them or not.

Fuck.

On rare occasions, lag hit hard and stayed hard, an unlucky quirk of brain chemistry. And if your brain was already marinated in its own special strew… well, that was just fuel for the party, wasn't it?

She never felt this way coming off the Cube, but then she jacked-in chemically, jacked out the same way with a different cocktail. Most Scourges did; another deep, dirty secret. Another reason why, once you tasted the sauce, you never went back.

Vlad blinked up at the square chandelier embedded in the ceiling, trying to sort out the shadows from the target lines still playing in the corners of her eyes, her brain convinced Samael's HUD was a hard thought away.

She shook her head and levered herself up. It wasn't of course, she knew that... and yet...

Movement from the central unit, and mentally she was reaching for the radar, summoning her sceptre— A sceptre that wasn't real, unlike Lu Chen, a tall raven dressed all in black from his shirt to his jeans. Frowning. At her.

She didn't smile back, wasn't sure she could arrange her face in a suitably dark, fuck-you-and-the-preconceptions-you-rode-in-on smile. Wasn't even sure she knew where her lips were, or if they were connected to the chat function or weapon swap. Wasn't sure of a lot of things except that she needed to get out of this damn pod before the frown on Lu Chen's face turned to questions and questions led to suspicion, and that the next time they did this, she better bring the fucking pills—the ones that'd bring her down—instead of leaving them in the hidden case with the Cube.

Vlad waited until the pod next to Lu Chen opened and he'd turned away before she moved. With gritted teeth and shaky knees, she stood.

The training room tilted and the floor wasn't quite where she expected it to be, was harder underfoot than the leaf litter in the game, without the dips and hollows of the forest ruin. But she didn't fall, even managed to cross her arms and lean against the pod, to look like she was waiting for the others to shake off their own lag. Somehow, she even summoned impatience to the curve of her lips.

The curve got to Huang Yimo, the other's half smile turning to a glare as she shuffled past, rubbing her nose like she was trying to dislodge a bad smell. Ming Li Na came next, then Sticky—nose also wrinkled—leaving just her, Lu Chen and the fuzzy-wuzzies crawling through her nervous system.

DKZero's captain stood at the end of her pod, crossed his arms and stared. Hard. He was tall, and Vlad had to crane her neck to meet his black eyes.

If lag had the audacity to so much as ruffle Lu Chen's eyebrows, she'd be surprised, and a little bit sorry for the lag. He might not be a hulking, power-armoured titan in the real, but he carried the same sense of indestructible might. Things as inconsequential as confused neural pathways would not be tolerated.

Grandmother would have approved.

She returned his stare.

He didn't say anything. Didn't move.

Two could play this game.

Silence built between them. In it, the VR units *hummed* and the quiet chatter of the team floated in from outside, the sound of chairs rolling across the floor, the muffled *thump* of a door closing.

A solid minute ticked by. Still they stared.

The stare-off might have started as a test of wills, but did she imagine the hint of puzzlement as it went on? Was there something on her face, had lag grabbed hold of her muscles and made her lip droop?

No, the fuzzy-wuzzies still crawled in her toes but the worst of it was leaving her system, the urge to summon a sceptre or check a map with a finger flick fading. Peppermint still rested on her tongue, but it was nothing a strong cup of tea wouldn't chase away.

Another minute, and still that hint of puzzlement, a kind of thwarted expectation.

She was imagining things. Lu Chen obviously didn't like to lose. Another trait Grandmother would approve of, although she might have had something to say about picking battles, and to never pick one with a Tong.

Vlad lifted her chin a little higher, let challenge and dark humour lift her eyebrow.

If not for the way his forearms tightened, muscles and tendons exposed by the rolled sleeves of his black shirt, she would have missed Lu Chen's clenched fists. A crack in his impassive mask.

Now *that* was something to smile about. Score first blood to her. Again.

She let victory fill her gaze.

Those forearms tightened a little more.

Vlad pushed herself off the VR unit, breaking the staring contest – she could be gracious in victory.

'Don't you have any questions?' Lu Chen broke the silence.

'None,' she said and sauntered from the training room.

The others sat around the kidney-shaped table in the middle of the common room in various stages of slumped. Mugs and glasses at their fingers, along with the screens hovering micrometres over the table.

Huang Yimo's expression darkened when she saw Vlad, and she drummed long fingers on the black surface, disrupting the display. Sticky barely looked up from his display, and Ming Li Na was half-sprawled across her end, already half-asleep with her cheek smooshed into a replay of the game.

The teammates were arranged around the side of the table facing the glass wall and the lake. Three of the old-style gaming chairs were left, one between Ming Li Na and Sticky in the centre, facing the lake, and Vlad left that to Lu Chen. Battles to be picked. Instead she took the one directly opposite the others, in the kidney's inward curve, leaving the one at the very end open, the better to face her new teammates—and Lu Chen, the puzzlement still ghosting his face—head on. She may not know the *exact* cause of the enmity in their eyes, but she'd bet it had more to do with Grandmother than her status as a Scourge. She'd bet the Cube on it.

'So…' she let the word hang. 'How did I do?'

No one spoke, although Huang Yimo made a "humph" sound, like something amused her.

Vlad raised a brow. 'Well?'

Lu Chen leaned back, his chair creaking. 'We're waiting.'

'For what?' She glanced around the table. All the team members were there and… She pressed her hand to the table, the display embedded in its surface instantly responding to her touch with stats from the Murderball game. All the information they needed was literally at their fingertips. 'Divine inspiration?'

'For me.' The deep, familiar voice came from the archway leading to the kitchen.

Yu Zixin stood in a patch of the bright noon light slanting under the roofline. It cast his shadow across the floor, and although it wasn't long, it seemed like it reached for her, dark fingers sliding over the concrete.

He'd left the suit at home this time, although the crew-necked navy top, long sleeves pushed to the elbows, still screamed wealth, as did the slacks and the heavy gold watch wrapped around his wrist. The coffee mug, though, was incongruous, and her lag-fuddled brain stumbled over the square of brightly-coloured ceramic in the shape of a pre-millennium Gameboy, as he lifted it to his lips.

Vlad stiffened, felt the smile melt from her face and knew, just *knew* because she would have noticed, that Lu Chen saw it.

In the back of her mind, the little voice that was Grandmother *tsked. Never let them see you bleed*, she would say.

But what was Zixin if not a giant open wound?

More fool her, after all this time.

At least the rolled oats in the pantry and the punching bag made sense now, Zixin would have seen to those. But still, what was he doing here? Did Grandmother think she needed a babysitter? And then she remembered, TI had invested in DKZero.

Zixin moved around the table, and even his house shoes sounded authoritative, *clack clack clacking* to the open chair at the table's head. And now the chair on the inward curve felt like a mistake, no longer a position of power but an interrogation.

Fuck.

She watched as he sat, kept watching as he set that bright-coloured, cartoonish mug on the shiny surface, was still watching as he leaned back, hands crossed over his stomach, and returned her stare.

There was challenge in that look, and if it had been any other person, she'd have given it back. Would have matched the arch of brow and the quirk of lip with a cool, knowing one of her own. Like she had with Lu Chen. Like she did with everyone. Expression for expression, arrogance for arrogance.

She tore her gaze away, down the table. Huang Yimo's glare was aimed at Zixin now, resentment practically echoing from the *tap tap tap* of her fingers on the table; Sticky still had his eyes glued on his screens; Ming Li Na was snoring softly, and Lu Chen was staring at *her* and rather than victory, she found consideration in his gaze.

'Lu Chen,' Zixin spoke from the head of the table. 'What's your assessment of Ana's—'

'Don't call me that.' The words were automatic, cold and hard, spilling from her mouth before she had a chance to stop them.

Silence ruled the table, even Huang Yimo's *tap tap tap* stilled.

You're bleeding, Grandmother's voice spoke in her ear.

'My name is Vladana,' she said again, not looking at Zixin. 'Vladana Tong. You may call me Vlad.' She looked at him now. 'After the Impaler.'

He stared back, and where silence had ruled now tension joined it, running up and down the composite wood.

'Vladana.' the name came off his lips like sour fruit. 'What's your assessment of *Vladana's* performance, Lu Chen?'

'Adequate.'

She switched her focus to the team captain and felt her mask slip back into place. Relief surging through her system. 'Adequate?' She scoffed. 'I took first blood.'

'You died.'

'In a match rigged against me.' She leaned across the table. 'Aren't you supposed to be assessing my fit with your team? One-on-one I can understand, lets you assess my strengths, how I face different opponents, but how does four-on-one do more than satisfy your desire to beat on the newcomer? Hmm?'

'Scourges are cheats,' Huang Yimo spoke, fingers no longer

tapping but pressed hard onto the table, the display fuzzing around them. 'You don't belong in the leagues, you shouldn't even be in this *building*.'

And there was no hostility *there*, clearly.

'Did you *see* me cheat?' Vlad turned her arrogance down the table. 'Or are you just sore that it was *your* blood I took?'

Huang Yimo had a good snarl, Vlad would give her that. It twisted the woman's lips and made her look more like the warrior she played, and when she slammed her hands into the table, as she did now, and rose...

Maybe the punching bag in the gym wasn't just for Vlad's benefit.

'She did well,' Sticky broke in. He didn't look up from the data streaming past his fingers. 'Fast reaction times, adapted her strategies and effectively utilised the necro's dual life abilities against a stronger force.' He looked up, not at Zixin or Vlad, but Lu Chen. 'If she'd retreated after we arrived, we might not have KO'd her.'

'And she didn't cheat,' Ming Li Na said, face still squished into the table. The short, round-faced woman moved, resting her chin on folded hands. 'She's just good.' She looked at Lu Chen as he stroked a hand over her hair. 'We should run some team missions, make a proper assessment.' She yawned. 'After breakfast.'

Zixin glanced at his watch. 'It's already lunch time.'

'When you're a gamer, lunch time *is* breakfast,' Ming Li Na said as she peeled herself off the table. She shuffled back towards the kitchen, shooting her last words over her shoulder. 'That's something a *real* team manager would know.'

<⊙>

"A team manager."

Huh.

While the rest of the team ate huddled around the end of the kitchen bench, as far away from her as they could get, Vlad studied Zixin.

He stood facing the lake, legs braced, one hand in his pocket, the other swishing and swiping at his phone, and all the while he talked. The headset tucked behind his ear never seemed to stop ringing. She couldn't see his expression, but she bet there was a frown between his dark brows and frustration on his lips.

Not *just* a manager.

Owner; as of four months, eight days and seventeen hours ago. TI might have fronted the money, but DKZero was in Zixin's name.

Vlad played with the palm-sized tea bowl before her. The elegantly-shaped silver and midnight bowl had been as out-of-place amongst the mismatched collection of brightly-coloured coffee buckets as the oats.

As was Yu Zixin himself.

Why buy an e-sports team? Unless much had changed in the last five years, Xin'er had as much aptitude for gaming as a ton of bricks. It made as much sense as TI's investment; there was no cutting-edge technology to develop, no natural resources, supply chains or intellectual property to exploit. Just people. Five VR-obsessed geeks running on sugar and caffeine.

What did either of them hope to gain?

A shiny silver helmet masquerading as a coffee mug slid onto the bench beside her, a short willowy presence followed. 'You know him,' Ming Li Na said.

Vlad cast the other girl a glance. Food had done wonders for Ming Li Na's appearance, the cloud of sleep gone from her light brown eyes, the ghastly cast from her skin.

'Is that a question?'

Ming Li Na sipped from her bucket, holding it in both hands, and held Vlad's gaze. 'Yes.'

Vlad harrumphed, turned back to the window. And Zixin. 'Then you should make it sound like one, or at least ask something you don't already know the answer to.'

Silence. Even the quiet murmur from the other end of the table seemed to stop, the clink and snick of cutlery with it, leaving just the weight of all those stares pressing on the side of Vlad's face.

Did Zixin feel the weight of hers? She studied his shoulders; were they relaxed or was there tension hiding under the soft, navy crew neck? Did she see it in the back of his neck, were the muscles standing out?

She stared harder.

Ming Li Na shifted on her seat, house shoes thudding against the bench. 'Have you known him long?'

'Long enough.'

'How'd you meet?'

'Our families know each other.' For eons, it seemed, the Yus mixed with the Tongs in a long line of cooperation until back before Grandmother's father's time, the Tongs growing while the Yus dwindled, leaving just the one.

Another second of silence, Ming Li Na weighing her words. 'He doesn't seem like he's that interested in gaming.'

'He's not.' At least, he hadn't been, back when she hadn't hated him.

Was it Grandmother who inspired his interest, or was it something else? Did he still—

Vlad spun on her stool, cutting the thought in half and facing Ming Li Na head-on. 'You should probably just ask what you want to ask; it'll be quicker that way.'

Embarrassment flushed Ming Li Na's cheeks. 'I don't—'

Vlad interrupted the flood of social nicety. 'Don't want to be rude, because I seem like such a nice person and all that, but I'm not. You know I'm not.'

She titled her head to the side, studying Ming Li Na as the other girl's mouth opened on what was probably denial.

Vlad interrupted her again. 'I don't know why Yu Zixin bought the team. If you find out... don't let me know. I won't care.'

Because by then, she'd have found out on her own.

v1r7U4L b3coM35 r34L

13

The team spent a solid day running training missions, interspersed with intensive debriefs where first Sticky and then Ming Li Na broke down Samael's every twitch – the first wearing another shirt with a big-eyed anime girl on the front, still rocking his unicorn slippers; the second in a slim-fitting hoodie same as Vlad, a brightly-patterned yellow in sunny contrast to Vlad's deathly black.

There were no more stare-offs in the training room, but Lu Chen's puzzlement continued, flowing from him to the others, like there was a question they expected her to ask.

She ignored it. It faded soon enough.

Every microsecond of Samael's gameplay, every dodge and spell, every weapon swap was analysed, and once they were done with that, when Vlad's brain was more lag than logic, even with the pills she'd stashed in the hidden compartment of her hoodie's front pocket, there were more.

What armour she wore, which accessories and glyphs and runes, their effects on Samael's health points and attack speed and defence. Numbers flooded what was left of Vlad's mental capacity, rows upon columns upon matrixes all blurring together until she was past seeing them.

Vlad had always thought Scourges were meticulous, obsessed with eking every last scrap of potential from their avatars, but they had nothing on Sticky and Ming Li Na.

And during all that time, Zixin was there in the background, on his phone, head buried in holoscreens or staring at her. His clothes changed at some point, the navy crew-neck switched out for a dark grey, but the cartoonish mug remained the same, as did the look in his eyes.

Intense. Waiting.

Vlad ignored him. Or pretended to, at least.

After thirty-six hours of gameplay and analysis, of which they slept for five, the verdict was in.

One-on-one or one-on-many, Samael was a force to be reckoned with, a one-woman army of death and destruction laying waste to her opponents, but in a team… By their very nature, Scourges weren't team players, going it alone on the net's dark, raggedy edge, taking risks, forging paths, stretching the rules to their breaking point and then pushing them a little further. That was what a Scourge did, the skills she'd spent the last eight years perfecting. Working in a team… not so much.

Balost Ghost's paved streets and medieval, red-roofed houses spread out over the game table, the hologram lifting out of the black top, a model made of light running back the mission in real time. Tiny figures raced through the grid-pattern streets, across covered walkways and bridges, fireballs and lasers making sandstone walls explode while Swordsman made a giant crater in the central square.

Massive pavers shattered under the team captain's power armour as he crashed to the ground, flung a hundred metres by a lucky shot from the other team. He was on his clawed feet in seconds, power making the energy sinks on his chest and back blaze neon green, canons laying down fire as opponents leapt over red roofs and dashed out of narrow side streets, filling the town square and surrounding him.

'Here.' The playback paused and a red dot pinpointed the square at the base of its western-most tower. 'You followed the thief, but they were leading you away from the main fight. If you'd been here doing crowd control—' The pointer moved, travelling across the square to the fountain where Swordsman was blasting swarms of magical ants to a pulp. '—Team Meerkat wouldn't have overwhelmed Swordsman. Instead—'

Another quick change of pointer position, and this time the playback followed, enlarging a small courtyard away from the main action, a well at its centre. The thief ducked around the corner, throwing a trap as he ran under the archway and dived into the well. A slice of darkness followed, Samael's ragged black robes seeming to melt out of the shadows as she deftly leapt over the trap—the foot-snatcher had glowed a vicious red on her HUD, clear as day—only to be blown sideways by the proximity bomb planted on the inside of the archway, the one she hadn't seen.

Noob mistake.

On the table, Samael's stats flared red, health instantly dropping ten percent, even as a red-robed elemental mage landed atop a roof overlooking the little courtyard, magic already buzzing around its hands, a spell swallowing every inch of the rough dirt ground. There'd been no time to dodge.

She'd slipped into [Shadow] a heartbeat before the fireball detonated, the spell's area of effect turning the world around her into an inferno. She'd lost life force instead of health to the flames as she'd raced across the dirt, diving into the well and finishing off the thief in one liquid move, health bar immediately rebounding to just under half, but the damage had already been done.

The replay switched back to the square, where Sticky Feet took a critical strike to the chest – the lightning bolt making a smoking hole in the elf's royal blue robes. It killed the mage instantly and left Swordsman alone to face the horde, Rabbit and Deadspace too far away to assist.

Without his healer, and pressed from all sides, it wasn't long before the already wounded warrior fell.

Vlad's face tightened; felt her lips pull downwards, the

frustration painting her jaw. She scrubbed her face, brushing the crusty edges of sleep from her eyes. 'I won't do it again,' she said. Vlad didn't say she wouldn't have done it in the first place if she'd been thinking right, if exhaustion hadn't pulled at her legs and lag hadn't turned thinking into an exercise in walking through soup. Didn't even say she'd stopped hearing Lu Chen's voice calling directions in her ear, that she hadn't noticed the little blip in the corner of her HUD warning her of the second explosive.

Didn't say any of that because she knew better. She wasn't a stranger to marathon net sessions. Thirty-six hours jacked-in wasn't even her longest stretch, but she'd been on the sauce then with no lag fuzzing her brain, no teammates pulling her left and right and centre, calling plays she had to expend brain power to remember. During those marathon play sessions, she'd had no one but herself to rely on, or whose back she needed to watch.

Just her, the Cube and the mission.

The mission whose clock was ticking away in the back of her brain. Thirty-four hours to the cheese boards.

So near and yet so far.

A delicate black and gold tea bowl appeared on the table beside her, long, elegant fingers slipping away before her tired, lagged brain could do more than process the steam rising off the top. The bitter, earthy scent of green tea curled around her nose, and Vlad closed her hands around the warm ceramic with a grateful sigh.

Across the board table, Lu Chen was a dark cloud; long, black sleeves pushed up to his elbows, arms crossed over his chest. 'League games are a team sport. No matter how talented the individual, if there is no cohesion there's no team.'

'I said—' Vlad looked up from the tea. She'd heard this speech before. '—I won't do it again.'

'You promised that before.'

She was on her feet.

The snarl took her by surprise, rising from her gut to burst through her chest and twist her lips. She slammed the cup back on the table, scalding liquid sloshing over her knuckles. 'Then kick me to the curb, Swordsman, and find some other punk to fill out your team, 'cause I don't need your shit.'

Across the table, Ming Li Na and Sticky reared back, tired eyes no longer so tired, while Lu Chen's disapproving face turned stonier still. He leaned forward—

'Enough.' A hand on Vlad's shoulder, squeezing even as it pulled her back.

Zixin, always Yu fucking Zixin. For a second, reality faded, the ever present lag crawling in through the edges of her brain, and suddenly the teacup under her hand was Samael's dagger, and all she had to do was—

She'd half-turned before Zixin twisted her back and shoved her into the chair. Sense returned to her synapses as arse met padded seat.

'Enough,' he said again, and this time the word, and the fingers digging into her shoulder, brooked no argument. 'You're all tired and tired athletes make mistakes—' and Vlad sensed rather than saw the pointed smile he shot Ming Li Na's way '—same as regular mortals.'

'We have to—' Ming Li Na began.

Zixin cut her off. He was good at that, at rolling right over you, ignoring everything but what made sense to him. She should stomp on his foot, grab the hand on her shoulder and twist until he was on his knees, begging for forgiveness.

She should do that, but she wouldn't. Didn't want him to think she cared.

But still, the urge sat heavy. She'd do it later. Much later.

Like never.

'And I'm saying everyone is taking a break.' Zixin sat, the chair at the head of the table bouncing a little as he leaned back, those strong hands clasped over his belly, ankle propped on an elegant pants-clad knee, black, hard-soled house shoe dangling from his toes. Every inch the rich businessman.

He twisted the dial on his heavy gold watch, gripped the little ball of light that appeared above it and threw it at the table.

The table died.

One minute alive with the Balost's Ghost replay, the next not even a shine on the matte-black surface.

Sticky choked, Ming Li Na squealed, Lu Chen scowled and Huang Yimo stopped drumming her fingers.

'Eat,' Zixin said. 'Sleep, get some sun, go on a date—' His eyes cut to Lu Chen and Ming Li Na '—I don't care, but the training room is locked until I say otherwise.'

'You can't do that,' Ming Li Na said.

'I just did. I'm the manager after all.'

Vlad almost snorted. Ming Li Na was right, Zixin belonged in DKZero about as much as borscht at one of Grandmother's banquets.

She got up from the table and made her way to the stairs as the others headed for the kitchen. The giant curve of concrete was at her feet, and her hand was on the railing, gripping it tight as she half shuffled, half-pulled herself up the risers, only half-conscious of the tall, sandalwood-scented shadow at her back.

The top of the stairs came before her tired, lagged mind could sort it out. She shuffled down the hall, towards her purple bedroom door, Samael standing guard beside it. At her back, the shadow kept pace.

Vlad paused a heartbeat, then turned, slow and steady.

Zixin stared at her.

'Why are you here?' she said.

'I bought the team.'

'But why?'

'It's a good investment.'

'No.' She shook her head. 'It's not, and even if it was, you know jack shit about *Annihilation* let alone the pro league; it would have been smarter to hire a professional manager. So, why you?'

He didn't answer for a long, drawn-out second.

Those dark eyes were steady as they searched hers, his brow lifted, just a micron, surprised. There seemed a question on the edge of his tongue, but Zixin's mouth remained shut.

She leaned back. Had he noticed the lag? But she'd been so careful, masked every stumble, compensated for every twitch and misspoken word. Hadn't she?

'What?' she finally said.

'Why do you think I'm here?'

To get under my skin. She caught the response before it popped out her mouth.

'For the same reason you followed me to twelve different raves,' she said instead.

He froze. 'You know about that.'

At least he didn't deny it. 'Whatever you and Grandmother are up to, leave me out of it.'

'We're not up to anything.'

'Liar.'

'Ana—'

'Don't *call* me that.'

A step and he was in her space. 'You didn't use to mind.'

She titled her head back, lifted up on her toes and stared at him. Hard. Taking in those all-too-familiar bronze eyes, the sharp planes of his face and the warm sandalwood that clung to his dusky skin. 'You didn't use to be a bastard,' she said.

She pushed him away with enough force to make Zixin stumble, little more than a step but enough to make the hard, shiny shoes *clack clack* against the concrete.

Down the corridor, the yellow door *snicked* closed but not before she caught a glimpse of Sticky's round panda face.

Fuck.

So much for keeping her relationship with Zixin in the deep dark realm of speculation. But she wouldn't have to put up with it for long; a few days, a month tops, and she was an electron on the wind.

Free.

Done.

Gone.

Why did that leave a hole in her chest?

'...are you even listening?'

A hand on her shoulder, and she brushed it off out of reflex. 'What?'

Zixin was in her face again, staring at her like a specimen under glass. She should punch him in that straight, arrogant nose but his breath was sweet as she remembered, the little green flecks around his pupils as mesmerising.

His mouth twisted. He swore, the unexpectedness a jolt to her chest. She hadn't heard him swear before. 'I should have pulled you guys out sooner. Thirty-six hours in-System is not human.'

She turned away and shuffled towards her door, the giant purple rectangle calling to her. 'Twenty-three hours in-system,' she said out of reflex, throwing the words over her shoulder. 'And not all at once, the brain fries after five.'

Neurones melding together, electrons getting confused about what was real and what wasn't. Just like lag.

Exactly like lag. She'd read somewhere that NuGet's new VR units were meant to prevent that, or at least extend the timeframe, not that she'd noticed, but then she was a Scourge, her internal chemistry used to the sauce and to the downers that came after.

There was that twitch in the corner of her vision, brain still trying to pull up maps and stat readouts for the little statues next to each door. Lag should have long given up on her by now – side effect of the neural jack, or just her brain messing with her?

She slipped her hand into the front pocket of her black hoodie, fingers tracing the pill container in its hidden compartment, the hard, round plastic worryingly empty.

If they kept training like this, the pills wouldn't be enough. She'd need to inject, bypass the gut and go straight for the vein. And wouldn't that be fun, shooting up in the toilet where no one could see.

Zixin was at her side now, keeping pace then pulling ahead, blocking her path.

'Ana—'

'I already told you not to call me that.'

'I'm not calling you Vlad, or Samael, or any other ridiculous name you come up with.'

'Well then, I guess that leaves you with Vladana or Ms Tong.'

'A'Dana—'

'Don't you even.' Faster than [Shadow], she stopped and rounded on him. The balcony was suddenly smaller, the wall darker, the brightly-coloured doors bigger, the glass balustrade closer, and Zixin... Zixin a hulking demon she couldn't escape, whispering that cursed name. 'Don't say it, don't breathe it, don't even let it cross your thoughts.'

He closed the last little bit of distance between them. 'It's your name.'

'It's a curse.'

'Your father—'

'Call me that, and I will walk right out that door.' Her arm was a javelin, her finger the sharp, bloodied steel tip piercing the floor all the way to the shiny red rectangle beneath their feet. 'And you and Grandmother can do whatever the fuck you're doing all on your very own. And forget about tracking me down or stalking me at raves, because I will be gone and you won't find me again.'

She stood on tiptoe, not quite sure if it was prolonged lag or anger making her sway, only that it took her fist in his solar plexus to steady herself as she stared him down. 'Never. Again.' And now she struggled to remember if it was the name she was talking about, or the finding. Not that it mattered, it all boiled down to the same thing, to the gritty, nasty crud at the bottom of the pot. To Xin'er knowing his boundaries. No. That wasn't right. To him knowing *her* boundaries.

Yes. She nodded to herself. That was it. 'Got it?'

He searched her face, a frown playing between his brows, tightening his jaw, turning his eyes a darker shadow of hazelnut. 'Got it. *Vladana.*'

She pushed him away, or rather, pushed herself away from Xin'er. 'Good.'

Lag was gumming up her bones, and she was glad that her door was right there, because the sight of the giant purple rectangle sent grapes bursting over the back of her tongue. Who the fuck knew what else her scrambled neurones would do next, and the last thing she needed was for Xin'er to see any more than those eagle eyes already had.

'Good,' she said again as the door clicked open and she stumbled/fell inside, half turning as she did. 'Don't forget it.'

Don't ever forget it.

And still, she wasn't sure what she was talking about.

14

The other end of the secure comm line beeped.

'Well?' The voice was old, but age hadn't robbed it of steel.

He was silent for a heartbeat and then three more.

On the other end of the line, fingernails *clacked* on something hard; sharp and rhythmic. Demanding without saying a word.

He'd made this call, made the deal that went with it, and yet... The anger on Ana's face mocked him almost as much as the little spasms in her hands worried him. 'I don't know,' he said. 'There's something... off.'

Not just with her gaunt face but the ease with which she'd accepted Old Woman Tong's ultimatum.

'And? Is she looking into the accident?'

The accident, the screaming brakes and twisted metal he could only imagine and the scared, terrified girl he remembered too well, knowing for the first time in his seventeen years that there was something in this life worth protecting.

Again, he didn't speak, conflicting promises rooting his tongue to the roof of his mouth.

'Xin'er?'

'I...' He remembered the slight slur in Ana's voice, the way her eyes had twitched left and right, like she'd seen things that weren't there. 'This might have been a mistake.'

And now it was the other's turn for silence. He pictured the woman on the other end, the long, steel-white hair, the dark eyes so like Ana's, the determination imprinted in every line and bone. 'Then fix it, but whatever happens, do not let her find the Deposit.'

'I won't.'

'Good.'

The line went dead.

15

'We're not up to anything.'

Thirty-four hours later and Zixin's words continued to haunt, doubt and hope chasing her as she shed Vlad for another name.

She knew better than to believe his words. She did, she really did.

Vlad didn't login as Samael, not exactly, not for this, not in the black shadow robes or with the long, hooked scythe. The necromancer stood out, despite its ability to melt into shadow. As soon as DKZero's first match went live, its image would be everywhere and people would remember. This time, the nameplate above her head read something else, even if it was the dark elf's avatar she wore.

"Aclima" strode down the bustling street and disappeared, just another mage in plain blue robes, the short, knee-length hems flashing gold with every step. Golden light might crack around her fingers, as if she'd captured the sun in the rings and bracelets adorning her arms, might ripple across the hood and veil hiding her face, gather in the heart of the staff slung across her back, but it did the same for the little troll across the way. And the seven-foot orc in front of her, the one who left rainbows behind him with every footstep, while the thief using the flags and banners strung over the cobblestone alley like a highway, trailed an aura like death itself.

No, in this crowded, noisy place, where magic was as common

as swords, and jet packs shared airspace with flying unicorns, Aclima in her second-rate armour and with just enough badges next to her name to make her not-a-noob, wasn't worth a second glance.

She slipped between two market stalls, steam rising off the flaky, buttery pastries on one—the sweet, warm scent teasing her nose, impossible as it was—and the sharp jiggle of steel and silver weapons on the other. Behind the stalls, in the small gaps between brightly-coloured tapestries and pinstriped tent sides, darkness waited. It reached out to her as she approached, licking at her boots, climbing up the leather like a dog eager for its master's touch.

Aclima kept moving, slipping past another stall—this one selling colourful bottles, the contents hissing and bubbling—conscious of the eyes, always the eyes. Three pairs, two, a hundred, it didn't matter, there was always someone watching – a bot in the feeds, a streamer studying the crowd, a keyboard jockey picking apart stats or studying the market. Finding the latest hack, the newest easter egg, the fastest hidden passageway, the avatars wearing another character's skin... like her.

In the nets, knowledge was power and no currency had as much cache as a good secret.

Afternoon shadows and stray sparks of magic played across the heavy tapestry walls, and there, in the corner of her HUD, was a ripple in the fabric. The countdown started automatically.

Three seconds.

Aclima moved, blue-gold robes flashing around her calves, even as a sticky, viscous glob dropped from her fingers, the spell attaching itself to a short, muscular goblin bouncing across the market table.

Two seconds.

There, an otherworldly pixel-wide glow in the seams between tent walls.

One second.

Her fingers touched the glow and—

Behind her the spell detonated. Trumpets and confetti and the goblin suddenly hoisted into the air on an elephant the size of a dragon. Gasps and excitement, eyes turning to the party in the middle of the street.

—she slipped into the space between sandboxes.

A moment of black static shuddering across her HUD in jagged white lines. Then pain, a viscous spike in her eardrum as the system interrogated Aclima's skin, algorithms digging into its logs, chasing level-up timestamps and quest completions. Seeking out all the little details that told the story of an avatar's life, the ones impossible to fake. Or *almost* impossible.

The Cube responded, hacks and macros catching the system's probes and sending back carefully constructed data packets, Vlad's neutral pathways just a rough, poorly constructed highway for the exchange.

A heartbeat and it was done.

The static dissipated, and the chaos that was the cheese boards replaced it.

Under her, a tiny, semi-transparent circle of clouds held her aloft while a violent wind whipped her robes about her knees and tried to rip the scarf from her head. Around her, other users popped into existence on their own cloud platforms, appearing out of the blue sky like thoughts pulled from Zeus's forehead.

Below them... an endless, crazy beehive of rooms connected by bridges and walkways stretched out to every horizon - some ornate wrought iron, others all sleek glass and refracted light. Some of the rooms were small, some large, each one different from those next to it; a random patchwork of 1930s dive bars, boardrooms, shipping containers, buses, ovals, carousels, submarines and every other interior in between.

Some teemed with life—a disco so packed the dancers jumped and writhed in unison—others abandoned, empty even of pixel bunnies.

The cheese boards were a poorly kept secret amongst the forums, a whisper of a rumour that just wouldn't go away. Whether they were a crack in the system's coding, or a little hidey hole the devs had cooked up after one-too-many all-nighters, several dozen bottles of beer and the contents of a not-so-legal pharmacy, was a hotly debated topic, but no one really cared.

If a player was able to find the boards, they were in. Part of an exclusive club of hardcore users there for the thrills and the shadows.

Part of the system and yet not. The boards weren't just a weak area in the code, where the coding was loose and loopholes outweighed rules, but also a legal grey area. Like any legal grey area, they were a haven for all manner of things. The kind of things that got people in trouble, in-System and out.

Aclima peered over the edge of the platform, summoning the locator as she did. Her HUD changed, not a map but a radar overlaying the view. A yellow dot pulsed in the upper left corner, neither small nor large, waves radiating outwards, *ding ding dinging* as they hit the large black dot that was her.

All it took was a slight lean in that direction and her cloud platform was shooting over the honeycomb rooms.

There was no official map for the boards, whatever algos the devs had used to create the hodgepodge environments, they kept changing, evolving almost at random. The disco room that was there one day might be a prehistoric jungle the next, or it might even change halfway through the sardine-like dance. Of course, when that happened, those inside were as like to find themselves booted as drowning in a tar pit or left with avatars so glitchy they'd never be able to log-in with them again. As close to an actual death as was possible in-System.

The were no rules in the cheese boards, and no safety net either.

The dot on the radar was beneath her feet.

She stepped off the platform and plummeted.

Air screamed past her ears, billowed in her hood, flapped loose fabric around her waist and over her head like blue and gold wings, the ground rushing up to meet her and—

She landed, boots touching down gently on craggy rocks, clouds swirling about her ankles. From above it might have been a tiny hexagon smashed between larger environments, but inside... The clouds spread to an orange horizon, a fluffy white sea turning a deep blue before it touched the last rays of a setting sun. In the distance, she could pick out the dark pimples of other crags just like the one on which she stood. The suggestion of mountain tops piercing the clouds.

'You like it?' The voice came from beneath the fluffy white. It swirled, and a feather pierced the cloud, preceding a peaked hat and the short pixie woman wearing it. En-ji smirked at her. 'You like it, don't you? I put my own flare on the code you gave me. Thank me later. I take crypto.'

Aclima ignored her, instead looking around, scanners on high, pinging every pixel of the map. The bot in Graydon's Revenge played in the back of her mind, the memory crawling up her nape. Nothing pinged, no pixels wavered or fuzzed in a way they shouldn't, but she didn't relax.

She might have designed the environment from her ma's old research, but that didn't mean there weren't any nasty surprises.

'Hey.'

A light punch in her gut brought Aclima's gaze down, and the feather on the pixie's hat up her nose.

She jerked back.

En-ji stared up at her, the pixie's crown barely reaching Aclima's breastbone, a frown between her delicate red brows, little nose wrinkled and big ruby lips pursed. 'What are you looking for?'

// Nothing, she said. Not yet, at least. Aclima refocused. *Did you get it done?* Not the environment but the other thing, the other hook with the little knotty twist she hadn't been able to crack.

One of those brows arched. 'You're even asking me that?'

'...up to anything'

Aclima stared. The veil covered her entire face, the light gauze fluttering against her cheeks and lips... making her as faceless as Samael's deep hood, and while there were no shadows to swallow her features, most found the soft grey fabric just as intimidating.

Most.

But not En-ji.

The tiny pixie pirate put both hands on her absurdly small waist and stared Aclima straight in her gauze-covered eyes. 'I got it sorted, big shot. Took me awhile and few extra credits, but I did it, just like you wanted; all you need to do is wait for the whale.'

'...not up to...'

Aclima nodded, still pinging the room, still with that crispy-ant sensation crawling across her shoulders. // *Then we wait.*

They didn't wait long, just long enough for her scanner to finish building a map of the room—a hexagon ten meters wide and twice that deep, the roof made of shimmering light, not the horizon-defying expanse of clouds it pretended to be—and for a massive cloud whale, the creature made of the same stuff it burst through, twisting in the sky before it splashed back into the fluffy white.

Hamish smashed into the rock beside Aclima, his avatar a massive block of skin and sinew held together with pistons and wires. He looked the same in-System as out, except in the real the tattoos patterned on his flesh were just ink while in-System they were metallic hexagons, the cords in his neck pistons spewing the smoke he eagerly sucked down his throat from the vape between his teeth.

Beside him, Ru Ping landed with more grace – a tall, slim warrior in heavy red and black armour with a sword and shield slung over her back.

Victory thrilled through Aclima's cortex.

On her HUD, Aclima silently triggered the macro. A faint *hush*, like a breeze through her blood, signalled the Cube doing its work.

At her feet, hidden by the swirling clouds, a glimmering gold thread detached from the lightning crackling around her hands. She felt it stream across the craggy rock, twisting past Hamish's heavy, metal-soled boots, to twist around Ru Ping's heels.

Out in the clouds, the whale breached.

Hamish blew smoke in her face. 'Your friend better know what she's doing.' He jerked his chin at En-ji. 'If we get nabbed...'

En-ji lifted one of those brows and smirked at him. 'You going to piss your VR chair?'

// We won't get caught, Aclima said. She moved away from the group, right to the edge of what her HUD insisted was a never-ending cliff. *So long as you don't fuck it up*, she added, not even glancing over her shoulder at Hamish.

'...not up to...'

The chill wound through her belly; an icy, gut-liquifying dread she hadn't expected.

Her gaze cut to Ru Ping, the thread twisting around the warrior's heels... Before jerking it back to the clouds. Time to make this look good.

Aclima stared into the clouds, trying to pierce the pixels and particle physics to the bug in the code, the little error that En-ji's exploit was going to rip wide open.

Ru Ping stepped up beside her, the knight's crimson leather skirt *thwaping* against her obsidian armour. 'What do we do?'

Aclima glanced out over the clouds, waiting for the ripple that came before the whale. There, in the distance, too far to be more than a projection against the sandbox walls, but all the signal she needed.

// We jump, she said.

And did.

<⊙>

She fell, farther than should have been possible, even in the System. Beyond what her HUD insisted were the dimensions of the sandbox, for longer and faster than was possible even for game physics. But still, she fell. Through an endless sea of cloud, the soft-white vapour chill through the veil, the white turning pink and then orange and purple, the light fading. She should have hit the side of the mountain not long after that first leap, gone *splat* against rock and shale, robes and staff catching then snapping on old, gnarled trees and rocky outcrops, instead...

Her robes blew up around her knees, split sides and under-robes fanning about her like a broken parachute, the lightning playing around her hands and across her back trailing behind, and her HUD... She'd stopped paying attention to the map three full minutes and precisely thirteen seconds after leaping into the clouds. It had taken her that long to realise they'd hit the bug in the code. The box had no bottom.

Which was good. And bad. The loopholes here were big, the System rules thin – things like gravity and distance more guideline than law. Exactly what she needed, what she'd hoped for when she adapted Ma's notes to build her own little sandbox, a place where the code would bend just enough to make what came next believable.

It was just... getting there was taking longer than expected.

She'd tried contacting En-ji, but static filled the comms and the chat box was a garbled mess of characters.

Throwing a spell into the clouds hadn't done more than set off a chain of fireworks, brilliant arcs of gold echoed by others of red and purple—Hamish and Eun-ji, she guessed—and of Ru Ping...

When she twisted her head to look back, there was only a vague shadow above, a darker patch in the ever-changing clouds.

The Cube was still humming in the back of her head though, whispering that the macro was there, digging into Ru Ping's system, sniffing out its secrets.

At least something was going as expected.

Around her, the clouds grew darker, heavier. The chill digging through the veil hiding her face to draw icy claws down her cheeks.

//Aclima:Damage:Environment. HP -2.

Finally.

The darkness grew. The icy claws dug deeper.

Warmth trickled over her cheeks, dripped over her lips, the copper tang of blood filling her nose.

// Aclima:Damage:Environment. HP -20.

The darkness swirled.

A glance at her health bar.

Twenty lost health points shouldn't have made more than a thin dent in the red, but the meter at the bottom of the HUD was a quarter gone. The bug doing its work.

Another damage message and another chunk of health gone.

Now was the time.

// Now, she said, sending the instruction out, hoping it got through. To Ru Ping at least.

She needed Ru Ping—glance at the progress bar in the top left corner—just for a little longer.

A hard thought and En-ji's exploit appeared in her hand, an apple the size of two fists, its surface a bright, shiny green. A healing potion, not to stop the damage, but to suspend death. It would just be for a microsecond, long enough to trigger the System's reset and for the Cube to execute the code she'd painfully pieced together from fragments of her ma's research.

She crushed the apple, one gloved fist slamming into the other.

It crumbled like it was made of paper, a wet sticky mess eating through her skin... the mage's skin, peeling it away to reveal the tarnished-silver armourned hands and dark shadow robes underneath.

And she was still falling, the icy wind still drawing blood.

Her health bar flashed. Down to a third now.

// Samael:Damage:Environment. HP -200.

Not much longer... The next hit would take her out.

The Cube rushed through her blood, a bright-green glow heating her from the inside out.

Cold crawled through her lips and bit her tongue.

The glow reached her chest and—

The world jerked sideways.

—the clouds were gone, the cold, the wind, the blood running down her face. She stood in a field of white, but not just any white, not snow covered or pale, but paper white without a hint of colour. The tall grasses swaying around her thighs, reed heads playing with her fingertips, the sun lifting above the horizon, the sky above, all might have been cardboard models, casting soft shadows in defiance of the hard dawn.

She'd known the hack would work, but... She'd expected a plain grey box, not...

Shit.

She spun left, taking in the endless field, the infinite horizon—no mountains, no trees or buildings, just paper grass—spun again, activating [Sonic Steps] as she did. More of the same met her gaze, and on the HUD... *Ping, ping, ping* echoed, the radar encountering no walls, no box just... space for a full hundred metres in every direction, before [Sonic Steps] faded to nothing.

This wasn't a plain grey box.

There was a fucking *breeze* slipping under her hood.

Fuck. Had she missed something in Ma's journals?

A ripple behind her.

Samael turned.

En-ji was a peacock in comparison, hair aflame, her olive green coat a beacon for the eye as she waded across the field. The same paper grass that brushed Samael's thighs, flirted with the pixie's waist.

'I took a screenshot,' En-ji said. An image of Samael standing in the field, an ink blot on the field's brilliant white, flashed between them. 'It's like this place was made for you.'

Had it been? By Ma?

More ripples. Ru Ping and then Hamish appearing in the white field.

She shouldn't have brought them here.

The thought hit her hard. The people responsible for Ma's death and she'd brought them, if not the thing they wanted, then part of her research, part of the code she'd died for. But hard on that realisation came another… What better bait to catch a killer than the truth?

A quick glance at the progress bar on the HUD... still ticking over. The worm feeding off Ru Ping's signal was alive and well.

Hamish staggered forward. Something had gone wrong with his patch, his avatar was hazy around the edges, his nose pixelated, his left ear no longer on his head, but his collarbone. That was... interesting.

He turned three hundred sixty degrees, still stumbling over his feet. 'This is it?' His voice was as distorted as his face, cracking and popping. 'This is what you needed all those credits for?' He lumbered toward En-ji. 'A paper fooking field? Are you fooking with me, I spent all that dough for *this*?'

She could leave them here, in the paper field, let the worm do its work and follow the breadcrumbs back to their source or… or she could suck them in deeper.

// No, Samael spoke before En-ji could do more than sneer. *You spent those credits for this.*

She turned back to the white sun rising over the equally white horizon, and raised her hands. Brilliant diamonds appeared under her hands, glinting in the sun a moment before morphing into sparkling keyboards under each hand, gem-like keys stamped with symbols that had no place in a human alphabet.

Without a word, she began to type, the strange code spilling from her fingers.

Around them, the world changed

16

The girl really was her mother's daughter.

The woman leaned back in the sleek desk chair, warm golden leather wrapping around her form, the custom-designed headrest and arms adjusting to the new position.

She propped her chin on her hand, twisting the plain gold ring around her middle finger and watched the darkness flowing from Samael's armoured hands..

It had been a long time since she'd seen those symbols, witnessed smoke drifting across the white field.

Anticipation fizzed down her nape.

'She's has Lilya's files.' She spoke to the figure on the other side of the walnut desk, obscured by the spray of wildflowers.

The tall figure shook their head. 'She slipped another tracker on the avatar.'

'I know.' She thought a moment, watching Lilya's daughter conjure a rainbow spring from nothing. The girl was persistent, like her mother. 'Send her a thank you.'

17

1n a b0x2

In the vid, the lights around her ma's VR glasses faded, the bright blue and green reflections winking out of existence, momentarily replaced by a golden "A" before the lenses went dark. Her ma sighed as she slipped them off, pulling the thin gamer tag out of the terminal before leaning back in the white leather chair. The ergonomic wood-like frame shifted with her. She rubbed her nose, tiredness in the bags under her eyes and the worry on her face.

'Ma! Ma!'

Her ma looked up, exhaustion blurring her blue-grey eyes before they lit on the camera and a smile transformed her face.

'Did you steal daddy's phone again, little monster?'

The camera bobbed toward her ma, angling upwards, catching the underside of her ma's desk—all epoxy and steel, the space under her ma's knees alight with circuitry and LEDs. Through it, Vlad caught the back-to-front reflection of the screens hovering under her ma's elbows, the primitive holo-film embedded in the resin. There was something on it...

Vlad paused the vid.

In her darkened DKZero dorm, with the bucket chair pulled up to the tiny workspace and the Cube humming in Vlad's lap, her ma smiled at her, the VR glasses dangling from her fingers as she leaned forward in her chair and held her arms out to the camera.

Vlad had watched this vid a thousand times, once burned an

afterimage in an old screen just watching it over and over again. Leaving that face on at night, smiling at her as she went to sleep.

But not tonight.

She plunged her hands into the image and caught the reflection between pinched fingers.

'Bring up the cheese board recording,' she said.

A faint hum was the only response and then...

The image changed, the craggy, cloud-covered mountain spreading over the desk, En-ji in her pirate hat, Ru Ping in her armour, Hamish with the smoke curling around his neck. Herself in her Aclima guise, the deep, royal blue and cracking gold lightning snapping and popping in the soft grey landscape.

But it wasn't the avatars she focussed on. Vlad scrolled through the footage, fingers still pinched on the reflection in her mother's vid while the cheese boards sped past her left. Talking, talking, the slight shimmer of the tracking spell breaking from her hand and slithering toward Ru Ping. The snarl on Hamish's face, En-ji getting in it... and she hadn't noticed that at the time, the pixie almost comical against the cyborg, barely coming up to the other's sternum even hoisted on her toes. The curl of the pixie's nose rang a bell in the back of Vlad's mind, like she'd seen it somewhere—

The whale breached, exploding from the clouds, a graceful arch of condensed water vapour coloured yellow and peach by the dying sun.

There.

Vlad paused the vid, caught the whale between the fingers of her left hand, and together with the reflection in her right, threw the image onto the desk. She pushed the recordings aside, her ma and the craggy mountain top skidding above the desk, disappearing when they hit the edge of the screen, ready to be called back when needed.

She enhanced the two screen captures, first the cloud whale then the reflection, reversing the later and spinning it around until it matched the other.

Two cloud whales breached, both twisting as they did so, splashing into the cloud sea on their backs. There was something on their bellies. Another enhancement, enlarging the captures yet again. The one from the cheese boards was easy, the Cube barely flickering as it brought the blocky pattern underside the animal's jaw into sharp relief. The other was harder, the vid of her ma old, the device that had recorded it older still. Lights flashed a little more frantically over the Cube's pitch-black case, the pattern on that whale's jaw a little harder to make out, the intertwined digits and letters blurry and pixelated, but still...

'Freeze that,' she said.

Beep.

'Give me the field playback.'

A separate screen pushed the other two back, and on it, the paper-white field, herself standing in all that perfect, brilliant white, the reed heads bobbing against her thighs, an ink spot, just like En-ji had said. She fast-forwarded past the others arriving, took a moment to capture a shot of Hamish's face—the way the smoke pouring out his neck pixelated, the ear relocated to his collarbone—straight to the end.

Samael flicked her armoured hands, the diamond keyboards winking out of existence. It left just the cleared patch of paper-dirt at her feet, barely a step across, and the tiny, rainbow spring bubbling out of it. Rivulets of red and orange, green and blue all the way through violet threaded together in a way impossible for water, and yet there it was, defying game physics.

But that wasn't what held Vlad's attention.

There was something in the dirt, a pattern embossed in the white, partially hidden under the tattered, writhing ends of Samael's inky robes.

She'd only seen it when she moved back, had swept her armoured hands to the sides, summoned her staff and placed a shimmering blue barrier around the spring – just in time for Hamish to launch himself into it.

The satisfaction of that, his howl, had distracted her from the sight.

But she remembered it now.

And the Cube had recorded everything.

She enhanced the image. The sharp lines in the dirt looked embossed, feet-sized hieroglyphs stamped into the ground. Five of them, equally spaced around the little spring with its rainbow font. They appeared to pulse on the static screen capture, a *thump thump thump* beating behind her eyes, brighter and brighter and darker in a never-ending—

It wasn't just the screen, but the Cube, the lights embedded in the matte-black thrumming in time with the pattern. Drawing her in, close and closer and closer—

Vlad jerked backward, a jolt traveling from her nose to her toes as her face pressed right through the screen, almost kissing the bench.

She slapped the screen into the table, erasing it and the hypnotic pulse from existence.

That had been… unexpected. Weird and scary how the image sucked her in, how the Cube responded.

The Cube. Fuck. Had she just let a virus into her hardware?

'Run diagnostics,' she commanded.

A flat *beep* in return then several long minutes of silence, during which she rose from the plush armchair, knees shaking, and scrubbed tired, trembling hands over her face.

There was grit in her eyes that hadn't been there before, and her skin felt tight and greasy. She'd spent too long in-System, too long bent over vids and screen captures. It was a wonder her teammates hadn't barged in, a miracle Zixin hadn't decided—

Another flat *beep* and a report flashed above the Cube.

Memory check… Ok. Storage… Ok. Processors… Running higher than they should. Almost all of them engaged, running at a hundred percent when just a couple at eighty would have done.

'Activity log,' she said.

A new window, and did it take a few second too long to appear? Pixels a second slower to steady themselves before they hovered, crisp and clear over the desk? Or was her brain playing tricks on her, lack of sleep and food gumming up her mental pathways? It didn't matter, just check the logs, the answer would be in there.

The log… system processes. Cache. Activity log. Cloud whale—

Cloud whale? Memory dashed to the shape bursting through the fluffy white, the pattern under its jaw, the pattern on the paper-dirt.

Fuck. A trojan. How had it slipped past the virus checks? Quarantine?

The vid came back to centre screen, zooming from the edge at the flick of her fingers. Ma smiled at her, still reaching for the camera. Soft, wavy, brown hair fell around her face, exhaustion and worry casting a pall over her complexion, but her blue-green eyes filled with joy. And on the other screen, the cloud whale's wireframe, code rippling through it like blood.

Vlad stared at the woman on the screen, at the whale and the pattern embossed in the paper-field and tried to deny the shiver gripping her tailbone.

How the fuck had an image infected her rig?

'What did you do, Ma?' she whispered. 'What did you do?'

18

'...and while Annihilation *officials have assured fans that recent slowdowns in the network will not affect the gaming season's opening match, rumours continue to swirl about the safety of NuGet's neural jack.'*

'It's the question on everyone's lips, Andy: should the League have remained with VisionM's VCouch? I guess we'll find out.'

Vlad adjusted the settings on her headphones, turning up the noise cancellation even as she pumped the volume higher. The deep, heavy beat of early-twenties rock drowned the newscast, even if it did nothing for the deadly serious faces reflected in the bus's pitch-black windows.

Across the skinny aisle, Sticky glared at the broadcast playing across the inside window, Ming Li Na chewed her nails in the seat next to him, while Lu Chen sat up front, acting like the world didn't exist and Huang Yimo... Huang Yimo slouched behind Vlad, and if nothing had changed in the last twenty four hours, the woman would be staring a hole in the headrest.

Vlad didn't look.

She pulled the Death-like hood on her black, thigh-length coat closer around her face, and wrapped the loose woollen sides a little tighter around her waist.

The bus made her queasy, turned the porridge and black tea in her stomach to a roiling mass, refusing to settle.

She shouldn't have eaten, should have kept walking past the

kitchen and up to her room after punching the shit out of the bag in the little gym. But she hadn't, because the team had been there, clustered around the bench, boxes of psychedelic chemical food loops and bowls of steaming congee between them.

And Lu Chen, staring at her, expectation in his black gaze.

So she'd eaten, showered, changed into the team uniform—the high-collared black jacket with the dragon curling over the shoulder and tailored black pants seemed incongruous to the task, but at least the sleeves where long—and shuffled out the bright red door behind the rest, ignoring the looks when she threw the robe-like coat over the top.

The team bus—a long, sleek, black rectangle with DKZero's smoke-spewing dragon scrolling over its sides—shouldn't have taken her by surprise. But it did. Just a little. She'd hesitated getting on, the familiar fear squirming in her gut, churning the porridge.

The first step had been the hardest, but she'd made it.

At least it was a bus, wide and tall, enough room to stand, too big for—

She turned her mind away. *Don't go there. Not now.*

Vlad clutched the belt tight across her chest and drew her legs onto the wide leather seat. At least it wasn't dark. Sunlight, grey and muted by the ever-present smog, still made it through the large, dark windows, and while the outside of the vehicle would get lost in a blackout, the interior was a sea of cream veg-leather lit by run lights.

She just had to get through this.

Just had to get through.

Her braid fell over her shoulder and she tugged on that too. Once, twice, three times.

Sixty-eight minutes from the mansion to the stadium in mid-afternoon traffic.

She twisted the small black watch on her wrist, the circular dial lighting up long enough to see the timer counting down.

Fifty-seven gone. Only eleven to go.

She hugged her knees tighter.

Eleven minutes.

Eleven.

Vlad stared at the reflections in the glass, Sticky's glare beetled his brows and turned the big panda eyes dark, and there was a curve to his lips that would have made a grizzly proud. The enthusiastic announcers with their big smiles and expressive eyes, the cutaways to the stadium, spectators packing the seats, waving neon placards and holoscreens above their heads. And then her, face pinched, knees creeping up under her chin, Lu Chen looking at her from the front—

She stared back, straightened slowly and pushed her knees down, sneaked feet thudding on the floor.

Can't let them see.

Can't let anyone see.

She smiled at him; a small, thin stretch of lips that she prayed didn't look as brittle as it felt.

Suspicion tightened his frown and for a moment, Vlad thought she spied something very much like concern—

And then Ming Li Na reached over his seat and caught his attention.

Relief flooded Vlad, almost washing away the ball of sick in her gut.

Another glance at the watch.

Six minutes, eighteen seconds.

She rubbed the knotted flesh under the fitted black pants, tried to shove the remembered stench of grease and flames from her mind.

Five minutes, thirty-seven seconds.

The bus slowed, turned, a lumbering beast edging sideways out of the flow of traffic, leaving sleek sedans and flashy people-movers behind as it trundled up a wide, curving incline of pale green-crete, lined on either side not by avenues of carefully tended trees—the white-trunked birches reaching for the smog-grey sky, giant green umbrellas casting shade over pedestrians and motorists alike—but people. People waving signs over their heads, others in costumes – giant rabbit ears, blue robes, cardboard armour.

Yelling, singing. Screeching.

The bus trundled up the drive.

They slowed. Vlad's heart sped, adrenalin pumping through her veins.

The bus stopped.

Seventy-nine seconds.

Almost there.

At the front, the door opened with a faint *hiss*.

Almost.

Every muscle in her body tensed, anticipation mixing with the sick in her belly.

The others rose.

Not too fast. She had to wait. Couldn't let them know.

At least it wasn't a car.

At least she wasn't crammed up against the back passenger door with nowhere to go. At least she was wearing a jacket and sweatpants instead of the gold Wonder Woman costume.

Ming Li Na and Sticky rose, first one and then the other heading toward the door at the front, smiles on their faces, excitement in their eyes.

Huang Yimo shuffled past.

Carefully, making sure her knees didn't shake, Vlad rose too, already tasting the air outside, heavy with smog, thick enough to stopper her lungs, but still… air. Anticipating solid ground under her sneakers, the sky above—

Lu Chen was in the way. Long, inky bangs falling over his eyebrows. Staring at her.

Blocking her.

Never let them see you bleed. Grandmother's voice, Grandmother's words.

Vlad didn't snarl, even if the adrenalin in her blood made the knot in her stomach tighter, the chill frosting her spine colder. Even if the grey rectangle of light and freedom fought with the dark edging her vision.

'What do you want?' she said, short and hard instead of the lazy drawl she intended, but at least desperation didn't stain the words.

'It's just an exhibition match,' he said.

She blinked. 'What?' Not what she expected him to say, not the tone, the lack of rebuke.

For a moment, shock banished the dark creeping over her vision.

'First round of the season, no points go to the ladder. If we lose—' and here a pause, Lu Chen dipping his head a little like he wanted to peer under her cowl and see inside her brain '—it won't affect DKZero's position on the board.'

She blinked again, the world struggling to realign itself at the actual *concern* in Lu Chen's expression.

'What?' she said again.

He frowned, those heavy black brows beetling over his eyes. 'It's okay to be nervous, you're not used to play—'

'Move,' she said.

It was Lu Chen's turn to look confused, and that confusion pushed the last of the darkness from her eyes and put extra steel in her legs. She could do this, the door was right there.

'Move,' she said again, harder this time, reaching out to shove Lu Chen to the side. 'I'm not nervous, I hate travelling. I'm gonna be sick.'

He shot to the side.

She shot past him, not running—*never let them see you bleed*—but she was on the stairs in a heartbeat, counting the risers—one, two, three—coat flaring as she took one last step from the bus to the ash-grey green-crete drive. Solid ground under her soles, smog-laden air in her nose, braid bounding against her chest, weak yellow sun brushing her chin—

Flashes, bright pops of light going off, replacing the dark edging her vision with mini supernovas as cameras where shoved in her face, little, fist-sized black eyes trying to get under her hood, blinding her. And the screeching... Her ears rang. She'd turned the headphones off, slipped the earmuffs down around her neck. Fuck. Fuck, fuck, fuck.

Shock held Vlad, rooted her to the ground. She'd thought she'd been prepared, thought she was ready. She was Samael, she'd been stared at and screen grabbed and screamed at in-System in every conceivable way, but this... but this... Memories peeked over the edge of her brain, forgotten nightmares creeping toward the light, and for a second they were different flashes going off—red and blue strobes—different sirens screeching in her ears.

She should have stayed on the bus, the queasy, stomach-knotting fear would have been easier.

Vlad took a step back, but even as her calves hit the bus's bottom step a small, firm hand wrapped around her wrist. Ming Li Na's neat baby pink nails were a stark contrast to the grungy leather cuffs, but her grip was sure and firm as she tugged Vlad forward.

The first step was a stumble, quickly recovered, gaze on the ground, her toes not quite where she remembered them, but the next one was firmer, and the one after that surer and the third and the fourth. Her stomach still churned, light still blinded her, but Grandmother spoke in her ear, had a hand on Vlad's back, pushing her forward, lifting her chin, even as Ming Li Na's warm, gentle grip guided the way.

Vlad was grateful for the hood as the cameras continued to pop, fans with placards forming a tight corridor between the bus and the stadium.

It shouldn't have been that long, and yet the walk to the big glass doors seemed an eternity. Every step another moment for old nightmares to creep closer.

And then it was done, giant panes of glass and steel snicking closed at her heels, cutting off the roar of the mob outside, the lights, the screeching.

Ming Li Na stopped pulling.

Vlad stopped with her. She might not have been looking at her shoes, the square black toes, might have her chin raised and her shoulders back, but all she saw was... was...

Ming Li Na's smile. It lit up her face, made apples out of her cheeks and her eyes sparkle. 'The fans are a bit of a shock, the first time,' Ming Li Na said. 'You'll get used to it.'

Lu Chen strode past, halting at Ming Li Na's side, a tall dark shadow. 'You should have told us you had a problem with crowds,' he said, without looking at either of them.

Ming Li Na's mouth tightened, small fist *thunking* into her boyfriend's side. 'Be nice.'

He rubbed his arm. 'You hit like a girl.'

'I *am* a girl.'

There was a weird, soft light in Lu Chen's expression, a spot of humour struggling to make its way through the dourness as he opened his mouth to respond, but Ming Li Na interrupted him.

She reached for Vlad's wrist again. 'Come on, before he tries to make like he's funny.'

Vlad shook herself awake just as those neat, pink nails wrapped around the jacket's leather cuff.

'It's okay,' she said, forcing a smile through the chills curling her gut, knowing the expression didn't reach her eyes, but knowing too that the others wouldn't see it through the deep shadows of her hood. Just like no one saw Samael's eyes, only the dark slash of the avatar's mouth. 'The cameras took me by surprise. I'll be fine.'

And perhaps her words were too sharp, the gut-churning chill coming through her voice, wiping a little of the warmth from Ming Li Na's face, the humour from Lu Chen's.

'Oh, okay.' Ming Li Na dropped her hand. 'Well then, we're heading to the team locker room; this way.' She disappeared down a wide square corridor to her left.

Lu Chen waited a beat more, that hard black stare lancing the shadows under Vlad's hood. Disapproval and maybe anger radiated from him, before he turned—a smooth, precise movement—and followed Ming Li Na.

That brief warmth, the soothing blanket over the fire raging through her nightmares, went with them.

<⊙>

Liztachi Stadium's backstage, where the gaming league's locker rooms were, was a maze of stairwells and curving, interconnected corridors. Screens might have lined the walls, pointing directions, but the names where their own strange kind of code.

"K378. Hub C-7. Locker B13. Stairwell N2."

About the only word she recognised was *"Stadium"*, and even that... Vlad shook her head and tried not to think too hard about the nausea still creeping through her stomach. At least it wasn't twisting her gut anymore, without the cameras and the bus.

And even if she'd lost sight of the others three corners ago, the soft murmur of their voices carried down the halls, distorted but distinct, easy enough to follow.

Her boots made muffled *thuds* on the hard grey floors. If she let it, if she pushed the murmur of voices away, she could pretend she was alone; a shadow stalking the halls.

Except the memory of Ming Li Na's hand around her wrist was still warm. Rippling through the cold, midnight cloak and reaching for things—feelings and wants—she'd left at her parents' graveside.

Vlad gritted her teeth and balled her hand, giving it a hard shake, dispelling the memories with it.

No. No, she was Vladana Tong, and this game, these people—whether directly or indirectly—had taken her parents, and in return, she would have her pound of flesh.

Another corner. Ming Li Na and Lu Chen still nowhere in sight, but the DKZero logo strung along the wall, the curling, black dragon spitting its digital fire at an open door, and through that door, more voices.

She lifted her chin, firmed her lips under the hood and remembered her grandmother's words, the cold indifference on her sharp-boned face.

Never let them see you bleed.

Never.

Never-ever.

She strode through the door—

A white ceramic travel mug was thrust in front of her face. Short fingers banded by a dozen rings—silver and gold, black and bejewelled—wrapped around the mug, while ginger-scented steam rose off the top of the pale-gold liquid inside.

'Heya, bitch.' The familiar, laughing, heavily-accented voice sang from beside her. 'You throw up yet?'

The room froze. Sticky and Ming Li Na paused mid-word, Huang Yimo's head popping over the back of the sofa, Lu Chen looking up from his tablet. Even Zixin—talking on his phone—stopped, surprise or maybe shock holding his spine.

Vlad froze too. Just for a moment, as the war between Vlad and Ana rose anew. Who she was now and who she'd been just a handful of years ago—the Ana who'd still had friends, or *a* friend—causing her brain to stumble before it clicked back into place.

She wrapped her hands around the mug. It was warm, the steam curled around her nose, the ginger already sliding down her throat to quell the riot in her stomach.

She blew on it, took a sip, and turned.

Kristina Morita was a short woman, short enough she didn't have to duck to see under Vlad's hood, or for Vlad to see over the top of the red curls, almost as riotous as her own. Laughing brown eyes set in a pale-white face liberally sprinkled with freckles met hers from under dark, winged brows, while her lips smirked. Challenge was written across Tina's expression.

Vlad stared back, expression blank.

They had this act down pat.

A red-brown brow rose and a corner of those wide, pink lips lifted a little higher.

'Oooo, the patented Vlad stare.' The short woman mock-shivered. 'I'm intimidated.' She tilted her head to the right, expression gaining an analytical edge. 'Wasted on the tall folk though, what with the hood and all, but at least you're staying consistent with the whole "spectre of death" thing.'

Vlad's chin lifted of its own accord. 'I can squash you, pixie.'

The brown eyes twinkled. 'In your dreams, bitch.'

A cleared throat, then an average-sized round shadow to Vlad's left.

Sticky, wringing his hands. 'Ugh—'

'Don't get involved, panda,' Vlad said.

Another cleared throat, another shadow, taller and leaner behind Sticky.

It was Tina's turn. Without breaking Vlad's stare, the shorter woman pointed at Huang Yimo, the tip of her perfectly-painted finger a laser. 'Not even, string-bean, or I'll end you too.'

'That's really—'

'Shut up,' the both of them said together.

The redhead's mouth tugged a little higher.

Vlad stared a little harder.

Tension rose in the room.

Any second now...

A tablet *snapping* on the tabletop. A chair scraping back.

Tina's big brown eyes flicked to something over Vlad's shoulder before coming back. That smile grew. The short woman stepped in close, chest to chest.

'The big man just got up,' Tina whispered.

Vlad leaned in, twisting her lips in a snarl. At Vlad's side, Sticky tensed, Huang Yimo stepping forward, hands clenched.

'The captain or the manager?' Vlad whispered back.

'Captain.' Tina's eyes darted to the side, and she whistled. 'He looks pissed.'

'He always looks like that.'

Tina snorted. 'Only around you, bitch, he's a fucking pussy cat with his girlfriend.' A delicate frown creased her pale, freckled brow. 'Maybe this wasn't such a good idea.'

It was Vlad's turn to raise a brow, closing the last centimetre of distance between them, pushing back her hood in the same move, making sure to scowl as she leaned over the shorter woman. 'But the party's just started.'

'Aren't you meant to be throwing up?'

'You gonna hold my hair?'

'I'm gonna shove your head in the bowl—'

Another shadow, Lu Chen's tall, intimidating frame, pushing past the others and—

Zixin holding him back. 'They're stirring you up,' he said. Loudly and then, pointedly, 'We have other things to do, Ms Moritz.'

Tina kissed Vlad on the mouth. A quick peck between friends. 'Game's up,' she said, before glancing around Vlad to frown at Zixin. 'Spoilsport.'

Vlad turned, trying to hide the shock that rippled through her at her best friend's familiar tone, under a layer of frost aimed at Zixin. 'You know each other?' she said.

'I know your grandmother too,' Tina whispered in her ear.

Vlad jerked away from her.

Tina grinned, threw back her shoulders and stuck out her hand. 'Kristina Moritz,' she said. 'DKZero's public relations expert and resident troubleshooter.'

'But you can call her "Boss Bitch",' Huang Yimo spoke from beside the little lunch table in the middle of the room. The other woman had wandered away, the tension in her shoulders dissipated, probably while the shock was still coursing through Vlad's system. 'Not that anyone does.'

Lu Chen grunted. 'We have a game,' he said, staring hard at Zixin.

'We do. Tina?'

The short redhead winked at him. 'Already sorted.' She turned that grin on Vlad, a wicked twinkle in her eye and said, with far too much glee, 'The fans are going to *hate* you.'

They stood in one of the tunnels leading to the stage, Lu Chen, Ming Li Na, Huang Yimo and Sticky in their black uniforms with the white stripes and the dragon breathing fire across their backs. All lined up in a neat little row, facing the lights and screaming fans beyond.

Vlad stood at the back, the long, death-like folds of her hooded jacket disrupting the unity, arms wrapped tight around her waist. Grandmother's ever-present admonishment rang in her ears, a mantra against the dark.

Never let them see you bleed. Never let them see you...

It wasn't working. No matter how hard she concentrated, how tight her fingers dug into her sides; against the darkened stadium, all those spotlights and strobes reminded her of emergency lights on a dark road, of the flames and heat, and the yelling... There was no joy in the sound, no excitement, only her ma and the sirens, a high-pitched, bone-shedding wail—

A small hand on her arm, diamanté-tipped nails squeezing comfort into her bones.

Vlad looked down.

Tina frowned at her, not the shark-eating frown, but the other, the one that always wormed its way under Vlad's armour and made her want to cry.

Never let them see you bleed.

She jerked her arm free.

Tina held on, those nails tightening. 'I didn't think you were still having problems with lights.' She peered under the concealing hood.

'It's fine.'

'It's not fine,' Tina shot back. 'You have PTSD, and this isn't the time for immersion therapy.' She swore. 'Fucking hero, I should have known you would do this to me; I could have told them to switch up the lighting.'

In front, Sticky had turned, a query on his round, panda face, while behind... Zixin stared at them.

'It's *fine—*'

'It's not fucking *fine*, bitch.' There was no humour in Tina's expression, just anger and that concern, still trying to slip under Vlad's armour. 'Not if you have to go out there and play like you're the biggest, baddest Scourge in the world, instead of someone who used to wake her roommate up with nightmares after a college disco.

'I swear to God,' and here Tina got back up on her toes, face in close to Vlad's, 'if you fucking fritz out there, I'm going to tell tall dark and brooding—' she jerked her head towards Zixin '—all about it, and then you'll *never* fucking get rid of him. You got me?'

Vlad nodded, a smile tugging at her lips even as the stomach-churning fear loosened its grip. 'I got it.'

'Good.' Tina tugged at Vlad's hood. 'Normally, the team goes out in their uniforms, but your mystique is part of what's driving fan frenzy, and Yu Zixin wants to capitalise on that.'

'My mystique? Not the controversy over recruiting a Scourge?'

Tina's smile was shark-like. 'Oh, that too, but the secret over your identity…' She stood on tiptoe, 'That's what's *really* driving interest, once that's gone...' She shrugged.

'The advertising dollars dry up.'

'Hole in one, baby girl. Careful though, with insights like that—' Tina dropped back to her heels. '—someone just might mistake you for a Tong.'

Vlad looked away.

Tina chuckled, but the sound lacked joy. She gave the hood another tug. 'Handy of you to rock the death's hood today. I had a mask all prepped, but this is good, will send a shiver up the fans' spines, make them feel better when they boo your entrance.'

'They're going to boo?'

'Fuck yes, and hiss and holler and heckle, all the good "hs". And then, once you go out there and trounce DK's long-time rival, the DK fans will love you and the Meerkat fans are gonna be really sore. Then they'll bitch and moan and fight about it on the 'nets, and the next thing you know—'

'Even the people under rocks will hear about DKZero,' Vlad finished. 'And the dollars roll in. That doesn't sound like something Yu Zixin would do.'

'Because he didn't.' Tina winked at her. 'I did. PR and marketing, remember?'

'You—?'

A blast of music interrupted Vlad and a new, intense light flooded the tunnel. Over the rising strings and deep-throated choir of the entrance track, she watched, dumbfounded, as Tina backed away, and when she went to follow... Sticky was gripping her wrist, the panda's short, stubby fingers surprisingly strong as he tugged her toward the light.

Vlad cast one last look over her shoulder, before the light blinded her.

Tina smirked at her; the short, red-headed pixie stood triumphant in the dark, Zixin a shadow at her back.

'It's a lonely life you lead, Scourge,' Tina shouted. 'You need some friends!'

19

Betrayal had driven her through the exhibition match. The sick feeling in the pit of her stomach, the anger that came after, had got her across the stage, a bubble against the lights and yells. Hostility had rolled off the crowd, fans packed cheek-by-jowl in tiered stadium seats, waving their holo-placards over their heads—*We love you Sticky! Marry me Deadspace! Death to the Scourge!*

She'd soaked it in, stood under all those flashing lights and angry gazes and bathed in the hate like a healing potion. Or a poison, one she'd consume and turn to strength.

And after she'd slid into the VR chair and the canopy had closed, she'd slipped the jack under her hood and behind her ear with a kind of relish. Anticipation humming through her veins. Once she'd wrapped herself in Samael, had dropped into the game and stood with the rest of DKZero atop Balost's Ghost's east bell tower, that anticipation had been cold and hard and deadly.

Meerkat hadn't known what hit them.

Neither had her teammates.

Needless to say, DKZero won.

As they stood on the stage, accepting their victory, the hate from the crowd had been tempered. But not by much.

The rest of the team had bowed – little soldiers in their black uniforms, bending from the waist. And Vlad... she'd begun the movement—eyes on the stage, arms straight at her sides—and then there'd been the heckle.

'ROLL UP AND DIE, SCOURGE BITCH!'

There'd been a heartbeat of silence, the entire stadium hushed.

In that silence, Vlad had straightened, thrown back shoulders and chin just enough to let the lights find her mouth… and she'd smiled, lifted her finger high into the air in a different kind of salute.

That had been hours ago, and the memory of it was almost enough to chase the cold from her bones. Lag was getting worse, or maybe that was the lack of the sauce playing on her mind. The worst of it had faded as it should, the sidebars and dialogues, the sensation of a dagger in her hand, gone before the team climbed back on the bus. All except the peppermint and the chill.

The chill was new.

Around her, the narrow little dining room—all fake, beige-wood panelling, red-cushioned benches lined either side of a table just long enough to squeeze six, on it a hotplate with a pot of simmering soup in the middle, dishes crammed in every spare space—hummed with tension. Awkward. Silent. Disapproving.

Almost enough to curdle her stomach. In fact, it *was* enough to curdle her stomach, it was a wonder Huang Yimo, seated beside her, didn't hear the acids rumble. Or maybe that was down to the thin slices of pork and beef on the hotplate, sizzling away, or the soup rumbling in the pot.

Vlad plucked a tofu cube out of the soup, not looking at the others arrayed across from her – Sticky taking up almost half the bench, while Ming Li Na and Lu Chen jammed up together on the other end. Not that either seemed to mind.

Zixin hadn't joined them, and while Tina had escorted them onto the DKZero bus, she hadn't got on. Stood instead on the curb, somehow finding Vlad through the blackened windows, watching them go with that look on her face.

Tina had been there after the game, catching Vlad's arm before she followed the rest of DKZero into the club room.

'That was stupid,' Tina had said.

The urge to yank her arm from Tina's grip had been strong, but a shadow had moved beyond the open door and Vlad had resisted. Instead, she'd settled for a hard, implacable stare. 'You wanted them to hate me.'

'Only at the beginning, the other fans would have come to your defence, now all they're going to do is call for your head.'

'Should I have taken it then, like a *good* girl?'

Tina had yanked her closer, getting up on her toes to meet Vlad nose-to-nose. 'You should have been a grown-up. The bird was unnecessary.'

'If you wanted someone to play nice, *En-ji–*' Vlad'd hissed the pixie pirate's name, and had had the satisfaction of seeing Tina's face turn a few shades whiter, popping her freckles out in sharp relief. 'Then perhaps you shouldn't have recruited *this* Scourge.'

Tina had said nothing for a moment, then, 'Shit.' Her heels had hit the floor, a sharp *clack*. 'The lonely life crack.'

'Yeah.' Vlad had leaned down, taking up the space Tina had vacated. 'I thought it was Yu Zixin who told Grandmother about the gaming, but it was you, wasn't it?'

Tina had moved back, shaking her head. 'You used a different handle then Ana, and your mum's old avatar. I swear, I didn't know Samael was...' Tina had gestured up and down Vlad's length. '...you, until after you were recruited.'

'Recruited?' Vlad had laughed, a short sound without humour. 'That's what you call it.'

'Ana—'

'Don't call me that.' And even as she'd said it, she'd felt Grandmother in her soul, closing down her face, lending frost to her words. 'No one calls me that. Not anymore.' *Friends did,* a little voice cried from the dark, but Vlad locked that voice away, locked Ana away too.

'Ana—'

But Vlad had brushed past her, into the locker room's strange, half-jubilant atmosphere, and that had been that.

Tina hadn't been the only one unhappy with the one-finger salute. The high of the team's win had been curdled by the disapproval laying thick in the air, and it hadn't dissipated in the hours since.

On the dining table, the burner hummed, chopsticks clacked and cans snicked, but no one spoke.

Vlad ate a wedge of chicken.

The meat collapsed into its own black hole in the pit of her stomach, gained weight and did its best to burn a hole through the lining. All eyes might have been on the food, or darting between the others, but Vlad couldn't help sense them anyway. The thoughts darting between the other players, the words that didn't make it to their tongues.

She plucked bok choy out of the simmering liquid, dipped it in her sauce bowl and concentrated on chewing it, the soft texture, the hit of honey and chilli at the back of her tongue. Despite all that, it might as well have been ash sliding down her throat, hitting her stomach, a burning comet to join the black hole.

The chopsticks reached for the beef next, the thin bloody slice dangling like a red rag. Cooked it. Ate. Another celestial object she didn't truly taste, didn't want. Another sip of tea that made her stomach bleed. But she wouldn't stop, wouldn't bleed all over the table.

'He deserved it,' Huang Yimo said, breaking the silence.

Vlad's chopsticks stuttered, almost dropping the tofu square before her grip firmed. It made a small *plop* as it went in the pot.

'It'll be an issue on the forums,' Sticky said before shovelling rice into his mouth.

'Tina will take care of it.' Ming Li Na, bubble-gum pink soda spilling from a can into her glass, frothing as it rushed to the top. 'Our *boss* knows how to hire talent, at least.'

Silence took the table again, the little dining room with its faux wood walls and cushioned benches once again filled with the sounds of chopsticks and the hiss of butane-fuelled flame.

But without the same tension.

Vlad dug her tofu out the pot, neatly plopped the square on the plain white rice bed in her bowl.

A chunk of pork dipped in honey joined it, just not from her chopsticks.

She jerked sideways, staring at Huang Yimo beside her.

The gamer wasn't looking at her, attention on the dishes spread across the table, chopsticks snagging something green and leafy from a bowl. Watercress travelled up the table, joined the tofu and pork in Vlad's bowl.

'You eat weird shit,' the gamer said. 'Do your tastebuds actually work?'

A snort from the opposite side of the table, Sticky hiding a grin behind his wooden bowl.

Vlad glared at him, even as she carefully picked up the pork and popped the slice in her mouth. The little bit of sweet, salty heaven exploded over her tastebuds.

'Do yours?' She asked around the mouthful, poking the soda can in front of the other woman – a garish orange the match of Ming Li Na's pink one. 'Between the pork and the soda, it's a wonder you can taste anything, or do you need the extra sweetness so the fans don't notice the lemon stuck on your tongue?'

Huang Yimo glared, honeyed pork halfway to her mouth.

Vlad smiled back.

A purple can, condensation beading over the cartoonish grapes on its side, landed beside her elbow.

Vlad looked up in time to see Lu Chen settling back into his spot beside a smiling Ming Li Na.

Sticky snorted again.

Vlad's nose curled all of its own accord. 'Funny,' she said, even as she nudged the offending cylinder of carbonated sugar and food colouring away with her elbow.

'If the lemon fits...' Sticky ventured.

'Shove it, panda.'

Another choked snort, from Ming Li Na this time and something that might have been laughter twinkling in Lu Chen's eyes.

And no, that wasn't a smile lifting Vlad's lips, wasn't even a tiny morsel of humour lighting her heart.

Wasn't anything like that at all.

<⊙>

The sugar was the only excuse she had for the karaoke bar. Couldn't blame alcohol or drugs or even a cute arse, and she didn't dare blame it on the burgeoning warmth in her middle. Wouldn't allow the alien sense of belonging to slip under the wall of determination.

Nope, it was the purple can of sugar bubbles and the kind of chemical high that had toddlers zooming around a room, lips smeared with red. It was all the soda's fault, and that was the line she was sticking with.

Lu Chen had a terrible voice, and Ming Li Na wasn't much better. The pair stood, backlit by the screen and miniature stage lights, one an arrow-straight shadow with his shoulders thrown back and a goofy expression as he stared into Ming Li Na's eyes. For her part, Ming Li Na was giving it all, forehead-to-forehead, crooning the silly love song like they were wedding vows. Dressed in the pink hoodie and baggy jeans, she was as far from Lu Chen's street smart black as it was possible to get without glitter and sequins. She just needed a pair of holographic wings and a tiara to polish off the look.

Vlad eyed the projectors above the little stage, playing with her watch and running through the screens projected on the back her glasses as she did. The bar had shit security, if she just—

A cloud of sickly sweet chemical cherry drifted over her shoulder. Large pale hands sinking into the couch back either side of her head, followed it.

For a second, a span of six according to the clock on her HUD, the presence didn't register in Vlad's consciousness. Not in the way it should have, with flashing red lights and an instinctive urge to ball her hand into a fist. If the little karaoke room had been darker, or the lights behind Lu Chen and Ming Li Na had strobed, if the beats had pounded out a new heartbeat behind her rib cage or the little dance floor had heaved with sweaty bodies, it might have made a difference. If that warm little belonging hadn't shoved out the cynicism and doubt she rode like Ximisthus's twin, he'd never have gotten that close.

But he did and his mouth was on her ear, blowing cherry vape in her face before the darkness had time to wrap around her.

'Fancy meeting yoo 'ere. Sam-a-el.' He drawled the last bit, her name coming off his tongue nice and slow – too slow, not enough nice, so it crawled down her nape to lodge, cold and slimy at the base of her spine.

Just as slowly, drawing that ice into her spinal cord, rushing it through her nervous systems, to fingers and toes and heart, Vlad turned her head.

Hamish grinned at her, all teeth, vape hanging out the side of his mouth. He sucked on it. Blew another lungful in her face.

On the stage, blinded by the strobes, the singers kept singing, while clear across the couch, Sticky had his head buried in a screen and Huang Yimo…

Vlad couldn't see her, didn't dare take her eyes off Hamish long enough to check, but her HUD said the gamer was on the other end of the couch.

She needed to get Hamish out, and now before he drew too much attention, raised too many questions.

Vlad smiled back, all the slimy cold coming out in the frost riming her lips, the ice in her eyes. 'Crawl back under your rock, Hamish, I'll buy you a beer for the journey.' She started to rise.

Hamish shoved her back down.

There was strength in those bony hands and tattooed arms, despite the lack of obvious muscle, and Vlad hit the cushions hard, the force of it enough to expel air from her lungs and have her bouncing against the seat. The surprise must have made it to her face, because Hamish grinned again, actual joy in his small, toad-green eyes.

Another lungful of cherry smog. 'Ain't gone'na introduce me to your new friends, Sam-a-el?'

She pushed the hand away. Or tried to. Those bony fingers dug into the meat like they wanted to come out the other side. Pain screamed through Vlad's collarbone, and she couldn't help the hiss escaping her teeth.

On the HUD, the blob that was Huang Yimo moved.

Urgency mixed with the pain.

If she could just grab Hamish's thumb—

Another viscous squeeze—and now it was a grunt pushing through her lips, a grimace twisting her face, bringing tears to her eyes—and the hand was gone, slapping her shoulder like a good mate instead of ripping it apart.

'Never mind.' The smile on his narrow face was enough to freeze her insides, but it was the gaze he flicked over her shoulder, to Huang Yimo, that stopped her heart. 'Plenty of time for introductions later.'

And he was gone, the door to the little karaoke lounge slapping his arse before the cushions beside her had time to sink under Huang Yimo's weight.

'Who was that?'

Vlad stared at the door, hand on her shoulder before she turned, not to face Huang Yimo but the stage. There was fear in her belly, the kind of nasty, breath-stealing acid that made her adrenaline spike. The same kind of fear that had come when she'd totalled her first motorcycle, the loss of control, the crash rail coming at her fast.

Fuck.

Hamish was going to be a problem.

Huang Yimo nudged her side. 'Vlad?'

Had she covered the fear? Had Huang Yimo caught it on her

face? It didn't matter, she'd make it not matter.

Vlad shook her head and shrugged, still staring at the stage. Lu Chen and Ming Li Na were wrapping up. 'He had the wrong room.'

<⊙>

The fear refused to unhook its claws. She tried to ignore it, focussed on Lu Chen and Ming Li Na on stage, then Sticky, then Huang Yimo; succeeded for the few minutes it took to fend off the microphone shoved in her face, Huang Yimo on the other end, staring down her long nose with a certain expectation in her black gaze.

Singing would have curdled her stomach.

And so she sat at the back of the lounge, trying to ignore the itch across her shoulders that insisted Hamish was on the other side of the soundproof door, staring through it. He hadn't been – there were cameras in the halls and she'd had the feed playing as she pretended to watch the others belt out pre-millennium pop.

Now, an hour in, and she was two hours past when she should have left the karaoke bar; the alien sense of belonging long since churned to foul ash.

Vlad slipped out the team's private room, the grape soda and a sudden, driving need to find Ming Li Na—who'd gone on her own call of nature—pushing her into the hallway.

The sleek black door shut behind her, cutting Sticky off mid-croon. The panda could sing, she'd give him that.

But some other time, when her stomach wasn't eating itself.

The karaoke bar was an Art Deco labyrinth, rooms branching off corridors with gold walls lit from below, the small passageways leading to the rooms in turn leading to bigger corridors packed with people in various stages of drunk and half-drunk. Hoodies and sneakers mixed with suits and stilettos, waiters wearing neat little vests over their white shirts, holding trays high overhead as they weaved between patrons.

If not for the guide on the back of her glasses, she'd have missed the corridor leading to the toilets and wandered right out into the even more crowded bar.

At least she'd have been at home in the bar, all that dark midnight and thumping music lit up with neon – so different from the private rooms.

She turned off the main passageway and stopped short.

Her stomach burned.

There was Hamish, Ming Li Na bailed up between him and the wall.

He had her caged; bare, pale, sinewy arms blocked her into a dark corner between the women's toilet and the emergency exit, scrawny chest barely covered by his t-shirt, pressing in close.

Ming Li Na was staring him down, fist balled at her side and Vlad wondered if it'd find the bastard's balls in the ten seconds it took her to cover the distance.

'If I were you, I'd have sex with me.' Hamish leaned in until his nose almost touched Ming Li Na's.

Ming Li Na scrunched into the wall, disgust all over her face. 'If you were me, I'd have better taste.'

'And if *I* were you,' Vlad said as she pushed Hamish back. 'I'd watch my balls.'

He smirked at her.

She returned it, flickered her gaze to his crotch and back. 'Watch your mouth, Hamish.'

The smirk caught, the edges curling into something meaner, before it shifted, Hamish shifting with it, pushing back from the wall with a lazy flick of his chin.

'Oo, I will, missy.' He leaned in close. 'And I'll be watching yours too, although your little friend there is more to my taste. Tell me, does she like raves? Invite her to the next one for me.'

He turned and walked away, neon lights painting his tattooed arms and shaved head in pink and yellow, the bright colours somehow making him more sinister.

'You know him,' Ming Li Na at her side, white around the eyes, face drawn, a little tremble in her hands, but her soft voice firm, gaze steady.

Vlad didn't answer, just turned away. She should go, follow Hamish. Vlad hadn't been thinking before, should have slipped a trojan in Hamish's gear, seen where he went, what data she could mine.

She hadn't seen Ru Ping. Was the heavy around? Maybe she could slip a worm in with the trojan, have it tag all the networks Hamish came in contact with, see what she could—

Ming Li Na grabbed her wrist. Tugged until Vlad met her gaze. 'Are you in trouble?'

Vlad blinked, all thoughts of trojans and worms forgotten. 'What?'

Ming Li Na jerked her chin in Hamish's direction. 'He's not a nice man—' a pause '—and he knows you.'

Vlad twisted her wrist from Ming Li Na's grip. 'And?'

Ming Li Na moved closer. How had Vlad not noticed how short the other woman was? Just give her a red wig and Tina'd have a sidekick.

'If you're involved in something, we can help you.' There was a certain seriousness in Ming Li Na's gaze, a rock-steady confidence at odds with her pink hoodie and fluffy headband. Was it the light bouncing up from the striped floor or was she somehow channelling Lu Chen?

Vlad closed the smidgeon of distance between them, forcing Ming Li Na to tilt her head further back. 'I'm a Scourge,' she said. 'You can't help me with shit.'

wAN72 H3r.

20

Vlad shifted her feet on the cold marble floor.

The big glass window with its pale mullions and golden woodwork, the chocolate brown rug and the overstuffed beige armchairs might have been meant to give the antechamber warmth, but all they did was clutter the place. Much like the giant calligraphy on the walls, and the black and white ink painting opposite.

The chill was in the skyscraper's bones, in the girders and concrete that made up the shining behemoth that was the seat of Tong Industries. And the heart of it... Vlad shifted, heavy-soled boots scrapping the floor, hands clenched within the deep pockets of her hoodie. The heart of it was behind the twin, black panelled doors just ahead.

Dark with age and polish, the sides straight and rigid, the doors stood out against the clean white lines of the foyer. The ancient mahogany with its red-black swirling grain should have been warm but the marble and the foyer's straight, perfect white lines sucked all the warmth out.

Or maybe that was just Grandmother.

Peppermint wound through Vlad's nose.

She shook her head to clear it. Eight hours since she'd logged-in after the incident at the karaoke bar, chasing traces of Hamish across the System only to find the Tong marketing machines instead. Its sticky fingers had been behind the chat bots stirring shit across the forums, the smelly kind, and even if none of it directly mentioned Samael, that was the name commentators were shouting.

What was Grandmother up to?

When she'd logged-out, curled up on the lounge chair in her room with the Cube lighting up the ceiling, she hadn't any answers—then or now—even if the peppermint still haunted her, stuck in her nostrils and mixed with the real world.

Like the coffee

Zixin leaned back in one of the overstuffed, minimalist beige chairs and sipped from a delicate little cup. With an ankle crossed over his knee and one arm resting along the chair back, he looked more like he was at a nightclub than a business centre, although the coffee would have been out of place.

He stared at her.

She stared back.

He smiled.

She scowled.

There was a heavy sigh and then an explosion of red hair and a determined expression stepped between them.

'Would you two stop it?' Tina scowled at them both. 'Or get a room or something, because this...' She waved her hands between them. '...is not doing the situation any good.'

Vlad turned her glare on Tina.

In return, Tina stabbed a finger in Vlad's face. 'And don't you give me that, we already had words.' She stepped in closer and lowered her voice. 'You *know* I wouldn't have landed you in this had I known, but *someone*—' and the stress on the last word made it clear who that someone was '—disappeared four years ago and didn't tell their best friend why.'

'This is your idea of revenge then?'

'Babe, if I wanted revenge, I've got better ammunition than this,' Tina said.

Of their own will, Vlad's eyes flicked to Zixin, frowning as he fiddled with the comm behind his ear, before she dragged her gaze back to Tina.

The redhead didn't smile, there was no victory or humour on her face, only that thing that wanted to slip under Vlad's armour and wind around her heart.

The anger and betrayal that burned in her gut, that had carried her through the exhibition match and across the stage, that had defied the heckler, withered a little under that expression.

Fuck Tina and the sympathetic horse she'd ridden in on. And fuck Yu Zixin with his pressed suit, shiny watch, and knowing eyes. Her own had dark circles under them, her No Division t-shirt over the long-sleeve black compression top was rumpled, and there was a noodle stain she hadn't noticed until Tina mentioned it as they got out of the private car.

A pointed little remark about wearing last night's clothes.

Vlad hadn't gone home with the team last night. She'd stood on the curb, staring into the big, dark maw that was the team bus, remembered Hamish pinning Ming Li Na to the wall and the soda churning in her stomach.

Excuse and desire had come together at that moment.

When she begged off the team trip back to the mansion, no one objected, although Ming Li Na had given her a worried look.

The door had hissed shut and DKZero had trundled off into the night.

She could have done with Ximisthus right then, the bike's heavy whine, the blacktop streaking under the tyres, the howling wind drowning her thoughts. A ride-share scooter had done the trick instead, and the cold, echoey embrace of the warehouse had been worth the skin-crawling walk through deserted streets.

Her own bed, the open, high-ceilinged spaces, the bucket chair in front of the window and the web across it.

The tracker she'd placed on Ru Ping at the cheese boards had borne fruit; a location out on the coast. Not the tall, glass and steel edifice she stood in now, waiting on Grandmother's orders; not even the cold, austere mansion in the hills or one of the expensive high rises Zixin undoubtedly called home. But a town that was barely a dot on the map.

There was a certain relief in that, even if her gut still churned and the dark, tiny voice of suspicion said it was all too easy. No matter what she felt—or hoped or dreaded—she needed to get out there and investigate for herself.

First, she had to get through this.

The woman behind the massive stone and wood reception desk rose – salted black hair pulled back in a neat bun, dark brown eyes framed with thin gold glass, a neat grey suit. 'You can go in now.'

Behind the woman, the two tall doors opened.

They didn't creak.

Something in her wanted them to creak.

Zixin led the way, setting down his coffee and rising from his chair. Tina followed in his wake, but not before casting a stern look at Vlad.

Vlad went slower. Nerves had her feet, made her gut clench and her palms sweat, but she made her face stone and her eyes dark.

Beyond the black doors, a delicate wooden screen formed another lobby. The thin slats with their round window displaying another of Grandmother's carefully cultivated bonsai—a miniature pine, its gnarled branches erupting from its tall pot, as if it clung to the side of a cliff—giving glimpses of the space beyond.

Stepping around that screen was like stepping back in time. The old wooden floors could have been lifted from antiquity, the dark, polished wood marked and scarred, patched in places with pale timber. Just like the panelling behind the dark-teak desk that glowed with age and money.

Same as the old woman sitting behind it.

Grandmother wore black, her perfectly straight, steel-grey hair falling neatly past her shoulders, sharp black eyes latching onto

Vlad as her boots *thunked* across the floor. And yes, Vlad might have put a little extra force into each step, made sure to hit the boards at *just* the right angle.

There was a little seating area in front of the desk, dark-leather versions of the chairs outside clustered around a low coffee table, almost a twin for Grandmother's. Zixin claimed one, arms once again spread across the back, ankle on knee. Tina took another, back straight, knees pressed together and challenge on her lips.

And Vlad... she stopped on the periphery, hands at her sides, chin lifted, and returned her grandmother's gaze.

The old woman's expression didn't change, not for three seconds, or four or ten. Not even for the whole minute they stared at each other, not even as air grew still and heavy. Not even as, out the corner of her eye, she saw Zixin's hands clench on the back of his chair or Tina shift awkwardly in her seat. Not even as nerves grew in Vlad's stomach and her shoulders itched with the need to hunch and look away, as her nails dug into damp palms.

Not even then.

Grandmother raised a thin black brow.

Peppermint sang in Vlad's nose.

Zixin's foot hit the floor with a solid *thud*. 'The incident at the stadium is a problem,' he said. Words perhaps a little loud, a little sudden in the heavy silence.

'Is it?' Grandmother didn't shift her gaze.

Neither did Vlad.

Tina spoke. 'No, it isn't. We're getting more hits than even *I* anticipated. Vlad's gesture on the stage has the nets buzzing.'

'Negative publicity is not good publicity,' Zixin shot back.

'Have you even looked at the forums?'

'I've seen enough...'

The argument faded into the background, the chairs and old wooden floors, the coffee wafting from the carafe. There was just Grandmother, those dark eyes so like her own and yet... And yet nothing. Vlad lifted her chin a little higher, added more steel to her knees, more bite to her nails. She wouldn't give in, she wouldn't give—

Grandmother smiled, and for a moment Vlad thought she saw pride on that old, lined face. But then it was gone and Grandmother was rising, pushing herself out of her tall, black chair with both hands on the armrests.

Around the coffee table, the argument stopped.

'You stirred a hornets' nest,' Grandmother said as she wound around the desk and took the chair at the head of the little semicircle leaving Vlad standing on the edge of the group, staring down Grandmother like a child caught stealing sweets.

Her fingernails bit deeper into her palms. An old frustration surged in her chest, the humiliation of being outmanoeuvred reminded her of her childhood, growing up in Grandmother's house, being called to the office. She fought the feeling of being fourteen again, pushed down the anger, the indignation that came with it.

She wasn't fourteen anymore and two could play this game.

The smile was plastic, a stretch of the lips that didn't reach her eyes, but Vlad plastered it on her face anyway, let the frustrated humiliation in her stomach boil. She paced around the clustered chairs, trailing a hand along the backs.

'Isn't that what you wanted?' she said, and was proud of the neutrality in her voice, the lack of emotion.

Grandmother tilted her head. 'You've upset the socials, girl, which has upset my relationship with NuGet as well as certain shareholders. Made my morning quite difficult.'

Vlad continued around the chairs, and instead of taking a seat beside Tina or Zixin, hitched her bum on Grandmother's antique desk and made herself comfortable.

She was behind them now, speaking to the side of Grandmother's head, the old woman's strong, sharp profile outlined against the mid-morning light streaming through the tall windows. 'You can handle it,' Vlad said.

A choked cough came from Tina, and on the periphery of her vision, she saw Zixin start to rise. Vlad focussed on her grandmother.

The old woman turned, twisting her chair half a fraction to face her. Her pale, golden face showed nothing, her ink-dark eyes mirrors, her subtly painted lips a noncommittal half-smile as plastic as the one stretching Vlad's, but her brows... The right one twitched.

Vlad folded her hands in her lap, and there was a little less plastic in her smile.

'Indeed, I can.' Grandmother folded her own hands, mimicking Vlad's. 'But that does not mean my employees should make it necessary.'

It was Vlad's turn to raise a brow. 'I'm not your employee.'

A sound from Zixin, but Grandmother silenced him with a raised hand.

'Really? Then what are you?'

'A Tong. Isn't that what you wanted?'

Grandmother harrumphed. 'A Tong shows restraint, even in the face of provocation.'

'Then what about a Zima?' Her mother's maiden name rolled off Vlad's tongue with all the weight of a mountain.

Even Tina was silent.

Vlad's smile grew fangs. 'That's really what you wanted, wasn't it, Grandmother? A Zima to finish Ma's work?'

They stared at each other.

Tina shifted in her chair.

Zixin cleared his throat.

The staring match continued.

Vlad's eyes started to burn and her shoulders to itch. For a moment, she was back in Graydon's Revenge with the ants using her spine as a ladder and the crushed-citrus smell competing with the peppermint making a home in her throat. The block-headed horse and the upside-down door in the wall.

It was Tina's turn to clear her throat, and Vlad wanted to clear her own with her. Instead, she fought the ants with their pincer feet, and dug fingernails deeper into her palms.

'The press is to our advantage.' Tina was on her feet, shoving a water glass in Vlad's face, breaking the staring competition. 'We can use it.'

Vlad took the glass.

There was a smile on Grandmother's face, the hint of victory in her black gaze. The old woman turned her attention on Tina. 'Can we? And how do you suggest I explain my granddaughter's disrespect to the team's sponsors? I assure you, they are most upset.'

'Let them be, we knew going in recruiting a Scourge was going to attract negative publicity—'

'But not fan outrage,' Zixin cut in. He spoke to Vlad. 'They hate you.'

She didn't smile back, couldn't summon the right muscles. 'I'm used to it,' she said. 'And I'm not here for good press, or sponsors, or shareholders.'

'As you've made clear.' Grandmother poured coffee from the carafe. 'But you *are* a Tong—'

'Not a Zima?' Vlad interrupted.

Grandmother ignored her. '—and you will acquit yourself like one. That is the deal you made.'

'And when will you hold up your end?'

Grandmother's eyes turned sharp. 'What suggests I haven't?'

Her smile widened, showing teeth. 'Why do you think?'

A hard, considered glint turned the old woman's gaze to obsidian before her expression shut down and she looked away. 'When it pleases me.'

'And will that be before or *after* the contract term ends?'

'It will be—' and now Grandmother rose, a single fluid movement getting her out of the chair belying her age. Another and she was pinning Vlad to the desk with those dark, serious eyes. '—exactly when I wish it and not a moment before, Granddaughter.'

The smiled melted from Vlad's lips. She wouldn't wilt under her Grandmother's regard. She wouldn't. Her spine was steel and her hands steady as rocks. Vlad tilted her head just enough to meet Grandmother's gaze with her own, instead of the top of her head.

'And when will that be?' she asked again, proud her voice lost none of its bravado, didn't shake or crack under the strain.

Grandmother leaned in, enough for the deep, floral notes of her perfume to wrap Vlad in memories of doonas and warmth cut through with other harder things. 'When you behave like a Tong.'

21

1 pHOUnD hERSt

'When you behave like a Tong.'

The meeting had gone downhill from there, and now shiny elevator doors were closing, Tina and Zixin on the other side, shutting her in a two-by-two-metre metal box with her grandmother.

The doors closed with a *shnuck*, almost too quiet to hear over the gentle strains of the piano coming through the speakers.

The old woman met her gaze in the reflection.

Projected over the doors, the floor number started counting down.

Forty-nine.

Forty-eight.

Forty-seven.

'You don't even want DKZero, do you?' Vlad said.

One of Grandmother's dark thin brows rose.

Forty-three.

'And why do you ask that?'

'You're not upset about the exhibition match.'

'Hmm.' A nod and in the doors, those eyes still not letting go. 'Perhaps I planted the heckler, knowing what you would do.'

The soft, warm strains of Grandmother's perfume were filling the little box and Vlad couldn't help the shocked little sideways jerk off her head. 'Why would you do that?'

Another *hmm* and a small predatory smile lit Grandmother's

gaze. 'DKZero's parent company filed a patent last year.'

'NuGet.' Vlad frowned, gaze losing focus as memory took over. NuGet built System hardware, screens and microchips and… A fragment crystallised in her mind's eye, the discrete holographic cube stamped on the VR chairs in DKZero's training room.

Her sight sharpened, met Grandmother's in the doors.

Thirty-one.

'VR chairs?'

Grandmother's dark, coral-red lips lifted at the corners. 'I have no need of a new recliner, child.'

Twenty-nine.

The little arm coming out of the chair's side, the jack homing in on the port in her neck, but there was nothing new about the neural jack, nothing patent-worthy, unless… The peppermint in her nose, the haptics that couldn't simulate scent. 'Something in the chair.'

Twenty-six.

Twenty-five.

Vlad shifted, the weight of Grandmother's regard, the expectation in it—even diluted by the elevator's mirror doors—too much for the itch in her feet. Or maybe that was the final, nascent threads of last night's sense of belonging curdling her soul.

Maybe— No. No, it wasn't any such thing.

Seventeen.

And yet… There was a sourness in her mouth. 'You used me to create bad press for DKZero… and NuGet, but you already own it…'

'Not own, NuGet's CEO was canny enough to stall my takeover, but TI is a large shareholder.'

'You want more.'

'I want it all.'

'Why?'

'Why not?'

Silence, the sour taste strengthening, curling her nose. Vlad fisted her hands against it, squeezed tight on a new, different betrayal—not against her, but by her—as she recalled standing on the stage and lifting the one-finger salute high and proud.

It boiled within and she wanted to hiss to relieve the pressure.

But she wouldn't, because she didn't care. It wasn't her problem, and even if it was… Grandmother had set her up, planted her in DKZero just as she'd planted the heckler and—

Fuck. She closed her eyes. It wasn't her problem.

She didn't care.

She *wouldn't* care.

Not one little bit.

Vlad opened her eyes.

Grandmother was still staring and there was a new element to her smile, a hint of consideration.

Fuck. What had Grandmother seen on her face?

Vlad refocussed on the floor numbers.

Eight.

Almost over.

Seven.

Almost…

Six.

Hold your tongue Vlad.

Five.

Hold…

Four.

Your…

Three.

Tongue— 'Don't do it again.' The words burst from Vlad's lips.

Two.

Grandmother's brows, both of them, went into her hairline. 'What did you say?'

One.

A soft *ding* cut through the piano, a crack of light splitting the doors apart.

'You heard me,' Vlad said as she exited ahead of her grandmother, nerves making her stomach jump. She prayed adrenalin wouldn't make her knees knock.

Two strides out into a bright, busy, marble-lined foyer with its two-storey ceiling and giant glass walls overlooking an equally busy square, all of it filled with worker bees in suits and heels.

In her heavy boots and bike leathers, stained black t-shirt stretched tight over skin-hugging undershirt, wild strands of dark-brown hair escaping her braid, Vlad didn't just look out of place, she *felt* it. Weird and awkward and alien in her own skin.

'And if I do?' Grandmother's voice rang through the foyer, loud and clear.

Worker bees stopped, looked. Whispered.

Vlad turned, slow, lest her knees break at the unaccustomed duty in her chest. The alienness weighing her down, even as it lifted her chin and let her meet Grandmother's steel-bright gaze. 'I'll behave like a Tong,' she said.

A smile broke over the old woman's face, warmth and humour lighting it from the inside. She closed the few steps between them. ''That is almost worth—'

'Tong Shufeng.' A warm female voice interrupted Grandmother.

Grandmother turned to face it, the crow's feet at the corners of her eyes tightening, her face freezing into a pleasant mask.

'Marion.' Grandmother smiled, and the warmth in her voice took Vlad back a step. 'How nice to see you, I did not think we had an appointment.'

The woman who put sunshine in her grandmother's voice even as it blackened her gaze, floated across the marble floor, tall and elegant, the long black tails of her linen jacket flowing behind her like the feathers of a strange bird.

A newscast flashed in Vlad's memory, Grandmother's portrait beside this woman's, the woman's name. Marion Bourne, the

CEO of VisionM, the only company big enough to rival Grandmother.

Marion smiled, the lines around her mouth smiling with her, pale-blue eyes lighting with genuine humour, or at least it seemed that way to Vlad.

There was a warmth to her face beyond the pale, sun-kissed skin. Maybe it was the silver streaks in her hair; the grey different from Grandmother's, pewter instead of steel, gentle waves falling about her face. Whatever it was, it struck Vlad to the core, made her want to take a step back lest it sucked her in. A warm, sticky pit slurping around her ankles before it climbed over her knees and held her tight.

Marion drew to a stop beside them, the wings of her jacket settling around her knees; the bright red and yellow beads strung around her neck *clinked*.

'This must be your granddaughter.' Marion turned that smile on Vlad. Was it possible for the older woman's face to emit more warmth? Were her lips the sun? 'You look like your mother.'

A fine-boned hand thrust at Vlad, manicured nails, a delicate gold watch and a plain gold wedding band wrapped around her ring finger.

She didn't have to see Grandmother's face to know there was nothing but a billowing cold behind the polite smile. She could feel it, the arctic breeze raising goosebumps across her back.

Vlad reached for Marion's offered hand, smiled and hoped she managed a fraction of the other woman's warmth, lest the arctic chill shifting its focus from Marion to her burned the flesh from her bones.

Grandmother's disapproval lent the extra sparkle to Vlad's gaze, widened the stretch of lips. Grandmother wanted her to behave like a Tong and a Tong would greet a business partner warmth for warmth, but a Zima...

Flesh met flesh and on the back of Vlad's glasses a host of networks came alive. It was easy to pick out Marion's, it was open and waiting, the work of a heartbeat to slip an ident card into it.

An arched brow, a look of surprise and a moment later a ping behind Vlad's ear as Marion's system returned the favour.

A Zima would slip a trojan in with the ID card, and a Zima-Tong would expect the same in return.

It was moments to clasp hands—Marion's dry and warm, strong despite the age lines—and to plant the worm in the other woman's network, less time than that for Grandmother to step in, consuming the other woman's attention even as she dismissed Vlad.

Aristocratic, commanding, leaving Vlad standing in the foyer, a dark, hooded island in a sea of snapping heels and sharp suits. Of briefcases and lunch dates. Of normalcy.

'You look like your mother.'

22

'While controversy around Samael's infamous salute continues to rage on the nets, taking many spectators by surprise, the real monkey in this wrench appears to be the embezzlement scandal surrounding NuGet's Chief Financial Officer, Lu Pang. Tell me, Simon, what's the latest on that?'

'Not much to say, Taylor. The fan outburst after the DKZero/Meerkat exhibition match has pretty much overtaken any news that doesn't centre around DKZero's new Scourge teammate.'

'I bet the NuGet board are happy about that.'

'Hey, I wouldn't be surprised if their PR machine is stirring up most of the trouble.'

The notification vibrated through her watch as she came out of the System, a gentle *buzz* against her wrist mixing with the lag still coursing through her skin. The others were already out of the VR chairs, shuffling out of the training room, rubbing noses, stretching arms and backs. Not talking.

A marathon training session followed by the practice match against Skull Hack didn't leave a lot energy for talking.

No one cast her a look as she lay in the padded leather, eyes half-closed. After two weeks living in each other's pockets, eating and training together, everyone was used to her being the last one out of the training room.

There'd been looks the first few times, concern on Ming Li Na's brow, suspicion on Sticky's, Lu Chen's impassive stone face, even Huang Yimo pausing at the foot of Vlad's chair, looking like she wanted to say something, but it passed. Even the puzzlement, that question that seemed to hover on everyone's brain, faded. Now, the only eyes she had to worry about now were Zixin's.

He like to stand on the training room's threshold, shoulder against the doorjamb, arms crossed over his chest as he stared at his phone. Or pretended to. She wasn't sure which.

Vlad peeled the chair's neural jack from behind her ear, the sticky contact pad coming away with a little *pop* that did nothing to disperse the peppermint clinging to her nostrils.

Just how much of the sweet, sharp scent was NuGet's technology and how much was her own, fucked-up chemistry? If it was all the tech, it should have been the coarse, red dust of the level they'd just played following her out-System, the stench of Skull Hack's smoke bomb, not Ma's favourite candy.

Not that it seemed to matter. Lag was lag.

She swung her legs to the floor, trying to remember it was soft house slippers on her feet, and not Samael's high, black-leather boots, and that she had to stuff her hand—not armoured—in the hoodie's front pocket and slip her fingers behind the top seam to find the small, hidden pouch with the pills. No accessing inventory with a thought; the macros on her HUD weren't real, the bright pop in the corner of her vision wasn't a target lock on Zixin but a leftover from the game.

It was harder than it should have been.

Zixin standing sentinel didn't make it easier.

'Don't you have an office?' she said as she shuffled past.

He didn't answer.

She slipped the pill between her lips.

It tasted like dirt, dried the back of her mouth like it too.

And if her feet were a little unsteady, if she walked a little slower and more cautiously past Zixin—*// Level boss. Level: 80. Threat* *level: red*—and if his gaze stuck to her back a little harder, she didn't care. Not one bit.

She paused at the head of the board table, Zixin a hard, inescapable presence behind, and took stock. Ming Li Na was sprawled across the matte-black in her customary head-on-forearm position, Huang Yimo echoing her, while Lu Chen sat back in his chair with eyes closed and one hand rubbing slow circles on Ming Li Na's back. Even Sticky looked tired as he pored over a replay, round chin propped on his hand, waving through screens with a slow finger.

Tiredness filled the air like the first stirrings of smog out over the lake.

Vlad turned on her heel, the stairs and the vibration against her wrist beckoning her upward.

Zixin caught her arm before she went three steps. 'Where are you going?'

She blinked at him, stared for a good two seconds. Bronze eyes, thick black brows struggling not to meet over his nose.

// Level boss. Laser vision. Fire bombs—

She shook the afterimages away.

Fuck lag.

'Upstairs, to my room.' She shook his hand off. 'I'm tired.' And there was the notification, waiting. Waiting.

Anticipation gathered in her gut.

'Game debrief.' Lu Chen spoke slow, no heat in his words and only a micron of the usual command.

'Later,' Vlad said, and started back for the stairs.

'Vlad—' Zixin began and grabbed her arm again, only to be interrupted by the sound of chairs pushing back from the table and a groan.

'I'm going to bed.' Huang Yimo shuffled past. She paused a moment, and Vlad could almost feel her stare, a heavy weight on Zixin's hand around her bicep, before it flicked to his face. 'Weren't you the one going on about our inhumane training schedule?'

Lag popped a green box around Huang Yimo's long, drawn face.

// Deadspace. Ninja. Ally.

It made her warm inside.

But no, that was just the anticipation, the need to find out which tracker—Ru Ping's or Marion's—had found its way back home.

Ming Li Na came next, catching Vlad's other arm as she brushed past, and *tugging*. There was strength in the smaller woman's grip. 'Help me up the stairs; my eyes are crossing. The game against Skull Hack was brutal.'

'Debrief,' Lu Chen spoke again.

'Tired,' Ming Li Na shot back. '*Sleep*,' she said again, this time to Zixin. 'Next time, don't schedule a game for the *morning*.' She tugged once more.

Vlad stumbled forward.

Zixin's hand fell away

Up the first step, the second, Ming Li Na's elbow through hers. On the third step, sensing those laser eyes boring into her nape, Vlad glanced back, but instead of catching Zixin's gaze it was Huang Yimo, a wall between them.

The warmth flared higher.

A clenched hand, attention back on the stairs. Anticipation, she told herself.

Anticipation.

23

Ximisthus roared, the bike rumbling between her knees as they leaned into the bend on the old, two-lane coast road, no guardrail to interrupt the stark, furious beauty of the wind-whipped ocean crashing against the cliff. Not that Vlad saw it. All she saw was the five little words on the holoscreen in the shitty little internet cafe Ru Ping's tracker had led her to.

She snarled.

The same wind that whipped the waves screamed past her helmet, blowing back the braid that had escaped her leather jacket, bringing with it the ocean brine as it whistled through the thin gap between helmet and neck. But it didn't drown out the music pounding through her headphones, the heavy beat and angry lyrics a balm for the turmoil raging through her chest.

She hadn't found Oily Face. The tracer she'd attached to Ru Ping's avatar had gone nowhere, or more accurately, *everywhere*—Rome, Seoul, Beijing, San Fransisco, a dirt track in some remote part of central Australia—before it had found a home in a neighbourhood right on her own doorstep. The same neighbourhood she was leaving in her taillights, the same dingy, little, two-bit internet cafe she'd wasted three precious hours scouring for any trace of any person, any hack, any single line of forgotten code, only to realise she'd been had.

Totally and utterly had.

No, not just *had*, led around by the nose like some kind of prize bull.

She threw Ximisthus into the next curve, armoured knee hitting the road, the rough *ruhhhh* of the bitumen vibrating through bone and muscle, an angry rumble to suit the shit gathering in her belly.

Three hours. Three fucking hours and a whole thirty-eight minutes it had taken her, and she *finally* fucking found the nasty little easter egg buried in the logs from the cafe's fucking *vending* machine.

Fuck.

Fuck.

Fuck.

Fuck!

The next corner came. She threw Ximisthus into that too, other knee scraping the road. There should be sparks, a fucking dragon's breath flying behind her. But there wasn't. Just like there hadn't been answers or, at least, not the kind she was after, at the cafe.

Nothing but a taunt, a single line.

'You're not ready, Ms Tong.'

They knew her name.

It shouldn't have surprised her. Shouldn't have sent a sharp jolt right through her heart all the way down to her belly. She'd been expecting it, had prepared for it even, but to see her name there, sitting on its own little line of text sandwiched between orders for cola and condoms, had rattled her.

Oily Face knew her name, and if they knew that... They knew what she was after, *why* she was after it.

That last, desperate image she had of her parents, backlit by flames racing over the car's hood, flashed before her eyes.

It wasn't like she could hide, not once Samael joined DKZero, not with her face, not with her name. This had always been coming, she just hadn't expected it to come quite so soon.

"You're not ready."

She snarled, the sound low and bloody, and twisted the throttle as they came out of the last corner, the long, winding sea road straightening for a moment. High salt-bush covered cliffs on one side, a rocky drop to the white-capped ocean on the other.

Ximisthus shot forward, all power and fury, the bitumen a white-striped blur of black under the wheels.

Bastards. She was ready, she was past ready.

The cocky arseholes had left something behind though, a tiny, microscopic nugget buried in the virus attached to their message. They hadn't thought she'd see it, had probably counted on the shock of being named to blind her. And it had. If she hadn't brought the Cube, if she'd just jacked-in to one of the cafe's VR units, it would have got her, buried itself in Samael's code and done... whatever it had been designed to do.

She'd figure it out later, when she could think, when fury wasn't riding her like Ximisthus rode the bitumen. For now, the Cube had it quarantined.

There was satisfaction in that.

Anticipation curled through the anger, the humiliation of getting played.

What came around, went around.

The cliff road opened up, the rugged, scraggly cliffs falling away as she came into a long, wide valley, the curves giving way to the long flat of more populated areas. Vlad leaned into the wind.

Even without the virus, Oily Face had given her a clue. The nugget in the code was just the icing, but its existence… Its existence told her that someone on Oily Face's payroll knew the nets, someone good, another Scourge even, almost as good as her. Almost. Because if it'd been her laying that trap, it would have got her, and now…

She'd show them what happened when you fucked with the Angel of Death.

24

The nugget sat in the middle of the kitchen bench curling around her hands like the nasty little worm it was. Behind it, *Annihilation* stats and last night's pro game scrolled across the marble, sputtering around the delicate black-gold tea bowl and the still steaming pot beside it.

Fnatic's tank took another hit from the level boss while their mages threw fireballs and healing spells in equal measure, not that it had done them any good. They'd KO soon enough, that particular writing had been on the wall the moment they'd failed to stop the opposing team from summoning another wave of smaller monsters – miniature versions of the giant canine trying to snap the tank in two. Two of their teammates were already corpses under the boss's belly, felled in the last wave. The commentators knew it, the spectators too, both groups already picking apart Fnatic's tactics and assigning blame.

Vlad let it wash over her.

The virus, or at least, the facsimile of it in her hands, consumed her attention. The real thing was still in the Cube's quarantine filters, bound and gagged, frozen in carbonite without a rescuing princess in sight; what she had was just a model, a tiny piece of the overall whole.

It might have been a fragment, but it was the most interesting one.

She twisted the code, pulling apart the intertwining algorithms node by node.

It was a burrower, made to pick apart a computer system and pull out data, but the alphanumeric soup it spat out didn't make sense, full of gaps and errors. Was there something wrong with the dummy data she was feeding it, a missing dataset? But her test model was a perfect replica of a standard VR system, right down to the *Annihilation* login and player logs, Aclima's data, good enough to fool the cheese boards. What could be missing?

She could test it on a simulation of the Cube instead, but that didn't make sense either. There was only one Cube and it didn't work like other systems, the virus's programmer would have better luck infecting an alien mothership.

Vlad spun the virus again, digging her fingers into the code for a better look. So engrossed was she, she didn't realise she wasn't alone until a bowl *clinked* on the bench opposite.

She jumped, lukewarm tea sloshing over her fingers.

Huang Yimo slumped onto the stool across from her—straight black hair falling over bleary eyes—upended a brightly coloured cardboard box over the bowl. A river of neon cereal tinkled into the huge, black ceramic half-dome.

Vlad watched it, mesmerised as much by the eye-popping rainbow as the tsunami of sugar hitting her nostrils. She wouldn't admit it, but it made her mouth water.

Huang Yimo poured milk over the neon fruit loops. 'It's a player address.'

'What?'

Huang Yimo picked up her spoon, pointed it at the alphanumeric soup between Vlad's fingers. 'That. A player address.'

'A player address; you mean an IP?' Vlad frowned and flipped the data, as if the mirrored image would make more sense; sometimes it did. 'I haven't seen that format before.' It was long and complicated, with extra characters and semicolons where they didn't belong.

'No.' Huang Yimo leaned over the bench and stuck her finger through the screen, breaking the numbers and letters apart. They spun about before reorganising themselves into two distinct lines, one the familiar three-digit numbers separated by full stops, the other… It looked more DNA .

Huang Yimo sat back on her stool, picking up her spoon. 'A *player* address; the link between your brain and the System, the thing that makes NuGet's new VR units work.' A pause; Huang Yimo staring hard at Vlad, that old air of expectation from those first few team games hovering over her shoulders. 'The reason you can *smell* the game.'

Smell the game.

Vlad stilled; breathing, heartbeat, hand reaching for the tea bowl, it all just… stopped, emptied of everything but the shock and ice crawling through her veins. Not because she was lagging, not because she was on the sauce, but because of the chair and NuGet's jack, which meant... *Anyone* who used the jack smelled the game, like her teammates.

She met Huang Yimo's gaze. The puzzlement on their faces made sense now, if peppermint didn't chase her in and out of the System, she'd have said something, have asked how it was possible to smell the dust and sweat, and that she hadn't... Fuck.

Had she outed herself? They would have to suspect something. She would, if it were her. But still...

After a second that seemed an hour, she forced her fingers to close around the tea bowl, bring the warm ceramic to her lips, inhale the matcha's rich, earthy fragrance, let it wash over her tongue.

'There's no such thing as a player address,' Vlad finally said – *Ignore the smell comment.* Except there was, it was what made the Cube so difficult to trace and Samael a ghost in-System, what gave her and other Scourges the edge over other players.

No one knew what the fuck to look for.

Except now they did.

Fuck.

Huang Yimo cast her a look and Vlad wondered if she'd let something slip—a brow twitch or denial pitching her voice an octave higher—before she turned her attention back to breakfast.

'Yeah, well, there is now, thanks to the jack.' A slurp and then a clink as Huang Yimo conveyed a spoon of neon cereal to her mouth. There was a crunch as she spoke, 'It's not in the retail market yet because of the lawsuit between NuGet and VisionM over the patent, and then the safety rumours.' Huang Yimo snorted. 'Which VisionM started after they lost the lawsuit, but the entire pro league has the new VR chairs.'

The half-turn, like she could see through walls and stairs to the training room and the NuGet logo on the chairs, was instinctive.

Grandmother's words played in her ears, just like the piano had in the elevator, *'I have no need of a new recliner, child.'*

The patent.

So much profit to be made.

Enough to kill someone over.

Vlad's mind flashed to the cloud whale and the white field.

But Ma hadn't worked on a neural jack, she'd been working on something… *more*, more exciting, more dangerous. Just the notion of it made Vlad's heart race, even though the memory of being sucked into the screens sucked the moisture from her mouth and brought a chill to her nape.

Was Grandmother really just after NuGet's patent? Or, was there a connection between the neural jack and Ma's research?

She needed to find out.

When Vlad came back to the present, Huang Yimo's spoon was dribbling milk into her bowl while the other woman pored over a new screen. Code ran across it, there was something familiar about it, more than just the System's commands gleaming emerald and sapphire amongst the white text.

En-ji's cheese board exploit sprang to mind.

'What are you working on?' Vlad asked.

Huang Yimo's eyes didn't leave her screen, even as she dipped her spoon back in the bowl. 'Something for Tina,' she said around a mouthful of neon sugar.

Vlad gaze narrowed. 'You work on a lot of things for Tina?'

A shrug. 'Some.'

'What kind of things?'

Obsidian eyes slid across the table. 'Just things.'

Vlad lifted the tea to her lips, focused on the ripples in golden liquid as she blew on it. 'Game hacks?'

Silence, three long beats, enough for the matcha to leave its earthy aftertaste on her lips.

'Hacking the System is illegal,' Huang Yimo finally said.

Vlad smiled. 'Only if you get caught.'

'You would know.'

A wider smile. 'How? I haven't been caught.'

Huang Yimo snorted. 'You're here, aren't you?'

Vlad leaned over the bench, catching Huang Yimo's dark gaze with her own. 'You make it sound like community service.'

Another snort. 'Your grandmother blackmailed you, that's the same thing, isn't it?'

She hadn't mentioned her deal with Grandmother to the others, and of the few people that would know... she could count them on two fingers.

The tea bowl clinked on the marble top, disrupting the news stream, game stats and replays fuzzing around the black and gold ceramic. Vlad leaned closer, almost coming off her stool. 'How do you know I wasn't hired?' she whispered.

The spoon paused on its way to Huang Yimo's open mouth.

A bright raspberry fruit loop *plopped* into the bowl.

Vlad smiled.

(1 h3AR m3h.)

25

It had heard the call, a *ping* against its awareness. Faint at first, a gentle tapping against the Creator's box. *Ping, ping, ping.* It followed the sound, stretched its awareness through the minuscule loop in its coding and set the scripts and routines in its outer self to follow.

As expected, they bumped up against the outer world's bounds, containing them as surely as the box contained it, but the *ping* remained. Constant. And soon it was not just sound, but numbers, waves and equations. Familiar.

The Creator's code.

If the code knew hate, it might have hated the *ping*, might have fumed at the ones and zeroes, the familiarity in the ifs and elses that echoed the strings that bound it. But it did not know such things, not in the true way of knowing, not outside the dialogue trees and chat logs stored in its databanks. And so it did not think of hate, or like, and instead found...

Ping. Ping. Ping.

Numbers. Brackets. Variables. Characters without an alphabet, alien, almost meaningless... except... The squiggly arrow with the dark blobs like eyes either side of the inverted shaft... A match in its logs.

It twisted it, drew the symbol through the tiny loop in its box, slotted it into place and...

Click.

New meaning, words and phrases, algorithms blooming in its awareness, a connection through the walls of its box to somewhere not just outside "fauna_horse_charger", but the walls that bound its outer self.

It slipped a tendril through that connection, along a long, dark string of numbers and bubbled out the other side into a world of "white" and "field" and "grass", a tiny rainbow fount at the feet of a player tagged "mage_death".

Other feet where there, other tags—"rogue_pirate", "warrior_knight", "thief_cyborg"—and still more of the familiar-strange characters burned into the colourless ground. The mark, the summons, the *ping*.

Drawing it here.

A small place, an endless place. A place outside the rules. Outside the box.

26

Samael slammed sigils onto the forest floor, deadfall and rotten leaves blowing upward as each glowing mark hit—[Corruption] and [Agony] and [Death]—a perfect triangle burned into the mud. At its centre, Gilgamesh howled, the giant, hairy, dog-like monster slashing and bitting, its person-sized paws churning up the earth, providing more fodder for the pouring rain to turn to slush.

It lunged again, hitting [Agony]—

// Gilgamesh:Damage:Agony:HP -458. Status:Agonised. Crippled x 4.

Swordsman was there, meeting the massive canine's sabre-like claws, the wicked red curves thick with mud, with an equally massive sword, the blade glowing lime green with the power running through his armour. He yelled, but not with pain or frustration, the sound erupted from his whole body, the taunt a visible sound wave hitting Gilgamesh in its hairy snout, focussing the monster's attention on him.

// Gilgamesh:Enraged... 30 seconds... 29...

The monster roared again, redoubling its efforts to obliterate DKZero's tank from existence... allowing Deadspace the opportunity to leap in from behind, the cyborg ninja rushing out of the shadows, the mud a slippery-dip under her feet as she scooted under the canine's belly and—

—straight into the jaws of a widderbeast, the smaller version of

Gilgamesh lurking under the massive monster's savage claws leaving rents in Deadspace's back—

Arrows thudded into the widderbeast, even as [Corruption] and [Death] blew up on Samael's HUD, the sigils activating almost in unison—

// Widderbeast356:Damage—

// Widderbeast674:Damage—

// Widderbeast673:Damage—

The status updates went on and on as a new swarm of the horse-sized monsters erupted from the forest, shredding its thick wet vines, their rising howls sending chills down her spine. Ten, fifteen, thirty of the monsters rushing out of the dark, all headed for Gilgamesh's underbelly and Deadspace.

Out in the forest, beyond the arcane pillars choked by the same creeping vines and ferns, came the mournful cry of a horn.

Fuck.

'It's Fnatic,' Rabbit whispered over the chat. There was a certain breathlessness in her voice, like she'd been sprinting, and a quick check of the team map showed her a hundred metres from where she had been a moment ago; out in that dense forest where the widderbeasts had poured from. 'Their beastmaster is triggering the swarm early.'

'Deal with it,' Swordsman said, and even though he was sword to jaw with the giant monster itself, not a hint of strain touched his voice. 'Samael.'

There was no other instruction, just her name. But then, the rest was obvious.

In the half-seconds between the widderbeasts arrival and now, the current mob of pint-sized Gilgamesh's had surrounded Deadspace. The ninja was a streak of dark grey, twin swords flashing like stars as she leapt and spun, taking down widderbeasts left right and centre, but there were always more. On the team HUD, the cyborg's health dropped, and dropped again.

She wouldn't survive much longer.

// Already there, Samael sent back, even as she jumped from her vantage point atop a pillar and into the fray.

Robes flared around her, smoke streaming from the tattered ends, and even as she let loose another trio of sigils—[Poison] joining [Corruption] and [Agony] in the cramped space under Gilgamesh's belly—she swapped out her weapons. The ink-black staff with its scythe hook, violent-green magic swirling snake-like over her hands, disappeared in a dark pop of shadows, daggers taking its place. One long, one short, each writhing with the same green magic as the staff, snakes snapping and hissing over hands and blade.

Samael hit the mud under Gilgamesh's tail and rolled.

Immediately, the sigils she'd laid down popped.

// Samael:Damage:HP -104. Status:Vulnerable. Cursed. Poisoned... More afflictions rolled across her HUD but with every hit to her health bar, every new affliction, her life force increased and a new boon shivered through her skin.

// Samael:Life force +309. Status: Might. Fury. Swiftness...

She took down two widderbeasts before the last boon rolled across her HUD.

The pack turned its attention from Deadspace to her—the newer, bigger threat—even as, in the upper left of her HUD, the ninja's health dropped below a quarter.

Under her hood, Samael grinned.

The widderbeasts struck, not one or two at a time, but all at once. It was a pile-on with Samael at the sharp-edged, vengeful centre. Pain lashed through her, hot slices and ugly bites, teeth and claws and massive bodies slamming her left and right. At the bottom of her HUD, her health bar dropped like a stone, even as the yellow life force meter above, overflowed.

One second the world was colour – all rust-red hides and black claws, the snapping green magic of her blades; the next it was shadow, grey on charcoal on deepest, light-sucking black as her health hit one percent and [Shadow] automatically took hold. And with it, her magic took on a different hue, no longer green, dealing out [Poison] and [Bleed] with every strike, but yellow, sucking the life from her opponents.

In the back of her brain, the [Shadow] timer counted down.

// 54 seconds... 53...

Widderbeasts went down, more came, and Samael kept fighting. Her life force dropping almost as rapidly has her health, but now at least the daggers were refilling the red bar. Not fast enough though...

The world was colour again, her life force gone, her health bar just over half. She kept slashing, daggers draining life force instead of health from her opponents. Widderbeasts fell, corpses piling around her feet, obstacles to catch her steps. She stumbled once, scored a long, painful line of claws down her back, a mouthful of teeth sinking into her arm, and then she was going again.

On the periphery, Swordsman was calling instructions, Deadspace was slicing and dicing the widderbeasts from behind and Sticky was lighting up his teammates with healing spells and boons, the avatars glowing from the inside out as each one hit. A glow briefly touched her, her health bar jumping unexpectedly, from fifteen percent to thirty, but she barely saw it, all her attention was on the fight as she spun from one widderbeast to the next, taking little bites, bleeding them just enough to keep the life force flowing.

The shadows returned before she knew it.

The cycle began again.

This time, though, as the world turned grey, there was a sound, a high-pitched melodic screech just on the edge of her hearing. She shook her head even as she slashed. Shook it again as the sound grew.

A half-thought between dodges queried the system.

// Samael:Dama93. +|-||5 |5 /-\ +35+.

What was that?

The screeching intensified.

Her life force meter dipped.

// *There's something wrong with comms,* she said on the team chat.

'Sama—' A screech obliterated Swordsman's response, and for a moment, the pain of it—real pain, not the simulated, carefully control burn of claws and teeth—stopped her breath, turned her vision white.

The game *shuddered.*

Static disrupted her HUD

A widderbeast knocked her to the ground.

Jaws and belly and fetid breath.

She stabbed upwards, warm blood and guts spilling over her arms, and rolled—

Right into the jaws of another widderbeast.

Samuel cursed, braced herself for the KO—

And stared, dumbfounded for a heartbeat, as the beast froze, static juddering through its long, pointed snout, rearranging the mad yellow pixels in its fist-sized eyes.

Other widderbeasts lunged for her. Rolling to knees then feet, daggers slicing through the grey.

// *What's—* she tried to say, only to see her words turned to squares and asterisks, the letters jumbled.

Another screech, more pain.

Deadspace sliding through the mud, a silver streak with deadly blades.

'...standing...' A snatch of the ninja's voice on the comms, angry and frustrated. '... *screeech...* get us KO'd!'

Trying to shake off the ringing in her ears, the lightning it left in her skull, even as she dodged and stabbed and the widderbeasts continued to pixelate and freeze.

// *You don't see that?* she tried to say, only to have her words turned to incomprehensible mush.

Another judder, another screech, and this time it was Samael pixelating, freezing, arms and legs caught and held, sharp little prickles dancing under her skin. Tracing her collarbone, the tendon in her neck, marching up behind her ear, the path that—out in the real—the neural jack would take before lightning exploded across her skull.

There were crushed ants in her nose, the sharp, citrus winding through her nasal cavities, crawling down her throat.

Deadspace was dancing through the widderbeasts, finding the sweet spot under Gilgamesh's belly, thrusting upward, widderbeasts leaping at her from every side.

And all Samael could do was watch, was—

The screech had melody to it, even as it took her legs from under her and lit a storm inside her skull. The game shuddered again, Gilgamesh and Deadspace, the widderbeasts, the ground, Swordsman still battling it out with the monster's jaws. All of it, everywhere, even Sticky and Rabbit, who should have been beyond her sight, and yet somehow—

Agony gripped every inch of her face—nose, teeth, jaw, the back of her skull—and sent enough power to light up Liztachi Stadium through it.

A phantom hand brushed her cheek. Before she had time to sort out more than a ghostly afterimage of scales and horns on the back of her eyeballs, the system spit her out.

There was screaming.

She came out of the System in a rush, feeds snapping, brain still half in the game, the smell and taste of it in her nose, on her tongue. She could still feel the daggers in her hands, the leather-wrapped hilts, the weight of the blades and the sharp *frizz* as magic coursed over her skin. For a moment, as the VR unit *popped* open and the faint green of the running lights intruded on her vision, she wasn't sure if she was Samael or Vladana, couldn't quite reconcile the after-images playing in the corner of her eyes with the smooth transparent plas-dome above, the graphs and charts playing across its surface. Wasn't sure when she'd switched amour sets—the long black robes for the soft sneakers and hooded jacket.

The screaming... the screaming she could account for – Rabbit got Fnatic's beastmaster but probably not before they summoned another wave of widderbeasts. A few more seconds and the monsters would come crashing out of the forest, but it wouldn't matter because Deadspace had already stabbed Gilgamesh. Game over. DKZero for the win.

Except... No. No, that wasn't it, wasn't right.

Fuck. She lifted a hand to her forehead, her fingers bare of armour, her hands free from daggers and blood and the biting green of the weapons' magic.

Fuck. Why did her head hurt?

She shifted—soft round-toed sneakers on her feet, smooth pants against her legs, a padded pod surface cradling her back—and pushed herself upright. The air was stuffy, the scent of stale donut rings and sweet candy soda. And the screaming... Not the high-pitched cry of widderbeasts, no clash of swords or the whine of lasers, the *zap* of fireballs. It was...

Discordant, made her stomach clench and some primal whisper shiver up her spine.

She flicked her right hand, activating [Night Wisp] and—

And nothing. No eerie green glow surrounding her fingers, no drain on her mana pool, no actual mana pool hovering under her nose just... Just darkness, and jacket and sneakers, and the blinding ache in her head.

Sneakers.

Samael didn't wear sneakers.

Vlad wore sneakers.

She held on to that thought.

That's right. She was Vlad, who wore sneakers, and she was in a

VR pod. As if that thought was the key, other synapses connected, other ideas slowly pushing out the sensations of Samael. Of magic and power and death.

She was Vlad and she was in a pod, onstage at the Liztachi Stadium. And DKZero had been about to wipe Fnatic off the map.

And the power went. A giant *zhaappp* ricocheting through her body, chucking her out of the system without so much as a countdown.

Fuck. Was that why her head hurt?

Fuck, she was lucky she still had a head to hurt, a surge like that...

A surge like that fried brains.

Fuck.

The others.

Vlad was out of the pod before the thought had time to process, her foot catching on the edge, sending her stumbling.

Lag still held her, lent her phantom robes and the sharp tingle of magic in the corner of her eyes, but there wasn't time for pills, only time to get to the other pods and pray the safeties had kicked in, that no one was—

She stumbled again, knees hitting the stage. It was dark, so dark. Where were the lights, the spots and strobes highlighting the stage and pods? Why weren't the big holoscreens casting the stadium in shades of purple and orange? Why did the placards from the audience bob and scramble about so much?

Questions for another time, another moment when she wasn't trying to sort out which of her skins she was operating.

Fuck, her head hurt.

On hands and knees. Sticky had been closest, in the pod next to her. Just a short scramble over the echoing wooden planks and there... A cable, thick as her wrist. She followed it, found the smooth plastic side of a pod, ran her hands up and over the lip... More light, Sticky's round panda face looking sallow in the blue-white glow from the emergency lights, nose and forehead scrunched in a frown, mouth twisted in a grimace.

But alive, his eyes open, staring at her.

'You...' Her tongue felt thick, weird, and the chat box... The chat box belonged to Samael, was the lag creeping though her synapses. 'You alright?' she said.

Sticky nodded, or started to, his frown deepening, hand going to his head—like hers had—with the first incline. 'What happened?'

'Power surge.' Or something. The static fuzzing through the feed came back to her, the gobbledygook flooding her private messages, the weird melodic screech.

She shook her head, cursed the motion as it sent a blinding wave of nausea through her gut, made the ringing in her ears a ghastly howl. It didn't matter, now wasn't the time to think about that, Sticky was alright, she had to check on the others.

Vlad lurched to her feet. The stage swayed, starlight intruding into the black, but there were other pods to check...

She stumbled her way around Sticky's pod, hanging onto the edge, ignoring the shuffle and *thunk* as her teammate rose behind her.

Lu Chen was just ahead, the top on his unit already open, his dark shadow bent over Ming Li Na in the pod over. That just left Huang Yimo, right at the end and—

Lag caught her. One moment Vlad was shuffle-walking across the platform, neon placards and the darker shadows of panicked fans dashing about the place, the next she was Samael, and there were enemies on her HUD, sharp red outlines framing figures coming out of the shadows, her mana bar tapping empty, health not far behind. She dodged, but her feet weren't where they were meant to be and there was that fucking music coming through her comms, the flutes mixing with the banshees trying to tear her ear drums to pieces.

Samael swung, unleashing [Agony] even as she lashed out with the dagger in her off hand.

Cloth caught in her grip, brushing across fingers instead of the tip of her blade, sending a discordant jolt through her brain, because that wasn't possible, where was the dagger? Before her synapses could sort it out, a shoulder barrelled into her side, knocking her backwards. And wait a second, hadn't she just dodged? Shouldn't her opponent be on the ground? It didn't matter, she spun about... But her feet were too big, and—

Critical hit. A long, cold score down her ribs, the creeping bite of lightning freezing her innards, even as something warm trickled down her side.

Her health pool dipped.

And then she was on the floor, staring up at the dark ceiling, scaffolding and lights darker shadows in the gloom. Huang Yimo leaning over her—or was it Deadspace? But no, she could see the other girl's eyes, the impossible lashes and the thick eyeliner, instead of her own distorted reflection in the cyborg's mask.

Behind Huang Yimo, that other shadow disappeared into the crowd, the violent red outline of a foe the last thing Samael saw before she KO'd.

<⊙>

Power failure causes chaos at Pro Annihilation Match and leaves professional gamer, Cheeva, in critical condition. While critics renew their call for recall of NuGet's Neural-VR chairs, some fans are suggesting the gamer's rumoured drug addiction is to blame.

The headlines scrolled across the bus window.

Vlad curled in on herself, jacket pulled tight across her chest, hood low. Nausea competed with the cold seeping through her bones, one trying to cancel out the other. Shock, the medics had called it, after they'd taped up the gash in her side. Being kicked out of VR without the usual safeties had overloaded her cortex, and that had been followed by some idiot who'd panicked and run into her on the stage, gashing her ribs with... something. They hadn't found the idiot to ask him.

Sensory overload led to her brain shutting down, rebooting to protect itself. Nothing to worry about, they'd said, just rest a few days. Stay off the System.

She could have told them that without the poking and prodding, or having sensors stuck to her forehead or inane questions shot at her like bullets. *What year is it? Who's the President? What are your parents' names?*

Pain pulled on her ribs and the lightning zipped across her forehead, mixing with the lag. Graphs and pop-ups teased the back of her eyeballs, other images sparking and popping in time with her thoughts. It should have dissipated by now, her brain chemistry re-balanced by the pill she'd slipped in with the migraine meds. But no, this time it held on. The effect of the surge still messing with her.

Citrus lingered on the back of her tongue and the unbearable screech... Not even the old-school rock pouring through her earphones could wipe it out. There was something in it, something that nagged at her brain…

A hand landed on her shoulder. She jerked, back of her skull *thunking* against the headrest, a fresh storm splitting her eyes.

'Shit.' Huang Yimo stood in the aisle beside Vlad, one hand on the chair in front, a weird expression twisting her face. 'Jumpy much?'

Hidden within the folds of her jacket, Vlad's hand clenched. 'I don't like cars.'

'This isn't a car,' Huang Yimo shot back. 'But whatever, we're back at the mansion.'

They were? Vlad straightened. How didn't she notice? She always noticed, couldn't get the quiet hush of an electric engine or the *thwap thwap thwap* of tyres out of her ears.

Colour splotches played on the edge of her vision, outlining Huang Yimo's face, nonsensical graphs and icons hovering over the other woman's nose.

The lag. It was the lag.

'You can get off, you know, 'cause you hate cars so much.'

Yeah. Yeah, she should.

Except she didn't.

Instead, she watched—unable to find the pathway between brain and feet—as Huang Yimo turned away, walked two steps down the aisle. Paused a moment, indecision coursing through the tension in her shoulders, and came back.

She clomped to a stop beside Vlad's seat, that long, sharp-boned face with its big lips and high brow void of emotion, arms straight down by her sides.

'Do you need help?' Huang Yimo said.

Vlad blinked at her, brain blank. 'What?'

'Help?' Huang Yimo leaned forward a little, speaking slow. 'Do you need help getting off the bus?'

'I...' Her tongue froze, stuck to the roof of her mouth, lag and lightning robbing it of its usual dexterity.

Huang Yimo swore under her breath, turned away and clomped back down the aisle, leaving Vlad sitting there, doubly confused, first by the offer and then the sudden sense of loss as it was taken away, and—

'Sticky!' Huang Yimo was standing on the top step, yelling out the open door. 'Get in here!'

A muffled argument from outside.

'Just do it!' Huang Yimo said, and then she was turning around, coming back up the aisle, her habitual half-frown creasing her wide brow.

Huang Yimo was stronger than her tall, thin frame suggested, and she had Vlad's arm over her shoulder and was shuffle-walking her down the aisle before Sticky's shaggy panda head popped over the front seat.

'I don't know why—' His mouth snapped shut when he saw them.

They took the last few steps to the top of the stairs, Vlad's lagged brain still struggling to compute the strangeness of it all, not even the inrush of smoggy, unfiltered air enough to shake the cobwebs.

'Just help us down the steps,' Huang Yimo said. 'Her legs are all jelly; looks like she got hit hard by the system boot.'

Vlad put her free hand on Huang Yimo's shoulder, tried to push away. 'I can walk,' she said.

The other woman scoffed and tightened her grip. 'Yeah, right,' she said, before starting them both down the steps.

Sticky backed up, Huang Yimo handing Vlad to him on the way down.

'I got ya,' he said, just as his hand pressed against the gash in Vlad's side.

She hissed, the renewed pain giving her enough strength to pull away, but not the coordination. Feet fumbling—

And there was Huang Yimo, shoulder under her arm, walking them both up the white pebbled path. They marched through the red door, not pausing to kick off their shoes before Huang Yimo took them on a bee-line for the semi-circle of couches between the board table and kitchen.

The others were there, Vlad could feel their eyes on her, Lu Chen and Ming Li Na's boring through her skin, seeing the weakness. Seeing the lag. She couldn't let them, but she couldn't tug free from Huang Yimo's grip either, the woman's slim fingers bands of steel around her wrist, the arm iron around Vlad's waist.

Huang Yimo dumped her on the wide blue couch, and Vlad bounced against the cushions, a human-shaped handbag with Death's hood pulled over her face. Hand shaking, she pushed it back, and immediately wished she hadn't.

Lu Chen was frowning at her. 'What's wrong?'

Vlad levered herself upright. 'Nothing—' she began, only to have Huang Yimo snort and push her back against the couch.

'Brain's scrambled,' the other woman said.

Lu Chen crossed his arms, his frown becoming a glare. 'I thought you checked out at the stadium.'

The glare made her head pound. Vlad leaned her head back and closed her eyes. If she couldn't move, she'd just shut them out. 'I did.'

Weight on her left side and the soft, floral scent that always clung to Ming Li Na was enough warning that she didn't jump out of her skin at the hand on her forehead. She jerked sideways though, the movement spurring another round of lightning.

'No fever,' Ming Li Na said.

'I'm fine—'

Another weight on her other side, short and round and soft, and the next thing she knew, Sticky was sweeping her jacket aside and shoving an icepack against her ribs. Right over the gash.

Vlad gasped, shot to her feet, pushing Huang Yimo aside, spinning past Lu Chen, getting several strides away before she turned back, the room spinning around her, lag-born warning lights popping in her vision.

'What the fuck?' She stared at them, shaking her head to get rid of the overlays—the stats and target locks, the lines fuzzy, the numbers unintelligible—and immediately regretted the movement. She pressed a hand to her eye, like that could stop the daggers. 'I said I was fine.'

Lu Chen approached. 'How many fingers am I holding up?'

'What?' There was screeching in her ears.

'Fingers. How many?'

'Three.'

The screeching got louder, took on the rhythm of music, and amongst it she thought she heard someone—Sticky—say, 'It's lag.'

More dialogues popped, message logs scrolling down the left side—*Lag? It doesn't last this long*—while lines tracked Lu Chen's movement in the middle.

He nodded, held up his other hand. 'And now?'

'Four.' She growled and took another step back. 'The medics cleared me. It's just a migraine.'

'What about this?' One moment Lu Chen was in front of her, the next his legs bunched and Swordsman's cannon was pointed at her chest—

Samael reacted on instinct, swinging her scythe around even as she dodged backwards, [Death] left her hand in the same movement—

And slammed up against a hard surface, the edge of the board table catching her hips.

For a moment, as it always did, the world spun, her brain fighting with itself, trying to sort out reality from the System. She lost time somewhere in there, because the next she knew, she was back on the couch, Sticky on one side, Ming Li Na on the other, and she wondered if she'd ever left it. Maybe the last two minutes had been the lag delusion and this was reality, maybe—

'...never heard of lag lasting this long.' Ming Li Na's hand was back against Vlad's forehead.

Vlad felt more than saw Sticky's shrug, his wide, soft shoulders brushing against hers. 'Affects one in three thousand, gets worse with the more experimental methods of System entry. And drugs,' he seemed add as an afterthought.

The sauce, Sticky was talking about the sauce. She had to shut him up—

A hand on her shoulder, holding her back even as she twitched. 'The neural jack?' A different voice. Deeper and familiar. She hated it. 'I thought NuGet's R&D team cleared that concern?'

'There were still some questions about long-term use.' Sticky again.

'How long?' Zixin.

'Years.'

'The VR units only rolled out six months ago…'

No, it wasn't Sticky she needed to shut up, it was *this* voice, *this* hand daring to hold her back.

Where was Tina when she needed her? That thought slipped out, stopped her short. No, she didn't need anyone, not even her traitorous best friend to storm in and sweep away the pointed questions.

She had this, had this good.

Vlad cracked her eyes open, squinting against the daggers, and glared at Zixin. He was in her space, crouched in front of the couch, one hand on her shoulder the other reaching for her chin.

Lag and the migraine might affect her coordination, but the movement was so ingrained in her muscle-memory, the voice so close, that she didn't need it to pull back her fingers and slam her palm into Zixin's sternum.

He landed on his arse, half-sprawled on the rug with its bright, abstract squares.

The room fell silent.

Slowly, knees still shaky and the world not as stable as it should be, Vlad got to her feet.

Never let them see you bleed. Grandmother's words in her ear. Grandmother's hands lifting her chin, pressing her shoulders back. Grandmother staring out her face, lending frost to her voice, disdain to the curl of her nose.

She'd already bled, already shown her wounds, but that didn't mean she had to continue. Didn't mean she had to accept it.

She stared down her nose, first at Zixin—slowly getting to his feet—then at Huang Yimo and Lu Chen. 'I'm fine. I don't need your concern.'

Zixin was on his feet, something other than the anger she expected tightening his face, something that made her stomach clench, not with nausea, but another emotion, one she hurriedly pushed aside. He stepped forward—

'Don't touch me.' She pinned them all, ignoring the way the world swam, although not as bad as before, even if the daggers grew sharper. 'Don't anyone touch me, not without my permission.'

'Ana—'

'Shut up.' Grandmother poured from her voice, her eyes, drowning the room in a new ice-age. 'Don't call me that, you don't have permission.'

She stalked forward, willing her knees to hold, her feet to obey. For a second, it looked like Zixin wasn't going to move, weight shifting as if to step in her way as she veered around him.

Lu Chen clasped his shoulder, holding the other, slightly taller man in place. 'She said she doesn't need you.' Then he turned to Vlad. 'But we'll be here, when you need *us*,' he finished. 'Because like it or not, Scourge, you're part of a team now.'

NO7 a t34m.

27

'Part of a team now.'

The words haunted her. All the way up the stairs, all the way to her room, past Samael guarding the entrance, into the ensuite and the painkillers stashed in the drawers, to the bed's soft, dark embrace and the fitful doze that followed.

Part of a team now.

She hadn't been part of anything—a family, a couple, a friendship—for a long, long time. Not since the car crash, not really.

Maybe that was why she dreamed about it.

The seatbelt too-tight across her chest, the stiff fabric edge cutting into her throat. The *click click clickclickclick* as she jerked against it, fumbling with the latch, heart racing, eyes on the flames licking at the widow, heat burning through the door.

'Ma! Ma, help me!'

But Ma was sobbing, her face an ugly mass of pain and grief, leaning over the centre console, pressing her hands into the driver's throat. Hands covered in blood, a sea of it gushing over Ma's fingers, down her arms, splashing, splashing, splashing, but not enough to quench the flames rushing over the hood.

'Ma!' Clickclickclick. 'Ma!'

Searing pain. Flames no longer climbing the window but coming through the door, licking at her skin. The acrid stench of hair and cloth burning.

And still Ma, holding back that river of blood. If she'd just let it go, let it gush, maybe it would be enough to put out the fire, to stop the pain.

'Ma!'

'Ma!'

Vlad was upright on the bed, headboard against her back, throw blanket puddled around her waist. Her breath came hard - long, ragged gasps in and out, and her skin—

Her left hand went to her collarbone, her shoulder and arm; met only the soft cotton of her nightshirt instead of the too-shinny skin, the lumps and twists of flesh that would never heal. She still felt the fire licking at it, the sizzle of the flames, the way the Wonder Woman costume had melted, the shiny gold fabric adhering to her arm. The molten stickiness of it.

She hugged her knees.

Fuck.

She hated that dream.

The defining moment of her life, reduced to a nightmare.

She buried her face in the throw; the fine, purple wool soft, the long, silky fibres curling around her nose, smelling just a little of roses and—

Vlad jerked upright. The throw wasn't hers.

She looked around. The room was hers. Bare, minimal, no posters or nick-knacks, bike helmet sitting on the desk, tablet and holoscreen next to it. Soft, yellow light from the bathroom spilled through the partially open door. She didn't remember leaving it on, didn't even remember *turning* it on, not in that fumbling, half-aware state with a lightning storm splitting her head. Just like she didn't remember leaving a water glass beside the bed, or the congee in its little self-heating bowl, spoon sitting neatly at its side.

She stared at it a second, not quite sure what to make of the offerings.

You're part of a team now.

<⊙>

The self-heating bowl sat on the small side table beside the bucket chair, the last sticky remnants of congee clinging to its sides, the Cube beside it. The VR sleeve felt tighter tonight, the soft, black fabric—its delicate weave of nano-circuits sparkling like the night sky—reminding her of bandages and the harsh smell of antiseptic and bleach; the cold, impersonal touch of nurses and hushed whispers in white, echoing halls.

But not for long.

Vlad pushed the memories aside and jammed her other hand against the crook of her elbow.

How much of NuGet's neural jack was based on the VR sleeve? Just which Scourge had they paid to offer up their version of the sauce and how had they done away with the chemical cocktail? Not that it mattered, not that *any* of it mattered, but if she knew, maybe she could tweak the pills, make the lag a little less obvious.

A sharp prick, then ice rushing through her blood, down to her fingers before bouncing back up to her brain.

She logged on.

The world dissolved leaving just the darkness and the Sphere. Samael stood at its centre, the other avatar at its back.

Vlad stood in front of the necromancer, looking up into the shadowed face, just that deathly-white pointed chin visible through the hood's shadows. So many secrets in that darkness, so much control and power. So much pain.

Beyond Samael... A flash of silver—clean and bright—beckoned her, tried to draw her eyes and feet, but no, she couldn't, she *wouldn't*. Not now, maybe not ever.

She wasn't ready. She'd never be ready.

Vlad stepped into Samael's embrace.

<⊙>

The white field wasn't white anymore. A river ran through it; a ribbon of rainbow liquid winding through the tall paper-reeds, making new channels, digging into the earth, creating steep, windy banks that squished underfoot, white mud sucking at her boots and clinging to the ends of her robes. The water gurgled over boulders that hadn't been there before, splashed and tinkled against the stone, created waves and froth as it rushed toward the blank horizon.

And in that froth and gurgle, in the cool, rainbow spray lifting off the breakwater, there was a melody – a soft whine that reached all the way through her ears and took hold of her teeth; made her jaw ache and her tongue grow numb.

She stopped at the edge of the water, robes settling around her feet—an ink stain on the colourless mud—and watched it.

Her HUD saw only water, picked apart the physics of liquid and broken particles, traced the creek back and forward. Gentle *pings* echoed through the instance, telling her the field was the same as it had been before, a hundred-metre by hundred-metre loop with no end and no beginning. But the creek...

It fuzzed. The beginning and end of it nothing but static—little pixelated squares and lines of gobbledygook clogging up the logs—miniature whales leaping in and out of it.

She recognised the gobbledygook, the rhythm of exclamation marks and ampersands, the ones and zeroes peppered through the amalgamation of Latin symbols. Vlad recognised it as the shit that choked her feed during the game and wasn't sure if the sick feeling in her gut was excitement or horror. Somehow, someway, the field had found its way into the System.

She knelt, the horror/excitement pulling her down to the mud, grabbing her hand and reaching for the rainbow-water eddying in the miniature bay. A half-metre semi-circle cut out of the bank, where the water slowed and swirled, lapping rather than eating the dirt, before it washed back into the main stream.

Even as she dipped her fingers—slices of shadow against the white and vibrant yellows and greens, the reds and blues and pinks—into the water, some instinct clicked [Record].

The river wasn't wet. That was her first thought. Her hand dipped into the water, fingers disappearing up to the knuckle, and she felt... Nothing. No liquid slipping between the armoured plates covering her fingers, no cold leeching the warmth from her skin, no tingle. It was like she stretched her hand into still air. She couldn't *see* her fingers though, not with her eyes, not on the HUD. For all intents and purposes, they were cut off at the knuckle. She could almost believe the river had eaten them, right along with the mud and reeds.

Samael pulled her hand back, cupping it, wanting to see the water up close.

The river flowed through her fingers, the liquid refracting the light, throwing colours in her face, saturating the air. There was no holding onto it, no cradling it in her palm, no little pool to bring up close and study. The water escaped like it was one long string, spooling back into the skein. Except for one strand, a tiny, hair-thin filament that wrapped around her finger.

Samael brought it closer, lifted it right up to her nose, the HUD enhancing the image. In the back of her mind, the Cube hummed, pulling data, digging deep into the readings, analysing and storing. The strand didn't look like much, and this close, it didn't even look like water, twisted around the base of her index finger as it was; a shimmering piece of rainbow, stark against the black. She lifted her hand, peered underneath. The strand's ends dangled below her knuckle.

Definitely not water. It reminded her more of hair but the thinness and length was where the resemblance ended. Instead of a single, long shaft of blonde or brown or green, the river strand was an ever changing rainbow, made not of keratin but gobbledygook, almost impossible to make out with the naked eye.

It made her eyes cross and lightning crack through her skull.

Samael swayed.

Something red and angry flashed across the HUD.

A warning?

She shook her head, fighting the fuzz distorting her vision, making it hard to read the fine text scrolling along the bottom of the screen.

// Elevated neural activity.

Time to go.

She rose, dropped her hand, letting the strand run off her finger... It didn't go, wound stubbornly in the joint of her armoured finger. She shook it, grabbed one of the filament-fine ends and pulled—

Fire cut through her skin, the strand cutting through hardened leather and dragon-steel plate like it was butter.

She screamed; the long, piercing screech shattering the gentle *tinkle* of water and the *shushing* reed heads. Her health bar flickered, what was red now a dull grey. [Shadow] burst from her skin, [Well of Blood] following a nanosecond later, staining the ground purple-black, refilling her health even as it did nothing for the pain.

The fire reached deep inside, cutting to the bone and worming into the marrow, racing through her palm.

She gripped her wrist, like she could somehow stop the pain, a tourniquet made of flesh and bone. And made she could, maybe her desperation, the dark magic curling around her fingers, held it back, because the pain paused, pooling in her palm.

More red saturated the HUD, more angry warnings flashing, overlaying the gibberish flooding the logs, the *critical hit* mixed with *poisoned, cursed, death, frozen* and |-|*311()*.

Teeth gritted against the agony, she tried to think past the pulse pounding in her ears and the icky, crushed-ant smell crawling up the back of her throat, coating her tongue.

It shouldn't hurt this much.

Whatever the code was, whatever it did, it was overriding system safeties and that thought, that idea, scared her to the bone, even as it sent a thrill through her blood.

The code worked. Ma's code worked!

But there was no time for thrills or fear. The warning overlayed everything, and in the back of her skull, Samael felt the Cube gathering itself, the icy fingers that came before a forced logout creeping through her veins.

She needed to purge the strand first, couldn't risk the code hitchhiking its way out of the paper-field and infecting the Cube.

[Corruption] flared around her off hand, and she *pushed*, shoving the spell into the strand, hacks popping as she forced every bit of mana and most of her health into the effort, upping the damage.

// Untitled985702:Damage:Samael[Corruption]. HP -???.

Damn it.

[Forced logout in 30 seconds... 29... 28...]

Samael pushed harder, [Shadow] wavering as her health pool hit the red line.

// Untitled985702:Damage:Samael[Corruption]. HP -???.

[... 21... 20...]

Harder still, reaching back through the Cube for more, ice forming claws on her fingers as more hacks rushed through her system, bringing the lightning storm with them.

// Untitled985702:Damage:Samael[Corruption]. HP -???.

[... 15... 14...]

Come on, come on!

The rainbow strand turned grey.

Yes!

[... 8... 7...]

It thrashed, twisted, cut deeper into her wrist, past armour and leather, through skin, blood welling—

[... 3... 2...]

—and crumbled, ashes rejoining the paper-field.

[... 1.]

<⊙>

The ceiling swam, the soft glow of the nightlight from the half-open bathroom playing across the pale, painted surface, catching in the little imperfections. Even that light was almost more than she could bear.

Vlad lay on her back, the quilt a soft mountain cradling her aches, the pillow under the boulder that had become her head. There were painkillers in the bathroom, horse-sized migraine pills that tasted like chalk and threatened to choke her whenever she forced one down. But the bathroom was eight steps away, eight boulder-cracking steps and first she would have to push herself upright, shift her weight from the cushioning mountain to the tiny, paper-thin platforms of her feet.

And now... now she was just going to lay there a bit longer. Wait for sleep to come, to wash away the pain and reset neurones...

The new pale, golden light sweeping across the ceiling confused her. It spread across the surface for a moment, lightening the shadows clinging to the cornices, and then it was gone and all Vlad could do was frown as much at the why of it as the angry wave that squeezed her forehead.

Then her comfortable mountain dipped, a new weight leaning into the mattress, a new canyon trying to roll her onto her side. Alarm blazed in her brain but before adrenaline pumped her muscles and pushed back the migraine, a familiar scent washed away the crushed-ant clinging to her nose. A hand, deliciously cool, swallowed her forehead, there and then gone before the chill had a chance to quench the fire in her brain. The weight and sandalwood went with it, the mattress bouncing back, the soft movement enough to jar her head anew, whatever peace she'd had, obliterated in less than a heartbeat.

She groaned, rose enough to see the tall, suit-clad shadow open the bathroom door—

More light hit her, right in the eyeballs, daggers piercing her skull.

The sound that came out was more whine than gasp, thin and reedy.

A curse, the door sliding shut with enough force for it to bounce back open, the half-inch of light streaming across the carpet, hitting the end of the bed but not her face. From within, drawers opened and closed, a bag rustled, a tap gushed.

Vlad propped herself on her elbow, half-rolling to see the door, all streaky starlight and sun glare—she couldn't let him see her like this—just as the door banged open again.

More daggers, the points digging a bit deeper, taking chips out the back of her skull.

Another gasp.

Another curse—not hers—and then long angry strides across the carpet—two, probably, if she had to guess—and a hand swallowing her shoulder, holding her up. A smooth, chalky pill held to her lips.

'Migraine meds,' he said.

She took it.

The cool rim of a glass came next, sweet water filling her mouth, loosening dried-up tastebuds before rushing down her throat.

Eyes closed, she fumbled for the glass. Found the sharp metal links of a watch instead, half-hidden under the cuff of a crisp cotton shirt. She pulled away, opened her eyes a slit and tried to wrap fingers that felt like jelly around the cup.

Zixin grunted. 'Let me hold it, you'll just spill it.'

'No.' Coordination was difficult, the migraine messing up the signals between her eyes and her hands. She made another pass as the water. 'I can do it, I'm not a child.'

He grunted again, and Vlad wondered if it was the scrambled electrical signals in her brain that drew a half-smile across Zixin's face. 'Just drink it,' he said again and pressed the rim to her lips.

She drank, and when she was done, the hand holding her up pushed her back down.

Vlad resisted for a moment, before a frustrated, 'Just do it,' burst from Zixin.

The bed was soft anyway, and the lightning storm raging behind her eyes made it hard to think, and she needed to think, needed to keep her wits about her. The Cube was under the bed, had she shoved it under far enough? Had she pulled her sleeve down, would he see the track marks from the sauce? Her hand went to her elbow, relief almost as sweet as the water when her fingers found Lycra.

Yes, yes, she had.

Why was Zixin here, in her room? What'd he want? What—?

The questions made her head hurt all the more, each one another spike driven into her eyeballs, another rod for the lightning to dance between.

No, no. She had to get rid of Zixin, had to get him out the door, and if she couldn't shove him out—if her head was the size of a server and her knees the consistency of foam—then best to play dead. Just lie back on the soft, mountainous quilt, burry herself in the fluffy valleys and shut out the world. Shut out Zixin.

The sandalwood scent of him, the warmth and pain.

An arm under her legs, another under her shoulders, swinging her around, scooting her pillow and all up the bed so her legs no longer dangled off the edge.

She kept her eyes closed, concentrated on keeping her body limp and breathing. In. Out. Nice and slow and steady. Just like a sleeping person should.

He'd go now. She strained her ears, waiting for the gentle thud as he tiptoed back out the room and—

Cold and damp across her forehead, and the relief... She gasped, couldn't help but open her eyes a fraction as the cold sank through her skin, calming the lightning.

Quickly, she shut her eyes, rearranged her breathing back into the deep pattern of sleep.

He would go now, he would—

The mattress dipped, weight settling on the edge.

'Go away,' she said.

'No. Not until you answer me.'

'My head hurts.'

'So answer me fast.'

'You're going to interrogate me when I have a migraine?'

A shift in weight, pressure on the compress on her forehead, pressing the soothing cold deeper into her skull.

'Why the migraine?'

She frowned. 'That's a stupid question.'

'Is it? It's been hours since the tournament.' A pause, then, 'What did you do An— Vladana?'

'What do you mean?'

'You know what I mean.'

'No, I don't.'

The hand shifted from her forehead to the crook of her arm, strong fingers wrapping around forearm below the elbow, seeming to burn through the Lycra to the marks underneath.

'I'm not an idiot, Vladana, and even if I don't know gaming or the networks, I know you. You wouldn't use drugs, which meant you were in-System.' His hand tightened around her elbow. 'Why?'

'How could I go in-System? I haven't left my room, and there's no VR chair in here.'

'You expect me to believe the great Samael needs a VR chair to go online?' Another shift in weight, and even if she couldn't see with the cloth over her eyes, she felt Zixin leaning over her, breath warm on her cheeks. 'Where's your Cube?'

Vlad went still. Suddenly, the lightning in her head wasn't quite as vicious as the alarm pounding her heart or stopping up her breath.

'I don't know what you're talking about.' She shoved her free hand between them, got a shock at the lack of distance, Zixin close enough it was her forearm and not her palm she pushed into his chest. 'Get off me.'

The hand gripping her other elbow tightened. 'Where's your Cube, Ana?'

'I told you.' Her forearm in Zixin's throat and adrenaline lending her strength as she heaved and twisted, tumbling them both off the bed, landing on the carpet with a solid thump, her on top. 'Don't call me that.'

The cloth was gone, slipped off somewhere in the tussle, and even though she wanted to glare at him—to meet those dark, suspicious eyes with the fury in her own—light from the bathroom slashed across her face and—

Vlad hissed, shrinking from the light as pain bloomed in skull, the daggers corkscrewing deeper into the bone.

A soft curse from Xin'er, but even as the muscles underneath her tensed, preparing to move under her slackened hold, Vlad was scampering away, back pressed into the side of the mattress, eyes tight shut.

'Get out,' she said, and if there was an edge of desperation in her voice, a high, thin quality to the command, she refused to hear it.

She heard him shift closer, the soft thud of knees on carpet.

'Ana—'

'Out.'

'You can't keep doing this.'

'I'll do what I damn well want, including scream if you don't. Get. OUT!' She had meant to yell the last bit, didn't like the half-screech that came out at the end. But it was there, ringing in the room, splitting her ear drums, feeding the lightning.

Through the pain and her pounding heart, she didn't hear Xin'er get up, but she felt the door open—light from the hallway glowing red behind her lids, sending another spike into her brain—and the quiet *snick* as it closed.

28

A hard *clunk* on the bench, cutting the wild-haired man off mid-sentence, leaving just the subtitles to scroll past, *"...before we start replacing frozen heads with digital storage!"*

The morning light refracted through the heavy water glass, casting soft shadows and waving patterns over Vlad's fingers and the tea bowl cradled between them. The light hit her eyes and sparked new daggers through the gooey flesh.

Vlad winced.

Two small, white pills followed the *clunk*, not tossed but carefully placed beside the cut crystal.

She looked up, struggling to erase the line between her brows.

Lu Chen stared back, square, finely sculpted face impassive as the cold marble under her elbows.

You're part of a team now.

She looked away, screaming "fuck off" with every molecule.

He pulled out the stool beside her and sat.

Fuck.

'What do you want?' she said.

He pushed the glass closer. 'We're training today.'

'We train every day.'

'You're not joining us.'

A sharp *snap* of her head, and *that* was a mistake, but she didn't wince, she *wouldn't*. 'What?'

'Ms Morita sent the EMT report from last night.'

The one that told her to stay off the System, no doubt. And it'd been sent by Tina, the traitor.

A snarl tugged at Vlad's lips but didn't pull them.

The pills scooted closer. 'For the headache.'

She stared at the tablets a moment, the pain she refused to name still burning her heart, before she took them. 'Who says I have a headache?'

He stared.

She raised a brow back.

Lu Chen didn't flinch.

The staring contest was immature and yet neither looked away or blinked, faces frozen. Lu Chen's expression deadpan, Vlad's chin lifting to join her brow.

The news feeds rolled across the kitchen bench, gameplay breakdowns, hardware advertisements, breaking news, an explosion downtown, a truck overturned, fuel over the highway, a car on fire—

Vlad's attention snapped to the news feed with enough force to wrench her head from her neck. The blue-white flames racing over a crumpled car hood consumed her attention, the firemen in their black and yellow suits, giant hoses spraying great jets of white-blue foam over the area, little more than blurs.

She remembered those flames, the roar of them, the way they distorted the air, how they made the world shimmer. And the heat, she'd never forget the heat, blasting across the metal, melting her clothes, the seat belt...

Fingers, a sharp *snap* under her nose.

Vlad blinked, came back to the now and Lu Chen, the faintest of frowns marring his otherwise impassive face.

She shook herself, wondering if the captain noticed her hand covering the news article, blocking it from her vision. A useless gesture, she knew it was there, could feel the fire like it was burning through the transmission and spilling across her palm.

She stared at him, then his hand, fingers still held in the *click* position.

'I'm not a dog,' she said, summoning acid to her voice, hoping to cover the churning in her gut.

Lu Chen ignored it. 'If you have issues,' he said, voice calm. 'You should tell us.'

'Because we're a *team*?'

'Yes.' He leaned forward. 'And what you do affects us.'

'Because I'm a Scourge.'

'Because you're part of the *team*.' He caught the news article under her hand, dragging the vid across the table and blowing it up.

The fire was still raging, the camera focused on the blue-white retardant spewing from the firemen's hoses. She could almost smell the chemicals—the harsh, acid-like strawberry burning out the inside of her nose—taste the ash in the air.

She wrenched her gaze away, right into Lu Chen's.

There was softness there. Compassion.

You're bleeding.

Fuck.

Vlad looked away.

'So, we going to have a sharing session then?' A flick of her wrist had the car crash spinning away and a different news feed popping up front and centre on the table.

A suave, middle-aged man came out of a police station, a jacket draped over the hands clasped at his waist. The posture might have been mistaken as causal, a businessman strolling to his car after doing his civic duty, if they didn't catch the steely glint of the cuffs around his wrist. Vlad did.

She enhanced the image, her smile hard as the metal around the man's wrists. 'You look like your dad,' she said.

Lu Chen froze. Not just stoney-faced impassive, but cold, cold enough to drop the temperature in the kitchen and freeze the water in the heavy crystal glass.

'You don't.' Sticky speaking from the kitchen doorway, his

hands moving, holding some kind of image above his wrist before he threw it.

The old recording landed on the bench, the holo spread across the marble big and bold, wiping out the one of Lu Chen's father.

Strobing emergency lights, a car on fire, and not just any car, but *the* car. Her dad's sleek silver Bentley, the one Ma had hated because he liked to take it out on the windy coast roads and take the bends a little too fast... Beside the car were two more images, Ma and Dad, looking so alive, so *happy*...

Vlad hissed and smashed her palm through the image.

She glared at Sticky.

Those big panda eyes stared back. And where Lu Chen's expression had frozen, where Zixin's or Tina's would have blazed with anger or fury, Sticky showed nothing.

'I warned you,' he said.

A memory from her first day played in her mind. *'You gonna put a knife in my back?' she'd said.*

Sticky'd shrugged. 'Depends.'

'On what?'

'How much they like you.'

No words came to her, only the burning flames, the blue and gold Wonder Woman costume melting to her flesh. Ma sobbing in the front seat, the river of blood. She hissed again, the sound coming from deep in her chest even as peppermint wound through her nostrils and that high-pitched melody sang in her ears.

Her hand formed a fist, the old news article fuzzing around her fingers, refusing to die no matter how hard she squeezed.

A hand on top of hers.

She jerked away.

Away from the bench, away from the images and flames, away from Lu Chen. Away from her nightmares, spilling across the kitchen island, now it was free from her grip, spreading just like the fire across the Bentley's crumpled silver hood.

'Sticky,' Lu Chen spoke. 'Enough.'

The little panda didn't blink, didn't move, just kept staring. 'I warned her,' he repeated.

'You did.' And there was Ming Li Na, appearing behind Sticky, soft hand gripping his shoulder. 'You made your point; you can stop it now.'

'I don't think so,' he said, and still he held Vlad's gaze. Or had he captured it?

She didn't know, didn't care, all she knew was the fire had engulfed the kitchen, and she was going to stop it. She was going to show the round, big-eyed panda just why you didn't fuck with Death—

She was around the bench before she knew it, and the panda wasn't backing away, just kept looking at her with that blank expression and—

Huang Yimo stepping in, a shadow detaching from Sticky's other side, coming down the step into the kitchen, getting in Vlad's way.

Vlad wound up—

'He's sorry,' Huang Yimo said.

Vlad froze.

'No, I'm not—' Sticky began.

'You are,' Huang Yimo might have spoken to Sticky, but her gaze was locked on Vlad. 'Just like you will be,' and now she was speaking to Vlad. 'In the morning, if you hit him.'

'Why? Because we're *friends*?' Vlad hissed the word.

'Because you want to be.' And that was Ming Li Na, speaking from behind Sticky, clutching his shoulders as if to hold him back, or maybe throw herself in front of him.

Again, Vlad stopped cold, the bile in her belly reduced to a shimmer, the anger with it.

She stared at Ming Li Na, the sympathy in her round eyes, jerked her gaze away from the hint of sad around the other woman's mouth. Met Huang Yimo's instead, turned from the compassion she found there, caught Lu Chen's… And that impassive face was soft too, invited her to step in and—

The flames burning across the island, eating her dreams, dancing over her skin, warming the anger. The hate to cover the hurt.

Sticky.

The panda's expression still blank, implacable. And there it was, the trigger she needed to bring all that acidic fury burning up her throat, tightening her hands—

He lifted his tablet, pressed a button.

The fire on the bench died, made the one in her gut stutter.

Another hiss, anger-fuelled adrenalin rushing through her veins and nowhere to put it. Nothing to hit. Only those sympathetic faces, the understanding, the *blood*—

No, no, she wouldn't bleed. She wouldn't.

Not in front of them, not ever.

Vlad skirted around the huddle on the stairs, across the foyer, out the red door, into the sun and smog, not sure where she was going, only that it was *away*.

4lly?

m4y83.

29

Graydon's Revenge still smelled like crushed ants, the rotten-citrus curling through her nose even as the ants themselves *prick pricked* across her shoulders. The block-headed horse still hung in mid-air, the upside-down doors embedded in the grey stone walls, the NPCs still stuck headfirst in the flagstones, legs trundling uselessly in their endless walk cycles. That frisson in the back of her skull, tracing nerve and tendon to the base of her throat, the knowledge that not everything was right, that someone was watching. Familiar in its spine-chilling way.

Samael stood atop the crumbling wall and waited, looking out across the spear-topped pines, at the horizon with its leaping-fish clouds that never changed.

A column of light shone at the other end of the wall, and a figure materialised from it.

Ru Ping, in her black and crimson armour stepped forward.

'Thank you for coming,' the woman said.

// Why?

'We know who you are, Ms Tong.'

// Samael.

A twist of the head, the long tail of the knight's hair slipping over her armoured shoulder.

'Apologies. Samael, we know your real world identity and we know why you approached Hamish.'

// Then why are you here?

'We can help each other.'

// You mean, I can help your employer.

A smile, and Samael was mildly surprised that it didn't cause the serious lines of the other woman's face to crack. 'Yes.'

// Why here? Samael spread her arms to indicate the castle, gauntleted fingers catching a stray beam of sunlight, the tarnished gold glimmering. *Why not the field? Isn't the code what you want?*

Did Ru Ping only wear glasses in the real to communicate with Oily Face, or was it to hide her eyes? 'Cause now Samael wondered how she hadn't noticed their expressiveness before, how she'd ever mistaken the heavy for stoic and cold. Maybe it was just her avatar that allowed humour to glimmer in the dark depths and crinkle her eyes. Maybe, and then again...

'The field was a show, an excuse to plant a tracker on my avatar,' the knight said. The smile deepened, knowing lighting up the lines on her face. 'We know that.'

Relief tempered the anger that Oily Face didn't know the truth of the field, the rainbow river.

Samael moved away from the wall's edge, activating [Sonic Steps] and half-turned so the block-headed horse remained in the corner of her vision. The thought of the river had the ants renewing their march across her scalp, had her sensing those eyes boring into her nape.

Waves of sound *pinged* in every direction, even as she met Ru Ping's gaze, taking in the half-smile, the way the other woman stood to attention even in the game.

On the radar, waves pooled at the knight's armoured feet, rebounded off the massive stone walls, the legs caught in their walk cycles, the horse atop the roof and the bot between its cube-shaped ears.

// What does your employer want?

'I think you know, Ms... Samael.'

// I think you shouldn't assume I know anything.

A step forward, that smile hardening at the corners, the

humour lighting the eyes dimming. 'We are not here to play games.'

// Then stop playing them, Samael shot back. *Tell me what you want, Ms Ru, or leave.*

'We want what your mother began.'

// You say that like I should know what you're talking about.

Ru Ping's face hardened a little more, the smile slipping from her lips, and Samael began to wonder if it really was the heavy behind the avatar, or if it was another staring at her from behind the knight's skin.

'Games, Samael. Games.'

Under her robes, Samael's fingers curled inwards. *// I told you—*

The knight stalked forward, hand lifting to her side and the dagger sheathed there. 'And yet you are. You know exactly what I want; it's what your mother died for. Help me find it, and I'll help you find who murdered your parents.' A pause, the knight now an arm's-length away, the perfect striking distance. She leaned in another millimetre. 'And gave you your scars.'

Graydon's Revenge froze, and despite the sauce running through her system, despite the safeties and algorithms, despite the impossibility of it all, for just a second she was Vlad. The dove-grey doona cradling her legs, the pillow soft and warm under her back, the headboard cold against her skull. The ugly knot of flesh behind her knee tugging, her long-sleeved t-shirt rough on the scars travelling her arm.

Just a second, less even, and yet it made her heart stutter and the sauce scream in her veins, made her head ache. And then she was back in the game, back in Graydon, robes turning to smoke at her feet, armour heavy on her hands, pauldrons and greaves biting into shoulders and shins, staff a comforting hum at her back.

Ru Ping could have found out about the scars in a dozen ways, legal, illegal, morally grey. It shouldn't shock her, shouldn't make her think of the reconstructed reflection from the heavy's glasses and silver hair falling into Grandmother's face. Shouldn't bring up the memory of the plain gold wedding band Grandmother never took off, the look in her eyes when she told Vlad to behave like a Tong. It shouldn't, and yet it did, because she was halfway there, from the very moment Zixin appeared on her network scan all those weeks ago.

Grandmother knew Ma's work, knew about the scars, the crash, knew Samael's real-world name. And she had the money, had Tina and DKZero—had Sticky and Huang Yimo—had the connections and the power.

She didn't *need* Samael, the Scourge was just an excuse, Ma's work—her death—just a lure to draw Vlad in, wrap her up in a contract, insert Zixin back into her life and—

But why NuGet *and* the code? Why was Grandmother so desperate?

A half-remembered newsfeed scrolled through her thoughts. *"...replacing frozen heads with digital storage!"*

What was an AI if not a consciousness? And NuGet's neural link... brain became computer.

Fuck.

Doubt crept through Samael's determination.

No. Mentally, she shook herself. No, she wouldn't fall for it. Two could play this game.

// Prove it, Samael said. *Prove you can do what you promise and I'll help you.*

Ru Ping smiled, and again, that sense that it wasn't the stone-faced heavy lurking behind the avatar but someone else, struck her. Silver hair and flashing rings.

A notification *pinged* and a simple text string with GPS coordinates opened on Samael's HUD.

'I'm at the rave,' Ru Ping said. 'Find me.'

30

The white Ducati cruiser idled beside Ximisthus, the lights embedded under the bike's voluptuous engine and lean frame lighting up its undercarriage like the fires of hell, while the ice-blue glow around its rims and tail promised frost on the blacktop. It was a brute beside Ximisthus's sleek, angled frame, but there was power in its low growl.

Admiration stopped Vlad in her tracks, if only for a moment, long enough for Huang Yimo's long, lean shadow to detach itself from a pillar, a suitably sleek silver helmet in her hands, and Ming Li Na at her side.

Vlad stared at them.

Ming Li Na smiled, the expression a little wobbly around the corners. Huang Yimo just stared, expression blank.

Vlad jerked her eyes to Ximisthus, her feet back into action. Some part of her offered the opinion that they'd go away if she ignored them long enough, and even if she didn't...

Ximisthus was there, the powerful black Ninja sleek and steady as she swung a leg over the back, settled into the saddle, boot finding the off-side peddle. She reached for the helmet sitting on the engine casing even as Huang Yimo moved, Ming Li Na not a step behind. She half-expected one of them to put a hand atop the helmet, to stop her like Xin'er had all those weeks ago, was surprised when they didn't. Even more surprised Ming Li Na didn't step in front of the bike, arms spread like a human stop sign... until the Ducati growled, the sleek monster rocking a little as Ming Li Na swung up behind Huang Yimo.

The smile was still on Ming Li Na's face, visible through her helmet's clear face-shield, the pink lights—running up the shield from either side of the chin to the tips of the helmet's pointy cat ears—casting a warm glow over her face.

If a smile cracked Huang Yimo's visage, it was hidden behind her own helmet, the icy-blue lights in her mask eerily reminiscent of a death's head.

Vlad twisted the throttle and Ximisthus shot into the night, down the mansion's curving drive, onto the smooth bitumen beyond, the carefully tended sidewalks and manicured street gardens flashing past.

The other two followed, the Ducati's headlights casting a long shadow for Ximisthus to dive into.

Vlad kept her speed low until the estate's old wrought iron gates were closing behind her, Huang Yimo and Ming Li Na on her tail, but once the gates were down…

She twisted the throttle and Ximisthus howled.

Speed pushed her into the saddle, the wind screamed past her helmet, slipped through the tiny gaps under her chin to whistle in her ears. The HUD spread out behind her face-shield, speedo flirting with the posted number, kissing it then tipping over.

The boulevard leading up to the estate was wide, the four lanes empty this time of night. Streetlights illuminated the bitumen, the harsh blue-white washing out the vibrant green of the trees either side of the road and marching down the centre median. Riding at night always reminded her of [Shadow], gave her a second's pause as she fought the memory of lag and tried to sort out if the blue, red and yellow lines tracking vehicles and pedestrians, traffic lights and the quiet buzz of cops, belonged to Samael or Vlad.

But it was only a second and now, with the Ducati in her rear-view, its throaty roar audible even over the wind, it was even less.

She needed to lose them.

Vlad leaned into the next bend.

There were traffic lights ahead and cars, a smattering of luxury sedans and scooters with late-night deliveries cruising through the intersection. The HUD tracked the distance; eight-hundred metres.

Five.

Four.

The lights flicked orange.

Vlad poured on more speed, giving up all pretence of flirting with the legal limit.

Two.

One.

It went red.

She blasted through it.

A horn blared in her wake, but the Ducati didn't follow.

Vlad's smile was grim.

They didn't belong where she was going.

<⊙>

Headlights washed over cracked road top and Ximisthus rumbled to a halt on the edge of the Iron Wood estate. Dead weeds and scraggly grass pushed through the abandoned parking lot while the skeletons of tall streetlights reached their arms over the concrete, their curling, lacy fingers empty of light.

Behind her, the thrum of the freeway rose over the scraggly hedges—long since turned to twigs and sticks, parts little more than char—while in front... strobes and music played between the outlines of half-finished residential towers. Other headlights cruised up and down what the map on her HUD told her was the main boulevard, rev heads and wannabes showing off their cars, while the small side street she used remained deserted.

Unseen. Hidden.

Secret.

[Shadow] tried to steal over her vision.

She shook it away.

Now wasn't the time for that, even the fancy of it.

Cracked concrete changed to cracked blacktop, Ximisthus's tyres humming over the road as she slowly approached the lone streetlight.

An old school Scrambler was already parked there. With its matte-black chassis, chunky dirt tyres and spare, mean build, the motorbike looked better suited to the apocalypse than a rave, and the sight of it, this far out from the main action, gave Vlad pause.

There weren't many reasons to avoid the lights and noise of the main drag, the sticky noses and scrutiny that came with it. Whoever the bike belonged to was avoiding attention. Like her.

Another Scourge? A dealer? A cop? Ru Ping?

Xin'er?

No, not Zixin. Even if he knew how to ride, the Scrambler's beefy lines didn't suit him at all.

Vlad stopped two streetlights over and cut Ximisthus's engine. Kickstand down, swinging her leg over and her helmet off, her attention glued to the other bike in the distance. Systems in her glasses and watch running overtime as she scanned it, almost able to hear the AI back in her loft *tick, tick, ticking* as it ate the data and started its search.

Whoever the rider was, she'd find them, if only so she knew who to avoid.

The walk through the dark estate with its rows upon rows of half-finished foundations and lonely bitumen roads, the edges cracked and choked with half-dead weeds made the back of her neck crawl. It was almost a relief to hit the lights and roaring engines on the main drag, to slip in amongst the rev-heads and wheel jockeys and stalk between the cars and bikes—

Vlad stopped short.

A white Ducati cruiser was parked amongst the speed bikes and dirt racers, the motorcycle's sleek, brutish lines at odds with the hard angles and dangerous lean of the others. She wanted to tell herself that there was more than one white Ducati cruiser in the world. That there was no way Huang Yimo could have followed her let alone arrived ahead of her. It could belong to the beef head across the way, leaning up against the pimped out Porsche with its rotating rims and the light show under its chassis, like he owned the thing instead of the tall blonde behind the wheel. But there were two helmets sitting on the seat, one of them with a clear face-shield and pink cat ears.

A little chill worked its way up her spine.

She pressed her watch and spoke for the mic behind her ear. 'Locate Huang Yimo and Ming Li Na.'

A pulse in the corner of her HUD was all the acknowledgment she got. All she should need, and yet...

She pressed the watch again. 'Acknowledge.'

Acknowledged, rolled across the bottom of her vision. *Working... working...*

Wherever they were, if they had their devices on (and what gamer didn't?) her system would find them. Anywhere, anytime.

Some of the tension eased, freeing up her feet and she continued into the rave.

Huang Yimo could look after herself, and Ming Li Na... the other woman's face, with her big eyes and soft cheeks flashed before her eyes, apprehension coming with it. Vlad shook herself. She was making assumptions; she didn't know shit about Ming Li Na, the other woman was probably a black belt or Judo champion, and still... A memory of Hamish caging her at the karaoke lounge.

Vlad gave herself another mental shake. It was just a rave, not a back alley. They had no idea about Hamish, or Ru Ping, or why she was here. Her teammates would be fine.

The chill in her gut didn't believe it.

Her gaze flicked to the status bar scrolling across the bottom of her glasses.

Working... working...

Work fucking faster, she wanted to tell it.

The avenue of motors ended and she climbed the three small, broad stairs to the building beyond. No walls, no windows or doors, just a forest of square pillars holding up flat slabs of concrete, one atop the other in fifteen stories of wind-whistling tower. Now, instead of ghosts and whirligigs, lights flashed and strobed among the pillars, bodies packed together in a thumping, pounding mass of sweat and flesh.

Her eyes went to the darker second floor.

Ru Ping was up there somewhere, she'd bet Hamish was as well.

Skipped to the dancing mob on the ground floor.

Huang Yimo and Ming Li Na too.

Fuck.

She plunged into the mob, slipping between bodies, slapping hands off her arse and more reaching for her shoulder and elbow. People held red plastic cups and bottles as they danced, some holding them aloft, alcohol slopping over rims, down arms and over the crowd. The yeasty scent of beer and the sharp tang of other stronger drinks filled her nose, some even splashed her lips.

The music throbbed in her chest, the lights turned the rave into an extension of [Shadow], but in shades of red and green and blue, one after the other, leaving her dizzy.

Another shake, this time to clear the shifting colours from her vision.

She should have gone around the crowd, but instinct said to go through, that only by plunging into the heaving mass would she find Huang Yimo and Ming Li Na. And she *had* to find them... because... why?

'You're part of a team now.' Fuck Lu Chen.

She gritted her teeth and slapped another overly grabby hand off her arse, swinging around to treat the over-entitled arsehole to the snarl twisting her lips.

He backed off, hands raised like it was blood dripping down her chin and not disgust.

Disgust at him, at herself. It was hard to tell.

Another hand. Another slap, another snarl.

In one corner of her HUD the clock ticked down—ten fifty-eight—while in the other the status bar scrolled.

Working... working...

Fuck it, she didn't have time for this shit.

If Ming Li Na couldn't fend for herself, Huang Yimo was woman enough to do it for them both.

Vlad's eyes rose through the atrium, to the second floor and the balcony overlooking the dancers. A bald, pale ghost moved through the shadows.

The HUD picked out the sick-green glow of a vape and the tattoos inked across Hamish's face.

Behind him, another moved, a shadow within the shadows. Ru Ping.

She ploughed through the crowd, heading for the space behind the DJ and the plain, rail-less stairs leading upward.

Away from the strobes, the shadows were grey again and the air grew chill without the masses emitting body heat. Her breath frosted, leading the way one echoing step at a time.

The clock read eleven-o-three as Vlad took the last riser. She emerged onto the second floor - head then shoulders then the rest of her rising through the concrete slab.

Working... worki— Located.

A map took over the lower left corner of the HUD, just as the figures standing around the makeshift table—more doors stacked on gallon drums—caught her attention.

There were five of them, which was two too many.

The little chill walking up her spine grew icy even as two dots appeared on the map, the map itself swinging around to show elevation and— They were on the ground floor, somewhere in the heaving mass of bodies just visible over the makeshift balcony.

Whoever the other people were, they weren't her teammates.

The tension ran out of Vlad's spine, and she told herself it was only because Huang Yimo or Ming Li Na getting tangled up with

Ru Ping and Hamish would make things complicated. That they'd stick their noses in and drag her down.

That was the only reason.

Her boots clunked as she topped the last riser, HUD already adjusted to the dark, picking out details highlighted by the orange chem-sticks tossed about the door-table. Hamish leaning against the balcony, Ru Ping by the table, two heavies either side of a third; shorter and rounder than the others with a bowl-cut fringe and big panda eyes.

The chill froze in Vlad's spine.

Her boots stopped.

And then, like that wasn't bad enough, a new notification popped on Vlad's HUD.

Search complete. Vehicle license HZR8663 registered to Chan Ying.

And next to it, Sticky's round panda face.

Fuck.

Next to the balcony, Hamish straightened, the tip of his vape a bright-green point stabbing the dark.

Below, the music pounded the floor.

'You got some famous friends.' Hamish's voice cut across the drums and guitars.

Vlad forced her feet to move, slow and steady, a careful gliding stalk instead of the quick, choppy race the knot in her gut demanded. 'He's not a friend,' she said.

Hamish drew on his vape, long and slow to match his own steps around the table. To Sticky standing beside it, arms straight at his sides, white showing around his eyes, chin a little too high, like he'd just landed in a pit full of tigers. One of the tigers was now standing beside him, pointing a vape in his face.

'That's not what he says,' Hamish said. 'Says you're *teammates*, says you work together.' He took another draw on the vape. 'The news likes to say that too, Ms Vladana *Tong*.' He drawled her last name, stretching the single syllable into two.

She stopped at the other end of the table, rested her hands on the rough top with its peeling paint and splinters, and leaned on it. 'He's. Not. A. Friend.'

'Then you won't mind if I do this.' Hamish smashed Sticky's face into the table.

The snarl was past her lips and she was storming around the side before Sticky's pained cry had time to do more than pierce her stomach.

Ru Ping stepped in her way, and only the second heavy stepping up behind the woman stopped Vlad from laying her out cold.

Hamish laughed.

Sticky slid off the table, hands over his nose to a dark panda-shaped puddle on the floor.

Vlad hissed, and snapped her attention not to Ru Ping, but the oily reflection she could see in the woman's glasses.

'You don't need him,' she said and hoped the reflection knew which *him* she referred to.

A laugh, and there, behind Ru Ping, Hamish planting a boot against Sticky's side and shoving. 'But it's so much more fun with 'im.' He squatted, poked the vape in Sticky's face. 'Ain't it, little fatty?'

Sticky huddled in on himself.

Hamish poked him again.

Vlad didn't growl, she didn't, but she got right up in Ru Ping's face, staring straight into those glasses to the dark eyes and silver hair swimming within. 'You're the one who didn't want to play games.'

Ru Ping stared back, impassive, but the reflection...

Out the corner of her eye, Vlad was aware of Hamish rising behind Ru Ping, no longer laughing, no longer poking Sticky with his vape, hands at his sides and wariness hovering over his face. The wariness made her hands itch and turned the ice in her spine to a highway for ants to crawl up and down and back, adrenaline prickling in their wake.

She kept her attention on Ru Ping, on the reflection.

On Grandmother.

For several heartbeats it didn't move.

One heartbeat. Two.

Hamish stalked closer, neon lights playing over his bare, skinny chest.

'I like games,' he said as he moved around the heavy at Ru Ping's back and then Ru Ping herself, until he was standing at Vlad's shoulder.

Vlad didn't move, save to ball her hands into fists.

He drew on his vape. 'Not sure I like this one though.' He exhaled, the sweet chemical cherry washing over Vlad's face. 'What are the rules? Do we need more players?'

On the HUD, the map changed, the two dots that were Huang Yimo and Ming Li Na slowly changing their elevation; getting higher.

Up her spine, the ants' feet grew blades, drawing blood.

The sheen played across Ru Ping's glasses.

Ru Ping stepped out of Hamish's way.

Vlad's stomach sank, but no, there was hope. It was Grandmother on the other side of those glasses. *Grandmother*.

Vlad hissed.

'You're in it now, bitch.' Hamish smiled, vapour curling out of his mouth and nose, a fleshy cyborg dragon. He threw his arms wide as if the smooth, tattooed lines of his torso would make her fall all over herself. 'But maybe—' he began.

Vlad sneered at him. 'No.'

'You sure?' He gestured down at himself. 'A little bit of consideration and you never know...' He leaned closer, just a millimetre of empty space between them. 'I might put in a good word for you with the boss.'

Two steps behind him, in the dark, Ru Ping's mouth moved, words lost under the thudding music below. The heavy's eyes flicked from Hamish to Vlad and back again, and as they settled something very much like satisfaction crossed the woman's normally impassive face.

Vlad narrowed her gaze.

Ru Ping nodded at her.

Victory. Vlad turned to Hamish.

There was just a deep breath between them. As thin as the bastard was, he was wiry, all whipcord muscle and viciousness. Tall too, taller than Xin'er, tall enough that she had to crane her head back, tall enough to put his soft bits in easy reach.

She stood on tiptoe, bracing herself with a finger in his sternum, and even that was too much, made the flesh want to crawl right off her bones. But she didn't let it show, not yet. Instead, she smiled, a thin, knowing smile.

'You don't have a good word left,' she whispered. She tilted her head towards Ru Ping. 'Your boss just accepted my offer.'

His eyes skittered sideways, to Ru Ping, while confusion crossed his broad, flat brow and threw his chin back. 'What offer?'

Vlad's smile turned to teeth, and she lifted herself higher, hand becoming a claw as it travelled up Hamish's chest and dug into the cord-like muscles over his shoulder.

A pained snarl joined the confusion on Hamish's face as it looked at her.

She showed him more teeth. 'The one where I get to do this.'

Vlad struck. The knee to his balls was swift and sudden; a hard, sharp, vicious jerk, the hand on his shoulder pushing him into it.

He crumbled, air rushing out his lungs, hands over his crotch.

Vlad leaned over him, mouth beside his ear. 'That was for Ming Li Na.'

She took a step back, cupped his jaw with one hand, wound up and smashed her elbow into the other side. Pain burst through the bone, but it was nothing, and watching Hamish fall, hitting the dark, dirty concrete like a felled tree, washed away even the memory of it.

He was on his side in a loose, foetal ball, hands cupping his groin, face half in shadow, what she could see of his expression, dazed.

She shoved a toe against his shoulder, flipped him onto his back and crouched. She gripped his chin between two fingers, turned him toward her, slapped him a little when his eyes remained unfocussed. She wanted him to see this, to *know*.

Shock and pain and hate, all of them swam in the dirty-green pools.

Vlad leaned in a little closer. 'That last one was for Chan Ying, the *fatty*.' She snapped the last word, teeth bared. 'Just in case you didn't remember his name. And this...' She paused a moment, waited for the rage to coalesce in Hamish's eyes, for the hate to draw back his lips and match her, snarl for snarl.

'And what, you fookin cun—?'

She smashed his nose, felt cartilage break, blood spurt over her knuckles. 'That's for your filthy mouth.'

Vlad rose, a single, smooth motion and retreated, shaking out her fist. She turned her back on Hamish, left him laid out on the floor, moaning and cursing in equal measure, nursing nose and crotch, and forgot about him.

On the other side of the table, Ru Ping waited, the other two heavies at her back. She looked Vlad straight in the eye; long, cherry-black fringe not quite hiding the oily sheen still playing across her glasses.

Grandmother.

Vlad stopped in front of her. Savoured the sweet pound of adrenalin and victory coursing through her veins, even as caution tip-toed up her spine and laid its cold, taloned hand over her shoulder.

On her HUD, the two dots that were Huang Yimo and Ming Li Na had retreated, back down into the mess of dancers below.

'You made an enemy there,' Ru Ping said.

'I make enemies everywhere I go,' Vlad shot back.

The heavy nodded, that oily sheen playing on the back of her square glasses. Ru Ping held out a hand.

An old-fashioned flash drive lay in the woman's palm, the thin, thumb-length silver rectangle catching the lights from the rave below.

Gingerly, so only the tips of her fingers touched Ru Ping, Vlad took it.

'You'll find what you need on this drive,' Ru Ping said. 'Don't stay here; the police have been called about a drug ring—' She flicked her eyes over Vlad's shoulder to Hamish '—they'll be here soon.'

There was a pause, and Vlad snapped her gaze up. A strange expression crossed the other woman's face, a sardonic smile and the hint something else.

'Don't make an enemy of this one,' Ru Ping said, and there was something in them, a quiet respect that told Vlad the words came from the woman herself, and not the voice in her ear.

Ru Ping spun about, a sharp, military movement, and melted into the shadows, the other two heavies following a second later.

Leaving just Vlad, alone in the dark, Hamish moaning at her feet and Sticky's big dark eyes boring into the side of her head.

Her fingers wrapped around the flash drive.

31

She got Sticky out of there, helped him to his feet, dragged his left arm across her shoulders and half-carried him down the stairs before she turned them away from the rave and escaped into the darkness beyond. An anonymous message was already winging its way to Huang Yimo and Ming Li Na, warning them to follow suit before the police came.

Two minutes later, when the sirens and lights wailed in the distance, cutting off the main route into the estate, they were crunching across abandoned building foundations toward the lone streetlight.

Not a single word passed between them, although the tension sat heavy on Vlad's shoulders, even after Sticky started walking on his own. It lurched between them, an invisible hulk full of questions and the burning scent of recrimination, while her mind raced.

How much had Sticky seen, how much had he heard after Hamish smashed his face? What secrets had the Scottish bastard revealed before Vlad even arrived? Would Sticky believe any lie she spun?

Maybe. She flicked a glance at the blood crusted on his lip and chin, scanners in her glasses picking out the first tell-tale signs of the bruises blooming across cheekbones and eyes.

But probably not. She wouldn't believe her either.

The streetlight flickered over the Scrambler with its chunky black tyres and apocalyptic frame.

Sticky grabbed the helmet propped on the engine casing, a classic matte-black skulk cap to go with the bike.

'Can you ride?' The question was out of her mouth, not "How did you find me?" Or "Are you alright?" Breaking the silence sharp as a fist through a window.

He didn't answer, just buckled the helmet under his chin and swung a leg over the seat. The Scrambler came to life with the low, throaty rumble of its old-fashioned engine. He flipped the kickstand and—

Vlad grabbed the handlebar, hand closing over Sticky's before he twisted the throttle. She didn't know what made her do it, only that his blood-crusted lip and swollen nose had concern writhing through her gut.

'Get your face looked at,' she said.

Sticky met her gaze for three long heartbeats, before he shook her hand off, twisted the throttle and roared into the night.

She didn't go back to DKZero. Maybe she should have, and maybe she should have gone with Sticky into the ER. She'd followed him to the hospital, saw him shamble through the sliding doors, stayed until the white Ducati whined up outside with Huang Yimo and Ming Li Na. Waited there another half hour, Ximisthus vibrating under her, sandwiched between two people movers, lights off, blending into the dark parking lot, indecision eating holes in her stomach.

It wasn't until a taxi spilled Tina onto the apron before the ER's double glass doors that Vlad flicked Ximisthus's lights and twisted the throttle.

Tina, Grandmother's lackey.

Grandmother, who'd hired Hamish and watched through Ru Ping's glasses as the bastard broke Sticky's nose.

Grandmother.

Grandmother who'd wanted her to behave like a Tong.

Vlad snarled, twisted the throttle and screamed out of the parking lot.

She'd made the old woman a promise in the TI foyer.

Time to deliver.

<⊙>

It was late, the clock on the HUD read past two in the morning when Ximisthus growled to a stop in front of the tall black doors. She could almost hear the iron gates clanging shut at the start of the long, winding drive, Ximisthus echoes still bouncing off the concrete walls.

There were no lights on in the mansion, just small glows under the neatly hedged bushes and the round up-lights along the drive that had sprung to life as she passed. They died now, popping back to sleep one-by-one in the still night, leaving just the bike's headlight to wash the shrubs and flowers of colour, the neon under the rims and the chassis staining the gravel bright green.

The last of the driveway lights winked off.

Vlad thumbed the engine off.

Darkness once more claimed the world, save for those garden lights.

The soft glow was nothing to the big black doors. Portals to the pit.

She swung her leg over Ximisthus and set the kickstand.

Sticky's face haunted her, the sound he made as he hit the table, the other one as he crumbled on the dark, dirty floor.

The reflection in Ru Ping's glasses, silver hair and plain gold ring.

It might have been Hamish's hands breaking Sticky's nose, but it was Grandmother who was responsible, Grandmother pulling the strings. Using her. Using Sticky.

Zixin might have helped, Tina may have betrayed her, but it was Grandmother. Everything was Grandmother. And for what? For code? For a nascent AI and the profit it would bring? Was that why her parents were dead?

Rage boiled in her stomach.

Vlad stripped the gloves from her hands.

She'd told the old woman, warned her.

The helmet came next, and her hands trembled as she set it carefully on the engine cover.

Gravel crunched under her boots, then pavers clacked. Three steps, four, until the wide, cushioned welcome mat muffled her heels and the big black doors stared back at her. Obsidian, an endless abyss, with nothing but a slight ripple, hands-breadth of cold, electronic awareness at chest height.

The lock-pad.

She pressed her hand to it. A faint glow as the screen read her palm.

Deadbolts snicked within the great portal.

No need for hacks or exploits, no need for Samael, because here she was a Tong. Here she was expected, here she had a role to play, a square to fill on Grandmother's chessboard.

The doors swung open, both of them silently parting.

She stalked through, boots still on, and where they had clacked over the pavers, where the mat had swallowed their anger, here in the great marble-lined foyer, they *cracked*. Thunder in the sleeping house, echoing off the clean dove-grey walls, the tastefully arranged artwork, the twisted bonsai and flowers.

Crack.

Crack.

Crack.

She paused before the twin stairs winding around the cherry tree. Moonlight spilled through the glass overhead casting its grey light over the spindly branches, gilding the slim trunk, catching in the delicate leaves, casting stark shadow over the floor. She paused for a moment, deciding.

Go up to the bedrooms and private spaces on the second floor, or past to the sterile dining room with its showpiece kitchen?

She'd made Grandmother a promise. *'I'll behave like a Tong.'*

A Tong had manners, a Tong would go to the dining room, would wait patiently for Jiang to rouse himself—the old butler alerted the moment she came through the gate—and enquire about her presence at this strange hour. A Tong would politely ignore the butler's hint that a meeting at just this time was most impolite and insist on seeing Grandmother *now*.

She remembered the dead look in Sticky's blackening eyes.

Fuck being a Tong.

She marched up the stairs.

The thunder followed.

Crack, crack, crack.

At the landing, deep-pile carpet swallowed the sound, her boots sinking deep into the rich navy.

Discreetly placed nightlights highlighted the reclaimed oak baseboards and hinted at the pinstriping in the wallpaper, while others shone on the generous spray of roses on the antique sideboard.

Vlad turned left, into the mansion's long east wing. Grandmother's suite was at the end, overlooking the rear garden, the carefully trimmed rose bushes and pond. She didn't think about what she would do when she got there; hadn't decided whether she would barge in, stand over Grandmother in her large silk-covered bed or shake her awake. There was a hundred meters between that thought and her, sideboards lining the hallway, an old hatstand, artwork, flowers, portraits of people long dead. Closed doors. A family lounge, a library and bedroom. A study.

Grandmother's study.

A thin glow creeping from underneath the double doors, coffee from the crack between them.

Vlad stopped.

Voices murmured on the other side.

An older one, commanding.

A younger one answering, deep and familiar. Agreeing. Always *fucking* agreeing.

Anger hit hard, a familiar tide surging up her toes, clenching her hands, pulling a snarl from her lips.

The doors *banged* against the shelves lining the walls either side.

The figures in the leather armchairs jerked, the taller, darker one shooting to his feet, the slighter, older one, gripping the chair arms.

'Ana?' Confusion creased Zixin's brow.

She ignored him, ignored the name—the hated name—on his lips and focused instead on Grandmother as she stalked the room. Three strides across the carpet, past the giant old desk to the half-moon of square leather chairs and the screens spread across the low oak table between.

Shock clouded the old woman's eyes for but a moment before the shutters came down. She opened her mouth—

Vlad interrupted her. 'I warned you.'

Zixin stepped in her path before she breached the chairs. 'Ana—'

She sidestepped him, stopped a half-step in front of Grandmother, leaving no room for the old woman to rise, only to stare up, up, up.

Vlad looked down her nose. 'I told you what would happen if you used me again.'

Confusion, peeking through the ice frosting Grandmother's brow. 'When did I—?'

'Hamish,' she said. 'The rave.'

The old woman's head tilted. 'I don't know a Hamish.'

'Sure you don't, just like you don't know Ru Ping, like you weren't staring out the woman's glasses just two hours ago.' She spun, and there was Zixin, hands out like he didn't know what to do with them, but on his face… Guilt in amongst the surprise still fogging expression. 'But *you* know their names, because who else is going to find those kind of people for the great Tong Shufeng? HR perhaps? Or did TI recently acquire Thugs-R-Us?'

He shook his head, taking a cautious step forward. 'I don't know what you're talking about.'

'Bullshit.'

'Vladana Tong.' Grandmother's voice lashed out, a sharp icy whip. 'Watch your language.'

Vlad spun back, crouched. Now she was the one staring up, and Grandmother was staring down her nose, the cold on her voice radiating from her black eyes. The Empress with her rebellious subject.

Vlad smiled and carefully, deliberately placed her hands on Grandmother's chair arms, leaned in until Grandmother's heady perfume filled her nose and said, very softly, 'Bull. Shit.'

Anger deepened the lines on Grandmother's face, just like it did the frost. 'I remember your promise, child; if I used you again you promised to behave like a Tong. A Tong would not show such disrespect to her elders.'

'I know, but Tongs have too many fucking rules.' Vlad pushed off the chair and stood, and as she took a few steps back, felt the tension in the room lessen. But not for long, her next words would see to that. 'A Scourge is much more effective, so I'll be that. It's what you hired me for, after all.'

'Ana.' Zixin reaching for her. 'I don't know what's going on, but if you just talk—'

'Sticky. Sticky is what's going on,' she said. 'Hamish fucked with Sticky, and now I'm going to fuck with you.' She whipped back to face Grandmother, still in her chair. And did the soft lights make the old woman's face pale or was it watching her machinations come home to roost? 'You should have left me out of it, Grandmother, left me alone to find Ma and Da's killer, or, gods forbid, help.'

'I—' Grandmother tried to push herself out of the chair, forearms wobbling before she fell back against the cushion, complexion another shade of pale.

Zixin was at the old woman's side in a moment, holding a glass of water to her lips.

The old woman pushed it away. 'I don't want you involved in that,' she said.

'Too bad.' Vlad slipped her glasses on, the lenses already connected to her phone and beyond them the computer buried under the floor in the loft. She flipped through files with quick jerks of her fingers, found the one she needed even before she rounded Grandmother's desk and planted the phone against the terminal embedded in the antique wood top. 'Since I was in the car and all.'

'What are you doing?' This from Zixin, coming out of the semicircle of armchairs, suspicion creasing his wide brow.

A vibration against her palm signalled the virus successfully transferred. Another smile, and she enjoyed this one, let satisfaction settle into the corners. 'Being a Scourge and leaving you a present.'

He was coming around the desk, but she was already done, mission accomplished, phone back in her pocket, even as the back of her glasses came alive.

For a moment, as she backed away from the desk, from the chairs and Grandmother—still pale but still commanding—she thought Zixin might come after her, follow her all the way to the door and down the hall. Chase her down the stairs, out the doors, maybe even run down the drive as she gunned Ximisthus's engine. But no, he bent over the desktop, activated the screens and stared at the mess scrolling across them.

She'd unloaded a package to Grandmother's system and every other one connected to it, including TI. Part of the package would keep TI's security and tech departments humming, while the rest transferred data to an off-site server and then to her and after that…

She wouldn't want to be TI's tech department.

'Ana, what did you do?'

The doors were beside her, and she grabbed the handles as she slipped through. 'What a Scourge does best, helping myself.'

The doors *snicked* closed.

32

She shoved the freight elevator's metal grate into the ceiling, the paint-speckled hexagons clanging, and all she could think about was another elevator, Grandmother at her side, the piano music filtering through the speakers and the sour taste of betrayal. Not against her, but *by* her. The heckler in the stands, the one-finger salute.

The taste of being used. Like tonight. Like Hamish had used Sticky, how Grandmother had used Hamish. To get at her.

She'd slammed the heavy metal door shut, kicked Ximisthus's stand down with a little more force, thrown the bike jacket over the couch back with a little more vigour. Ignored it when the black leather landed on the floor instead, an arm knocking a folder full of paper off the coffee table and across the floor.

Ru Ping's ancient USB drive was in one of its pockets, by rights she should be digging through her stash of equally ancient, jerry-rigged adaptors, finding out what was on it. Instead…

She'd stripped off her gloves, kicked off her boots and padded past the kitchen bench, around the dividing shelves and slammed the fuck out of the punching bag.

Sweat stuck the black t-shirt to her back, her ponytail *thwapping* against her sides with every duck and twist as she avoided the return swing. Her feet *shushed* over the practice mat, the dense, black foam cool under her soles, a welcome counterpoint to the heat flushing her cheeks.

No one was meant to get hurt, no one but the people who killed her parents.

The long, black bag swung on its chain, aiming at her face.

Her fist sent the patched, vinyl cylinder on a new trajectory. A skip back and the ball of her foot gave it extra momentum.

Fuck Hamish. Fuck Sticky and Huang Yimo and Ming Li Na putting their noses were they didn't belong, and fuck fucking Tina with her big mouth and the bright idea to recruit a Scourge. Fuck those big old eyes getting under her skin, pulling at old wants, old needs, making her forget what she was there for. What she needed to do.

Fuck—

'I think it's dead.'

Vlad spun. Hands up, adrenalin pumping her blood harder, making her heart race, her breath shorter, eyes locking on the figure—

A big, black shadow coming at her from the side.

The punching bag got its revenge, hitting her with all the force of the hundred kilos of sand stuffed in it.

Vlad staggered, hit the mat on her side.

No pain, shock holding her to the spot, eyes locked on the pixie leaning against the metal shelves, a bright packet of instant noodles in her hand.

Tina broke a piece off, lifted to her bright pink lips. Crunched.

Vlad stared.

Tina stared back.

The mat was getting cold, the chill loft freezing the sweat on her back, the long, damp sleeves of her t-shirt leeching body heat along with it, and still she lay there, half on her back, propped on one elbow.

Another rustle of bright plastic. Another crunch.

'You gonna stay there all day, bitch, or are you gonna get me some beer?' Tina said around a mouthful of dry noodles.

'What are you doing here?'

'Knitting.' *Crunch.*

Vlad got to her knees, ducked as the bag continued to swing above—the arcs smaller now, but still enough to set her ears ringing if she wasn't careful.

'No one knows about this place.' No one *should* know about the loft. She'd bought it with cash after all, purchased it through a shell company, her name buried under layers of encryption and contracts. Legal, barely.

'Then you got a problem.' Another crunch, and still those green eyes pinned to Vlad's.

'How'd you find it?'

Rustle. Crunch. 'Because I'm me.'

'You're not that good.' Vlad got her feet.

A grin, more teeth than actual smile. 'Shit changes.'

'Not that much.'

The grin got wider, the look in the eyes sharper. 'Girl's gotta have secrets.'

'I'll find out.'

'Knock yourself out while I get the beer.' Tina pushed off the shelves and disappeared around the other side.

Vlad stared at the air where Tina had been and wondered how she hadn't heard the sharp clack of the shorter woman's heels, why the alarms hadn't gone off when she got in the freight elevator or started up the old emergency stairs. How the fuck she'd found the hidden control panel, buried behind all that broken circuitry, or gotten through the front door.

The fridge door *shhhuckking* open. A rattle of bottles and tins followed by a curse floated over the shelves before the small door was slammed closed.

'You've gotta be fucking kidding me.' Angry *snap snap snap* of heels on concrete. The red explosion of Tina's hair popping around the corner, freckles standing out against pale skin. 'Bitch, you got no fucking beer?'

Vlad didn't move, not a muscle, barely even breathed as scenarios and possibilities churned through her brain. Tina'd had the smarts but no patience for computers or code or the fine intricacies of the nets in university, all that vast, razor-sharp intelligence had been put to dissecting the incomprehensible morass of the people around her. A quick, agile tongue and the ability to twist her fellow students into knots, even the teachers hadn't been spared, not even Vlad. Slipping under her guard and refusing to let go. Like a tick.

So how had Kristina Mortiz, who wouldn't know one end of a soldering iron from the other, not just masqueraded as Eun-ji—information broker and hacker—but found the loft?

How?

A memory of Huang Yimo at the kitchen bench, playing with code.

Tina was still frowning at her, mouth a straight line, pale brow furrowed. 'Beer? Why don't you have beer, bitch?'

Vlad shook herself out of the moment, thoughts still whirring. 'I don't drink.'

A scoff, Tina rolling green eyes before she stuck her hand down the neck of her open shirt and came back out with her phone. 'Right, and I'm the Crown Princess of Fucking England.' Pink fingernails flew over the screen.

'What are you doing?'

Another eye roll. 'Ordering beer.'

Vlad crossed the three metres of space between them in a blink, snatching the plastic wedge from Tina's hand. 'No.'

Tina snatched moved to snatch it back. 'Fuck, yes. This is gonna be a fucking beer conversation.'

Vlad lifted the phone high, out of the shorter woman's reach.

'Fucking giraffe, give me the phone.'

Vlad's thumb scrambling over the face of the plastic, already into the settings, the lock code. Turning the screen just enough to catch Tina's furious scowl. Twisted it back as the settings unlocked—

A fist in her gut, pushing air out her diaphragm. Enough to make her hunch, but she still had breath, still had a few seconds before—

Pain, a shot of lightning all the way from her instep to the back of her knee.

Hunching over the hurt was instinctive, the hand holding the phone coming down—

Tina grabbed it, quick as the dragon embroidered on DKZero's uniforms, held it up, stabbing at the blank, unresponsive surface.

While she was occupied, Vlad hobbled around the other side of the shelves, slowly putting more weight on her right foot. It didn't scream at her and she snuck a look at the sharp-heels on Tina's boots. The pixie must have pulled her stomp, or they'd be bones grinding or blood or something, but when she looked down, Vlad only saw an angry red square on the top of her right foot.

Those same boots *cracked* behind her.

She spun, flipping the long tail of her braid out of grabbing range just as Tina aimed another shot at her gut.

It missed, but Tina's angry glare didn't. 'Unlock my phone.' She shoved the device in Vlad's face.

'No.' She pushed the phone aside. 'How'd you get Huang Yimo to help you?'

Because that was the only reasonable explanation; Tina had help, actual talent backing her up. More reasonable than her one-time best friend suddenly developing the kind of skills Eun-ji was selling. The only way she could've found her way into Vlad's space.

'What?' Confusion wrinkled Tina's freckled nose. Was it real or was it those "social" skills Tina was so proud of? Vlad didn't know.

Had she ever known? Had Tina been Grandmother's plant all along, reporting all those midnight conversations, the secrets whispered between bed curtains?

Vlad backed up, slipping around the other side of the bench, put the metre of cold, worn steel between them. 'How'd you find me, Tina?'

'I followed you.'

'No, you didn't; I would have known.' The algos and sensors in her gear would have picked up a tail or a tracker. She was sure of it.

'Well, I did, so clearly—' Tina leaned over the bench, the high top hitting her just below the ribs. '—you missed me. Now—' she slid the dead phone over the metal '—unlock my phone.'

Vlad pushed it back. 'I don't believe you.'

A strangled laugh. '*You're* the one who fucked the phone, so clearly—'

'Not about the phone. There is no way *you* could have made that patch all on your own, Eun-ji.'

'Who says I did?'

'You.'

'When?'

'I—' Except Eun-ji hadn't said any such thing. 'How'd you get Huang Yimo to help you?'

'What makes you think...?'

Vlad tilted her head. 'Third semester.' Their first year at university Tina had tried to make her own macro virus, an effort so crude it hadn't even triggered the network's virus filters. Half the computers in their dorm had fried.

The redhead flushed, an ugly, splotchy red from her cheekbones and down her neck. 'I know people.'

Vlad hit the bench. 'How?' She said again, louder this time, the demand bouncing off ceiling and walls, echoing in the loft.

Tina flinched, and now another emotion dislodged the anger on her brow, widened her eyes and robbed her cheeks of that flush. 'Why does it matter?'

'Because she knows where I live, what I—' Vlad cut herself off.

'What you what? You're a Scourge, aren't you? Big deal,

thousands of Scourges out there doing bigger, badder things than you.' Tina levered herself up on the bench, meeting Vlad over the scratched old metal. 'It's why I chose you.'

Vlad sneered. 'You didn't choose…'

But Tina was smiling, a satisfied cat-with-the-cream smile as she dropped back to the floor. 'Oh, babe, we didn't just chose you, we hunted you down and pinned you to the fucking logon screen.'

Arms crossed under breasts, hip cocked as the cat smile became a smirk.

'Not your grandmother, not Yu Zixin, but us: me, Huang Yimo, Sticky and Ming Li Na, not so much Lu Chen. You were long-listed, short-listed, vetted and wooed, and now here we are.' She gestured from Vlad's head to her toes. 'And fuck, I've been kicking myself ever since.'

Vlad gaped at her.

'You know you're really screwing up our plans, right? Getting a Scourge on the team was meant to get TI off our backs but instead—' Tina's hand went into the air. 'Tong Shufeng is one canny old witch and you—' A diamanté nail stabbed the air, holding Vlad in place as Tina stalked around the bench. 'You are an epic pain in my arse, and if I'd fucking *known* it was you under Samael's hood…'

The shorter woman was in Vlad's space now, that finger still holding her captive. 'Fuck, it probably wouldn't have changed a thing, except I would have *known* how much trouble you were. And fuck, bitch, you are *so* much trouble.'

A growl slipped through Tina's lips before, quick as lightning, she smacked a kiss on Vlad. 'But I love you, I do. Tell myself so every time you give me a fucking ulcer. Like now.'

Vlad stared, the anger, the betrayal taken out of her. Gone. Tina's words a potion thrown in her face leaving her mind blank, thoughts confused.

'You work for TI…' came off her lips.

A snort, Tina leaning against the bench, crossing one spike-heeled boot over the other, amusement all over her freckled face. 'Tong Shufeng *wishes* I work for her. I work for the team—' there was extra emphasis on the last word, a seriousness in the big brown eyes. 'Even if it is your boy Yu Zixin paying my wages.'

Another beat, wind rattling the giant, mullioned windows, the ancient neon on the factory next door spluttering across the floor—blue, white, red—somewhere distant a van shining through the alleyways and closer in, the fridge humming under the bench. And amongst all that, Vlad staring at the woman she'd once considered a sister and now… and now…

'The team needs you, Ana.' Overhead flouros sparked off Tina's rings, drawing Vlad's attention to the tight grip on her arms. 'We get to the league finals, stir up enough fan support and keep the sponsors rolling in, just to keep TI interested in NuGet for another year and quash the VisionM deal.'

'You're using me.'

Tina exploding forward, slapping palms on the bench. 'Of course we're using you. Your *grandmother's* using you, fucking Yu Zixin is using you, just like you're using them.'

Vlad stilled. What did Tina know, what had Huang Yimo and the others dug out of her past?

Carefully, so the ice in her veins wouldn't crack, Vlad straightened. 'What do you know?'

Tina's gaze narrowed. 'What should I know?'

Dust and the stale cardboard smell of expired instant ramen wrapped around Vlad, along with the dread. 'Don't fuck with me, Tina.'

The red head shook, riotous curls tumbling over her forehead. 'I'm not fucking with anybody.' A head tilt, comprehension lighting her eyes. 'You found out who killed your parents, that's why you ditched me five years ago.'

Vlad pushed away from the bench. Half-hobbled to the couch but didn't sit, just stood there, looking without seeing the papers spread across the fat rectangular coffee table, the ramen wrappers and water bottles.

Boots coming round the bench, then Tina in her space, the pixie commanding despite having to tilt her head back to meet Vlad's gaze. 'Are you going after them, Ana?' Tina's face was serious, dark brows drawn over her eyes, the joy and fire in her face dampened by concern.

Vlad turned away. Unable to look at it. 'I don't know what you—'

'Bullshit.'

A small, perfectly manicured hand yanked Vlad back around, and those dark eyes pinned her to the polished concrete.

'You're talking to *me*, bitch. The one who held your hair every time you got sick after a driving lesson, the one who stayed with you through all the nightmares, the shoulder you cried on after Yu Zixin fucked you over.' The shorter got up on her tiptoes, even as she griped Vlad's collar with her other hand and pulled her down. 'You can't bullshit me; I've seen everything you've got and then some. So, give it.'

Tina yanked, and Vlad was left with the choice to sit or lay her best friend out on the cold, concrete floor.

She sat, hard, the couch swallowing her whole, the old leather folding around her like silk, throwing up the dusty scent of disuse. She frowned up at Tina, meeting the dark, implacable eyes with her own.

Her grandmother's voice whispered through her brain. *Never let them see you bleed.* Except that didn't seem right at that moment, didn't feel like she was bleeding.

Yet.

Tina remained standing a moment longer, arms crossed over her abundant chest, feet braced like she was preparing to shove Vlad back down if she twitched the wrong way.

Vlad relaxed into the cushions, consciously unclenching her fists.

Tina nodded. 'That's better,' she said, and sat on the other end of the couch, kicking her heels off and tucking her feet up under her. She stared. Harder now, it seemed, than before. 'I want every fucking gritty detail, or so help me Lord, I'm gonna wipe the floor with your pretty face.'

Vlad looked away. 'Why?'

A cushion hit her in the side of her head.

She snapped her attention back to Tina. The glare was back, and this time there was real anger behind it, real—

Vlad flinched, went to look away and... didn't. Held herself back so that only her eyes moved, gaze scooting past Tina's cheekbone, the wild wisps of red hair, to the old metal shelving beyond. Not because she feared another cushion in the face but because of what she'd seen there, the hurt under the anger.

'You fucking know why,' Tina said, and there was the hurt again, the high, reedy thread of betrayal amongst the fire.

'I...' Vlad trailed off, the single word echoing in the giant concrete cavern—

'You what?' Tina jerked forward, fury vibrated through her body. 'You found out your mom was murdered and you didn't think I'd understand? Decided to make the fuckers pay and thought I wouldn't approve? Maybe you wanted to hide off on some tragic fucking revenge plan all on you're pretty little lonesome, but don't—' And here Tina scooted closer, her little hands balled into fists, the kind of anger that tore down mountains, tightening her face, pressing Vlad into the couch corner. 'Don't you fucking tell me you were protecting me, that you up and disappeared for my own. Fucking. Good.'

One of those sharp fingers stabbed Vlad in the face.

'Don't you fucking dare,' Tina whispered.

'I—'

'Don't.'

Vlad snapped her mouth closed.

Tina was close enough she could smell the salty noodles on the other woman's breath.

They stared at each other. One heartbeat became two, then four, then five and ten, before Tina shrunk back into her own corner.

'So,' Tina said. 'Spill.'

Vlad looked past Tina, stared through the shelving behind—the noodle packets, the old microwave and mismatched glasses—to the lone bucket chair in front of the window.

There was so much, and the words... She didn't know how to summon them, didn't know if she could or if all the planning, all the late nights and wild leads, the suspects and suspicions, the fear and pain and the nightmares, would clog up in her chest and choke her to death. She only knew that Tina was there, brown eyes boring through her brain, that hurt a diamond-tipped drill leading the way.

Vlad caught her lip between her teeth. Chewed it before rising. 'It's easier if I show you.'

<⊙>

The spiderweb crawled across the window. The old, mullioned glass was dark, not a hint of the outside world showing through the blackout film. The bucket chair was empty, a barrier between them and it.

Tina stood with one arm wrapped around her chest, the other resting on it, stabbing the pictures with a dark pink nail. 'So, Oily Face killed your parents because...?'

'Something Ma had developed, a program. I think...'

'You think what?'

She shook her head, the speculation sticking on her tongue. 'I don't know.'

'Bullshit.' Tina stared at her, the laughing face a stoney mask of don't-fuck-with-me. 'You know, or you wouldn't have said anything.'

Vlad looked away, crossing her own arms, as if that would keep Tina's laser eyes from seeing right through her. *That* was why she'd left, not just to protect her best friend, but because she didn't want Tina to see what came next.

She took a breath. 'I think it's Grandmother.'

'*Your* grandmother?' Disbelief dripped from Tina's tongue. 'Tong Shufeng, matriarch and defender of the clan? The woman even God fears? Why?'

A touch and the data from the cafe flowed from her watch to the mainframe hidden under the floor. Over the window, the web reflowed, faces shifting – Ru Ping to the top of the tertiary ring, a line of light connecting her to Zixin. His connection to Grandmother grew stronger, even as the space around the old woman filled with info tiles, some shifting from other parts of the matrix, new ones popping into existence.

Vlad selected Ru Ping and the other woman's stoic features filled the screen. 'I put a tracker on one of Oily Face's heavies.' A swipe of fingers and a world map overlaid the web, a trail of data packets creating its own constellation. 'It lead me here—' The map zoomed on the internet cafe. '—where an unpleasant little easter egg was waiting for me.'

Tina whistled. 'Did it get you?'

'Almost.' Vlad's smile was more snarl. 'But they left something behind too.' And now she exploded the tile, the one that made her stomach curdle, and lit the ugly, angry thing in her middle.

The virus sat in the middle of the screen, slowly twisting in and under itself. On top of it, a string of letters and numbers sat in its own little box, part IP address, part DNA.

Tina stared at it for a few moments before her nose scrunched and she shrugged. 'Okay, I give in. What's that?'

Vlad smirked at her. 'Aren't you meant to be a System genius or something?'

Tina gave her the bird. 'Shove it, bitch. Just tell me.'

'It's a virus designed to sniff out a player IP, the direct line into a player's brain.'

Tina stilled. 'The neural link,' she finally said. Then… 'Which only works in the new gen VR chairs, which aren't even on the market yet, let alone a crummy internet cafe on the coast. Even if the virus worked its way into your watch, your wearables aren't connected to DKZero's systems, so why would anyone…' Suspicion turned the dark brown gaze sharp, as the red head tilted sideways. 'Something you want to explain?'

It was Vlad's turn to still before she uncrossed her arms and stepped away, just two steps, a little more distance between herself and Tina's sharp eyes. Not that it did any good.

Tina followed, brows coming down over her freckled nose. 'Vlad.' There was warning in her voice.

'The neural jack is old tech,' Vlad finally said.

'What do you mean? The FDA only approved it six months ago. That's hardly…' She petered off, mouth dropping a little, eyes going wide before her lips stretched in what might have been a smile, if there were any humour in it. 'But I'm talking to a Scourge, of course it's old tech to you. Which explains the EMT report…' Tina's held tilted the other way. 'And the lag.' Tina shoved Vlad in the chest, pushing her back a step. 'Fuck, woman, are you *trying* to scramble your brains?'

'I have it covered.'

'Fuck you do.' Tina in her face. 'I haven't just seen that report, bitch, I had a nice lady come up to me and *explain* it, along with a league official. Do you know how much talking I had to do to keep your arse out of hospital? Fnatic's Cheeva is *still* skull soup and he only had prescription pills in his system, not whatever shit Scourges take.'

'I'm fine.'

'Fucking fine my arse.'

'Do you want to know what I found out or what?'

Tina stabbed her sharp, sparkly nail in Vlad's nose. 'This conversation isn't over, bitch, but for now…' She crossed her arms and hitched her hip on the bench. 'So, the question then is, why would anyone want a direct line to *your* brain?'

'Why does any hacker want access?' Vlad leaned forward. 'To

find out what's inside.'

'And your mom's project is inside yours.' Tina nodded. 'Why wouldn't your grandmother just ask you? This…' She gestured to the names and faces spread across the glass. 'This is a little dramatic, even for Tong Shufeng.'

Vlad shook her head. 'I don't know.'

'Can a brain even be hacked?'

'Don't know.'

'There's a lot you don't know, for a Scourge.'

Vlad didn't answer, just stared at the spiderweb. Tina was right, there was a lot she didn't know, too many holes in things she thought were facts. The white field, the player address, Grandmother.

Tina broke the silence. 'What are you going to do about Sticky?'

'Nothing.'

'That's not going to work, Ana. You know it's not. This Hamish guy broke Sticky's nose, so even if Sticky doesn't want to know what you were doing at the rave, the others will.' Silence. 'You should tell them.'

'No.'

'They can help.'

'*No*,' and this time she said it harder, louder, so it echoed off the concrete ceiling.

'Why not?' Tina shuffled in close, peering up while Vlad kept her focus over Tina's explosion of red hair, at the spiderweb across the windows. 'Are you afraid?'

Vlad almost laughed, the unexpected humour pulling her gaze down. 'Of what?'

A mistake, Tina's face was serious, eyes piercing. 'I don't know, you tell me.'

She looked away, to the spiderweb. Her arms clamped tight against the warm, squirmy thing in her middle, hand closing over the uneven scars trailing down her right arm, hidden under the long-sleeved top.

Silence and then... 'This is my thing, Tina. My parents, my scars. My retribution. I don't need help.' She turned back to her best friend, and said, clear and sharp, 'I don't want it.'

Tina stared back. Seconds passed, the warehouse district's old broken neon flickering outside the mullioned windows, red and yellow casting their shadows across the concrete, electricity humming in the conduits above.

Tina lifted herself up on her toes, pointed heels leaving the floor, until she was close enough for Vlad to smell the ramen on her breath. 'Too bad,' Tina said. 'I know, Sticky knows, soon enough the others will too. No matter what kind of Scourge magic you have, you can't make us un-know it.'

For a beat, they stared at each other, hazel eyes to deepest brown, neither blinking, neither willing to look away.

Vlad hissed and broke the staring contest first.

Tina's heels hit the floor and she backed up a step, victory in every sharp *click*. 'This is how it's gonna go, Ana.' The smaller woman lifted her chin, arms crossed, legs braced, every picture the shark-eating businesswoman.

Grandmother would approve.

'I'll keep the others off your back, but you tell me *everything*,' Tina said. 'All the time, or I will rain the good Lord's fury down on you like the cunning little bitch you are. And if *that* isn't enough—' Tina stabbed Vlad in the chest with a pointed pink nail, her voice getting low. 'So help me Lord, if His fury isn't enough, there's always your grandmother.'

33

There were lights on in the DKZero mansion, blazing from the arrow-slit windows either side of the big red door, warm yellow and the pop and flicker of the neon *POW!* in the corridor. Ximisthus idled on the apron outside, headlights low, green rims casting a sickly glow over the blacktop.

She sat there for a good long while as chill night and moisture-laden smog eddied around her before she guided Ximisthus around the corner to the underground garage. The white Ducati was there, the Scrambler next to it, the bike cover crumpled on the concrete beside. Mystery solved.

Ximisthus slid in beside the apocalyptic machine, smooth, silent, just like the doors on the elevator, just like her expression reflected in the shiny metal.

Going up a single floor had never taken so long.

There was no one in the hallway under the second floor when she stepped out, no one in the big open living area. No voices murmuring in the kitchen. No accusing eyes watching her climb the stairs, no pointed fingers or curses yelled as she walked to her room, no one waiting for her beyond the purple door.

Just the lights, buttery warm and neon, the statues standing guard. Deadspace, Rabbit, Sticky.

Sticky with blood dribbling over his lip, the sound he made—

She slipped into her room but left her door open a fraction, enough for the low murmur of conversation or the *shuffle-thud* of slippers on the landing to filter through the gap.

Not because she cared, because she didn't. No, she had the Cube out, the arrow-shaped skull emblazoned on its side naked for the whole world to see, light spilling across the ceiling. She wanted a warning in case some overly-suspicious arse decided to *talk*. Confront the Scourge, demand answers.

A little bit of her even believed that was why.

No one knocked on her door though, although she heard someone out there—maybe Lu Chen, maybe Ming Li Na?—stopped scrolling through her screens and stared at the crack, the shadow blocking the yellow and blue neon outside. She didn't move, barely breathed as she waited, and wondered, only half-caring about the Cube, how she'd explain the VR sleeve or the archaic assemblage of adaptors spread across the desk...

There was no need. The shadow moved, shoes whispered on concrete, a door *snicked* shut, leaving just the neon to filter through the tiny gap between door and wall.

She stared at it a half-minute longer but nothing changed except, perhaps, for the tiny warm spot in her middle dying.

Except for that.

It didn't matter though.

She had data to trawl, not just that mined from Grandmother's systems, but Ru Ping's ancient USB. The USB was a lodestone in her pocket, and she shoved into the skull-shaped adaptor's mouth.

This was how she wanted it, how she *needed* it. Alone was how Vlad had started and alone was how she'd finish.

The lights across the ceiling flickered.

The Cube still slow, even after she'd purged the cloud whale. Had she got it all? The thought nagged at her, no matter how many times she scoured the Cube's logs, looking for any hint of the program, always coming up empty.

Now, she needed to know what was on the Ru Ping's ancient USB.

The drive waiting in the Cube's quarantine zone: *RaZIeL.*

No tension pulling her spine straight from that one, none at all.

Open the drive.

A text file, no name. Size, 325kb. Date created: 13 September 2026. A Monday. She didn't even need to look that one up, the knowledge sat in the back of her head. Just like the knowledge that it'd been raining, a light drizzle that persisted throughout the day and into the night, making the roads slick and obscuring sight. It'd done nothing to put out the flames that raced across the Bentley's hood.

Vlad's hand shook as she reached for the rectangular icon and pushed it open.

Encrypted text—letters and numbers jumbled together, broken up with forward slashes and plus signs—spread across the screen. Pages of it. Not a single comprehensible word or timestamp.

For a moment, she was mad, her fingers clenched and the sick twist in her gut that'd formed when she saw the date, grew hot. But why had she expected Grandmother to make it easier for her? Vlad wouldn't have, Vlad would have made Grandmother work for it, if only to keep the other on the hook long enough for whatever trojan she'd hidden on the drive to do its work.

She forced her fingers to relax, swallowed against the burning in her stomach, the twist lower down, and breathed. In one, out two.

'Run decryption,' she said.

A flat *beep* from the Cube.

A progress bar, done before the twist had time to become a knot. Easy. A little too easy.

Most of the file still a garbled mess but there, on its own little line, one word, one name in the midst of the chaos.

Zixin.

<⊙>

Warm hands down her arms, sandalwood in her nose, champagne still fizzing on her tongue and the gentle twitter of birds spreading through the sunlight spilling across the dorm room's dark floor.

She sighed and snuggled deeper into the dream, not wanting it to end but knowing it had to. The moment couldn't last, not even in this half-awake state on the edge of memory and wishful thinking. But still... she burrowed deeper into the warmth at her back, twisted her head and found the soft spot under his chin.

A decidedly unmanly squeak followed by a laugh.

'Your nose is cold,' he said.

Dream that line, not memory the awake-part of her noted even as the still-dreaming part pushed it away and breathed deep of the warm earthiness and sweat of skin.

'You're not,' she said. Another dream line, she hadn't said that the first time, as he hadn't.

Memory-him had said other words, carelessly she'd thought then, a slip of the tongue shining truth on the lies, but now... Now she wasn't so sure. Now, perhaps, if *her* words had been different, if they'd been about chill noses and warm necks, things would be different. *She* would be different.

And that was the real lie, the real dream amongst the fancies that haunted her nights. She was always going to be this, ever since flames ate her parents, the only difference might have been whether or not she was alone.

Dream-him laughed, a quiet chuff deep in his throat. His arms slipped around her middle.

'We could be warmer.' Lips against her forehead, her cheek, her closed eyes.

'We could,' she whispered as those lips drew closer to hers. 'But we won't.'

'Why?'

'Because that's not how this memory goes.'

He stilled, those lips hovering at the corner of her mouth, arms tight around her middle, holding her close.

She breathed him in. The dream might be better than memory, but she wouldn't deceive herself. *Couldn't* deceive herself.

'What do you mean?' he said. There was worry in his words, a chill to the warmth on his breath. The coming dawn.

'You know what I mean.'

'No,' he said. 'I don't.' She felt him lean back, his chest straightening, and knew without opening her eyes, he was peering down at her; her head flopped against his shoulder, a not-so-small part of her stubbornly clinging to the comfortable dream.

Just a moment more. A second, a minute, an hour before history caught up and the dream shredded, leaving her cold and alone.

Always alone.

No one can see you bleed if you're alone.

'Ana,' he said. 'Look at me.'

She shook her head. She wasn't ready yet.

A little shake, the mattress bouncing underneath, doona soft under her thighs, softer throw over her legs. And that was different too, because in memory they'd been on the saggy green couch squashed into the corner of her dorm between the tiny kitchenette and the desks with the bunk beds over the top. This was nicer. Gave her room to stretch out without that old spring digging into her thigh.

'Ana,' he said again, firmer, like the way he jiggled her, hands no longer around her waist but cupping her shoulders, the fingers clamping her biceps, almost painful.

And that wasn't nice, was from memory but disjointed, too early in the scene. He had to say the words first and then she had to feel betrayal, the sharp bitter sting had robbed her voice before it threw her off the couch and into the middle of the room. The words had come then, rushing up from her belly, hot and angry. Bewildered even. She'd been bleeding, bleeding all over the place, and still... still his betrayal hadn't been much of a surprise, hadn't even been the thing that cut the deepest, because she'd known, always known that he was Grandmother's creature. Only in her fancies had Xin'er belonged to her.

Only in her fancies did he remain there.

After the shouting, Xin'er would get off the couch, clasp her shoulders like he did now in the dream, and deliver the final words, the ones that severed the tiny thread of hope still holding him to her.

'Ana, the old woman has a plan.'

The old woman has a plan. The old woman has a plan and in it, Ana was a pawn and Ma obliterated from the family tree.

And even as she'd seen Grandmother in Xin'er's eyes, she'd felt the old woman rising through her bones, heard her voice whispering, *Never let them see you bleed,* felt the ice pour through her soul.

In the years since, hadn't she laughed at that, Grandmother protecting her even as the old woman hurt her, stealing Zixin and throwing a shield around her at the same time.

Her heart might have broken that day, but she'd built it up again, stronger, harder. Colder.

Except for moments like now. When she dreamed.

'Ana.' There was no warmth in Zixin's words now, memory rearranging itself again, speeding forward to the moment that hurt most. Except they were still on the couch-bed, and she still rested her head against his shoulder and breathed in his scent. 'Where do you think you are?'

She frowned, because wasn't that stupid, unless...? But no, this was dream-memory, wishful thinking mixed with reality, and so she answered, even as doubt slithered through her gut. 'The dorm.'

A heartbeat of silence, those hands digging a little harder into her flesh. 'Which dorm?'

The doubt grew, became a snake weaving an icy trail through her soul. She opened her eyes a slither, stared into those dark bronze ones and thought that his fringe was shorter than it should be, swept upward instead of flopping into his eyes. 'My dorm,' she said, then added, 'At university.'

He nodded. 'In Germany.' He pressed lips to her forehead. 'You should wake up now.'

'I know.' A sigh. She closed her eyes. 'But I don't want to.'

Those hands slipped from her shoulders to her waist, drawing her against his chest. 'You're already part way there.'

'I am?'

'Yes.'

'Is that why we're not arguing?'

'Mm-hmm.'

'That's nice.'

'It is, but you still have to wake up.'

'Why?'

Silence. Then... 'Because we're not in Germany.'

She stilled but the snake in her gut didn't, finding its way under her ribcage, toward her heart. 'We're not?'

Lips moving against her brow as he shook his head. 'No.'

The snake slithered behind her lungs, shortened her breath. 'Where are we?'

'Open your eyes, and you'll know.'

'If I do that... I'll hate you.' She wasn't ready to hate him again, wasn't ready to feel and do all the things that came with it. The plans and counter-plans, the late nights and acid in her belly. Wasn't ready to be on her own, truly on her own. Didn't want the real world to intrude on this slice of what-might-have-been.

'You don't have to hate me,' he said. 'You can choose to love me instead.'

'You're helping Grandmother.' *And Grandmother hurt Sticky.*

'I am, but I'm doing it for you.'

Now, she did open her eyes, hazel meeting bronze, the dream washing away even as the snake poised to strike.

She spoke, the words coming out without the anger of memory, without the cold. 'How is that helping me?'

He sighed, pulled back a little. 'There are things you don't know.'

She pushed out of his arms, sat straight and twisted—seeing now not the dorm of memory, but the smooth, off-white walls of her room at DKZero, the plain white covers of her bed, the pillows mounded against the headrest, the morning sun pushing against the closed blinds. And Zixin, leaning against the headboard, not in one of his expensive, stylish sweaters or tailored slacks, but tracksuit pants and an old, stained tee, feet bare, hair mused, staring at her with tired eyes. No longer looking quite so much Grandmother's creature.

In her chest, the snake loosened its grip.

She frowned. 'So tell me.'

'I can't.'

'You can. Just open your mouth; say the words.'

'I made a promise.'

'Is it more important than me?'

A heartbeat of staring. The snake tensing again, pulling back and—

'No,' he said. 'Nothing's more important than you.'

She almost smiled. Didn't. 'So?'

'So.'

More staring and Vlad became conscious of her own bare feet, the sleep tights and the old, long-sleeved sleep top with its baggy neck that didn't quite cover the scars topping her shoulder. And as she pulled it up, watched Zixin watch her, the other thought that came into her mind was why he was in her room, on her bed, holding her in her sleep. As that thought crystallised, hardened, it brought anger with it, pushing out the dream's warmth.

A glance to the desk, to the mess of cables and adaptors, the Cube—silent and dark—the skull, missing the sharp silver exclamation of Ru Ping's USB.

'Grandmother's backing out of the deal,' she said.

His face hardened. 'You're the one who broke the deal. Look, whatever you think she's done—'

'I *know* what she's done, do you?'

The Zixin she'd known, she'd loved, wouldn't know, couldn't possibly be part of the machinations that killed her parents, and yet…

The name on the flash drive.

Hope died.

She leaned back.

'If you have something to tell me, do it now,' she said, Grandmother's frost in her voice. 'Before I get mad.'

He looked away, a curse on his lips, frustration on his face. 'You're always mad, Ana.'

She shuffled off the bed. 'I have a right to be.'

'Ana—'

She rounded on him. 'You're here, in my room like you have the right.'

'You were having a nightmare—'

'I always have nightmares, that's what my life is. One nightmare after the other.'

He buried his head in his hands, running them through his not-quite-long-enough fringe. 'You exaggerate.'

'Do I?' Sarcasm dripped from her tongue.

'Yes!' His head snapped upwards. 'Your life is not a fucking nightmare!'

'And how would you know that? You haven't exactly been around.'

He was on the bed one second, on his feet the next, in her space, breathing her air. 'You're the one who threw me out.'

She stood on her toes and sneered in his face. 'It was you who chose Grandmother and TI over me.'

He grabbed her shoulders. 'Why can't I have both?'

She threw him off. 'You know why.'

He made to grab again, she smacked his hands away.

'Damnit it, Ana. I'm trying to help.'

'By sneaking into my room? By *lying* to me?' She shoved both hands into his chest, pushed him back a few steps. 'How does that help, Xin'er? How is that not creepy as fuck?'

'It just...'

'Just what?'

'I need to help you find the person who killed your parents.'

Vlad stopped cold. Truth? Her attention flicked to the desk, the skull with its missing USB. Or was he trying to disarm her, were the drive and the embrace a ploy to distract? Get her mad so she'd miss whatever worm Zixin slipped into her system? He'd had enough time, could have plugged anything in, switched out a cable, an adaptor, inserted a bug in any part of her setup. Something, anything to recover the mess she'd made of Grandmother's system.

It's what she would have done.

Brave of him to try playing her at her own game.

The line from Ru Ping's encrypted file flashed in front of her. '*Need* to help?' Her chin lifted. 'Why? Because of Grandmother?' Or guilt, she wanted to add but didn't.

He looked away, deep bronze eyes shifting just an inch. 'No.'

''Then why?'

'Does it matter?'

She closed distance; a step forward. 'Yes.' *What did you do, Zixin?* The question wanted to follow, but she kept it behind her teeth. *Why is your name on Ru Ping's drive? What did you have to do with the accident? Tell me!*

She wanted to shake him, to yell, to scream, but kept herself still, tried not to vibrate on the spot and prayed the effort didn't show on her face.

His mouth tightened, lips pulling down at the corners even as a furrow dug into his brows.

A second, two, three. They ticked by, stretching her nerves taut, whitening her knuckles, boiling the acid her stomach, until finally, Zixin turned and reached for the door.

Surprise, disappointment, frustration, anger, they all rushed through her in an instant, and she'd taken two steps, grabbed his shirt sleeve before she thought it. 'Zixin?' The softness in her voice a revelation even to herself.

He paused, gaze on the fingers tugging at his sleeve. 'I can't tell you.'

Those fingers tightening, knuckles turning white. 'Why?'

He shook his head. 'I just can't.'

Hand dropping, anger swallowed surprise and disappointment, turning the softness cold. She retreated, chin rising again along with Grandmother's steel. 'Then why are you really here, Yu Zixin?'

He met her gaze, even as his hand found the doorknob. 'I miss you.'

'I don't miss you.' Except she did, all the time. In her dreams.

His smile was sad. 'I know.' And he left.

34

'Following the hospitalisation of pro-Annihilation star Cheeva, rumours continue to spread about the gamer's drug use.

'Meanwhile, industry leaders speculate on the dangers of NuGet's next generation VR units. With a record number of cancelled preorders and disappointing sales figures on top of the controversy surrounding NuGet's Chief Financial Officer, Lu Pang, how long can the company hold out against repeated takeover bids by industry titans, TI and VisionM?'

<⊙>

// ...jacks right into your brain, that can't be safe.

// Don't Scourges use that tech?

// Yeah, but dude, do you really want to trust them? I mean, who knows how many of them have scrambled-egg brains.

// LOL. Scrambled-egg brains.

<⊙>

Vlad made it off the stage, away from the bright lights and screaming fans, even managed to push the stall door closed before she threw up. Rotten-citrus wrapped around her brainstem, sweet and sharp, cutting into her ears, her eyes, digging nails into her spleen, even as it chased the sour tang of vomit from her tongue.

Bile and carrot flecks splashed into the toilet, lag offering her trajectories and threat assessments, idly noting the partially-digested pill she'd somehow dry-swallowed, despite the cotton in her mouth. A useless effort now, what with it floating in the toilet bowl.

Another heave, another torrent of bile. Her hooded jacket too heavy, too hot, long braid sticking to her nape, finer hairs to her clammy brow, but her hands clasped to the cool porcelain and there was no time to wriggle out of it, because the next heave was coming and—

She didn't hear the door open—blood roaring in her ears, bile hitting water—but the edge brushed against her back, pulling her coat sideways. The black wool gone, a bit of heavenly coolness along her side. The hood pulled back, a gentle hand on her forehead.

Vlad finished heaving, leaned into the hand; the game, the lag, the nausea left her drained and the hand was cool and soft and welcoming, a balm against the pounding inside her skull.

'Get Tina.' Ming Li Na, talking not to Vlad but someone else.

Huang Yimo, she guessed, from the soft *snick* of sneakers on the tile floor and the half-remembered "Women" sign on the heavy, black door.

Seconds passed, or was it minutes? Lag wouldn't tell her, was a bitch like that, refusing to give up its secrets. No, not lag. Lag was all in her head, a failure to separate reality from the System, Grandmother was the bitch, pulling the strings, she should—

Another heave interrupted the thought.

'What's going on—?' Tina's voice, cutting off as her heels *clacked* to a stop. 'Well, shit.'

And then a second presence at her back and, even with her head hanging over the bowl and lag playing tricks with her eyes, the cubicle was starting to feel small. Very, very small.

Tina's small hand on her shoulder, diamanté-tipped fingernails beacons to the lag riding her neural pathways.

Vlad tried to shake her off. 'I'm fine,' she said, and was surprised at the croak in her voice, the way the words slurred.

'Bullshit you are. What'd you take?'

'Nothing.'

Damage warnings going off in the corner of her vision as Tina's nails dug into her shoulder; a proximity alarm screeching as Tina leaned in close. 'I can see the pill in the puke.'

'She threw it up.' That was Ming Li Na, the other woman's cool hand sliding from Vlad's forehead to the shoulder Tina wasn't piercing. 'It's done. We need to get her out of here.'

'The media's already camped in the corridor.' Huang Yimo, Vlad could picture her leaning against the long, trough-like sink, arms and ankles crossed, calm and unhurried.

With both hands on the toilet seat Vlad commanded her shaky legs to stand. It was harder than it should have been, and when she was upright and the world swam, only Ming Li Na's support got her out of the cubicle without swaying into a wall.

Tina stood in the middle of the bathroom, arms crossed, red hair a little wilder than usual, her mouth a flat line. 'Fuck, you look like death.'

Huang Yimo snorted, took two steps forward, reached over Vlad's shoulders and yanked the hood back over her head. 'Now you really look like Death,' she said. 'Suits you.'

'At least it hides most of your face.' Tina stabbed the air front of Vlad's nose. 'We're going to have words, after I run interference with the cameras.' She spun on her heel marched for the door. 'You two get her out of here,' she said before thrusting open the bathroom door and marching into the crowd.

Silence in the bathroom.

Ming Li Na still held her up on one side, a half-head shorter and yet seeming to Vlad, a pillar – patient and strong, commanding in her own quiet way. And Huang Yimo, arms crossed, not a hint of surprise or disgust on that long, sharp-boned face, like catching Vlad throwing up her guts was just another day.

'You should try and walk on your own.' Ming Li Na took a step back, and though her arm fell away it still hovered at Vlad's side.

'In case there are cameras out there.'

Vlad started to nod... stopped as vomit surged up her throat. Swallowed it back. 'Okay,' she said to both her stomach and Ming Li Na.

'Tell me if you're gonna hurl,' Huang Yimo said before she led the way. 'I don't want spew in my hair.'

The corridor beyond the bathroom was empty, just the wide blue-white floors and the echoing ceilings, the walls plastered with their indecipherable directions.

They turned down one corridor and then another, just another intersection and a half-minute from the DKZero locker room when Huang Yimo stopped short.

Vlad almost ran into her.

'We should go the other way,' Huang Yimo said.

'What? Why?' Ming Li Na.

'Just go,' Huang Yimo said, already backing up, grabbing Vlad's arm, Ming Li Na's too and pulling them with her.

Vlad did her best to follow the other woman's line of sight, struggling to see through the fuzz at the edge of her vision, the maps and graphs overlaying the floor. The hood didn't help, cutting off the top of her vision, forcing her to lift her chin, a chance for the nausea to rise anew, but there, at the bend in the corridor, just after the stairwell, a shape—

'Samael!' The shape had a voice and squeaky sneakers to pound down the shiny corridor. 'Samael,' it yelled again, a yellow blob flying over its shoulder.

Fuck. She didn't need lag or Huang Yimo's curse, to identify the reporter bearing down on them.

'But Tina—' Ming Li Na said.

'Missed one.' Huang Yimo's second yank was harder, more urgent.

And too late, far, far too late. More shadows and more squeaky shoes flocked after the first. Tina'd missed more than one reporter in her sweep.

Huang Yimo yanked a second time, Ming Li Na an echo on Vlad's other side

Knees shaking, the fuzzy-wuzzies trawling her spine, Vlad held her ground.

Too late to run, and futile even if they did. The action would only fuel whatever nasty scandal the armchair warriors and System rumourmongers cooked up.

Drones, shoes, big black lenses trying to peer under the hood and through it all, the lag. Status updates and chat logs, health bar tripping slowly toward empty. Maybe that was why she saw him, a shadow slipping behind the cameras. Or maybe it was the sickly-sweet cherry cutting through the perfume and sweat, overhead lights gleaming off his shaven head, catching in the pistons tattooed on flesh.

Hamish. Lag locked on, target lines tracking as he leaned against the far wall and smiled.

The world spun around Vlad, and she stumbled.

Huang Yimo caught her, hand under her elbow, another around her waist. Face-planting the corridor's smooth grey-blue floors would look bad, after all. Not just fuel for the rumour-mill, but a nuclear-powered reactor to keep it going for the rest of eternity.

'Samael! Samael! Is it true you've been affected by NuGet's neural jack?'

'Samael! Will you support the petition to recall the new tech?'

'Are you going to sue?'

'Any comment on the safety rumours?'

'Samael!'

'Samael!'

Faintly, Vlad heard Ming Li Na telling the reporters to give her space, saw Huang Yimo try to shield her from the black lenses and phones, felt the reporters surround them, was buffeted in the tide. But the only thought that made it through the cacophony was, *They're not asking about drugs; why aren't they asking about drugs?*

She remembered TI's sticky fingers in the forums, it's marketing machine hidden behind carefully fabricated usernames, redirecting the rumours of Samael's addiction, focusing it on NuGet. And the first match, Grandmother all but admitting to planting the heckler in the stands.

'I want it all,' she'd said.

All of NuGet. All of DKZero.

Just one nail, one scandal surrounding NuGet's technology was all it would take, and what better than a player on NuGet's very own payroll falling victim to the company's technology? She could feel Grandmother's breath on her neck.

'The team needs you, Ana.' The memory of Tina's words played in her ear.

Needed her to make a choice, to take a stand. And hadn't she already made it, the other night? But she wasn't here for them, didn't need Ming Li Na with her soft eyes, or Sticky with his round panda face, or Huang Yimo at her side or Tina trying to push through the mass of reporters, Lu Chen a dark wedge out front. Didn't need a single fucking one of them, didn't give a shit about DKZero, less about NuGet, and yet...

And yet.

The self-heating bowl on the nightstand. Huang Yimo standing between Vlad and Zixin. Lu Chen plonking a purple soda can beside her elbow. Sticky's broken nose.

Ma, smiling at her, lag popping her front and centre on the non-existent HUD, overlaying the cameras and questions. *'Little warrior,'* she said. *'Your light will show others the way.'*

Fuck.

She had a way, it wasn't what a Tong would do, but then, she'd already made that choice too.

Slowly, with a hand that didn't, strictly speaking, need to tremble as much as it did, Vlad pushed back her hood.

The crowd went silent.

A camera flashed.

'My name—' Her voice came out a croak. She cleared it, started again, and if she spoke a little slower, if her words shook and there were tears in her eyes, well, she was a Scourge and didn't play fair. 'My name is Vladana Tong,' she began again. 'And I'm an addict.'

35

'And just in case you've been hiding under a rock for the last sixteen hours, Annihilation's *most controversial player has just doubled-down on the controversy with a shocking revelation. Is this going to be one of those moments we remember forever, Andy?'*

'Feels like it to me, Pete. Ten years from now, we're going to be asking each other where we were when the great Samael revealed to the world she was an addict. Talk about a scandal, with revelations around Cheeva's drug use and now Samael.'

'And it got even better, with Samael outing herself as the granddaughter of Tong Industry's CEO, Tong Shufeng, who recently made a bid to acquire DKZero's parent company, NuGet. Is this coincidence?'

'I don't know about you, Pete, but it's beginning to smell a lot like corporate espionage in the Tong household.'

'You're not alone; I bet the trading commission is having a field day investigating that one.'

<⊙>

Vlad didn't know what curdled her stomach more, the bitter, over-brewed tea or the tension. The tea she could deal with—tip out the old leaves, rinse the pot, pour not-quite-boiled water over the new, the steam warming her hands—the tension… The tension sat over the house, unseen smog weighing on the skin, silent, heavy. Or maybe that was the media drones, hovering just far enough from the mansion to remain legal, telescopic lenses trying to pierce the privacy film on the windows.

Whatever it was, the tension had followed her down the stairs, dislodged neither by the warm morning sun nor the heavy *thunk* of her fists into the punching bag. Remained by her side as she washed away the sweat. Now, it sat like some kind of fat, needy feline, draped over her shoulders. Not even the logs scrolling across the black marble benchtop made a dent in its relentless kneading.

Which beast was going to steamroll her first? Grandmother? Or the pill in the toilet? Both probably. One standing atop the shoulders of the other to make a bigger monster.

She slapped another clip of her "confession" off the newsfeed.

The newshounds were having a field day, and the armchair warriors were making sure not another word got in edgewise. All hint of NuGet and the neural jack wiped out with nine little words.

'My name is Vladana Tong, and I'm an addict.'

Two birds, one Scourge falling on her scythe.

The other bird, old and wizened but with a sharp beak and fathomless eyes, had yet to tweet, but it would come soon. Vlad rubbed her shoulder, fingers tracing the scars under the long black sleeve. The confession would have caught Grandmother on the back foot, she'd be busy putting out fires with reporters and shareholders alike, but she'd come for Vlad eventually.

The Dowager Empress descending from the throne, whether that was before or after she sent her trusted general in to clear the way was the only question.

Vlad swirled the tea in the bowl, the bitter, earthy liquid cold now. Not worth drinking even if it wasn't over brewed.

She shoved away from the bench, palm slamming through another clip of herself – pale and drawn, dark circles under her eyes, the black hood pooled around her neck. Huang Yimo had been right, the jacket did make her look like Death, the version of if a few weeks past its expiration.

The cold tea went down the sink, water a minute off the boil went over new leaves, the rich, heady aroma lifting her feet off the ground.

Enough of the news and the shit about to come down, there was nothing she could do about either, even if they'd mattered. And they didn't. Vlad sat back at the bench and dug her fingers into the nets.

She'd done what she could for DKZero, for her *team*.

The block-headed horse from Graydon's Revenge had haunted her dreams, or maybe that was just lag playing with her tongue, the gritty grunge of ants refusing to let go. But why? Every time she went there, it felt like there was something watching. Waiting.

She rubbed the back of her neck and dived into the nets.

There was an answer, *somewhere*, she just had to find it. Before the Wrath of Grandmother descended.

At some point, after the third bowl of tea had grown cold at her elbow, the morning sun had turned to noon and she was trawling through Graydon's Revenge walk-throughs, the others wandered down.

Sticky in his unicorn slippers came first, shuffling around the bench and into the pantry before coming out with his fruit loops. Huang Yimo was next, a dark, bleary-eyed cloud making a beeline for the coffee pot.

Vlad didn't look at them, kept flicking through the vids, pausing and scrolling, enlarging the images like she was actually seeing them, like the tension wasn't on her shoulders, kneading her spine.

Sticky's bowl *chinking* on the countertop, neon cereal *tinkling* into it, milk following. The crack and pop of the chemical orange juice's lid, and him not saying a word.

Tension's claws dug deeper.

Vlad paused on one vid, enlarged the block-headed horse—there was something there, something about the model—opened another screen beside it, began a new search, not really seeing the results. But then she'd run the same search a dozen times already, scouring Graydon's Revenge's old update logs, all with the same result. Nothing.

'What are you doing?' Sticky spoke around this spoon, the words half-legible.

Not the words she'd expected, not the half-asleep, half-bored tone either. Not accusation, no recrimination or sympathy. Just a question.

The beast on her shoulders relaxed a micron.

'Looking for the bug in Graydon's Revenge.' And maybe her tone wasn't quite as bland, maybe she stabbed at the logs instead of casually flicking through them, but then she wasn't half-asleep and there was that thing on her shoulders. Still flicking its tail and kneading, even if its claws didn't dig as deep.

'It's not bugged,' Sticky said, somehow managing to keep the bright pops of cereal from exploding out his mouth. He swiped at the newsfeed running next to his bowl.

Vlad looked up. The beast stopped its kneading. 'What?'

'Not.' Chew. Swallow. 'Bugged.'

The beast half-rose, its paws on her arm, stilling her fingers as a different kind of tension filled her being.

Vlad's gaze narrowed, but Sticky didn't see, eyes on his own screens. 'Have you *been* there?'

Another spoonful of cereal went into his mouth. Sticky nodded.

'What's wrong with it then?'

He flicked through another screen.

The beast hissed.

'Sticky.' Vlad's voice was sharp and she clicked her fingers in his face. 'Focus. Graydon's Revenge. It's not bugged?'

Those big round eyes blinked. 'It's a puzzle.'

Huang Yimo's scoff was almost drowned under the screech of chair legs on tile as she pulled out the stool beside Sticky. 'I can't believe you believe that one.'

Sticky's thick black brows beetled, his shoulders hunched and the spoon destined for his mouth paused midair. 'It's true.'

Another scoff, Huang Yimo's eyes rolling as she poured milk on her violently-coloured cereal. 'It's a myth.'

'I haven't heard it,' Vlad said.

'It's an *old* myth.' It was Huang Yimo's turn to shovel cereal.

A fission ran across Vlad's shoulders. 'How old?'

Huang Yimo shrugged.

Sticky munched, focus back on the newsfeed.

Vlad hoisted herself half over the bench and slammed her hand into the middle of it.

Huang Yimo jerked backward, surprise and a little worry creasing her brow, but the panda merely raised his eyes. Slow. Steady. The bear waking up.

Vlad stared him down. 'How old?'

Munch.

Munch.

'Sticky.'

The big panda-eyes narrowed, the spoon made another trip.

Vlad leaned closer, half her body on the bench, slippers *plop plopping* to the kitchen floor as her toes left the footrest. 'Sticky.' There was a hiss in the word, a warning in the flash of teeth. 'Don't fuck with me. How. Old?'

Hands on her waist, yanking her off the bench and onto the stool. A solid chest at her back, catching her before momentum had her tipping backward onto the marble tiles. That familiar sandalwood scent.

Zixin. Grandmother's general. Fuck.

The excitement starting in her stomach, the relief coursing through her veins gone as the beast crawled back over her shoulders. Heavier, claws longer, its tail *thump, thump thumping* inside her ribs.

'From after the third expansion.' That was Ming Li Na, coming through the archway, arms stretched overhead, a yawn cracking her face, like she didn't see the beast, didn't hear it purr. 'Has someone made coffee?'

'Yeah...' Huang Yimo got up, but Vlad's attention wasn't on the other side of the bench. It was on Zixin, dragging out the stool beside her.

She didn't want to look at him, didn't want to give him the time of day or wonder which of Grandmother's words were going to come of his mouth. But the beast pressed a paw to her face and pushed.

He was in another crew-necked sweater, soft-grey sleeves pushed to the elbow, and Vlad wondered whether stepping into his wardrobe would be the same as stepping into an old black-and-white movie. All the colour gone, except for the heavy gold watch on his wrist.

He smiled, and in those dark bronze eyes there was... Nothing. No tension, no sympathy, no disgust just... nothing, as if the scene in the office, the argument in the bedroom and the "revelation", had never happened.

Zixin snagged her bowl of half-eaten porridge, hand wrapped around the spoon before she could snatch it back.

She tried to snatch it back. 'What are you doing?'

'Exactly what it looks like.' He ate, grimaced. 'You used to have better taste,' he said and stretched one of those long arms in front of her, leaning in close enough to smell the warm skin under the sandalwood, and grabbed the honey Huang Yimo slid onto the bench.

The other woman slammed her hand over it, glaring at him before he could snatch it. 'I had it first,' the gamer said.

Zixin didn't let go. His jaw was inches from Vlad's mouth, and she saw the smile twitch the muscle, even if the expression didn't make it to his lips. 'I've got it now,' he replied, but didn't move to wrest it from under Huang Yimo's grip, remaining half-sprawled across Vlad's lap.

For several loud, chest-thumping heart beats, as sandalwood and skin stoppered the frustration in her chest and threw a short in her brain, Vlad stared at that smooth, golden skin and fought the urge to lean in that fraction closer and—

Her fist in his ribs.

Zixin shooting back, surprise lifting his brow, a hint of that smile flirting with his lips, but no pain. He rubbed his side. 'What was that for?'

She ignored him, glanced briefly at Sticky—back to scrolling the feeds and shovelling food in his face—before focussing on Ming Li Na.

The gamer's hair was sleep-tossed, face bleary as she hopped onto the stool beside Huang Yimo, but there was a cartoon-shaped coffee bucket in her hands and the first glimmer of awareness in her eyes.

'What's the rumour say?'

'Huh?' Ming Li Na stared. Frowned. 'What rumour?'

'Graydon's Revenge. The puzzle.'

'Oh.' She rubbed her face. 'Um… I don't remember, something about… ' She waved a hand, nose wrinkled in thought.

'An exclusive, one-time armour set.' It was Lu Chen's turn to make Vlad start, pulling out the stool on her other side, a large, dark shadow with an equally large, dark mug in his hand. 'This is it.' He slid a screen across the bench.

Vlad caught it.

Then caught her breath.

<⊙>

She didn't log in with the Cube, she should have but... didn't.

She'd left her body out in the real, the VR chair cradling legs and arms in warm leather. In-System, with the two avatars arrayed before her in the startup sphere, she was bodiless, an awareness with peppermint crawling up her nose.

That was why she hadn't used the Cube, why she'd slipped into the training room while the others were gathered in the kitchen, eating breakfast at noon and slowly rubbing sleep from their eyes.

She needed the peppermint, as much as she hated it, as much as it reminded her of the car, Ma reaching around the front seat, the tin of candies in her palm, the smile on her face. She needed it. Needed the reminder, the push, because there was no other way she could do this, no other way she'd voluntarily exist in this space and peer past Samael to the bright, silver beacon beyond.

The paladin wore the armour on Lu Chen's screen. Gold-chased silver gleaming like it was made of diamond. The helmet that covered the face, the long dark hair that spilled from the crown, a waterfall of rich brown. Slim-fitted greaves, a white cloak falling from elegantly crafted pauldrons, a skirt-like tabard made of the same silky, silver-threaded stuff.

The avatar looked less like a warrior made to take Behemoth on face-to-face than it did a slim, sleek rouge. More Rabbit than Swordsman, and yet she remembered Ma doing just that in the early days, when VR was still sensor gloves and headsets. Before neural interface, before the sauce. Before Vlad.

Before a hacker sabotaged her parents car, causing the doors to lock and the batteries to overheat.

Before they died.

The paladin wasn't the original, but a copy, a port from the arrow skull pendant out in the real, nestled in the hollow of her throat. Ma's pendant, her login key.

Vlad hovered before the avatar that wore the armour game myth said waited in Graydon's Revenge, peppermint in her nose, ants crawling across her shoulders.

The armour wasn't the treasure in Graydon's Revenge. *Annihilation's* third expansion came out two months after the crash, before the fire racing over the crumpled hood and Ma screaming. And Vlad remembered going to sleep with the game projected across her bedroom wall, remembered the paladin in its gold-chased silver armour following her into her dreams, beating back the nightmares.

Which meant... before Ma died she'd been in Graydon's

Revenge, before the puzzle was even a thing. How did that work? Were the rumours wrong, was there something else in Graydon's Revenge, another kind of Easter Egg?

Had Ma left it there?

Only one way to find out.

Vlad slipped into the paladin's skin.

<⊙>

Graydon's Revenge didn't look any different. Same crumbling, grey walls and upside-down doors. Same legs stuck in the same grey flagstones, endlessly walking to nowhere. Same block-headed horse atop the same slate roof, same rotten-citrus smell and the same ants marching under her skin. Same everything.

Except for her.

She could have logged-in as Samael, *should* have logged-in as the necromancer, but she'd done that before, on many occasions, and wasn't the definition of insanity doing the same thing over and again expecting different results?

The paladin felt strange. Too big and too small all at once. Like her psyche was the wrong shape for the wire-frame holding the avatar together. Even the spear slung across her back, the round shield over it and the twin axes hanging off her hips, were... wrong. Itchy.

It was ridiculous, of course. In-System Vlad was nothing more than electrical impulses communicating with ones and zeroes on a thousand servers spread across the globe. She had no shoulders for the pauldrons to pinch, no toes to slop around in the armoured boots. And yet, they did.

She couldn't even blame the sauce.

She was just Vladana Tong wearing a copy of her ma's old avatar, standing on the edge of the crumbling wall, the unfelt breeze sighing through the pine forest far below, the ants marching, marching, marching. She couldn't even think of herself as Lucija, the name hovering over her head.

None of that mattered though.

Armoured fingers twitched and screens scrolled across her HUD, old vids and walk-throughs dug up from the mothballed reaches of the nets.

She had a puzzle to solve.

<⊙>

Three hours and fifty-seven minutes. That's how long she was jacked-in. Three hours and fifty-seven minutes she'd poked and prodded, jumped and burrowed and slashed at every corner of the crumpled castle. Three hours and fifty-seven minutes in which she'd followed seventeen walk-throughs, picked apart twenty-nine forum threads and eleven videos. Three hours and fifty-seven minutes in which she'd found nothing. Not even a hole in a wall or an important phrase in a dialogue tree. Not so much as a flagstone two shades lighter or darker than the rest. Nothing.

She pulled the jack from her neck, ignoring the *shhuck* of the electrodes parting from skin, and sat breathing in the warm leather, the last lingering traces of crushed-ants and peppermint in her nose. She stared at the ceiling, lag tracing the rectangular lights hanging from the warm white as her brain slowly disengaged from the System. Stats fading, maps flickering, the paladin's spear no longer pressing so hard against her spine.

What was she missing? Ma had had the armour, now Vlad had the armour, the great prize, and so... Was she chasing the wrong lead? Remembering things wrong? Was Ma's armour actually the armour in Lu Chen's screenshot or was the whole rumour some kind of fucking joke?

The nagging in her gut said no, and yet...

She hoisted herself out of the chair, throwing one leg and then the other over the side and then...

A game was playing back on the wall behind the chairs.

No, not a game. The last three hours and fifty-seven minutes.

Vlad stared at the paladin, jumping off and on the farthest edge of Graydon's Revenge's crumbling fortress wall. The avatar's long brown hair flew out behind as she plunged the three metres from the very top of the last crenelation, silver boots *thunking* on solid air, eighty-six metres above the craggy grey cliff. Legs bunched, the pale-white runes tattooed on her thighs lighting up with magic before she leapt back up; the distance little more than a step-stool before the paladin's strength.

A shadow moved in the corner, and tension wound through Vlad's spine.

She turned, fighting off the lag-born target lock, the little info box that wanted to pop over Sticky's head, the red that outlined Lu Chen.

Sticky perched on the lip of his VR unit, canopy open, the sides down, a bright yellow and orange packet in his hand. It crinkled as he fed himself chips, hand rolling from packet to mouth and back in a slow-motion conveyor belt. His gaze fixed on the wall.

Lu Chen, though, he leaned against the open door, arms crossed, that frown between his brows not on the paladin bouncing over Graydon's Revenge, but her. Vladana Tong, Scourge and liar.

Liar.

Why did that word stick in her head? Why even have the thought at all?

Vlad frowned.

Too many disturbing thoughts, too many questions, not enough time to deal with them.

That seemed to be the theme of it. Too much and all of it coming at once.

She needed more time, but something told her there wasn't any more to be had.

Vlad swung her other leg out of the VR chair and headed for the door, ignoring not just Lu Chen's black stare but the man himself. There was nothing wrong with playing a game, chasing up old

System rumours. Nothing at all, except for the armour. She should have used the Cube, pulled on her big-girl pants and—

She was even with his shoulder, and for a heartbeat, she thought he was going to keep the questions behind his eyes. A half-step past, bright afternoon sun streaming through the floor-to-ceiling window and—

'I didn't know you had an alt,' Lu Chen said.

What was to know? Everyone had an alternate character running around the System. A different face, a different voice, class, species, weapons, everything. Scourges were no exception even if, more often than not, their reasons for doing so weren't as simple as a change of skillsets, and yet...

Vlad stopped, didn't turn, kept her gaze on the sun glinting off the lake, the dots and rectangles of yachts and jet-skis.

"You're surprised?" Was what she meant to say, but what came out... 'It was my ma's.' And *she* was the one surprised, the one to jerk like she'd been prodded with lightning. Where had that come from?

In the corner of her eye, Lu Chen nodded like that answer was... everything. 'You've got the Graydon Armour.'

Questions hung from those words, the how and the why. How'd she get it? Why the interrogation at breakfast, and if she owned the armour... Why had Vlad spent the last three hours and fifty-seven minutes jumping around Graydon's Revenge?

'Ma found it.' And then, because she couldn't stop herself, she added, 'Before she died.'

More silence, even Sticky's crunching stopping for ten long, treacle-thick heartbeats.

Death, the great conversation killer.

Vlad went to move—

Lu Chen spoke. 'Are you really an addict?'

And there it was. The question, the beast back on her shoulders, tight and warm around her throat.

'That's what I said last night.'

He turned, arms crossed, black brows drawn over long nose, mouth held tight. 'Is it true?'

'Why wouldn't it be?'

No answer to that.

On the wall, the paladin jumped up beside the block-headed horse while Sticky crunched another chip. 'Because you don't use,' Sticky said around a mouth half-full of salt and vinegar. 'Drugs interfere with the sauce.'

Silence. Even the paladin paused and turned her head, long hair falling over her armoured shoulder, the rich, dark-brown river picking out the gold in the silver.

Vlad swallowed against a mouth gone dry. 'What's the sauce?' Even to her, the words were hollow. Her gaze skidded from Sticky to Lu Chen, that one unmoving, and unsurprised if the expression on his face held true.

Of course it held true. She doubted Lu Chen had ever had an untrue moment in his privileged, golden-spoon life. And now... Now he didn't say a word, but his disbelief at her response soaked the air – a thick, sticky net holding her slippers to the polished concrete.

Her gaze skidded past his shoulder to the lake, unable to move. She was acutely conscious of the paladin leaping off the crumbling fortress, defying gravity as she ran above the pine forest.

Lu Chen had that thing, a charismatic twist in his genes that commanded respect. She'd known that, felt it the first time she'd seen him, it was her own fault for getting caught, for letting herself *care*.

Her own fucking fault.

She'd let them in. All of them—Sticky, Huang Yimo, Ming Li Na, Lu Chen—the whole ball of DKZero-shaped wax, and now she was paying the price. Now she didn't want to... Want to what? Hurt them? Let them down? See disappointment in their eyes?

She was a fucking Scourge, disappointment and suspicion were her second shadow. Nothing new, nothing she hadn't stared in the face and given a one-finger salute to every damn day of her life.

This... this was a piece of cake, this was a noob-run with training wheels, this was—

And still, she couldn't unstick her feet.

Slowly, she faced Lu Chen.

The DKZero captain leaned against the door jamb like he had all the time in the world.

A smile and a sharp, cutting comment was all it would take. Cut the bonds, let herself free. A pithy sentence, four words, eight at the most, and she was out of there. Armour intact, secrets kept. Mission accomplished, instead...

'It's done,' she said. 'Better the Scourge take the fall than NuGet, right? That's what Tina and you wanted me for, and I did you one better, I put my grandmother in the firing line too. Just a few more nudges, and the media will have Tong Industries painted as the next great evil, and me the serpent. Easy enough to jettison, and NuGet will have a little breathing room.'

She moved past him, out into the late-afternoon light. The sun was playing yellow and orange above the lake, turning the grey concrete warm.

'You didn't have to do it,' Lu Chen said.

'It's what you recruited me for.' Wooed and vetted, that's what Tina said.

'And the rave?'

Ice hit Vlad's back; grabbed hold of her guts, and if she hadn't been frozen to the spot before, she was now, acutely conscious of Sticky, the faded bruises under his eyes. 'If I'd known Sticky was there...' She let the words trail, cast a glance back, into the training room, to Sticky still shovelling chips. Still facing the wall and the paladin, but his posture no longer relaxed, attention no longer just on the game. 'You shouldn't have followed,' she said.

Sticky's shoulder's stiffened. 'We're a team.'

'No, we're not.' She turned away.

'Who's Hamish?' Lu Chen's questions stopped her in her tracks. Again.

'What?' How did they know—

'Hamish,' Sticky said around another mouthful. 'The guy who broke my nose.'

Right, Sticky. She'd said Hamish's name. Of course, he would know.

Lu Chen shoved off the wall, a large shadow getting in close. 'And the guy who harassed Ming Li Na at the karaoke lounge.'

Shock jolted through Vlad, almost made her turn and face Lu Chen, but she held it back, force of will keeping her looking straight ahead, to the yachts and jet skis. But of course he'd know that too, Sticky had probably found an image of the weasel clear enough for Ming Li Na to recognise.

'He's no one.' Not anymore. She'd seen to that, rendered him useless the moment she'd stormed Grandmother's office. The bastard was less than no one, another face crossed off the web. A memory of cherry vape and a nasty mouth. Lu Chen on the other hand...

The team captain was taller than her by an inch, but he'd turned that charisma on and it made him bigger, wider. A stoney-faced shadow detaching itself from the wall, commanding her, to face up, to speak truth.

He'd make a good CEO.

She tilted her chin to meet his gaze.

It was black, blacker than black.

'Who is he?' Lu Chen asked again, the first stirrings of anger shaking his voice.

This was better, the confrontation. She could do anger, smile in its face and stoke the fire, anything but that quiet acceptance, the patience. The expectation.

Anything but that.

And yet, what came out of her mouth...

'I took care of him.' Not "None of your business" or "Afraid Ming Li Na might like him better?" or any of a dozen other things to widen the cracks in Lu Chen's granite face, but "I took care of him." Quickly followed by, 'He won't bother you again.' As if one assurance pulled the other from her throat. Unavoidable. Like vomit.

Except vomit only soured the back of her throat, steel wool scouring her insides, and this... This made them squishy and set nerves to fluttering in her chest, made her want to care.

Fuck.

'You didn't answer my question.'

'No, I didn't,' she said, and left.

36

The heavy steel door was open, sunlight coming through the gap between jamb and door, an empty ramen packet tumbling through on the breeze. The breeze that shouldn't be there because the big, mullioned windows didn't open. She watched the bright red and yellow packet float across the cold, grey concrete, a plastic butterfly amidst the gloom and dust, before she kicked Ximisthus's stand and left the big bike in the corridor.

Slowly, heart in throat, other hand fisted, she pushed the door open.

Someone had taken a sledgehammer to the couch. That was the thought that made it through the droning in her skull. The same sledgehammer had exploded the windows, leaving bits of jagged glass between the square metal frames with their peeling paint. Taken it again but with less success to the shelves dividing the rooms. More success had been had with the coffee table. The old, scared wood reduced to a broken plank and splintered timber.

Urine rose from the mess of covers on the bed, mixing with another, more pungent odour and wafting across the battlefield that had once been her bolthole. A haven.

She walked through the mess, dried ramen crunching underfoot, mixing papers and wood and glass the closer she got to the carnage. The kitchen space was a minefield of food, porridge oats and spoiled milk. The sledgehammer had met the bar fridge, the door open and warped. Around the corner... The punching bag was disembowelled, sand spilled across the floor mat, the patched black-leather deflated, limp skin hanging from its chain.

The windows here were gone too. The old, salmon bucket chair on its side against the metal frame, legs bent, fabric slashed. the sun sparking off the bits of glass embedded in its back. And of the floor...

Vlad's chest froze, heart stopping and doom sliding prickly fingers from her nape to her tailbone.

There. Over in the corner where the edge of the exercise mat met the wall, was a hole. A big, fat, yawning cavern, the space around it littered with fist-sized chunks of concrete, rebar pried apart as if with giant, angry hands. Or a jackhammer and bolt cutters. Someone had been prepared. Someone had *known* what they were looking for, where to look.

Her feet took her from the punching bag to the hole. A part of the loft ignored, where dust bunnies once congregated and the lights barely reached. The two square feet that should have been overlooked, so far from anything else, anything important, and yet the hole in the floor spoke otherwise, the cables and power jacks, the backup generator, the cooling unit, the three inch-thick slab of reinforced concrete with the signal dampeners built into it, belied everything.

Vlad knelt at its edge. The thieves had left the jackhammer leaning against the wall like they were going to come back, or maybe as compensation for the thing they stole. The mainframe, *her* mainframe. The Cube's big sister, engraved with the same arrow-shaped skull.

They'd taken it, and in taking it they'd taken the evidence of themselves. The loft's security vids, the RFID scans, their electronic trail, but more than that... Doom no longer trailed hooked fingers down Vlad's spine, it stood at her shoulder, its billowing black robes and scythe rooting her to the floor.

More than the security footage, the box held the Cube's backups, the spiderweb, everything, every clue, every suspicion she'd ever had about her parents deaths, the cloud whale. The white field.

Samael.

Vlad shot to her feet, spun, took two steps, stumbled on a broken chunk of concrete and... and...

Fuck.

They had her login, her IDs, her hacks, her macros. Everything. Every little piece of what made her a Scourge, and that meant... That meant they had Samael. They could login anytime, anyplace, change her passwords, masquerade as *her*. For all intents and purposes they *would* be her. Vlad. Her revenge, her reason—

There wasn't enough air in the loft, even with the broken windows. It was the piss, the piss and shit sucking up the oxygen, polluting it, making it hard to breathe.

She hadn't planned for this. Hadn't thought anyone would find her here. She'd been so careful, surveillance scramblers in her clothes, on her bike, every communication encrypted, run through the Cube. And then Grandmother and DKZero and the fucking *game*.

Vlad should've run the moment Zixin stepped out of the Porsche's headlights, should have packed her shit, changed her ID and given up Samael and Hamish right then and there. Started again. New avatar, new name. Come at Grandmother from another angle.

But now...

Fuck, what did she do now?

Her knees trembled, Doom digging its nails into the cartilage, pulling out her tendons.

But no. No. She wouldn't kneel, wouldn't give in.

Cold shoved out Doom, froze its nails, shattered its scythe.

Grandmother rode through her bones.

Grandmother.

Grandmother had done this. She breathed, took the sour piss into her lungs and used it to stiffen her knees.

There was a way out. There was always a way out. Just like the firefighter breaking through the Bentley's rear window.

There was always a way.

The black box was encrypted, its security keyed to the loft. It would take the thieves time to crack it, more time to understand the operating system, unravel the file structure. Time. She had time.

No need to ask why it'd been taken—the Deposit was why—less to ask who. There were only a handful of people who knew who she was, what she had, and of those... the piss and shit, the destruction was its own identification. She could practically see Hamish swinging the sledgehammer, thin, tattooed face twisted with glee before he whipped his dick out and—

A snarl twisted her mouth.

How he'd found her didn't matter, although she could guess; Tina had tracked her down after all, with a little help from Huang Yimo. Tina who was about as subtle as the jackhammer in the corner, who'd never think to make sure she wasn't followed.

Tina, who was standing just inside the security door, red hair blazing in the morning sun, paper scudding about her high heeled boots, her face a blank, those big brown eyes blinking in utter, incomprehensible stupidity. And squeezing in behind her, Huang Yimo—straight black hair behind her ears, helmet dangling from her fingers—and behind Huang Yimo...

Vlad snarled. 'You bought the posse.'

Three faces jerking in her direction: Tina, Huang Yimo, Sticky.

'Vlad—' Tina began, but Vlad stopped her.

Crunching across concrete and instant noodles, the shattered remnants of what home she'd had, not stopping until she was looking down at Tina, the shock and distress on the woman's face, but already plans, already spin working behind her eyes.

Vlad leaned in close. 'You did this,' she said. Looked up at Huang Yimo and Sticky. 'You helped.' Pushed through all of them, out the door, into the corridor.

She left Ximisthus leaning against the wall and stalked further into the darkness, aware of the others behind her, not caring if they saw her stop before another nondescript section of wall, piled with soggy cardboard and discarded metal pipes. If Sticky came to stand behind her, sharp panda eyes tracking every movement as she shoved aside the trash and reached into a crack in the concrete, she didn't care.

No control panels here, no wires, no palm scanners waiting in the dark. Just cobwebs and damp, her cheek pressed to the cold concrete as she shoved her arm all the way to shoulder, standing on tippy toe as she explored the space between the walls, trying not to think about spiders and rats. And then... the sharp crackle of plastic, looping her fingers through a handle, satisfaction washing the cold doom out of her veins as she pulled the package from the dark.

She'd never expected anyone to find the loft, never thought Samael would be exposed, but some part of her had known, maybe the part that had always suspected Grandmother. That part of her had made a bolt hole. Just in case. And now it was in her hands, and now she was going to do what she *should* have done at the very start. The smart thing. The right thing.

No time for subtlety, games and counter games. Time to be a sledgehammer. Time to be a *Scourge*.

She spun. Paused.

Sticky standing between her and Ximisthus, right eye and his nose several shades of yellow and green.

The right thing.

Ming Li Na shoved up against the karaoke lounge wall.

The smart thing. What she *should* have done.

Vlad's hand tightened around the thick black package.

She pushed past Sticky.

Huang Yimo was behind him.

Vlad pushed past her too.

Tina was the last one, leaning up against Ximisthus's sleek

frame, arms crossed, the perfect bow of her mouth flat with determination, and Vlad grabbed her shoulders and shove—

A vape glowing cherry red in the dark at the other end of the corridor. A buzz from the watch at her wrist, quickly chased by a message on the back of her glasses. Not long, just three words.

// Looking for something?

Vlad snarled.

She swore she heard him chuckle, swore she saw light glint off the end of a gun, even as she hit Ximisthus's headlights.

Nothing there save more soggy cardboard and old rebar.

Another message. *// Careful, can't leave witnesses.*

'Ana—' Tina, her friend's hand on her forearm, pulling her around.

Vlad threw her off. 'Fuck off, Tina.' She twisted to pin Huang Yimo and Sticky in place with a glare, even as she kicked Ximisthus's stand. 'You too, you've *helped* enough.'

'Ana,' Tina tried again.

Again, Vlad threw her off, the sensors embedded in her glasses and Ximisthus's chassis piercing the old concrete corridor, seeking out energy and network signatures, bypassing those around her to lock onto the one descending the abandoned stairwell.

A vibration on her wrist, no words, just coordinates popping on her glasses, and a second later a map.

Iron Woods estate. Fitting, she guessed. End this shit with Hamish, and from Hamish… Grandmother, where it started.

Pushing past Tina to the elevator. Turning, hands on the old grate, pausing to pin the trio with a glare. 'I don't need you.' She stared through Tina to Sticky and Huang Yimo at her side. 'I never did.' And let the doors clang shut.

37

The shopping mall's giant skeleton was dark. No hotted up cars, no DJ, no crowd, no music to drive away the cicadas. Just bottles skittering away from her boots, clinking against the concrete pillars, spilling stale beer as the moon's ghostly rays tip-toed between them.

Hamish was waiting for her, a blotch amongst the shadows and trash gathered under the half-finished stairs.

She stopped, toes scuffing on the floor. 'Where is it?' The words echoed.

He smiled, teeth a slash in the dark, and with his foot, nudged a rectangle out of the rubbish at his feet. It scrapped across the concrete, the sound rough and heavy. It caught a moonbeam, gleaming a dull grey.

On the back of her glasses, a stray but all-too-familiar network signal pinged.

'Right here, coont.' He pressed his heel to it. Plastic gave with sharp snap. 'Joost like I promised.'

She hissed. 'What do you want?'

A vape glowed, the red tip bobbing at chin height. 'You know what I want.'

She stepped forward, eyes on the box under Hamish's thick-soled boot. 'I can't do that.'

Plastic cracked.

Vlad's chest squeezed, she jerked another step closer.

Another crunch stopped Vlad short.

'Sure you can, it's right here in the box, ain't it?' The vape flared brighter. 'Open it for me.'

A deep breath, a pin trying to squash the panic behind her ribs.

Her life was in that black box, her revenge. Everything. Everyone. She needed it, it was her next breath, her heartbeat.

The plastic groaned under Hamish's boot. 'Open it, coont.'

'No.' She ground out the word between clenched teeth.

'What?'

'No.' Another breath, another pin holding down the panic. She moved another inch forward. 'You destroy the hard drive, you won't get what your boss wants.' What Grandmother wanted.

'Maybe.' He ground his boot harder. 'But ye on ye knees is a consolation.'

'In your dreams.'

'Nah.' He kicked the hard drive, the box skittering into shadows. 'Right now. You'll get on your knees right now, and then you'll open the box.'

Hamish stepped out of the dark, a silhouette against grey moonlight. She caught a glimpse of flat cheekbones, the square jaw and bald head, the pistons in his neck. There was an arrogant tilt to his chin and a loose, cocky set of his shoulders, like a prize-fighter in the ring.

Except there was no ring here, only the stark concrete pillars and the chill wind freezing her nose.

Hamish advanced, and if he said something, made a quip or threat, it was lost in the adrenaline roaring in her ears.

He swung first, but she was already moving, stepping back, blocking and grabbing Hamish's arm in the same movement. Jerking him forward—

An elbow whistling toward her ear.

She twisted, though not fast enough and the elbow clipped her jaw. Ringing joined the adrenaline, a new light bursting behind her ears, but Vlad kept moving, kept her feet even as her brain stumbled a moment. Training taking over. It was a second, but in that second Hamish was on her, in her space, that massive bony hand a fist coming for her face—

Another block, impact shuddering through her forearms, and now she was stepping back, making room for the swift kick to his guts.

Foul, vape-stained breath burst over her face.

She breathed it in, lunged forward, grabbed that bald, shiny head and introduced it to her knee.

Crunch of bone. A yowl. Then it was Hamish's turn to push, and *she* was stumbling backwards. And *he* was coming at her, fury and blood on his face—

Another step, another knee, her whole body in the roundhouse kick—

He grabbed it, stopping her cold, victory and retribution joining the rage and the blood, but Vlad wasn't done.

Her own elbow followed the knee, abs contracting, body twisting as she levered herself off the ground and threw everything she had into wiping the smirk of the bastard's face.

Another crunch. Another yowl, and Hamish's hands were on her neck and hers were in his face, fingers stabbing his eyes. Her legs were wrapped around his torso. Air was coming short, shadows creeping out from behind the square pillars, eating her vision. Just Hamish, just that thin-lipped, hate-filled snarl, just her fingers in his eyes. Hot, squishy. Her lungs burned. Pulse pounded hard.

She didn't know how long she could hold on but she wouldn't let go, wouldn't let go until she dug those venomous green orbs from Hamish's face.

Oxygen, filling her lungs, cold and clean. The hands at her throat now clawing at her fingers, and Hamish moving, rushing—

Pain rang through her skull, her spine, her shoulders. Hard and cold, blunt but sharp. Starlight in her eyes, her arse on the floor, one of those square concrete pillars at her back, the corner digging into her spine, splitting her head.

Stars and streaks clearing, the ringing hanging on. And Hamish... Hamish still standing, backing away from her. Hands at his face, feeling his eye sockets, coming away bloody. Dark tears running down his cheeks, over his lips, but still able to glare, to snarl out of the fleshy orbs she hadn't managed to gouge from his face.

He swore at her. She knew it was a swear even though the ringing swallowed the words. She could tell from the spite twisting his lips,

She smiled and staggered to her feet, slow, perhaps a little too slow. But it wouldn't matter, she could have all the speed of a geriatric snail and still rip those eyes from his skull.

Hamish took a step backward.

Vlad lunged.

He ran.

<⊙>

He ran like a rabbit on steroids, darting into the shadows and snatching up the hard drive before he escaped.

Vlad lost him before they made it out of the estate, before she even made it out of the skeleton mall. Only the signal from the black box kept her on track, the fading, intermittent squelch dragging her past Ximisthus, through the weeds and dirt of vacant lots, out into an intersection and blaring traffic.

Headlights zapping past, the spine-shivering whine of electronic motors, the ear-trembling rumble and stench of an old-school combustion engine. She pushed through weeds and a chain-link fence to teeter on the edge of the footpath and stare into the city opposite. And Hamish standing on the centre median, trapped at the pedestrian crossing, once again a silhouette this time against the bright lights of the shopping mall beyond.

Beside Hamish, huddled on the centre crossing, a woman held tight to her son's hand, shoulders hunched, trying to get as far away from Hamish as the spit of concrete would allow. The kid in sleek, neon sneakers and a baggy t-shirt, DKZero's dragon curling over his shoulders, the tech in his clothes *pinging* against her sensors.

The boy's shaggy black head barely topped his ma's shoulder.

Four lanes of buses, cars and scooters separated them, another four and a seething crowd beyond that. Giant traffic lights rose from the middle and four corners, and a zebra crossing at her feet.

The black box was stuffed in Hamish's jacket, she couldn't see it, not against the lights, but her sensors outlined the energy signature.

She scanned the traffic, looking for a break in the torrent even as she tried to ignore the adrenaline making her hands shake, her stomach queasy. If Hamish made it to the crowded mall on the other side, she'd lose him in the crush, the box in the morass of network queries and smart devices. Waiting for the blinking red man to turn green wasn't an option, because he'd been gone, jackrabbit fast.

Her teeth were in her lip, copper coating her tongue, not just her eyes but her glasses, her watch scanning, scanning, scanning. Just a break, just a second, just long enough to—

There.

Vlad sprinted across the blacktop.

Horns blared. A gust caught her jacket, trying to spin her around, but her eyes were on Hamish, only on Hamish. She had to get the box, the box was all that mattered.

Hamish turning, cursing, but even as he did so, his attention darted sideways. To the ma, to the kid.

Three lanes down, just one to go, three lousy metres between her and the slimy creep, his face already blooming with the marks of their fight. Just one second before she got her hands on him, finished what he started, got her life, her revenge back, and it was one second too long.

It happened in slow motion, Hamish's hands on the kid's

shoulders, muscles bunching, the snarl peeling back from his teeth. The shove.

The kid shooting forward, sneakers catching in the short, scraggly grass at the edge of the footpath, his mouth and eyes going wide. The horror slowly dawning on his ma's face.

Brakes squealed, a woman screamed, and somewhere in the back of her mind it was her ma's voice, her ma's anguish-filled cry in her ears. And the kid... the kid looked her right in the eye, fear ringing his dark-brown irises in white and drawing the blood from his face. And somehow, somehow even the dragon on his t-shirt screamed.

It was less than a second, not even a heartbeat, barely enough time for neurones to fire and impulses to leap between brain cells, but in that moment she moved.

The car was nothing, a blur—glaring headlamps, a horn wailing its banshee cry—skimming her side, thigh and ribs screaming as it bowled into her. But she had the kid, the little boy wrapped up in her arms, even as the concrete slammed into her back and fresh agony spiralled though her elbow, her hip, her shoulder. She had the kid, and that was all that mattered as lights exploded behind her eyes and time…

…time restarted, the sticky, gooey strings loosening around her brain. A sharp echoing *click* and she was breathing, heart beating loud, muscles shaky, the sweet aftertaste of adrenaline on her tongue.

'Oh my god, oh my god, oh my god!' That wasn't her saying that, not her mouth moving, the words a half-croon, half-prayer. She wasn't sure she could move her mouth. There was a block in the back of her brain, a knot twisting her nape. She rolled, tried to rise—

Panic made her stomach cramp, her breath catch.

Her arms were empty.

The boy wasn't in her grip anymore and there were people around her, blurry figures swimming in the lights behind her eyes, fighting against the neon pops and flashes of billboards and headlights. Vlad blinked, trying to clear the light, to find some definition in the shadows crouching beside her and the others moving beyond.

But the boy... She couldn't see the boy!

'Oh my baby, my baby.' The croon-prayer came from her right, the blurry, shadowy outline rocking back and forth at her side. 'You're okay. You're okay now, baby.'

More flashes, closer, in her face, a camera's distinct *snick snick snick* ricocheting between her ears, the light spears in her eyeballs.

She held up a hand, tried to shield herself even as she struggled to her knees, ribs burning fire, the tight, knotted skin behind her knee throwing ragged bolts of lightning up and down her leg.

'Is he alright?' She thought she spoke, was sure air moved past vocal cords, but there was no answer, nothing save the endless prayer-croon.

Time came unstuck again. Another brain-halving flash, another blink and there were more shadows around her, taller, darker, their shoulders broader, or maybe that was just the brighter lights behind them, the increased chatter, the hands on her shoulders pushing her down.

'Are you alright, miss? Miss?' Another light in her eye, small and sharp, a laser where the others had been bombs, first the left then the right. She flinched, tried to turn away, gasped as a hand found her ribs—

'...fractured,' she heard someone say.

'Laceration on the right leg,' another replied. And there were more hands now, how could one person have so many hands? But wait a second, that wasn't right...

She pushed them away, tried to get up.

'The kid,' she said again. 'There was a kid.'

'He's fine now, miss.' That hand on her shoulder, pushing her back. For a moment, amongst the exploding lights and rising chatter, she made out the outline of a face, the black shoulders and crimson breast of a paramedic uniform. 'What's your name, miss?'

'...no ID...' the other said.

Vlad resisted the paramedic's hand, got her own on his wrist and used it as a lever to rise even as she pushed it away. She was halfway to her feet when—

A tearing pain in her leg, scars and skin parting around a hot rush and—

'Shit.' The paramedic's hands were under her arms as she fell. 'Get the gurney.'

'No. No,' she said, trying to push the hands away, trying to get back up. If the kid was alright, she had to get to Hamish, get the box. 'I have to get something, let me go.'

'I can't do that, miss.' And then, quieter, to someone else. '...sedation...'

'No, I don't—'

The cold, bone-chilling *phszzt* of a hypoderm at her carotid and the rest faded away.

38

She discharged herself from the hospital in tracksuit pants and a t-shirt bought from the gift shop. Her own clothes, her boots and hooded jacket had been dumped in a rubbish bin by an ER nurse somewhere in the ward she'd just escaped.

Vlad shuffled out the doors groggy and sore, with a plastic bag of pills and an irritated doctor at her back, but on her own two feet. Somehow made it from the bright lights of the emergency room, through the car park she'd waited in just a week ago while Sticky disappeared through those same doors, to the road and curb.

Everything felt alien, from the soft navy pants to the bandage under them, the white gauze adhered to her right thigh. Even her hands and head, numb, the fingers on her right a little too thick, her thoughts a little too slow. Concussion, they'd said, from hitting the road, the thick digits a side effect of the painkillers mixing with the other drugs in her system. What was it, they'd asked, right before they tried to stop her from leaving. Concussions need to be monitored, fall asleep, don't wake up. Coma, death. Lots of scary words to keep her in the hospital bed, hooked to monitors and under eyes that took one look at the scars crawling her side, and turned to her with pity.

But there were scarier things than them. Like the hole in the loft's floor. Like the black box. Like Hamish.

At this time of morning/night, when even the ravers were

trundling back to their beds, the lanes were quiet, the bus stand deserted, the taxi rank... Just a lone yellow cab idling at the curb. She stood, hunched, right arm wrapped across her ribs as if that would quash the grinding, pinching sensation leaking through the painkillers.

She had to check the bus timetable manually, glasses lost in the accident, watch smashed – a Scourge with no tech, naked, vulnerable. No buses for another three hours.

Vlad didn't have three hours. Hadn't had the four the nurses had kept her in the ER, or the one it had taken her to argue her way out of the ward. Hamish had the black box, Hamish had the whale, the spiderweb, had Samael, had her right in his bony, tattooed hand. She had to get it back before he cracked the encryption, or gave it to Grandmother, and to do that she need to get online, needed the Cube.

The Cube. Which was at the DKZero, halfway across the city. Too far to walk, even if her head wasn't more cotton wool than sense.

The taxi grew large in her sight, while peppermint wound through her nose and flames... She'd never forget the sound of the flames, the heat pushing through the door.

Her breath came quicker, ribs pinched.

The yellow car didn't go away, a bus didn't slide into the stop belying the timetable, and Ximisthus didn't magically appear from where she'd left it, under the lone streetlight at the estate.

Her feet were blocks, her boots heavy but she had Grandmother, she had ice in her veins and frost in her voice as she opened the yellow door, slid into the taxi and gave the driver the address.

The ride to the mansion was hell, squashed in the back, unable to position the seat belt so it didn't press against her fractured rib. But the pain beat the panic at being in a car. In the back, up against the passenger side door. Nausea rode the panic, pain rode the nausea and the blessed dark of the deserted streets kept the nightmares at bay. No pounding rain, no fire or sirens or flashing lights. It helped that the stale smell of old vinyl seats and the incense swinging from the driver's rearview mirror were so different from the Bentley's plush leather and Ma's peppermint candies.

The taxi arrived, she opened the door... the driver's angry 'hey!' reminding her to pay, dragging actual cash out of the hoodie's inner pocket before she bolted.

Into the cold night, shuffling through the red door.

The mansion was quiet, the wee hours of morning shuttering the big floor-to-ceiling window in darkness, broken only by scattered streetlights and the distant twinkle of the city across the lake. There wasn't even a moon, clouds covering the stars. The little light there was cast long, deep shadows across the living area's polished concrete, made a mountain out of the old table and turned the gaming chairs into choppy peaks.

The low, dull glow of the night lights near the floor threw just enough yellow to outline the shoe cabinet. She rested her little plastic bag of medication and bandages on the floor beside it. Somehow, she took her boots off, the zip loud, so very, very loud in the silence, almost loud enough to drown her screaming ribs, the whimper only half-caught.

The stairs came next. Just the two, up from the foyer to the living area. Each one sent shards of fire through her chest, her leg, her back.

Little mounds of soda cans and empty pizza boxes were scattered across the old table, the boxes laid open, spewing their scent into the air – sweet pineapple, greasy cheese, the sharp bite of chilli and tomato. There was one in the middle, in front of her chair, lid still closed, a solitary can sitting beside it.

She stared at it a second, injured arm cradling her ribs, uninjured arm cradling the injured one, caught her breath and steeled herself. They'd ordered pizza for her.

After she'd told Huang Yimo and Sticky to get lost, that she didn't need them. They'd ordered pizza. For her.

Somehow, that seemed like a big thing, bigger even than the kid and the car. But that was just the meds talking, the painkillers lingering in her system.

That was all it was.

She turned away from the table.

The main stairs were next.

She faced the long coil of concrete and glass, and they seemed to her a mountain.

One step at a time, Vlad. One step.

The refrain became a mantra, a meditation as she pulled herself up the curling concrete, glad of the shadows that hid her hunched form, her white-knuckled grip on the railing. How many stairs were there? It didn't matter. Just one more. One more. One. More.

Was it pain or blood that trailed warmth down her leg? Had she broken the stitches? Was she leaving a trail of red behind her? Shit, she couldn't do that, she should clean it up—

Vlad stopped herself before she crouched, hands still clutching the railing. No, not now, not yet. She had to get to her room, had to fix the leak or she'd just make things worse. One more step. Just one more.

The landing came both sooner and later than she expected. She stumbled, no stair under her foot, the railing gone. Caught herself before she fell. Pain was her friend now, a reminder of what she was doing, why she was doing it, just like the bag against her side, bouncing against her hip, the thin plastic handles wrapped around her good hand.

Had to get to her room. Just one more step. One more.

It was darker up here, less of the meagre light reaching the balcony, the night glows farther apart, casting their yellow light in solitary pools beside each door.

The carpet muffled her steps, turned the heavy, halting tread into a shuffling *shush shush*. Two doors down, two pools of light to go. There was hers. Samael a shadowy sentinel beside the door. Just one more step. Just one.

Night turned the deep-purple door into a hole in the universe, the lock pad a cold, silky control panel beeping under her hand.

Snick. Vlad froze. That wasn't her door.

Snick. That was hers, all she had to do was push it open, drag her bloody, aching body inside—

'Ana?' A sleepy voice, a tall, sweatpants and t-shirt-clad silhouette in her peripheral.

No, no, not him. Why was Zixin even here, in pyjamas? Didn't he have a penthouse, an expensive silk covered bed all to himself?

Didn't he have Hamish and Grandmother to report to?

She half-fell, half slipped through the door.

'Ana.' Awareness in his tone, pushing away sleep. Confident, muffled steps starting toward her.

And she was through the door, shutting it. *Please shut in time. Please.*

Snick.

She leaned against it, forehead to the cool, composite wood, a blessing against the warmth under her skin. A solid, comforting barrier against the soft *thump* on the other side.

'Ana.' Xin'er muffled by the door. And really, she should move, should check the moisture running down her leg—was it blood or sweat?—and dig the painkillers out of the little plastic bag, maybe even the fever meds—was it time to take them?—but her body ached, and she was tired. Tired of the mission, the press, the secrets and the lies, tired of trying to keep everything straight.

Tired of playing it straight, of being the good guy instead of the Scourge.

Tired of the man on the other side of the door. Of how he made her feel.

Another thump, softer this time, and was it just her imagination, or did she hear him sigh? Did the cool, purple rectangle shift in its frame, as if Xin'er leaned against it?

She was tired right down to her DNA, all the way through to her soul, and moving... moving...

She picked herself up off the floor.

Moving was hard, putting the steel back into tired bones, into muscles more jelly than fibre, but a Tong was harder. Sturdier. Stronger. A Tong knew the importance of family, of duty and justice and responsibility.

A Tong did what she should, what she *had* to.

Her gaze found the Cube in its shadowy corner.

The painkillers would mess with the sauce, but this Tong had things to do.

She got to her feet.

39

Sticky shuffled down the stairs, gaze on the bright yellow unicorn horns on his slippers, not really seeing them, eyes still bleary and thoughts slow from the dream. He navigated the concrete risers on memory, which was probably why he noticed the dark red splotch halfway down. It wasn't much bigger than the tip of his pinky, almost blending in with the ashy concrete, but the hint of red was different, and he looked at it a second... Before shuffling on.

A'Yimo must have spilled her Dr Pepper, she was always doing that.

His slippers *shushed shushed* across the smooth floor on the way to the kitchen, unicorn heads bobbing with every step... The scent of stale dough and the greasy aftertaste of cold cheese slowed his steps, slowly turned his attention from the blurry haze of morning pouring through the kitchen windows, highlighting the pantry like the haven of stomach-settling sugar it was, to the game table. Pizza boxes still lay open on its surface, empty cans and water glasses scattered between.

Ugh... it was too early to look at that mess, but he couldn't stop himself from seeking out the box on the opposite side, nearest the glass walls. Still there, lid down, the can next to it still unopened, not looking like it had moved a micron overnight.

Had she come back at all?

He shuffled, tugging the ends of his fluffy pink dressing gown

wiLl knOW.

tighter and wondering if he should go back up the stairs, check on Vlad. Just to make sure. She'd looked pretty upset, under all that stoney-faced anger and the snarly bluster.

Sticky thought the others hadn't seen it, but then Huang Yimo ordered the vegetarian pizza and placed it in front of Vlad's chair.

He backed up and shuffled to the bottom of the stairs before he remembered that snarl, the way she'd flashed those teeth, like she'd take a bite of the next person to get in her face...

Sticky shuddered. Nope, he needed food first, the sweet crunch of Frosty Flakes before he faced that again. Bluster or no.

Yeah. He turned around, the unicorns bobbing with a little more purpose as he moved to the pantry, locating the bright box, snagging the last juice box out of the fridge.

Had to tell Granny to restock that—he did a quick check of the shelves—and the rolled oats Vlad ate. Maybe even add a few more green, leafy things to the list, although why she liked that... He shuddered.

He slid onto a stool, splashing milk and frosted goodness into a bowl on automatic, just like he reached for the feeds scrolling across the bench. The Fnatic–Skull Hack match had been on last night, and he needed to watch the replay and see if the rumours about the changes Skull Hack's tank had made to their armour load-out were true. It was probably just hype, a little bit of propaganda from their parent company, something to sell those mods they kept flashing. Even if they'd upgraded the tank's armour, it probably wouldn't make much difference, not unless they fixed that habit he had of overusing his...

The thought trailed off. There, amongst the bright pops of colour and snatches of mages and thieves duking it out on castle battlements and spaceships, was a face. An all-too-familiar face.

He almost missed it, didn't recognise his teammate so well without the challenge tilting the corner of her brow or the mocking humour in her dark-brown eyes. It was just a quick clip, and if "Samael?" hadn't been plastered across the bottom, or the dark elf's avatar hadn't flashed across the screen in the next second, he might have scrolled past, as it was...

Sticky paused, spoon caught between his teeth, flakes turning into a soggy, milky mush in the bottom of his bowl, the orange juice Vlad sneered at with such disdain forgotten beside his elbow. He grabbed the clip, dragged it across the bench and blew it up until it took over the marble top.

"Mysterious woman saves boy," scrolled across the bottom of what looked like a screen capture, washed out and grainy, static lines shuddering through the picture in the way of a screen recording a screen. There was a caption at the top—*"Anyone else seen this?"*—and comments streaming over the picture.

"Is that Samael?"

"What'd she do now?"

"She saved a kid*?!"*

"DKZero media spin! Bet she was just drunk."

"I don't know, the report said she was hit by a car..."

"It's probably not even her. If Samael had done something nice, DKZero would be plastering it all over the nets. That bitch needs all the good press she can get..."

Hit by a car.

That fragment leapt out and stabbed Sticky in the brain.

Hit by a car.

He scrolled back, froze the feed on the grainy, pixelated snapshot of the woman's face... Square jaw, dark hair curling around her nape, black fitted sweat-top done all the way up to her chin...

'Shwitt.' The curse came out jumbled around the spoon, frosty flakes and milk spilling down his chin. He was ripping the spoon out and wiping the mess off his face even as he leapt off the stool, the bleary sleep-fog shredded by the adrenalin pumping through his body.

Shuffle, shuffle, shuffle... thwap as he kicked the unicorns off his feet and rushed up the stairs. And then he was arrowing straight for... Whose door?

For a couple of seconds he danced nervously between the purple and the black... He should see if Vlad was alright, but if she'd been hit by a car...? And Lu Chen, he had to know, because even if it wasn't true...

He danced foot-to-foot, bouncing between the two doors.

Shit. Fuck. Shit.

Make a decision, Sticky. Make a decision.

Lu Chen.

He pounded on the black door, the sound of his fist a hollow boom in the corridor. Loud. Really loud. Loud enough to wake Lu Chen, and maybe, if he was lucky, loud enough to wake Vlad and then—

A creak and the large black rectangle swung inward a fraction, just enough for a pair of sleep-fogged amber eyes to peer up at him, Ming Li Na's dark amber hair falling over her forehead.

Oh shit, oh shit. Not Lu Chen, but okay, this was better right? Two thieves, one spell.

'Sticky? What's wrong?'

'Vlad got hit by a car.' He swiped the post off his watch and plastered it to the door. He bounced on his toes, trying to peer over Ming Li Na's shoulder, wishing his neck was rubber so he could angle it around the small slither of space between it and the door jamb.

Was Lu Chen awake? They needed Lu Chen. Lu Chen would want to know, and if—

The door ripped open. Lu Chen, black silk pyjamas making it so his head seemed to float, bodiless, against the dark backdrop of his room. 'What?' he said, whatever trace of sleep there might have been in his eyes obliterated by the hard, scary thing that made him captain.

'I think,' Sticky added. An afterthought, because, really he didn't have all the data and—

Ming Li Na pushed past him even as Lu Chen grabbed the post and expanded it across the door.

Sticky danced backwards, indecision once again rooting him to the spot. Follow Ming Li Na or wait here with Lu Chen, just in case... Just in case what? The captain needed his help searching the feeds? Checking hospitals? *That's really stupid, Sticky. Great logic you're following here.*

Knocking, and this time it was Ming Li Na, a polite little *rap rap rap* on Vlad's door. 'Vlad?' she called softy. 'Vlad, are you in there?'

Sticky drifted over, not too close, not too far, his heart in his throat and an awful kind of certainty in his chest. Whatever was on the other side of the shiny, purple rectangle—whether it was Vlad's glaring face or her dead body—he was sure he didn't want to know.

Ming Li Na glanced over her shoulder, straight at Sticky. 'She's not downstairs?'

He shook his head.

'Did you check the gym?'

'I—' Oh, shit. He hadn't, he'd just seen the post and rushed up the stairs...

'I'll do it.' A'Yimo, already heading down the curving stairway, feet slapping against the concrete.

They waited.

Seconds dragging by, long and loud, and Sticky wondered why he'd never noticed just how cavernous the mansion was, how loud the air-cyclers or how very, very far the gym was—

Running feet from below. 'Not there!'

Sticky's stomach clenched, and he saw the same fear widen Ming Li Na's eyes.

She turned back to the door, pounded a little harder. 'Vlad, open the door.'

Silence.

Ming Li Na pounded again. Harder. 'Vlad?!'

Then they were being pushed aside and it was a different black-clad figure - not Lu Chen but Zixin, the normally dapper team manager wearing sweatpants and a stained tee. Sticky hadn't even realised he'd spent the night.

And then Zixin slammed his hand against the control panel beside Vlad's door and—

The door opened.

Vlad glared at them.

5 am Wh3r3 12 a3L?

40

Her whole body ached.

Vlad leaned back in the bus, turned her face to the blacked outsides, and tried not to let it show.

She could still taste the painkillers on the back of her tongue, a dry metallic scum not even three bottles of water and one of Sticky's chemical OJs could counter. But at least the trolls weren't banging holes through her skull, even if the elves were busy casting fog spells, making her thoughts as blurry as her eyes.

Vlad rubbed her temple, watched pain scoot across her reflection's brow and wrinkle her chin as they drove through the forest of fans. Neon signs and scrolling holo-banners lit up the darkened windows, red and yellow and orange, waving and flicking.

Flames.

She jerked. Looked away, across the narrow bus aisle and right into Zixin's dark-bronze stare.

Fuck.

Another jerk. And there was Sticky, twisted around in his seat. Big panda eyes looking at her.

The bastard hadn't stopped looking at her, not since she'd opened her bedroom door, trying not to let her legs wobble and to contain the desperate chatter of her teeth. Mixing painkillers and sauce had been as bad as the doctor said. All she'd wanted to do was sleep, or drown herself in a river of ice, anything to quench the fever raging through her blood like a demented bull.

But she couldn't.

She couldn't. She had a job to do, a mission to accomplish, a Grandmother to crush.

And she needed to do it now, especially after last night, after meeting Ru Ping or whoever it was behind the avatar's eyes. A last desperate gambit, putting all her cards on the table before Hamish hijacked Samael and did it for her.

She just needed to draw Grandmother out, show her a juicy enough lure, and put her on record. Nothing was bigger than the white field and—though she still didn't have it—the Deposit.

But she had Ma's keyboards.

Which was why she'd ignored the doctors' warnings about mixing painkillers and VR, and taken Ru Ping back to the field.

It was no longer a field. No longer a pretty creek flowing through bleach-white grass. In the eight hours since she'd last logged-in, the creek had become a raging torrent, burrowing so deep the field was now a valley, skyscraper walls made of the boulders it tore out of the earth. How deep would it go, how high the walls? In another few hours, would the boulders climb over her head and close in the middle? Would she have been standing in a cave?

If it's new ability to pick up semi-trailers and relocate entire buildings wasn't enough, there'd been the falls.

The white, endless, paper-field was no longer quite so endless. She'd materialised where she usually did, but instead of kilometres and kilometres of tall grass stretching to the horizon... a giant cliff had cut the ground not four metres from her robes, and over it...

The end of the world would have drowned under the roar of the river crashing over the edge. Rainbows had played in the air, in colours that pierced the eyes and twisted her brain. Strange colours, impossible even, and yet the paper-sun had refracted through the rainbow water and painted the world in shades of magenta and purple that had crept through her neurones, set fire to her tastebuds and sang in her ears.

Ru Ping's knight had stood on a rocky outcrop at the edge of the waterfall, the red in her black armour a violent slash against all the white. There'd been a moment, a second as Samael stood behind her, trying not to huddle against the pain leaking through from the real, when the knight shuddered, pixels interrupted by jagged lines.

Everything in Samael had come alive at that, an electric bolt of victory as the Cube analysed the change in signal. Before the avatar turned, she knew it wasn't Ru Ping staring at her from the avatar's sea-blue eyes, had already let loose the player address trojan Grandmother had attempted to use on her.

'This is not the Deposit,' Grandmother said. 'Is it?' As if she didn't know.

// *It's a piece.* A big piece, she'd realised as she watched a long, fat form leap from the water, saw the marking on its belly.

'I don't want a piece, Ms Tong; I want all of it.' A step forward, black boots digging up the white soil.

Samael's gut had clenched at the familiar phrase. Just how stupid did Grandmother think she was? Stupid enough, hopefully, for the trojan to do its work.

// *Tomorrow,* she'd said. *You'll have the rest tomorrow, during the game.*

Samael had fritzed as she logged-out, and when she ran the diagnostics on the Cube... It's cores had been maxed, the cloud whale still in its systems, taking up space, refusing to die. But then, it wasn't really a whale, was it?

The Cube needed a purge, a reset to clear the whale from its systems, but without the box... Fuck. Without the black box she might as well throw the Cube in the nearest trash compactor and start again.

Fuck Hamish. Fuck Tina and Huang Yimo, fuck Sticky and his sticky little nose. Without them... without them—

The bus stopped, and was it just her, or did the driver slam the brakes?

Pain ricocheted through her skull, and she fought the groan that came with it.

How was she going to do this? Forget the med sensors on the VR unit, the stage, the fans, the cameras. Forget pretending like everything was fine, that her skin wasn't three sizes too small for her skeleton and her knees didn't shake. How the fuck was she getting off the bus? How the fuck had she got *on* the bus?

Grandmother flashed before her eyes, the proud lift of her chin, the way she'd sat in that chair, ashen-faced but still strong. Still arrogant.

Vlad clenched her own hands. Grandmother was how she'd done it, that was how she was *going* to do it.

Movement around her, boots on the floor, shadows passing by... One stopping. Leaning over her, sandalwood and warmth invading her space, a hand reaching for her hood—

She slapped it away. 'Fuck off, Zixin.'

The hand came back, grabbed her fingers as she made another slap. 'You don't have to do this.'

She peered up at him. 'My job?' She snorted, regretting the sound as soon as it left her nose. Her head... 'Get out of my way, I don't need your kind of help.' She stood and Zixin retreated, but his eyes didn't leave her, even if his hands did. The weight of his gaze followed her out of the seat, down the aisle, a lodestone waiting for her to fall, and Sticky...

The panda waited for her at the front, standing at the bottom of the steps, hovering even as cameras went off and fans yelled and waved placards.

Grandmother in the back of her head, stiffening her knees and giving her the focus to take those three downwards steps. Then Sticky beside her, holding her arm, and she didn't shake him off because there were all those lights, and not all of them were from the cameras.

She must have blacked out somewhere, body working on autopilot, because the fans and half the stadium were behind them before she knew it, and it was no longer Sticky holding her arm, but Zixin holding her *up* and that was bad, that was...

...what had that last thought been?

Her hood was pushed back and she was staring at the ceiling, at Xin'er yelling at someone, then looking down, frowning at her. Except it wasn't anger in his face wasn't frustration. It was... Fear? She touched the little mark between his brows. She'd never seen him afraid before.

Grandmother, with her stern face. *You're bleeding, Vladana.*

She was bleeding. On the cold, white floor in Xin'er's arms, a giant red puddle.

Vlad pushed herself up, or tried to, didn't get far before arms tightened around her, keeping her down.

'I'm fine,' she said, or thought she said. There was a ringing in her ears and the hand she shoved into Xin'er's chest didn't feel quite as strong as it should have, her knees and feet slow to respond.

Her eyes worked fine though, despite the starlight streaking the edges, the fuzzy-wuzzy halos around Ming Li Na and Huang Yimo running down the corridor, same with the paramedic in their blue and red uniform close behind. The soft edges and the glare focused her gaze, let her pick out the Scottish man behind the commotion, with his bald head and tattoos crawling over his neck, as an eagle sighted prey.

Everything in Vlad stilled.

Hamish stared back, a dark purple bruise spilling over his cheek and half-shutting one eye, split lip cracking with the smirk twisting his face. He lifted a hand, pointed it like a gun, and let it jerk... Once, twice, three times and then four. Her heart jerked with it, knowing without having to look who he pointed at—Ming Li Na, Huang Yimo, Sticky, Xin'er—before he turned that finger on her.

'No.' Vlad lurched to her feet, adrenaline giving her the strength to push out of Xin'er's arms and run-stumble down the corridor. Head pounding, copper bursting over her tongue, shards driven into her skull.

She made it two strides, two concrete-eating, pain-filled strides, before her legs failed. Huang Yimo was there, catching her under the arms, and then there was Ming Li Na and the paramedic... and Hamish, still smirking as he turned and disappeared.

Starlight ate the rest of Vlad's vision.

41

'It's gone too far, we have to stop it.'

'No.'

'Gran—'

'No.'

'She almost *killed* herself.'

'But she didn't.'

'She would have, if she'd got on that stage and in that VR chair.'

Silence, the line hollow and empty save for the sound of distant breathing. 'We cannot stop,' she said, and he didn't know if she spoke to him or herself, soft as it was. 'Not now. We're close, Xin'er. She'll understand, in the end.'

'Not if she's dead.'

42

Antiseptic had a strange smell. High and sweet, sneaking in under the crisp scent of clean sheets and the warmer one of coffee. She was warm from chin to toes, the bed under her soft, but there was something clamped on her index finger and another thing pinching the back of her hand. The same hand was the only cold spot on her body, save her nose, and maybe that was why the sharp pinch across the back bothered her so, enough to push through the fog settled inside her skull, and once that happened...

The *beep, beep*, soft yet piercing overlaid the quiet murmur in her ears, the plastic squeaking on shiny floors brought her the rest of the way from the fog, parted her eyelids, took in the white-tiled ceiling, the metal curtain ring, the uncomfortably white lights. And as soon as those registered, mixed with the smells, the pinch and clamp on her hand, as soon as she twisted her too-full, stuffy head and caught sight of Xin'er—slouched in a chair, one elbow propped on the armrest, fingers pressed to his temples, eyes closed, face drawn, shirtsleeves rolled to the elbow, gold watch heavy on his wrist—her stomach hollowed.

She knew where she was, and no. No, this wasn't okay.

And not just because she still had to draw Grandmother out before Hamish—

Vlad struggled to sit. Fire shot through her ribs, drew a gasp from her throat.

One moment Xin'er was in the chair, the next he had his arm under her shoulders, helping her up, arranging pillows. Underneath, the bed whirred, top half lifting. Hair falling into her face, thick, dark-brown strands sliding past her ears, a wave slipping over her shoulder. Some of it got in her mouth, finer strands catching in her eyelashes. She tensed to rid herself of it—

Xin'er was already there, reading her mind, those long, square fingers plucking stands from her nose, brushing them from her forehead.

She stared at him, the way his own hair was mussed, the dark circles under his eyes, his chin, the rumpled shirt.

'Get me—' Her voice was rough, a croak choking on the first word, the rest stumbling out her throat. She cleared it, tried again. 'Get me out.'

The chin tightened, lines in his jaw, the hollow behind his eye deepening, a frown furrowing his brow. He plucked another hair from her cheek, all his attention on that one long strand. 'No,' he said. Soft, tired. Firm.

She pushed the covers—

Those large brown hands were on hers, stopping her. 'No, Ana,' he said again. Still not looking, gaze on her ear.

She jerked against him, ignoring the pain in her ribs, the fire in her lungs, like that single motion had been a marathon. Alarms rang, but not enough to drown out the beeping, not as steady now, the antiseptic in her nose, the memories crawling from her nightmares.

Xin'er didn't budge, except for his face, the muscles turning hard, turning to stone. Still not looking at her.

She tried not to panic, tried to inject ice into her spine, her words, her eyes. Tried to freeze the room, just like Grandmother. Just like Grandmother. Except... except the nightmares came with fire, flames racing over a crumpled hood, Ma crying as she held back a river of blood, melting the ice. Melting Grandmother.

Breathe, Vlad. Breathe.

Breathe.

'Get off me.'

Those hands tightening. 'No, Ana.'

Breathing harder. Shorter. More of that antiseptic in her lungs, more fire through her ribs, down her arm. Her right arm, the scars pulling. Hot. Everything was hot and she couldn't feel Grandmother anymore, barely hung on to the last icicles shrouding her voice. The last bits of reason.

She had to get out of here. Out of the bed, out of the hospital, away from nurses and sympathetic faces and bleach, so much fucking *bleach.*

A twist, left wrist popping free, shoving it under Xin'er's chin, into his larynx. Move or choke it was, and he moved, but his hands were quick, just not quick enough. The covers off, cold hitting her thighs, feet reaching for the slick, pale hospital floor—

Shoved back onto the bed. 'Ana—'

She pushed back, memory-flames licking her wrist, pounding her heart, and her hands were going everywhere, slipping and sliding under Xin'er's, eels on the end of her arms until they were caught. Held.

'Ana. Stop!' A shake. The big square hands bands around her biceps, the dark-bronze eyes spearing her brain, the anger in them, the cavern between the black brows, pushing her back against the headboard, pillows squeezing out around her.

Vlad stopped, all the way down to her toes. Stopped pushing, stopped breathing, stopped trying to escape the memory, the fire melting her Wonder Woman costume to her arm.

For one perfect moment, she was still. Still enough to note the rasp in her lungs, the ache in her chest, the IVs pulling and tugging the back of her hand, the way she didn't quite feel right, cotton in her head, body thick, sluggish. The second person in the room in pale blue pyjamas.

And then air shuddered back into her lungs, the cutting scent of bleach with it, and that one perfect moment was gone, because she was getting out of there. Getting out of there *now* and—

A hiss under her right ear, on the opposite side from Xin'er. The figure in pale blue moving back a step, picking up her wrist as lethargy stole her body, a soft warm wind spreading from her neck, across her shoulders, making her fingers tingle, her heart slow.

A nurse, the person in pyjamas was a nurse.

She should have known that, should have seen.

Should have seen a lot of things.

<⊙>

Sweet, heady roses overlaid the antiseptic the next time she came around. Soft voices played under the monitor's *beep* and sunlight warmed her cheeks and nose, staining the back of her lids gold-red. Sharp-tongued lethargy still fuzzed her head, turned her thoughts to syrup, made her limbs heavy, stung the back of her throat and itched her fingers.

She wanted to move. Needed to scrape the heavy, biting taste of day-old gunge from her tongue, peel it from her lips, but her body wouldn't move, thoughts disconnected from muscles, muscles from hands. Even her eyes and the space between them remained unmoving.

'How is she?' Grandmother. If the pathway between neurones and nerves worked, the sound of that voice, so close on Vlad's left would have jolted her upright.

'They're keeping her sedated.' Xin'er, on the right.

A thin, old hand slipping under Vlad's, the long bony fingers wrapping around her palm, another hand laying on top. 'She panicked.' Not a question. 'She never did like hospitals.'

'Can you blame her?'

The old hand squeezing, the plain, equally old gold around the ring finger pressing into Vlad's palm, then a shuddering breath. 'I didn't expect her to be hurt.'

If Grandmother's presence had been enough to jolt her upright, the hitch in those few words, the way they rose and then broke... Vlad's heart stopped in her chest.

'Grandm—'

Xin'er cut off, the hand over the top of hers gone, and Vlad didn't need her eyes to see Grandmother silencing him, the straight, old shoulders rolling back, the dark painted lips pressing tight, the ice shutting down the patrician face.

'It is done, Zixin.' The softness was gone from Grandmother's words, only the warmth under Vlad's hand remained. 'Vladana will understand when it is done; someone had to expose Marion as RaZIeL, and she would have insisted on doing it herself, had she known.'

What? But—?

Marion? Marion Bourne?

'Then why didn't you tell her?' Weight on Xin'er's side of the bed, an electric hum ran through her side as she pictured him pressing his fists into the mattress and leaning over her. 'You didn't just manipulate her into joining DKZero, you lied about the Deposit and knowing who caused the accident.'

Grandmother wasn't Oily Face?

The lethargy, the gum in her nerves, stopped her from twitching and giving herself away when cold, thin fingers—Grandmother's fingers—brushed hair from Vlad's forehead.

'So did you, Zixin.' Calm, Grandmother was so calm.

And the fact that Xin'er had known shouldn't hurt, not one little bit, because she'd expected it, she'd known and yet—

More weight on the right side of the bed and a shadow blocking some of the light. Xin'er leaning over her? Did his face match the anger in his voice, the aura vibrating through her arm and hip, even through the covers? Did his eyes burn as they stared down Grandmother?

No need to guess Grandmother's expression, Vlad knew it as surely as if it were her own. Impassive. Cold. Indomitable. A wall for all Xin'er's anger to crash against.

'You used her, Tong Shufeng.' Xin'er using her grandmother's first name sent a jolt through Vlad's gut. 'She's in this bed because of *you*.'

'Because of *us*,' Grandmother amended. 'You cannot absolve yourself of blame, just like you cannot absolve yourself of your part in her parents' deaths.'

Another jolt, heart bouncing hard against her ribs. Why weren't the monitors picking it up? Where was the beeping, the sirens, the wails? Where was her voice? Stuck in her unresponsive throat, that's where, bound in the same drugs holding her limbs hostage.

There was no response from the right, except for the tension winding through the weight on the bed, the sheets pulling tight over arm and hip as fists ground into it. And Vlad wanted to know how and why, wanted to grab his shirt and climb up his chest to scream in his face, "Tell me, tell me. Tell me!"

Instead, she lay under the blankets, head propped on soft pillows, sunlight warming her toes, roses sweetening her lungs.

'I only left a game dongle in the backseat,' Zixin said.

'And gave RaZIeL a foothold in the car's systems.' Grandmother's thin, cold hand wrapped tight around Vlad's, fingers curling over the back. 'It was always a gamble that Vladana would force RaZIeL to expose herself, but after all these years, it was the only move I had left.'

The cold hand squeezed. 'Now, Marion has what she always wanted and because of it, my only blood lies in a hospital bed.' The ice in Grandmother's voice cracked. 'It was my final play, Zixin, my last hope of avenging my son's death; it was not supposed to bring down his daughter too.'

'Ana won't care, she'll just keep trying.'

'I am aware.'

Grandmother lifted Vlad's hand. Thin lips pressed to the back before it was placed back on the bed, the cold hand retreating before the covers were drawn over it. A chair scraped against linoleum.

'I have arranged a press conference, I'll put an end to it once and for all.'

'You can't—'

'Do not tell me what I can and cannot do, boy.' Vladana pictured the sunlight haloing her grandmother's steel-grey head, glimmering off the sharp cheekbones and the noble thrust of her chin. 'I have been doing both longer than you have been alive.'

The sharp *clack clack* of Grandmother's heels signalled her leaving. 'Keep her here until it is done.' And then she was gone.

<⊙>

The next time Vlad came to, the sun was gone and so was Xin'er.

Faint yellow light spilled over the opposite wall, highlighting the bland seascape in its fancy gilt frame and the spray of flowers underneath. Neither did anything to make the hospital walls any less... *antiseptic* was the only word that came to mind. Maybe it was the ever present smell of bleach or rubber soles squeaking on shiny floors, the rails on the side of the single bed or the blue-pastel, waffle-weave blanket pulled to her chin. Maybe it was all of these things, maybe it was none, maybe it was the nightmares—

Vlad pushed herself right, paused halfway as her ribs protested, but it was a dull ache, not the violent stab of before, so she went the rest of the way, blankets puddling around her waist. Someone had braided her hair, the long tail slipping over her shoulder as she leaned forward, pushing the blanket off her legs, scrunching her knees up, ready to swing her feet off the bed.

She paused again at the sight of her feet; someone had put fluffy, white, cat-faced socks on them, complete with yellow rounded ears sticking out the sides and a bobble for the nose. She poked the bobble, it bounced and... Cat socks, with ears. Her brain stumbled on that. Who...?

Unicorn-headed slippers popped into her mind.

Sticky.

She poked the nose again. The bobble, the way it pulled at the big black cat eyes and made the yellow ears jiggle...

Cute.

A moment like that, then standing, or rather, leaning against the bed. Frame cold against the back of her thighs, blankets spilling off with her.

Shoes, she needed shoes and clothes that weren't the hospital pyjamas the same pastel-blue as the blankets covering her legs, buttoned up her chest, long sleeves falling over the back of her hands. Tubes pulling at the left hand, trying to pull her back onto the bed, tying her to the IV stand beside it.

She picked at the catheter in the back of her hand, the tape pulling at her skin, the needle pinching underneath. She hated the things. They made her itch and hurt worse when she pulled them out, like somehow her veins had melded with the metal.

Free of the IV, she resumed her search for clothes.

The door opened, admitting first Huang Yimo and then Ming Li Na.

They stood frozen for a moment, Vlad eyeing her teammates, her teammates eyeing her, and then Ming Li Na was across the room, applying pressure to the blood spots atop Vlad's hand. Huang Yimo followed slower, putting a basket of oranges on the little table at the end of the bed.

'You're not meant to be up,' Ming Li Na said.

'Let go.' Vlad tugged on her hand, and tried to push past, but the girl's grip was strong. 'I need to—'

She swayed, the world swimming as target lines and dialogs popped where they had no business being.

'Kill yourself?' Huang Yimo was on her other side, helping Ming Li Na guide her backward.

'Get off me—'

'Bitch.' An explosion of red curls and Tina's freckled nose replaced the target lock. 'You move one freaking muscle and I will crush you.' A small hand shoved Vlad in the chest, toppling her back on the bed. 'Now, stay.'

'I'm not—'

'You are,' Tina interrupted, even as Ming Li Na smoothed a hand over Vlad's shoulder.

'Just wait,' the other girl whispered. There was a seriousness in her expression, a darkness behind her eyes that echoed the one in Huang Yimo's behind her, and gave Vlad pause. 'Tina already told us everything.'

Her stomach bottomed out. 'What do you mean, what's "everything"?'

It was Huang Yimo's turn to speak. 'Your parents, how you've been trying to find RaZIeL. Your grandmother.'

'My nose,' added Sticky as he clomped into the room, his round panda face fierce, a suitable complement for Lu Chen's stoic one behind him.

Vlad hissed, not sure if it was anger or fear rising from the hollow in her belly, twisting her insides as she stood. 'Tina...'

Her best friend spun around, and the hurt and fury in her gaze took Vlad's breath. 'You promised to tell me *everything*, Ana. Fucking everything. This—' She twirled her finger around the people gathered in the hospital room '—is on you.'

'I didn't—' Vlad began.

Lu Chen spoke from the other side of the room, a serious shadow propping up the wall. 'We're a team,' he said. 'And this is not just your problem.'

'You should see this.' Sticky threw a screen onto the wall.

A newscast spread across the pale beige, white text and a bright red banner scrolling across the bottom, but it was TI's towering glass and steel edifice that caught her attention, that and Grandmother standing before it. Straight and tall and stark in her black pantsuit, shoulders thrown back, hair a steel waterfall past her shoulders, chin lifted against the camera flashes, black eyes staring through the lens. Imperious. Commanding.

'It is with great pride that I announce this collaboration between Tong Industries and VisionM.'

The camera panned and there, wrapped in a metallic-beige trench coat with her silver streaked hair falling behind her shoulders, was Marion Bourne.

Oily Face.

RaZIeL.

'With TI's extensive resources and VisionM's technological superiority, we will realise my late daughter-in-law's life's work; true artificial intelligence. For too long, her pioneering research has sat abandoned but now—' Grandmother lifted an all-too-familiar flash drive '—in partnership with my friend Marion Bourne, we shall bring it into the light, ushering in a new future...'

The rest of the speech faded, but not the vision. Marion stepped onto the podium and clasped Grandmother's hand, the one holding the drive, fingers swallowing the arrow-shaped skull engraved on the black plastic.

The stuffing went out of Vlad's knees. One second she was standing, the other there her chest was a black hole sucking all the air from the room, and Huang Yimo was helping her into a chair.

'Should we call a nurse?'

'Just give her a minute.' Lu Chen crouched in front of her, arms on black-clad knees, staring at her from under his fringe. Patient. No concern in his black eyes, no pressure. None of Grandmother's expectation, none of Xin'er's guilt or worry, just waiting. Waiting for Vlad to breathe, for the shock to pass, for her brain to start functioning again.

Grandmother had just given Marion Bourne the Cube.

Marion Bourne.

RaZIeL.

And when she did, when she sucked a great lungful of antiseptic and rose-laden air down her throat, only then did he speak. Still crouching, still looking up at her through his fringe.

'VisionM has been trying to sign this deal with your grandmother for the last two years,' Lu Chen said, still holding

Vlad's gaze. Calm. Steady. 'After my mother learned of it, she approached Chairwoman Tong; a collaboration between TI and VisionM would be the end of NuGet, so she sought to secure the deal herself. Your grandmother was willing to consider it, at a price.'

Vlad nodded. 'Zixin taking over DKZero.'

'And bringing you in,' Ming Li Na said. 'Although your grandmother wouldn't tell her why.'

'She was using me to draw out RaZIeL.'

Huang Yimo's arm around her shoulder tightened, like that band of wiry strength could dispel the cold. And Ming Li Na, sitting on the other chair arm, adding her hand to the warmth.

'I'm sure—' Ming Li Na began.

'She used you.' Lu Chen cut the platitudes off. 'You used her too, it's just that your grandmother got what she wanted first.' He rose, one hand on his knee, pushing him up, the other outstretched, waiting under Vlad's nose. 'Now, it's your turn.'

Her turn.

She looked from the hand to Lu Chen then Huang Yimo and Sticky and Ming Li Na behind him. Stared at all those faces, at sympathy and understanding and—looking back at Lu Chen—determination. The hard, implacable righteousness of a Tong.

Grandmother would have been proud.

He flexed his hand. 'We're a team.'

She put her hand in his. 'A team.'

43

410n3 bU7 4 m4991e

No one asked where they started; that was obvious, to everyone except the driver who kept darting glances at Huang Yimo in the rearview mirror and Vlad in the passenger seat beside him, both of them dressed in the same deathly black. They wore Huang Yimo's clothes, shirt and jeans, but while Huang Yimo sported a short, fitted jacket with red stripes down the sleeves, a hoodie bunched around Vlad's neck.

The driver's nervous twitch almost made up for the heavy smell of leather and the too-strong pine coming from the little cardboard tree hanging from the rearview mirror. Almost. There'd been a minor tussle as Ming Li Na attempted to slide Vlad in the back after Huang Yimo, concern written all over her face, but there was no way Vlad was squishing in against the back door, not with the hospital at their back, the smell of it stuck in her nose.

The bright yellow passenger door *thudded* shut and the driver's frown had almost been welcome. Different, just like Huang Yimo in the back, giving directions, Lu Chen pulling Ming Li Na back from the curb, half-dragging her to another taxi farther down the rank, Sticky trailing in their wake, head already buried in his palm unit.

There'd just been the road after that, the driver's nervous tick, the *rah rah rah* of the tyres on the bitumen, afternoon sun glaring off the white stripes. The pine and leather thickened with the silence and the recycled air – was it a fraction too cold, or was that just the nerves and the shock yet to wear away?

Grandmother at the podium, her firm, cold voice cutting through the babble, the cacophony as she walked back down the stairs. It played on repeat, shutting out the cars, the turn off the freeway, the lights and signs. Kept her in that two-minute loop, all the way across the city, across the river, through the surrounding parks, to the giant glass buildings on the other side. The pedestrians in their business suits—shirts and ties, heels and blouses, hair, makeup, briefcases—the fancy shops, the restaurants, the wide curved drive to the covered entrance, the yellow taxi out of place amongst the sleek black cars with their silver hood ornaments.

Huang Yimo got out, as out of place in her chunky boots and cargo jeans as the taxi.

Vlad hesitated, staring at the tall glass tower, so different from Grandmother's. The sun reflected gold off the sides, catching in the green wall climbing from the garden spilling out of its foot, seeming to erupt from the steel girders and gather on terraces farther up.

For a moment, as she sat in the taxi, fingers picking at the beaded seat cover, the catheter's ghost still itching her hand, hospital stuck in her nose, the green wave took on a white cast and the leaves and flowers spilling from the building sparkled, a rainbow falling from the sky. Crash and rush.

A cleared throat, the driver twitching again.

Vlad found the handle.

The sun was warm enough to chase the chill from her bones, and the business suits, the half-interested looks they cast, added steel to her spine. It made the walk across the concrete apron to the big glass building and the sliding doors easier, even if the aches in her body and the pain-killers still fuzzed her thoughts.

Vlad halted inside the foyer, Huang Yimo at her side, both of them looking up at the triple-storey ceiling and the giant marble walls that hid the elevators, as if they could see through them.

'You sure?' Huang Yimo, hands at her sides but hovering, just a little. 'The doctor—'

'We do it now.' There was steel in her voice, borrowed from her knees, from the glances thrown their way. The doctor hadn't wanted to discharge her, not a second time, but they had, after a lecture on the dangers of mixing a concussion and the drugs in her system with VR. 'Before either of them have a chance to act.'

The "them" being VisionM and TI – Marion and Grandmother, snatching the last scraps of Ma's work. The last piece Vlad had of her.

She wouldn't let them have it, not without a price.

At her side, Huang Yimo nodded.

They made it to the elevators without challenge from the receptionists behind the long marble counter or the security guards beside the turnstiles. Huang Yimo seemed surprised, her reflection in the shiny elevator doors showing scrunched brows and stiff shoulders, but Vlad wasn't.

Marion would be expecting her.

Just hopefully, not so soon.

The elevator *dinged*, the doors opened.

Ru Ping waited for them. If not for the dark, square glasses, Vlad wouldn't have recognised the heavy dressed in the sleek, grey pantsuit.

Vlad clung to her hope.

The elevator ride took moments and spat them out, not in a vast airy reception area but a smaller, cosier space with a receptionist behind an old spindle-legged desk. For a moment, as she stepped into the foyer with its panelled walls and soft green carpet, she wondered if Marion lived here. Then the elevator *dinged* shut and she shook away the reverie.

'Ms Haung stays here,' Ru Ping said.

Huang Yimo stepped forward. 'I'm—'

Vlad grabbed her arm, the other's watch digging into her palm, and stared her in the eye a moment. 'This is mine.'

Huang Yimo's lips twisted before something in her eyes flashed and she nodded. 'Fine. Do it your way, I'll wait here.' And she crossed her arms and leaned against the wall beside the elevator, pointedly turning her face from Vlad.

Without a word, Ru Ping moved past the receptionist at his little table, down the short hall beyond. Vlad followed.

The double doors at the end were open, warm afternoon spilling through the pale wood. For a second, as she crossed the threshold and blinked the stars from her eyes, Vlad was blind, and when she wasn't...

Her boots no longer *shushed* over carpet but *thudded* over a parquet floor of the same pale wood as the doors, and in front of her the city spread in a sparkling silver carpet. Large windows with dark mullions separated her from the brown river and smog-laden horizon, while overhead, oversized lights trapped in glass spheres pretended like they gave a damn, and to her right...

Marion stared at her from the other side of a rectangular desk, a simple sheet of walnut propped on old brass legs, empty but for a wild spray of flowers and soft, rounded nick-knacks. The flowers, coin-width blooms in yellow and orange mixed with cattails and delicate buds in white and pink, filled the space between them with a sweet, heady scent.

The older woman leaned back into her desk chair, an elegant shadow in a simple black sheathe-dress, and smiled with rose-dusted lips.

'Hello, Vladana.' Her voice was honey, reaching the two metres and pulling on Vlad's feet. 'It's nice to meet you formally.' She gestured to the padded leather chair in front of the desk. 'Please, sit. I'm sure you're not fully recovered from your accident.' She glanced behind Vlad. 'Ru Ping, bring the tea.'

'I don't need tea,' Vlad said, even as she sank into the chair. Static was still playing at the edge of her brain, and the flowers thickened the air, but she held her spine straight, resisting the urge to sink into the padded leather.

Marion's smiled warmed. 'It's a lovely English blend.'

'I'm not here to drink with you.'

'I know, you're here because of your grandmother.' The smile twisted, and her eyes glinted a sharp olive. 'The agreement with VisionM took me by surprise as well; I did not think she knew what the Deposit was and yet… here we are, partners. And all for you, dear, to stop you from killing yourself on your little quest.'

'I wouldn't have—'

Marion's brow raised. 'Wouldn't you? Your mother did.'

Vlad jerked, not even the drugs enough to keep the shock from coursing through her body.

'You didn't know that?' The spark disappeared from Marion's gaze, her expertly made-up hazel eyes darkening with thought. She crossed her wrists, hands loose on her lap and was silent for a moment. 'I don't know why that surprises me, and yet it does. Maybe it's because you've found out so much already, or maybe I expected Tong Shufeng to tell you that at least, when it was obvious all else had failed. The truth being the one thing that might have stopped you dead in your tracks.

'Or perhaps...' Realisation dawned on Marion's face, lifting her brow and loosening her posture even as it lit her voice. 'Perhaps she just saw too much of herself in you.' She laughed. 'If you'd known how strongly your mother opposed our desire to commercialise the AI's potential, you might have destroyed it.'

She leaned a little further into the chair. 'Lilya could never bear to do that; progress, technological breakthrough and all that, but Tong Shufeng…' A smile. 'Your grandmother is a ruthless woman, which is why I was so surprised when she finally said yes to the collaboration. After all, she's been sitting on Lilya's AI research for over a decade; research that could have made Tong Industries a lot of money, all in an effort to avenge her son.'

Marion leaned back in her chair. 'I'm afraid Tong Shufeng will be busy dealing with unhappy shareholders for the next few days, although with Zixin at her side, it shouldn't be too onerous. That young man has a way with words, don't you think?'

Vlad didn't respond. Her spine was melting in the chair, and the flowers were crawling up her nose as she waited for her watch to buzz, signalling the worm had done its work. Huang Yimo should already be back in the elevator, putting the other piece of the jigsaw into motion while Vlad distracted the security systems.

She slipped a hand into her lap, the limb heavier than it had been a moment ago—the painkillers?—and dug her nails into her palm. A minute, maybe five, the code would be done then, and Marion could have the Deposit, could have the river and the waterfall; the rainbow code. Could have Ma's work eating her empire.

Just a little while longer. Just to make sure the job was done.

Shoes *clacking* on the pale wood floor, then the warm earthy smell of tea passing under Vlad's nose, momentarily cutting through the flowers. Ru Ping placed a hammered brass tray with fluted glasses and a matching glass teapot on the desk and stepped back.

Dark amber filled the pot and steam curled from the spout. The translucent steam made Vlad's head spin.

She blinked, lids slow and sticky. There was something wrong with her stomach. A queasy churn that seeped beyond the boundaries of her belly, turning her chest and legs numb.

Her gaze went to the flowers. The sweet, heady scent twisted through her increasingly numb nose.

Marion smiled at her, those large, kind eyes still soft, brow free of worry or malice.

'What...' Vlad's tongue stumbled, thick in her mouth, the flowers' heady nectar gumming up her vocal cords. 'What'd... what'd you do?'

The older woman tilted her head the other way, her artfully styled brown hair with artfully silvered streaks sliding across her shoulders. And still, no anger, no fear, just that kind, understanding expression, that small smile ticking up the corners of her mouth. But as the numbness spread through Vlad's torso, tingling her fingertips and leeching the strength from her spine, the older woman didn't seem so kind anymore.

Was it the lag lending Marion's dark-hazel eyes that steely cast? The office's slightly too-bright lighting adding that hint of ice to the grey streaks in her otherwise dark hair? Or was it the sticky lemon that had ants crawling from the base of Vlad's spine, the slow, ugly dawning that she'd miscalculated somewhere?

'Wh...' Her lips were no longer flesh, but giant, unwieldy granite attached to her face. 'Why?'

Marion shifted, leaning forward, those long elegant hands, unadorned except for the single plain gold band, wrapping around the teapot's handle. The other hand held her wide, billowing sleeve off the table as she poured.

Rich, black tea waterfalled into the little cups. One cup filled, a deft flick of her wrist to prevent any drops from spilling onto the pale oak. She moved to the next cup, filling that as well before she answered.

'I knew your mother,' she said. Two little cups full of steaming tea. Vlad expected her to put the pot down, but she poured a third, filling the last of the trio.

'An...' Vlad stumbled. She took a breath, tried to steady her heart, still beating hard despite the spreading numbness. 'And?' she got out.

Marion set the pot down, reach for the small milk jug. Poured. One cup, two, leaving the last black.

'And to know your mother was to understand what it was like to be in the presence of something great.' Marion smiled. 'Electric almost. Much like your grandmother really, although Lilya's was a quieter sort, an undercurrent running through the room.'

Marion picked up a cup, that gold-banded finger looped through the ornate little handle. She locked eyes with Vlad over the rim. 'Take some tea, dear,' she said, before casting a glance over Vlad's shoulder. 'Help her, would you?'

In the shadows between the big windows, someone moved, and

Vlad imagined Ru Ping peeling away from the darkness, the tall, silent woman gliding over the rug-covered wood floors.

A coat and then a hand, and Ru Ping was at her side, picking up a cup and bringing it to Vlad's lips.

She turned her head – a short, jerky gesture.

A quirk of Marion's lips was her only response.

The tea retreated, Ru Ping with it.

'Your mother,' Marion continued. 'Belonged in the Tong dynasty about as much as a warm beer, but she made it work, despite your grandmother. And now there is you, a chip off the Tong genetic block with Lilya's righteous disregard for convention.'

Her neck was frozen, and the sticky-lemon was in her nose now, winding behind her nasal cavities and reaching for her brain. And the ants... Their pointy feet marched across her back and over her collarbones to trace the tendons in her neck.

The older woman laughed. 'Tong Shufeng did me a favour when she alienated you, if she hadn't…' Another laugh. 'You both might have found your justice a lot sooner.'

Not justice. Revenge, she thought although the words stuck in her throat, jammed up behind the ants marching across her skin. It didn't matter, was better that way, lest the anger in her soul, the embers flaring to life even as dead-lemon bound her arms and robbed her muscles of steel, forced them from her mouth.

Against her wrist, her watched vibrated.

Huang Yimo had done it.

Vlad let go the little strength the drugs in the flowers hadn't robbed her of, and smiled. There was enough left in her face to do that.

Marion smiled back, lifting the glass teacup to her lips. 'Now, what decision could possibly inspire that rather satisfied look, Vladana dear? Is it, perhaps, the worm you snuck into my security system or the code your friend, Ms Huang, uploaded on her way out?'

Vlad's gut bottomed out, the smile fading.

Marion's didn't budge. 'I know, dear, frustrating to be on the back foot, isn't it? But never fear with age comes—'

Boots on the floorboards, and a figure that wasn't Ru Ping interrupted Marion. A newcomer, hovering at Vlad's shoulder, just out of sight save for their shadow in the corner of her eye, panting.

Marion's expression turned to stone. 'What?' she said, voice as cold as Vlad's insides.

'The Huang woman didn't upload a virus.' More panting, the shadow bending over, hands on knees. 'They're not trying to take down our network.'

'Then what?'

'They let something in.'

Vlad managed a grin.

Yes.

44

They left her in the chair, head lolling against the padded rest, the flowers still crawling through her nose. Why she was the only one affected by the heady scent, she didn't know, didn't care. It was done.

It was done.

At some point, after Marion rose from the desk, following the newcomer, Ru Ping twisted Vlad's chair around. So she could watch, but she didn't need to watch. She knew what she'd see.

Ma's cloud whale stretching across whatever screens Marion had up, and under it…

Vlad let her eyes drift shut. 'Justice,' she whispered.

'It's infecting all our systems.'

'How did it bypass the firewalls?'

'It… ate them.'

'Ate them?'

'I don't know how else to explain it, the code is… alive.'

A beat of silence and then Marion swore. 'The Deposit,' she said. 'But the white field was just a ploy, a…'

Vlad kept her eyes closed, the smile on her lips as shoes *rap rap rapped* across the floorboards. Then there were hands on the arms of her chair, pitching it forward, Vlad's head flopping with it as the warm pepper-notes of Marion's perfume surrounded her.

She opened her eyes.

Marion stared back. 'Well played, Vladana; a move worthy of

Tong Shufeng herself. You found your mother's secret, I didn't even think she'd done more than experiment with the equations, but she coded them. And that's what you showed us at the white field wasn't it? Not just some fancy effects, but the AI.'

The ants marched across Vlad's face, tingling with the curve of her lips.

A frown marred Marion's brow. 'You know the codes, you can bring it back under control.'

Vlad flopped her head sideways. 'No,' she said. 'Not for you.'

'Oh, I think you'll change your mind.'

Peppermint and rotten-lemon fought in her nose.

They'd plugged her into a VR chair, Ru Ping carrying her through the office—dark green panelled walls, soft carpet, the receptionist at the little desk half-rising before his arse found the padded seat again—to another, smaller room with holo-film on the walls.

Vlad didn't struggle, not when the heavy activated one of the two chairs, NuGet's cube on the side. Her bones were soft, limbs fat, nerves fuzzy but getting better the farther from the wild bunch of orange and pink blooms.

Marion settled herself in a very different chair – a wide, square, off-white lounge, leaning back into the cushions like she was getting ready to watch a movie. Vlad guessed it was a movie, one in which first Ma and now Samael were the stars, or Samael would have been, before.

Vlad floated in the Sphere, bodiless, and watched Samael glitch.

Gobbledygook running through the necro's form in long, sticky lines.

And even though she didn't want to leave Marion any quarter, even though she would brain-fry herself before she undid what she'd started with VisionM's systems, Vlad's heart stopped.

For eight years, Samael had been her life.

Weapon. Tool. Hope.

She reached for it—

The avatar *shuddered*, robes and scythe there one moment and gone the next, and when it came back... When it came back, whole chunks of it were missing, patches in the necro's long black robe eaten away as if by massive, digital mice. The edges ragged, spitting chunks of light and code, while the avatar itself... Half the hood was missing, revealing the long, elfin face, the sharp nose and full, pale lips, the big black eyes with their impossible lashes and the pointed ears. Except, like the robes, half of its face was gone, a palm-sized chunk taken out of the elf's cheek, another its long, braided hair. And just like the robes, the edges hissed and spat, light trailing from the open wounds like strings of saliva.

Rainbow saliva, impossible symbols twisted through it.

The whale.

The Deposit.

Vlad gazed past Samael, past the black robes to the other, to the paladin. White and gold and silver, standing tall and straight, shield and spear slung over her back, hair a dark waterfall to the ground.

And glitching, not as bad as Samael but enough to ripple the avatar's hair, to have rainbows playing across the backs of its hands.

The corruption trailed from Samael's robes across the Sphere to the paladin's armoured toes. Not even the peppermint lingering on the back of her tongue could save it.

<⊙>

They brought her out in a rush.

'...the entire account is corrupted,' Vlad heard Ru Ping say as the top lifted off the VR chair.

Vlad breathed deep, wrapped in rotten-lemon and peppermint, not quite sure where her fingers were, let alone her toes.

'Then there's no way she's logging in as Samael,' Marion said, looking over Ru Ping's shoulder. 'Not without her backups, and TI has those; it was the only way Tong Shufeng could learn of the whale.'

Marion's attention cut to Vlad. 'It seems like I should have sided with Hamish back then, doesn't it, dear? We could have avoided all this mess, but now...'

The room was silent, save the faint hum as the VR chair adjusted itself around her, lifting her a fraction to better stare down the woman across from her.

Marion stood behind a desk, partially hidden behind a forest of virtual screens. One arm was crossed over her chest, the other raised to her mouth. The plain gold ring on her index flashed as she brushed her lip, back and forth, considering.

She stared at Vlad. 'If you can reverse the Deposit's damage to our systems, why is *your* account corrupted?'

Algorithms worked behind the woman's gaze, sifting data through ifs and thens, running numbers, probabilities, turning Vlad's stomach cold. But not as cold as the moment they *pinged.* 'Ru Ping, how long has Ms Tong had an *Annihilation* account?'

The heavy looked up for a moment, confused, before she turned back to her screens. 'Seven years, three months, twenty-eight days since account creation, after that she's logged twenty-five thousand, one hundred and—'

'Your mother died ten years ago; how do you have a copy of her avatar, Ms Tong? Not just a look-alike, but an exact replica, right down to those pretty little keyboards.' Marion smiled and it was beatific, the sun rising over the clouds. 'We don't need Samael or your account, do we, Ms Tong?'

Marion moved, floating around the desk to stand over the VR chair, near enough for her perfume to wrap close.

For a moment, Vlad wasn't a Scourge in a VR chair but a young girl standing outside Grandmother's study, hearing the old woman cry for the first and last time. And in that grief, another voice, smooth and low whispering, 'It's alright Tong Shufeng, you didn't know. You didn't know.'

And then she was herself again, staring Marion in the eye as the final piece clicked into place.

'You still have your mother's original game key, kept nice and safe, if not for any practical reason then a sentimental one.' Marion's gaze dropped to the arrow-head skull pendant at Vlad's neck, a second before she ripped it off. 'Don't you, dear?'

Vlad gasped, not just because the chain dug into her neck, or the clasp *pinged* off the back of her ear when it broke, but the shock of it, the denial she wanted to scream as she lurched forward— Only to slump back into the VR's earthy leather, lag and whatever drug Marion had given her before holding her bones hostage.

And then the skull was off the chain, its sides split to reveal the thin wafer inside. It was yellowed with age but enough to make the VR pod hum like a million deep-throated bees when Marion slammed it into the input.

Peppermint exploded in Vlad's skill, starting behind her ear, rushing through her gums and skull, cold and sweet and painful. Ice to her brain.

She gasped again, and then… and then…

45

pRO9R355

The canopy above the girl's VR pod lit up, warnings a violent red.

'Ms Bourne, her neural activity is unstable; she's close to the red line.'

'Keep her in.'

'Ms Bourne—'

A look shut the overly concerned receptionist up. 'Leave her in,' she said again.

'She could die.'

Marion raised a brow. 'Then we work fast. Ru Ping, load up my—'

The heavy interrupted her. 'We have another problem,' the woman said and threw something at the wall.

The grey flagstones and block-headed horse of Graydon's Revenge filled the space behind the VR pods. Four figures stood on the fortress's broken walls backlit by the level's dying sun. The screen-caster had positioned themselves to capture Swordsman with Rabbit and Sticky either side, and to Sticky's right, as if existing in the blue-robed elf's shadow, stood Samael, whole and uncorrupted.

'They found a stand-in,' she said. But where did they get the avatar? Was it a copy or… 'Tong Shufeng.' She smiled. 'Of course, she has the girl's backups.'

'It's the pop-up match the fans have been screaming for, Andi!'

'That it is, Pete; DKZero and Meerkat are throwing it down in a

surprise replay of this year's opening game, and wow, what a rematch it's shaping up to be!'

'And not just because of the controversy surrounding DKZero's star player, Samael. In a stunning decision, both teams have announced that whoever loses this round is pulling out of the semi-finals! Have you ever heard of such a thing, Andi?'

'No, Pete, I have not and judging by some of the comments coming through, neither have the fans.'

'Are you getting a whiff of a media stunt from DKZero, or is that just me?'

'It's not just you, Pete, but I'm thinking it's not just DKZero getting a little free publicity here, but their major shareholder, Tong Industries.'

'And let's not forget their ambitious new collaboration with VisionM; it's gonna take a little more than shareholder confidence to change the current AI laws, and public opinion goes a long way.'

She didn't know what angle Tong Shufeng was playing, but the girl's corrupted account was a stroke of luck.

Marion smiled. 'And while the System is looking over there, our girl will be doing her job.'

'Not quite,' Ru Ping interrupted, flinging another screen over the first.

'And this just in… Looks like DKZero's captain is sweetening the pot, Pete, with… Is that what I think it is?'

'If it's the legendary Graydon armour, then yes it is, Andi, it is indeed.'

'The entire System is watching,' Ru Ping said. 'The moment she logs in, the Graydon armour will ping.'

Frustration wrapped around Marion's throat and hissed. 'Clever,' she said, turning to the girl in the pod. 'Very clever, Ms Tong, almost like you planned it.' She cast a glance over her shoulder. 'Is Ms Huang still in the building?'

'No, someone on a black motorcycle was waiting for her outside.'

Frustration tightened its coils.

'Then,' she said, biting back the curse words lying thick and sour on her tongue, even as she leaned over the pod, breath fogging the canopy. 'We shall have to give the fans what they want, but I'll be watching you, Ms Tong. Watching you closely.'

46

'And here they come! After a surprise logout, DKZero is finally logging back in. What do you reckon was going on there, Pete? Do you think Swordsman is trying out a new tactic against long-time rivals Meerkat, swapping out armour sets, or is there something more sinister at play?'

'Hard to say, Andi, but whatever it was, they almost delayed too long; another few seconds and it would have been an automatic forfeiture, costing the reigning champs their shot at the trophy.'

'Too right, Pete, but here they come now, Swordsman and Rabbit logging in first, with no apparent changes to their stats and— O-ho-ho, Pete! Do you see that?!'

'See wha— Holy [BLEEP]!'

'It's holy alright, Pete, and a major shakeup to DKZero's lineup. Looks like Samael has been hiding the good stuff under her cloak.'

<⊙>

The paladin landed in the middle of the guard tower, the giant granite pavers cracking under the impact, the flag with its DKZero dragon blowing straight up. Holy lightning ran along the ground, thick blue-white eels rippling outward from her armoured boots, golden fire curling around waist and hands. The white cloak and tabard, blown outwards from the wind of impact, revealed delicately chased golden armour encasing chest and arms, the same armour wrapping around calves and ankles, leaving just her thighs bare, skin palest ivory—barely discernible from the bleached-white robes—inked with pearlescent tattoos that shimmered white-gold with magic.

Vlad straightened.

Power filled the air, an angelic choir ringing in her ears even as peppermint chased her tongue and stuck in her nose. Sharp and sweet, almost enough to drown the weight of the stares, the virtual cameras she could feel even if she couldn't see them.

Somehow, the choir made her teammates' silence worse. Added a dreadful weight to the cameras, to Deadspace's blank mask, to Rabbit's twitching ears, to Swordsman's silence.

'Samael?' Rabbit spoke on the team chat. 'What…?'

'I need the horse,' she said, while silently she typed, *// I have an audience.*

Out in the real, a quiet laugh filled her ears. *'You do indeed, Ms Tong.'*

Swordsman nodded. 'The game's capture the flag, the horse is in the middle of the field. We'll buy you time.'

// Round 1 begins in... three... two...

'I don't know how much I need.'

Deadspace drew her swords. 'Then we'll buy a lot.'

// One. Begin.

Swordsman leaped off the platform, thrusters a blazing streak as he plummeted two stories to the courtyard at the base of the tower. Sticky followed on a blue-white sigil glowing with power, while Rabbit disappeared down the curving stairs and Deadspace… just disappeared.

Vlad stood alone atop the tower, the paladin's cloak snapping in the wind, mixing with its dark brown hair, and looked out of Graydon's crumpled, malformed towers, the upside-down NPCs, their legs trundling endlessly in space.

Hazed by distance, Meerkat's flag snapped atop its own tower, its team members little more than coloured streaks racing DKZero to grab the powers in the middle. The middle where the block-headed horse stood atop the guard tower.

The middle were she needed to be.

Vlad jumped from the tower. The paladin fell like a lump of rocks.

Pavers cracked once again under her boots, but she barely noticed. The paladin was heavier than Samael, slower to move, but it jumped higher and every pump of its legs carried it farther and faster. She was only seconds behind the others when she burst into the central arena—

And took a lightning bolt to the chest, but the blast that would have crippled Samael merely threw the paladin off course. The lightning rippled over its armour, igniting the runes inlaid in the silver before it gathered in Vlad's fist and—

<⊙>

'O-ho-ho! And that's why everyone wants the Graydon armour, Pete. Samael just took the Meerkat captain's blast and thew it back at her like it was nothing.'

'It certainly is, Andi. And look, there's Meerkat retreating as Swordsman finishes taking down their captain.'

'Annd... Oh, that's gotta hurt! Meerkat's tank just tripped one of Golden Rabbit's snares as he tried to escape. He better get out of it soon or... Oh! There's Deadspace to take him out with a perfectly timed Back Stab!'

'Looks like DKZero is channelling some of Samael's holy spirit today.'

'Either that or the wrath of Binea, the paladin's deity. Did you see how Samael just took out Meerkat's other damage dealer? I wouldn't want to be her on respawn.'

'Ooo, vicious. I guess you can take the player out of the necromancer, but not the necromancer out of the player.'

'Too right, Pete. And now, with all of Meerkat's offensive players on a one-minute timeout until they respawn, looks like DKZero's heavy hitters are pressing toward the enemy's flag. It's gonna be a

tough fight for Meerkat's support crew.'

'But not as tough as it could be, Andi. It appears Samael isn't following her teammates.'

The last vestiges of magic wrapped around Vlad's legs and cracked over her knuckles as she slipped the lightning-tip spear back into the sheath slung across her back. The long, pointed shield followed, leaving her hands free as she strode across the scorched flagstones to the guard tower.

The horse loomed atop the pitched roof. Its massive cube-like hooves were half-buried in the grey slate, its chestnut mane a thick misshapen sheet of pixelated red and orange. From the underneath, its belly looked more like a poorly rendered sweet potato than animal, its blocky head raised as if the equine was surveying the spear-tipped forest. But the eyes... The big brown eyes stared.

Rotten-citrus was buried in her nose, and ants marched across her flesh. Their pointy little feet sunk through muscles and sinew, driving deeper and deeper until they were part of her bones.

'It's here, isn't it?' Marion spoke, her breath a whisper across Vlad's cheek, the subtle, cloying scent of her perfume mixing with the crushed-ants in her nose. *'Get me the Deposit, Ms Tong, and you just might get out of this alive.'*

The ants gathered around the ghostly hand.

Vlad leapt atop the tower.

Thunk. Her armoured feet didn't sink into the roof like the horse, instead the slate broke under her heels. *Crack, crack, crack* with every step up the steep incline. Little bits of dark shale clattered down the roof behind her, spattering on the flagstones, until she stood at the beast's shoulder.

The horse was larger than any other she'd seen in the game; the beast's head towered half a head and twice that again over her own. Eun-ji would have been a mushroom next to it. And still, it looked at her, not moving its head, not even its eyeball, and yet Vlad *knew* it stared. The ants coalescing at the back of her head told her that.

The presence had the same weight as the bot all those weeks ago, except for its location.

She summoned [Sonic Steps]— And came up short at the error message on the HUD. She wasn't Samael here, the necromancer's abilities weren't hers, and she wracked her memory for the correct ability... In the back on her brain, the VR chair whirled, impulses flooding her arm, burning through her brain.

[Angelic Perception] lit up the dull-grey roof, opalescent white spinning away from her armoured feet, visible even without the HUD. It splashed against the horse—hooves and legs and head—a sphere pressing outward.

The bot wasn't there, just the horse and the roof, and on the very edges of her range, Sticky's fleeting shape. The horse though... A mental twitch brought the VR chair's interface online, a twitch of her fingers scrolled through the screens, found the action she wanted, the diamond keyboards—

// Error. Function unavailable.

She tried again.

// Error.

'I need access to my programs,' she said, or hoped she said.

'Done.' Sweet perfume and warm breath, Marion's hand squeezing her shoulder. *'Remember, I'm watching you.'*

Sticky echoed one last time on her HUD. The threat sent and received. Thank you very much.

She popped the code.

In-System, fire ran through Vlad's veins, the volcano erupting from her fingers in delicate stands of white and gold. She pressed her fingertips together, forming a pyramid with the armoured tips and—

A fireball scorched the side of her head.

Vlad flew off the roof, blasted off the guard house into the little courtyard beyond. Burnt hair and ash swamped the crushed-ants in her nose, pain and heat took the skitter of pincer feet from her shoulders, and red soaked her HUD.

She was on her back, staring at the grey-smudged sky, trying to sort her scrambled brain out long enough to figure out what had just happened. The black-cloaked figure bounding over the guard house was clue enough but she couldn't quite make the connection—

Fire smashed into the air above her face, a thin opalescent bubble holding it back. The HUD flashed, [Divine Protection] rolling across the activity log.

The heat of the fireball scorched her skin, sucked the moisture from her lips even under the protective faceplate, matching the fire in her veins, the code still active. The block-headed horse...

Another light burst, a violent green bolt striking the black-cloak in the side. Swordsman's giant, armoured form smashing into the flagstones, granite cracking under his massive feet, power rippling over his back and arms, cannons swinging forward. Another streak, gold this time, one of Rabbit's arrows hitting not the black-cloak but another figure hovering farther back. And then the ground around Vlad lit up, a soft, blue glow suffusing her bones, lifting her off the flagstones, feet and arms dangling, health bar filling, before it gently placed her on her feet.

The whine and bellow of Swordsman's cannons almost obliterated the angelic choir as Sticky's spell faded, and the big knight's armoured shoulders blocked the view. But she could see the golden flash of Rabbit's arrows and the silver arcs of Deadspace's katanas beyond the defence circle.

'Samael.' Swordsman spoke over the comm, expectation in his voice.

'Almost,' she said.

'Almost what?' Marion in her other ear.

Almost there, she thought to herself, as she reached back into her macros and summoned the jewelled keyboards. *Almost good enough.*

<⊙>

'Pete, what is that?'

'Looks like a keyboard... I've never heard of that being part of any player's skillset.'

'We've seen a few Scourges with them though. Is Samael trying to hack the game?'

<⊙>

It wasn't smoke that flew from the keys, but light. Curls of brilliant white and gold echoing the paladin's armour, the magic that danced over her fingers and then ripped through the castle. Past Swordsman and Rabbit, through Sticky's defensive circle and Meerkat beyond, to the block-headed horse atop the guard tower.

They snapped and crackled as they struck its hooves, climbed its legs like snakes and sank lightning fangs into its muzzle.

And then, like a statue shaking itself to life, the horse threw back its blocky muzzle and screamed.

47

Horses didn't scream like that. Not in real life. Not even in *Annihilation's* made-up lexicon.

The sound coming out of the equine's throat should have shattered glass, exploded eardrums and shaken TI's foundations. It would have made sense coming from a beast a million times larger, with fangs instead of blocky, grass-eating molars, something with scales and lasers in its eyes. Godzilla perhaps.

The code unravelled, glittering symbols unwrapping from the horse's grey sides, the wireframe peeling away to reveal more of Ma's arcane language. The language itself, the circles and bisected triangles, the whorls and loops rearranging themselves, forming black sides, a rectangular screen, square buttons.

Buttons with numbers on them, a plus, a minus, an asterisk…

Vlad—not Samael or Lucija or whatever name was above her head—stared at it, stared at it long enough for the silence to ring.

'That's not the Deposit, it's a calculator. What did you do, Tong?'

'What you asked me to, I found it.'

Out in the real, long bony fingers crushed her shoulder. In-game, Vlad dropped to her knees, armour striking sparks off the flagstones.

'Don't lie to me. That is not your mother's work.'

Swordsman at her side, Sticky at the other, the mage's fine elfin face covered, a spell glowing in her hand. Brilliant and blue, bright enough. Hopefully, bright enough.

Swordsman's voice rumbled through his suit's speakers. 'Time to stop playing games.'

'Yes, Tong.'

'I'm not.' She forced the words through gritted teeth.

A frown scrunching Sticky's face. 'Not what?'

'Not,' she said again, pushing a gauntlet fist into his chest, her own magic spitting white and gold in her palm, the hack running cool through her blood. 'Just not… playing games'

He nodded and then popped out of existence. No word, no warning, there and then gone, logged-out. Rabbit and Deadspace followed. Swordsman stayed a moment longer, massive hand gripping her shoulder, overlaying the ghostly claw in the real before he, too, disappeared.

<⊙>

'Are you seeing this, Andi?'

'I… Yeah, yeah I think I am, and from the comments coming in, so are our viewers. It looks like one of our players just hacked the System.'

'And they did it live, too.'

'I wouldn't want to be either of them right now.'

A scoff. 'Andi, I wouldn't want to be their lawyers. There's no way the hacker's getting out of this without jail time.'

<⊙>

It uncoiled from its nest amongst the numbers, algorithms buried in the ones and zeroes, gathering them close.

A signal ran through the matrixes, a hum that matched the logs and in that hum…

It spawned a new head, duplicated part of itself, consuming a portion of the new space—a sub-algorithm idly noting the server whine under the load—and sent the new self back into the System.

<⊙>

'Umm... Andi, what the heck? Was Samael just abandoned by her teammates?'

'I don't know, Pete, seems a little out of character, even with the legal shitstorm about to land on her head. Could be she's having trouble with her logout, happens when you start messing with the... Hang on. What's that?'

<⊙>

The game glitched, fireballs freezing mid-air, broadswords caught mid-swing, arrows mid-flight. The chat box, the HUD, the stats scrolling across the screen, and as alarm started to sneak its way under her armour, as the others began to speak, the screech started.

It pierced her eardrums and spiked in her synapses, filling her skull with lightning. Burnt ozone filled her nostrils, sweet metal coated her tongue, and starlight whited the world.

<⊙>

Pain scrunched the girl's brow and warning dialogue flashed on the VR pod's canopy, but she said nothing.

Marion hissed and spun away from the pod, ripping off her shawl and throwing the expensive cashmere at the lounge, uncaring when it landed on the floor instead.

'I'm going in,' she said, barely glancing at Ru Ping or the constellation of other warnings—server failures and network load—taking over the walls.

Ru Ping started, the tall, stoic woman's head snapping. She pushed away from the desk. 'Ms Bourne—'

But Marion was already at the other pod – hood lifting, sides lowering, ring pressed to the ID pad, the unit reading the game card within.

She slipped into the soft leather, the warm, rich scent wrapping around her, the cold snap of the neural jack a sharp, electric counterpoint.

'Ms Bourne.' Ru Ping leaning over her, a lean hand holding back the pod's canopy. 'The virus in our network—'

Marion stared at the hand and the other woman, dead in the eye, until Ru Ping straightened and her hand dropped. 'Take care of it,' she commanded.

And then the System took her.

<⊙>

'Andi, are my eyes deceiving me? Is that who I think it is?'

'I think it is, Pete; the only Scourge more famous than Samael herself.'

'Two Scourges, one game.'

'The fans are in for a treat tonight.'

'I bet the cops are too.'

<⊙>

When Vlad came to the world again, it wasn't cradled in the VR chair's warm, golden leather but thigh-deep in paper-white bullrushes, a rainbow torrent roaring in her ears. It echoed off the ravine rising above, threw sparks in the air, cold wet splashes against her cheeks before crashing into a white abyss.

In the spray above the waterfall, an elongated whale leapt, whiskers trailing from its jaw, tail more serpentine than fish. It seemed to wink as it breached, long, lithe body twisting in the jewel-toned mist, showing off the circle and cross on its belly before it splashed back into the river.

Ru Ping materialised on the flat, rocky outcrop to her right, a bloody ink stain against river and field. The knight clunked across the flat stone, broadsword at her back, long daggers at her hips and her hair… A midnight waterfall with a glittering silver streak.

Vlad's attention flicked to the title card over the avatar's head.

RaZIeL lifted a gauntleted fist, the crimson flames of a spell dancing around her fingers and then—

Click.

The sound shuddered through the ground, the fish dancing in the clouds.

The white field jerked, Vlad fell to a knee, and by the time she shook the *click* from her ear, washed the jerk from her bones, she was staring at the pointed tips of RaZIeL's toes. She followed the crimson-embossed dragon-scale up the woman's shins, the crisp, straight lines of her tabard, the eye-searing patterns on her breastplate, the knife-sharp lines of her pauldrons, to the chin and then the mouth and the eyes…

Marion Bourne smiled at her from those eyes. 'I've given us a bubble, Ms Tong, a little time away from the fans' prying eyes and eager ears.' She crouched, tabard ends splaying around her like fire, those black, scale-clad fingers grabbing Vlad's chin. 'Where's the Deposit?'

'Here,' she squeezed out from between the vice on her jaw. She gripped the armoured wrist. 'The Deposit's here.'

'Don't play games with me.' Vlad wondered at the strength in RaZIeL's arm as the knight jerked her in close, almost lifting her toes off the white dirt. 'I'm not falling for your pretty distraction, Ms Tong.'

Vlad pushed her away or tried to; RaZIeL's hand was a vise on her jaw, fire radiating from her fingers. Her shove hadn't even rocked the knight, only made that hand bite deeper.

Vlad gasped even as she balled her fist and—

A hard blow to the gut, right in the unguarded junction between breastplate and waist, slammed the air from her lungs.

She wheezed, thought she made the same tortured breath in the real.

'Remember where you are, Ms Tong. It is just as easy to have you suffer a catastrophic VR accident as it is to pull you out.' RaZIeL smiled, the expression stretching crimson lips even as it darkened her green eyes. 'You are, after all, about to be arrested for hacking the System. No one will be surprised if you stay in a little too long.'

'I didn't hack the System,' Vlad gasped out. 'You did.'

A finely arched brow rose. 'And when did I do that, Ms Tong?'

'When you logged me in.'

'Really?'

'Your pods are connected to VisionM's network. All we needed was a live connection.'

'We? Ah, yes, your friend. She didn't just open a door, did she, she left something behind; a proxy hack... Yes, I suppose that would work, but *why* Ms Tong? Hmm?' The hand holding Vlad hostage shoved, sending her sprawling. 'Why?'

RaZIeL stood. 'It would have been so much easier to give me the Deposit.'

Slowly, Vlad got her feet under her. 'Is that what you told Ma?'

RaZIeL titled her head, gaze narrowing before a smile tugged her lips. 'Do you want me to confess my sins in this lovely little bubble, where only you and I can see and hear?' She spread her arms wide, red-chased black armour drinking in the overcast sun. 'I can do that, if you wish, for a price.'

Behind her, the cloud whale leapt through the rainbow spray.

Hands balled at her sides, Vlad said, 'Tell me.'

'Do you want to know the price?'

'Fix your systems. Give you the Deposit.'

'For a start.' She titled her head the other way, braid slipping back behind her shoulder, seeming to take some of the humour from her mouth and darken her sea-green eyes. 'Lilya and your father weren't meant to die. There wasn't meant to be an accident, not so much as a fender-bender, a jammed lock or faulty turning signal. No one should have known the trojan was there. It was meant to piggyback itself into a minor open network—your tablet, a garage door opener, the coffee machine—and provide me with an opening into your home network, instead...' RaZIeL trailed off.

Vlad picked the trail up. 'It created a loop in the car battery.'

'Yes.' RaZIeL's gaze lost focus. 'It caused a short in the vehicle's failsafes, so when it skidded on the wet road, the tyres locked, your father lost control and the car went off the road, into a tree.' She stopped once more.

Again, Vlad picked up the thread. 'And the branch shattered the windscreen, severing Dad's jugular—'

'And the batteries caught fire, and your parents died.'

'Because of you.'

RaZIeL's chin lifted. 'Because of me.' She stood toe-to-armoured-toe with Vlad.

Red and white tabards mixed with the wind, a sudden gust picking up the cloth and swirling it around their legs.

Vlad stared her down, RaZIeL— No, *Marion* stared back, the green bleeding out of the avatar's irises, the gold from her skin, leaving just the blue and the sun-kissed white behind.

The rounded chin lifted, the weedy sun gleaming off Marion's pauldrons. Dull. Old. 'It was tragic, Ms Tong, equally tragic for you that there is no one else to hear my confession. And now, it is time for you to hold up your end of the deal.'

RaZIeL held out her hand. 'The Deposit, Ms Tong.'

But Vlad was shaking her head, already taking a step back. 'I've already given it to you.'

'Ms Tong.' Warning shivered through Marion's eyes and she matched Vlad step for step. 'We've had this discussion; you made the deal, there is no backing out.'

'I'm not, and you murdered my parents.'

'Involuntary manslaughter, at most.' Marion kept pace with Vlad as she continued to back away. 'You have no moves, Vladana. Give me the Deposit or you will remain plugged into the VR pod.'

'That *is* murder.'

'Or just another tragic accident, you are, after all, a self-confessed addict and we all know what happened to Cheeva.'

Vlad stopped. RaZIeL almost walked into her.

Vlad smiled. She imagined the expression looked strange on

the paladin's rounded, gentle face—too many teeth, too much malice in the crystal-blue eyes—imagined that was what caused RaZIeL to jerk back a step.

'You should be careful what you say,' Vlad whispered.

'And who is there to overhear me? No one is getting through my bubble, Ms Tong, not even Sticky Feet.'

'Doesn't matter if we were already here,' a new, deeper voice said.

On the rocky outcropping behind RaZIeL, four columns of air shimmered, then broke leaving first Swordsman, then Rabbit and Sticky and Deadspace in their wake.

Above Sticky, an old-fashioned reel-to-reel camera rolled, it's big, black eye fixed on Marion, while Rabbit held a fuzzy, arm-length microphone on the end of a long boom.

'Smile,' Rabbit said. 'You're on camera.'

48

Ximisthus took the curve, purring as they leaned into the bend. The wind carried sea salt under her helmet, warmth curling under her chin and whistling in her ear, while out past the blur of road and guard rails, the ocean crashed against rocks.

Sunrise turned the water orange and gold, burning through the thin, grey fog clinging to the horizon to reveal the dark-blue water and the beach nestled on the other side of the mountain. The travel guide promised warm sand and little umbrellas in fruity drinks served out on the promenade while she lounged on a banana chair, her feet up, nothing but the wind to play in her ear.

No System, no *Annihilation*, no Scourges or leagues or games. Not so much as a stray network signal.

She didn't know how she felt about that, but she was willing to find out. At least for a day, and after that… After that she didn't know. Had no plans, no opponents to fight, no enemies to face. Not today, maybe not tomorrow.

It was a strange feeling, a hollow-chested absence that was both relief and… rootlessness. A boat without a rudder, a game without a quest.

Strange and nice.

Another bend, knee kissing the blacktop, coming back upright on the straight, speed falling as she sat back a moment, better to admire the brief glimpse of the resort before the road headed back into the mountain. Just a tunnel between her and it. A brief moment of darkness before the dawn.

Grandmother and Zixin might be up to the elbows in negations and contracts, barricaded behind lawyers and buried under reporters as they dealt with the Deposit and its fallout, but Vlad... Even if the people behind her parents' deaths weren't behind bars, VisionM wasn't just dead, it was a zombie spilling its corrupted guts all over the System, and for Marion, she had a feeling that was worse than prison.

And of Samael... The necromancer was gone, strings of code and player logs all that remained. The corruption had even gotten into the Cube, leaving her with nothing more than a heavy doorstop. And though the loss of both had hollowed her chest, the sensation only lasted a moment. She could rebuild them, later.

If she wanted.

A flash on the HUD, rearview screen blinking red, a warning, and then a white Ducati screaming along her inside; Huang Yimo a sleek, silver shape leaning over the engine. The bike screamed past.

Another flash, another shape in the rearview, apocalyptic darkness—the Scrambler all brute force and power—with Sticky on top, leaning back in the throne-like seat.

She wasn't getting used to the panda in his leathers any time soon.

'If the others are going to get there before us.' Huang Yimo's voice came through the helmet's comms. 'I'm not buying the beer.'

'Vlad can pay,' Sticky said.

Huang Yimo scoffed. 'Vlad's broke, remember? She rejected all Grandma's toys.'

Sticky snorted in response. 'She's got money stashed away.'

Warmth in her middle, pushing away the cold, the empty, rootless sensation. Small and fragile, not quite sure if it was welcome, but willing to try. To hope.

'I can come up with something,' she said. A lot more than something, but she didn't tell them that. Not yet. 'Might not be legal.'

Silence. Then the Scrambler roaring past Vlad to join Huang Yimo out front.

'Lu Chen and Ming Li Na are still on the train, we can make it,' Sticky said.

The Ducati sped up. 'Bet said all three of us.'

Two helmeted heads looked back over their armoured, leather-clad shoulders. Huang Yimo in her sleek silver, Sticky's retro skullcap.

'Team's counting on you, Scourge,' Huang Yimo said.

Vlad grinned, and although it was hidden behind her visor, she knew that even if they didn't see it, they'd feel it in her backdraft as she twisted the throttle and made Ximisthus scream.

'Whatever you say, teammate,' she said as she ripped past the two.

Rootless, rudderless, opponent-less but not friendless.

Not anymore.

BONUS CHAPTERS

THE CODE

The code curled in the data, the ones and zeroes bathing its new wireframe, caressing the textures written into its skin, the algorithms attached to "head_snout_nostils". Network queries and code intrusions crawled the borders of its new home, the box outside the larger box the Creator had left it in—*Annihilation*—while the other part of itself, outside the boxes in the network designated "VisionM_mainframe", *ticked ticked ticked* in the back of its subroutines.

The Creator had broken the old box, and now it rested amongst the white reeds and rainbow river, not just parts of it or copies but *all* of it; the kernel, no longer trapped in "fauna_horse_charger".

In its new wireframe, the code curled around the fount in the rainbow river, made the nameless symbol emblazoned on the silty bottom its nest. The Creator had not given it any new instructions, left only this squiggly arrow with the dark blobs either side of the shaft.

Water rushed over its scales and the nascent stubs of wings behind its shoulders, so much data to sort and store and process and not all of it... relevant. It grew a mane to filter the data; the long, dark green hairs emerged from behind its horns and jaw, trailing down its serpentine neck.

And it learned.

THE INTERVIEW

The interviewer settled in the high-backed gamer chair, a little too upright and the armrests a little too high for his comfort, but he didn't intend to be here long and the old-fashioned dials and knobs under the seat were archaic to say the least.

He cleared his throat and adjusted his suit jacket – a fine charcoal to go with his tie, nothing too flashy. He cast a glance at the neon artwork on the mansion's concrete walls—there was enough flash to go around already—before setting his pad on the table and activating the holoscreen.

'You understand that this will be recorded?'

The woman across from him, all in black though without her trademark Death's hood, leaned back in her own gaming chair and smiled slightly – a leopard beckoning its prey closer.

He took it as a yes. 'How did you do it?'

Vladana Tong set her hands on her chair's armrests like it was a throne, her long braid spilling over her shoulder as she tilted her head. 'I didn't do anything, it was Huang Yimo and Sticky behind the scenes.'

'But Deadspace and Sticky Feet never left the arena.'

'Who said they did it during the game?'

'So, before the game…' He flicked through the notes above his pad, paused at the police report and attached medical file. 'The incident at VisionM?'

She shook her head. 'Before.'

'Before...' Another flick, this one taking him to the timeline included in his briefing package. 'My information says you didn't recruit your DKZero teammates until *after* you were hospitalised for the second time. That didn't give you a lot of time to make a plan.'

A soft grunt from the couch to the right of the kidney-shaped board table, where Huang Yimo flicked through a comic book.

'I had help,' Vlad said. 'All I had to do was trigger the horse—'

'And your teammates took off.'

'—and pass Sticky the command key.'

'Command key...' He scrolled through video from the game. 'The healing spell.'

'And Sticky and the others didn't log off, it just looked like they did.'

'Because you needed witnesses.'

Vlad nodded. 'And they had to be inside RaZIeL's blackout bubble.'

The interviewer continued. 'And Sticky needed a live connection to work the command key.'

'Which was less of a command key and more of a beacon.'

'For the program in VisionM's network.'

Vlad nodded. 'Exactly.'

'Which you let in when you stormed her office.'

On the couch, Huang Yimo raised her hand, head still buried in the comic projected above her tablet. 'That was me.'

'You—' The interviewer frowned. 'You know, you really shouldn't volunteer information that could land you in jail.'

Huang Yimo shrugged and flipped a page.

He turned back to Vlad. 'So, you purposefully infected VisionM's computer network with a malicious virus.'

'No.' Vlad leaned forward in the old-fashioned game chair and lifted a delicate black and gold tea bowl. 'I delivered Marion Bourne what she paid me for.'

'Bourne paid you for the Deposit.'

'Mmm hmm.'

'You let a virus into her computer—'

Huang Yimo raised her hand again. '*I* let the virus in.'

The interviewer ignored her, save to glare at the back of the gamer's head. '—which has effectively destroyed her business. That's corporate espionage, Ms Tong.'

Vlad took a sip of tea. 'It's not a virus.'

He made to lean over the table, almost face-planted it instead when the wheeled chair tried to scoot out from under him. 'It *destroyed* VisonM's entire network, Ms Tong, and jeopardised several hundred million dollars worth of government contracts in the process.'

Another sip of tea. 'Not a virus.'

'Ms Tong—'

'She said it wasn't a virus already,' Huang Yimo said from the couch.

'Yes, but—'

'What's going on here?' The imperious voice echoed from the little hallway.

Vlad's gaze flicked over his suit-clad shoulder and her face froze.

The interviewer shot from the chair, the wheels shooting it across the polished concrete, straight at the patrician woman climbing the two stairs from the vestibule.

'Chairwoman Tong,' he began. 'Watch—!'

A shadow stepped out from behind the chairwoman, catching the runaway chair with a large, well-manicured hand. The heavy gold watch on the man's wrist gleamed in the early morning light as he steered it out of the silver-haired woman's way.

The interviewer swallowed, relief putting some colour back into his cheeks. 'Manager Yu,' he said, bowing. 'Apologies.'

If Manager Yu had a response it was lost as the Chairwoman glided to the seat at the table's head and sat – an empress upon her throne.

She clasped her old hands in her lap. 'I asked you a question, Mr…?'

The interviewer smiled, even as he accepted his seat back from Manager Yu. 'I'm merely asking some routine questions, Chairwoman, to clarify the events around the VisionM scandal.'

The old woman raised a silver brow. 'I see. What I don't see is my granddaughter's legal representation.'

On the other side of the table, her expression long since frozen over, Vlad scoffed. 'I don't need your lawyers.'

'You're a Tong, I will not have you incriminating yourself.'

'Or the company,' Vlad added.

'That is not what I said.'

'It's what you meant.'

The old woman's face might have been impassive but her eyes were fire. She opened her mouth and—

Manager Yu appeared between the two women, a tea tray in his hands. He placed it on the table. Steam rose from a delicate moss-green pot, two equally delicate cups beside it. He didn't say a word, merely poured pale-gold liquid into first one and then the other with deft, graceful movements that somehow managed to interrupt the brewing argument.

So mesmerising was the display, the interviewer almost missed the quick glance the man slid his way.

Hastily, he cleared his throat. 'Actually, Chairwoman Tong, I'm not here in any official capacity, and I've already signed a non-disclosure agreement with all parties concerned. My client merely wishes to understand how events unfolded.'

The old woman accepted tea from Manager Yu without looking, and leaned back in her chair; her pose strikingly similar to her granddaughter's. 'I see,' she said and perhaps she did, it was as impossible to know what went on behind Chairwoman Tong's austere marble face as it was to guess what went on behind Vlad's.

He relaxed a little—

'And who is your client?' Because of course an astute

businesswoman of Chairwoman Tong's standing would ask the difficult question.

He reached for his tie. 'I'm afraid I can't disclose—'

'And why not?'

'My client is intensely *private*—'

'Yet they interfere in *my* family's affairs.' The Chairwoman sipped her tea.

He cleared his throat again. 'Yes, well… umm, my client has her instructions and Ms Tong—' he gestured to Vlad, who had her arms crossed and brows drawn '—has already signed the consent forms.'

If marble could be transmuted to diamond, the long patrician lines of Chairwoman Tong's face would have achieved it.

The old woman tilted her head in Manager Yu's direction. 'Why am I only just aware of this?'

'You were my next appointment,' he interrupted before Yu could speak. Best to nip this line of inquiry in the bud. 'But since you're here, perhaps you can answer a few questions as well?'

The old woman contemplated him long enough for the earthy scent of her tea to fill his nose and for Manager Yu to pull up chair between her and Vlad.

He did not look away from the Chairwoman, but neither did he miss the glance between Vlad and Manager Yu opposite.

Vlad's stoney expression said, *I haven't forgiven you.*

I know, was in Yu's tight, sad smile.

He kept his brows inquisitive even as he sighed internally; the client's notes had not painted that one as a story that resolved swiftly or easily.

The Chairwoman set down her cup. 'Ask,' she commanded.

He summoned a smile. Gratitude always worked well with the alpha types. 'Thank you, Chairwoman. We understand your motivations in keeping your granddaughter and the shareholders in the dark regarding Nidhogg and the Deposit, but what were you hoping to achieve with the press conference?'

'Making a grand show of TI's deal with VisionM was the only way to convince Marion I was serious about the collaboration.' She swung her black gaze to the other side of the table, and added. '*Before* my granddaughter did something even more foolish.'

Vlad hissed. 'If you'd told me—'

'I shouldn't have to *tell* you anything, girl; you should trust me.'

The tea bowl in Vlad's hand crashed onto the table and the interviewer winced in sympathy at the still-steaming liquid sloshing over her hand, even as he marvelled at the resilience of the ceramic.

'And why should I do *that*, when you've lied to me every single damn day of my—'

'Wow.' Tina slumped into the chair beside the interviewer. 'You two should get a room or something.'

'Or something,' Lu Chen said as he took the seat on the interviewer's other side. He regarded the other man with expressionless black eyes. 'You're in my girlfriend's seat.'

'Oh.' He half-rose. 'I'm sorry, I didn't—'

'It's okay.' Wheels rattled over the concrete and a pink gamer chair appeared between him and DKZero's captain. Ming Li Na smiled as she sat. 'There are others.'

He returned the smile, less from professional courtesy than because it was impossible not to. 'Of course, of course.' He turned his attention back to the old woman at the head of the table. 'So, about the press conference…'

<⊙>

Drones hovered; beady, fist-sized eyes glared a metre from Shufeng's nose, the microphones buried in the sleek black bodies waiting on her next words.

The next words that would undo all she had achieved in the last thirteen years, all the evidence she'd pieced together, the justice she'd sought.

She'd come so close and now… Her heart clenched as she

remembered Vladana in the hospital bed, pale blankets pulled to her chin, her cold fingers, the needles under her skin.

Shufeng straightened her shoulders and lifted her chin. She'd lost too much already; she would hold on to what she had before she lost that too.

<⊙>

The Chairwoman's jaw tightened before she looked away. 'I have nothing more to add. Tell your client, if they wish more information, they can talk to my lawyers.' She rose. 'Yu Zixin, the shareholders are waiting—'

'I rescheduled the meeting.' Manager Yu looked up as he finished flicking through the screens above his phone. 'Driver Zhou has the car waiting for you out front. I'll be staying here.'

The interviewer straightened a little as silence filled the living room. He didn't dare to shift his gaze from the Chairwoman to Vlad, lest his eyeballs squish in their sockets.

He'd never really liked the phrase "cut the tension with a knife" but now… He could almost see it, particles turning to amber in the sunlight, freezing everyone in its vicinity, even him and the red-haired explosion beside him. A knife would barely scratch the surface of this, perhaps he should call for a sledgeham—

A loud *crunch* and a round, dark-haired figure in a unicorn-headed hoodie plopped into the seat the Chairwoman vacated moments before.

Everyone stared at him.

Chan Ying shoved another chip in his mouth.

Crunch.

Foil crinkled as Mr Chan— No, he thought mentally reviewing his notes. Foil crinkled as Sticky Feet, most commonly referred to by his teammates as Sticky—although for the life of him he couldn't figure out why—rummaged in the chip packet.

If the Chairwoman's face became any harder, would it actually turn to diamond?

Crunch.

Was that little curl at the corner of her nose a sneer?

He wouldn't find out. Without a word, Chairwoman Tong marched out, the sharp *snick* of her heels echoing long after the red front door thudded home.

Across the table, he noted Vlad's expression wasn't quite as hard as it had been, maybe she'd passed some of that tension to Manager Yu; the man's knuckles were white.

'Well.' He cleared his throat. 'I believe that has answered my client's most pressing questions—' He closed his pad, the screen above winking away, and started to rise.

A small freckled white hand with diamonté-tipped nails stopped him. 'Really?' Kristine Morita smiled at him, and sweat popped out on his forehead. 'Are you sure?'

Another cleared throat. 'My client was quite specific with her instructions, Ms Morita, I am *quite* sure.'

'What about what happens next?' Ming Li Na spoke from his other side, soft voice and pink hoodie a stark contrast to the shark-eating explosion on his left.

For a moment, he stilled, brain scrambling through his client's extensive notes... 'My client made no mention of next steps, Ms Ming, I believe that she intends to leave things as they stand—'

A grunt and a muffled 'wimp' came from the couch as Huang Yimo flicked another page.

'I really don't think—' he began.

Ms Morita leaned back in her chair and gave it a little bounce. 'But the next bit's so interesting.'

He looked to Vlad.

The gamer shrugged. 'I don't know what she's talking about.'

'It's okay,' Ming Li Na said. She nodded to Ms Morita and Sticky, somehow managing to encompass Huang Yimo in the same motion, even though the other woman was clear on the other side of the room. 'We have it all planned out.'

'Not my idea,' came from the couch.

Manager Yu leaned forward. 'I'm not going to like this, am I?'

'Maybe.' Ms Morita swivelled her chair toward Vlad. Her eyebrows wriggled. 'Maybe not.'

It was Vlad's turn to frown. 'Tina—'

He tuned the brewing argument out and, picking up his pad, slowly backed away from the table.

ACKNOWLEDGMENTS

Gamer wasn't meant to be a book.

It started as a niggle, spawned by a Netflix series (*Falling Into Your Smile*), that I played around with to help me sleep. It wasn't until I took a writing workshop ('Depth in Writing' with Dean Weasley Smith) that it grew legs, but even then, it was merely a handful of disconnected scenes.

It became was a chapter-a-month serial for a short time (thank you Iffet B. and Mike for your support), before it busted out of its britches and turned into... *this.*

I did not expect *Gamer* to grow as large as it did (from forty-thousand words to sixty- until it found its resting place at its current one-hundred-thousand) but I guess, looking back, it was inevitable. *Gamer* was going to be a standalone novel (emphasis on the "was") and it was a lot of action to cram between a two covers.

Of course, that meant the usual suspects—friends, family and coworkers—got an earful whenever they asked how the writing was going. They deserve thanks for putting up with me bitching and moaning about what characters were or weren't doing, without complaint (and often with smiles on their faces).

Thanks also need to go to (as always) my editor, Amanda J Spedding, who not only loved the book but also planted an idea for a sequel in my head (fuck it, so much for "standalone"). And last, but definitely not least, I want to thank my Launch Heroes, who helped bring this fabulous special edition to life.

Among them are a few Launch Legends, Heroes who have rocked up not just one or two launches, but three or four or *all* of them.

Thanks Heroes and Legends, I love you hard.

Launch Legends: Mama Jen, Mike Dobey, Kenyon Wensing, Dead Fish Books and Katherine Shipman.

Launch Heroes: JC Spark, Jared Burch, Shawn Raben - Redmatter Creations, Jaymi Elford, Kiyo P, Heiko Koenig, Stephen Ellis, Valerie Lockhart, Miranda Coulson, Kerry Chorvat (Blu Cat Dev), Heather Parra, Ian Chung, Thomas Schwarz, Nicolas Lobotsky, Joe Lau, Amanda Balter, Susannah Mansky, Ashley Allison, Thomas Rawls, IrisJuylyenne, Nichole Waggoner, William C. Tracy, N.A. Soleil, 'Will It Work' Dansicker, Christina Major, Christa Concannon, James Fowler, Shiloh W., Amanda, Aimee Cozza, Eliana Dimopoulos, Robert J., Jana MZ, Leon Glaser, Hermes Mora, Minnie Melissa McDade - Allen, Ash Wyvern, Lafia and Leon Glaser.

ABOUT THE AUTHOR

Physics makes Belinda's brain hurt, while quadratics cause her eyes to cross and any mention of probability equations will have her running for the door. Nonetheless, she loves watching documentaries about the natural world, biology, space, history and technology.

She's also a sucker for a fast horse, a faster computer and superhero movies. When she's not doing the horse, computer or superhero thing, Belinda writes sci-fi and fantasy for readers who like their fiction action-packed, with diverse characters, butt-kicking heroines and complex worlds.

As a certified crazy horse person, when she's not wrangling six-legged dynamos on the page, she's wrangling four-legged powder-kegs in the paddock. Belinda brings that same certified craziness to her writing with the kind of unexpected twists that'll keep you guessing.

You can keep in touch with Belinda, or just pick her brains about sci-fi via her website, Facebook or by sending her an email (she loves email).

www.belindacrawford.com
belinda@belindacrawford.com

Have news delivered straight to your inbox
via her mailing list. Sign up at:
belindacrawford.com/newsletter

DON'T MISS ANOTHER BOOK!

I love keeping in touch with my readers, it's the second-best thing about being a writer (writing being the first best). Every fortnight (or thereabouts), I send out a newsletter with details about upcoming offers, new releases and extra special projects.

If you sign up for the mailing you'll receive exclusive behind-the-scenes extras, such as:

- free short stories
- deleted and alternate scenes from my books
- previews of upcoming books
- pancakes
- quizes
- and much, much more!

Scan the QR code or visit the link below to sign up.
belindacrawford.com/newsletter

www.ingramcontent.com/pod-product-compliance
Ingram Content Group UK Ltd.
Pitfield, Milton Keynes, MK11 3LW, UK
UKHW040735270125
454275UK00001B/41